The Epic Saga of

The Master of Whitehall

Continues with these
Other Titles
by
Rick H. Veal

Lexi's Legacy

Dale's Descent

Charlotte Ann's Coven

James' Journey

Other Works Include

Jennifer's Ghost: A Tale of Ghostly Love

Hannah's Heartache

Taylor's Tale

(Master of Whitehall Novelettes)

~ Praise from readers and reviewers for ~

Katelyn's Chronicles

This is not your typical Vampire and human love story. Kudos to you Mr. Veal ... for not only writing one great female character, you wrote two.

Fab, Fun & Tantalizing Reads

This timeless story personifies a magnitude of emotions that range from heartache, lust, revenge, and ultimately LOVE. The author effortlessly fuses the worlds of the natural with the supernatural, while still making the storyline pleasantly believable. This is not a traditional vampire novel. It absolutely stands above the rest.

Stephanie Beetham – Reader/Reviewer

... this book was awesome! It gives a totally new spin to vampires and what we typically expect from them. I definitely recommend The Master of Whitehall to anyone that loves YA or paranormal romance!

Mom of Two Book Reviews

... an intriguing vampire romance that captured my imagination, and is completely unique to any other stories I have read in the past.

Book Reviews by Lynn

What made **The Master of Whitehall** *stand out was the attention to detail during the 'changing' between human and Vampire.*

Loaded Shelves Blog

... in every way a true love story.

Paranormal Romance Guild

... far more interestingly, is that this is a book written by a male author, in a first-person female character's voice. The author got so under the skin of Katelyn, espoused her sensibilities so well, that I was totally blindsided by his gender.

MeganBlogs

A truly unique story ... not your everyday vampire book ... a refreshing change.

The Kainas Book Blog

The love between the two characters is simple and pure. I found myself captivated by the beautiful descriptions and world that the author has created.

Winter Haven Books

The author has done a wonderful job in capturing the sensuality that makes most of us intrigued by vampire lore. A real literary treat.

R&M Fab Book Reviews

I HAD to know what happened next. The story was that engaging. I even remember thinking that I would finish this one, and then I would be done, but now I have to read the next book. I grew to care about the characters, and they became real to me.

Christine Grey, Reader/Reviewer

... a beautiful tale of the gift of love.

Mama's Reading Break

~ Praise from readers and reviewers for ~

Katelyn's Chronicles

This is not your typical Vampire and human love story. Kudos to you Mr. Veal ... for not only writing one great female character, you wrote two.

Fab, Fun & Tantalizing Reads

This timeless story personifies a magnitude of emotions that range from heartache, lust, revenge, and ultimately LOVE. The author effortlessly fuses the worlds of the natural with the supernatural, while still making the storyline pleasantly believable. This is not a traditional vampire novel. It absolutely stands above the rest.

Stephanie Beetham – Reader/Reviewer

... this book was awesome! It gives a totally new spin to vampires and what we typically expect from them. I definitely recommend The Master of Whitehall to anyone that loves YA or paranormal romance!

Mom of Two Book Reviews

... an intriguing vampire romance that captured my imagination, and is completely unique to any other stories I have read in the past.

Book Reviews by Lynn

What made **The Master of Whitehall** *stand out was the attention to detail during the 'changing' between human and Vampire.*

Loaded Shelves Blog

... in every way a true love story.

Paranormal Romance Guild

... far more interestingly, is that this is a book written by a male author, in a first-person female character's voice. The author got so under the skin of Katelyn, espoused her sensibilities so well, that I was totally blindsided by his gender.

MeganBlogs

A truly unique story ... not your everyday vampire book ... a refreshing change.

The Kainas Book Blog

The love between the two characters is simple and pure. I found myself captivated by the beautiful descriptions and world that the author has created.

Winter Haven Books

The author has done a wonderful job in capturing the sensuality that makes most of us intrigued by vampire lore. A real literary treat.

R&M Fab Book Reviews

I HAD to know what happened next. The story was that engaging. I even remember thinking that I would finish this one, and then I would be done, but now I have to read the next book. I grew to care about the characters, and they became real to me.

Christine Grey, Reader/Reviewer

... a beautiful tale of the gift of love.

Mama's Reading Break

Veal's writing style is somewhat different in that he writes in a niche between Gothic horror and modern day vampire literature that no other author has delved into yet. He is one of only a small handful of authors who adhere to the classical, lethal vampire instead of the more romanticized versions portrayed in current literature. His characters are not the modern whitewashed version of vampires but more of a cross between Bram Stoker's vampires and the ones found in present day paranormal literature. While they are likable they are ***NOT*** human and the body count that piles up is astounding even though the vast majority of the victims are criminals of the worst sort.

Douglas C. Meeks,
Amazon Top 100 Reviewer

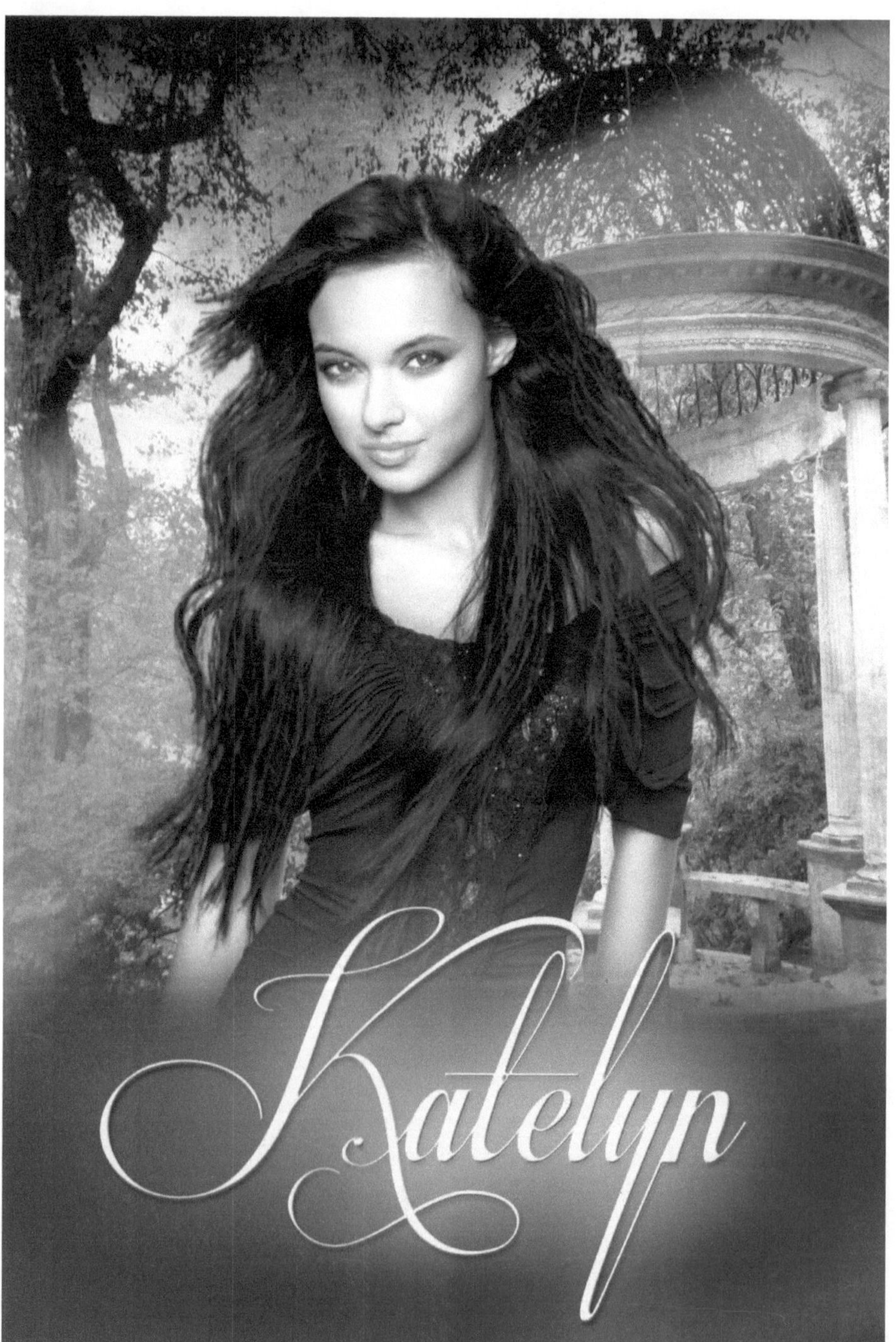
Katelyn

The Master

of

Whitehall

Katelyn's Chronicles

Book One

Rick H. Veal

Published by Virgin Vampire

The Master of Whitehall: Katelyn's Chronicles

Cover Art and Cover Layout by
Deborah Taylor, DCA Graphics, Inc.
www.dcagraphics.com
Cover photo of Whitehall House courtesy of
Adam Padgett
www.adampadgettweddings.com
All other decorative art courtesy of
Karen Watson, The Graphics Fairy, LLC
www.graphicsfairy.blogspot.com
Body text set in Palatino 12 pt.
Library of Congress Control Number: 2012911405
ISBN: 0-9981044-0-X
ISBN 13: 978-0-9981044-0-9
Printed in the United States of America

Thank you for your purchase, for comments, or to obtain further copies, please contact the author at author@prtcnet.com.

Omnibus Edition
June 2021
10 9 8 7 6 5 4 3 2 1

~ Acknowledgements ~

I have heard it said that no one writes a book by themselves and that has certainly proven true in this case. So many of my friends have helped in numerous ways, to all of you, thanks! I cannot name all of you but would be very remiss if I did not name some of you.

First and most importantly, to the memory of my parents, Hoyt and Hazel, thank you for having been such great parents and for the Life Lessons you taught me; many of which I didn't realize the importance of until after you had departed this life. This work is lovingly dedicated to you!

Thank you so much to my very special friend Billie Jo Mitchell. Her wealth of medical knowledge as an experienced registered nurse was absolutely priceless to me in my research.

I offer my special gratitude to Debbie Taylor, friend and artist, for her many artistic talents in producing and designing the beautiful cover. You are always able to take what I see in my mind's eye, put it on canvas, and turn it into an eye-catching, breath-taking work of art. You are a real Blessing to me!

A special thanks to Adam Padgett of Adam Padgett Weddings for the gracious permission to use his photograph of Whitehall house on the cover.

To Karen Watson at The Graphics Fairy, thank you so much for all the wonderful antique graphics that you have gathered together into one place and made them easy to use.

For my sixth grade art teacher who always said "Whatever you do, think big, and then do it big!" While your name has long since passed from my memory, your words have stayed with me my entire life, inspiring me in so many different endeavors. You accomplished what teachers everywhere set out to do, you touched my life.

I owe a special debt of gratitude to my college English Professor, Dr. John Wright, for teaching me not only how to write, but to enjoy writing; thank you, sir!

Coat of Arms

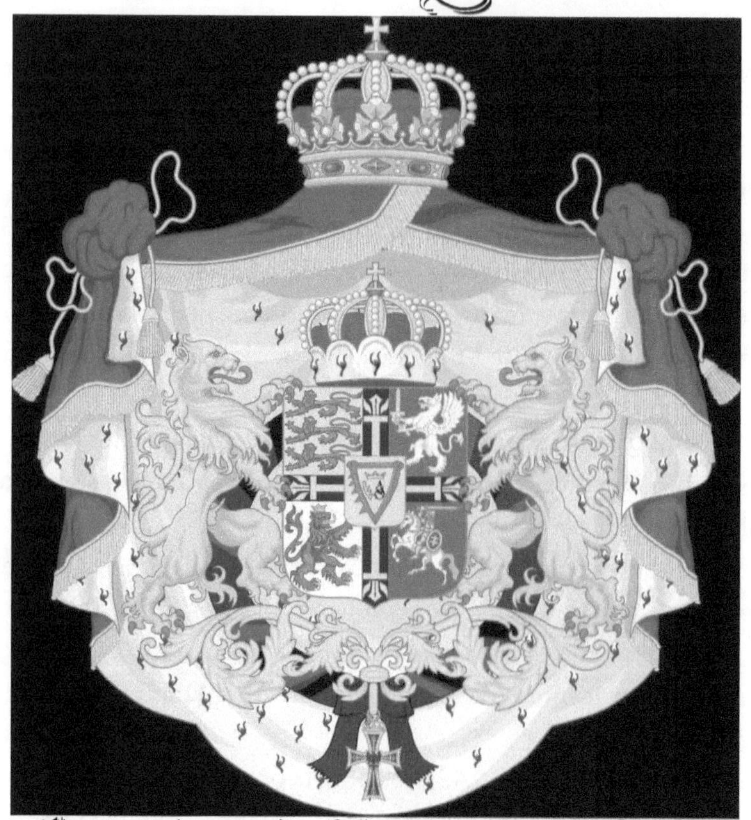

Granted by the Keeper of the Arms
To the Family of

Dubois

In the year of our Lord 1070
The Forth year of the reign of
William the First, King of England

Chapter One

I slowly opened my eyes upon complete darkness. I was scared beyond belief … but I didn't know why. I began turning round and round in the total blackness, straining my eyes, trying to see something … anything … but there was only the impenetrable night. I squinted, trying hard to gather in even the tiniest bit of light. I shivered uncontrollably as I suddenly realized the heavy murkiness that surrounded me was a cold dark fog of pure evil that wrapped itself around me like a sodden blanket. I could feel the touch of terror on my skin as the cloud moved and swirled, constantly changing, hiding my path, closing in so that I couldn't see anything. The only feeling I had was that of a continued heaviness of heart as the darkness bore down unrelentingly upon me. I struggled with sluggish movements, to slowly make my way through it; I had to get out of it. I tried to make my legs move but they seemed to be locked in place, held by an unseen force. I tried desperately to push my way out of the darkness, but apparently moved nowhere, so I gave up and stood still.

As I continued to stand there the darkness slowly began to fade to gray with just the tiniest hint of light making its way through. Gradually it began to grow lighter, becoming a reddish color, until it finally became a translucent pink. I began to move through it a little easier, even as it still closed in on my every step. It shrouded me, like a heavy weight, pressing into my very soul, so close that it was making it almost impossible to move.

All of a sudden I became aware of an unseen entity close by, sharing the darkness with me. It radiated an invisible strength, as if someone, or something, was standing right beside me. Then it reached out and put its hands on my shoulders … hands that were as cold as death … gripping me tightly. It was a strong presence that began pushing me forward. When I pushed back, resisting it, it moved to my front and began pulling me forward. I tried to resist once again and it moved around behind me, pushing tenaciously once again, making it impossible for me to stay in one place. It led me as I surrendered to its guidance, first left then right and finally straight ahead moving through a maze that I could not see. I realized I could not make myself stop now; I was completely under its control as it moved me along faster, forward into the opaque cloud.

I could feel and hear my heart as it raced in my chest, pumping so hard I thought it would burst as the pain radiated out through my entire body. My breathing became fast and shallow … it was difficult to breathe … the tightness in my chest was gripping me ever closer. I had to make my lungs work. I could not, would not, die all alone in this dark, forsaken place.

My legs felt like lead weights as I once again tried to force them to move. I made a concentrated effort to lift first one then the other as I stubbornly pushed on through the darkness taking one small step at a time; the weight of the thick darkness still lying heavily upon my shoulders. I was determined I would come out of this, even if the only path was through it.

All of a sudden my thinking abruptly shifted, now I wanted more than anything to stop. I didn't want to go on but now I couldn't stop. I became confused … I knew I had to continue on, deeper and deeper into the stirring clouds, there was no other way out. But I also knew there was something ahead that I did not want to face, an unknown that *was* known, and I was suddenly afraid, wracked with dread of what lay ahead. I wished I could just close my eyes again and lay down in the thick darkness. But that unseen force was on me again, once more pushing and pulling, making me move forward.

"Please," I silently cried out to it, *"I don't want to keep going, I want to stop, just let me stay here in the dark … I don't want to see what's ahead … please don't make me go any further."*

A sinister foreboding began to rise up in me, gripping me, sending chills throughout my body. I abruptly remembered what was waiting for me in the light at the other end of the darkness. Terror filled me, I tried to resist the pulling force, doing all I could to get free and run back into the darkness. I wanted to cry out but no sound came. A sudden flash of hope rose in me, as the darkness began to lift away. Maybe, I hoped, that awful thing wouldn't be waiting for me. Maybe this time it would be different. But deep inside my heart I knew that it would always be the same. It would never change ... it could never change.

As that realization sank home to me, the haze, moving like it had been blown by an unseen wind, suddenly cleared away completely. Then, as if a stage curtain had been drawn aside, the same terrible scene as always opened in front of me once again. Just like every time before, I stood there looking down at the bodies of my parents. They lay there like two discarded dolls, broken and covered in their own blood. They both stared up at me with their wide lifeless eyes, clouded with death. They looked like they were begging for my help, seemingly asking 'why did this happen', the fear of dying, still on their faces, was now forever etched in my mind.

I stood there over them, frozen solidly, the horror now racing unabated through me. I wanted to run away, to get as far away from this tragedy as possible. But I was unable to move, my body was locked rigidly in place. Sensing my total helplessness, I surrendered to it and simply stood there, my heart and soul being torn apart inside me, knowing there was nothing I could do.

Then, as had happened so many times before, the tears began welling up in my eyes, clouding my vision. I continued standing there looking at the frightful, blood covered sight as my tears spilled over and began to flow like a river down my face. The more the tears flowed, the more it seemed as if a dam had broken inside me. Then an uncontrollable scream, following the tears, rose up from within the depths of my soul, full force and unstoppable, bursting out of the very center of my being. I screamed again and again, as loud as I could, unable to stop, barely able to breathe, hoping the screams would make it all go away.

As I continued helplessly screaming, I heard the voice of my Aunt 'Chele, far in the distance, but drawing closer, as it cut through the darkness of my terror. My eyes finally popped open as she came running through the bedroom door letting it slam against the wall. I was still shaking uncontrollably, gripped with fear as she raced toward me.

"Katelyn! … Katelyn! … Darling wake up, it's the nightmare again, it's going to be alright sweetie! I've got you baby … I'm right here and I promise I won't let anything hurt you! You're going to be alright now," she cried as she wrapped her arms lovingly around me, holding me tightly, rocking me gently in her arms as she stroked my hair and my back.

I slowly came fully awake, trying to shake away the terror that still filled me. I looked deep into her eyes and I saw her love for me filling them. With the tears still streaming down my face, I felt like a little child that had been hopelessly lost, and then suddenly found. I cuddled as deeply as I could into her loving embrace, wrapping my arms tightly around her. She held me there as I fought to shake off the sleep and the terrible nightmare that always came with it.

"Oh my God, Aunt 'Chele," I sobbed, "it's still so real … still so awful," I said as I wept into her hair, "I can still see them so clear and plain with that look of fear on their faces, lying there broken and dead, begging me to help them. It keeps ripping me apart, it hurts so much and there's nothing I can do to help them! Why couldn't I have been there? If I just hadn't stopped for lunch, maybe I could have done something! I feel so totally confused and helpless."

"Now, now, Katelyn," she said as she continued holding me, lovingly rubbing my back while she slowly rocked me in her arms, "there's nothing you could have done to prevent what happened. Darling, if you had been there you might have died along with them. Please don't blame yourself, that's the last thing they would have wanted. You know they loved you more than anything and wanted only the best for you."

I slowly untangled myself from the security of her hug, knowing she was right. I reached for my pillow, hugging it close to me, and rolling over I buried my face into it, bursting into tears once again. While I cried, grieving for my poor dead parents, I once again became the poor little girl lost in the dark.

Chapter Two

My name is Katelyn Corbin, I'm twenty-one years old and a senior in college – or at least I will be in a few hours when I get to school. The nightmare I was having was about the murder of my parents last April. They worked in a small grocery store we owned located in Marietta, Georgia, a suburb of Atlanta, and were killed there during a robbery.

Two men came into the store, high on drugs and demanding money. My parents tried to give them all the money they had, but when they got scared and couldn't move fast enough one of the men shot both of them several times. They then wrecked the cash register getting away with only sixty-eight dollars, a handful of change, and two grocery bags they stuffed with snacks. In the end, all told, my poor parent's lives were worth less than a hundred dollars.

I had the misfortune to be the one to have to find their bodies that awful day. It was early spring and I was almost finished with classes for the year. Summer vacation would be starting in about two weeks and my two best friends, Beth and Tiffany, and I were planning a trip to Pensacola Beach to begin it properly. The three of us and several of our friends had stopped after class at the Marietta Dinner … the best kept dinning secret in the greater metro Atlanta area … for a late lunch and spent a couple of extra hours chatting and enjoying ourselves in the warm sunshine. During lunch we had all decided to go up toward Dalton, to the National Forest and go hiking the following weekend.

When I got back to the store that afternoon I ran in laughing and happily calling out, "Hey Mom! Dad! Guess what *I'm* doing this weekend?" and going toward the back counter I abruptly stopped, frozen in place as time came to a screeching halt, my soul suddenly ripping wide open inside me. My mind refused to believe what my eyes were seeing, and I was suddenly filled with confusion. There was blood everywhere, it was splashed and splattered on everything, and my parents were lying there in the center of it all. I started crying and screaming as I ran to them, kneeling beside each one of them, calling out to them, trying to help, but there was nothing I could do. I saw my Dad's arm stretched out toward my mother almost like he had tried to help her as a final act. They were both dead and I knew it. I remember how cold they both felt lying there together. There was so much blood everywhere, it seemed to cover everything.

I somehow managed to reach the telephone on the counter and dial 9-1-1. The operator sounded so calm when she answered, "911, what is your emergency please?"

I struggled to answer but all that came out was a tearful whisper, "Help me … please … someone help me …" and then I dropped the phone.

I slid back down the counter, sitting in the gory mess beside my parents, confused and crying helplessly. I covered my face with my hands hoping to block out the terrible sight in front of me. My hands felt sticky and wet so I took them away from my face and looked at them. They were covered in blood and it was all over my arms, too. I tried to wipe them clean on my shirt and jeans. The more I wiped the more it seemed to spread, I just couldn't get their blood off of me. I cried out with a plaintive wail as the pain tore through me again, my tears washing the blood across my cheeks and down my face.

When the Marietta Police arrived they carefully removed me from that terrible scene and walked with me to the front of the store where I couldn't see anything going on in the back. The young officer was so nice to me. She found a chair for me to sit in and then she took a seat facing me.

"Ma'am," she began slowly, "I have to ask you some questions now … can you understand me?"

"Yes, ma'am," I replied through the haze, "you need to ask me something."

"Very good," she started, "my name is Officer Hemmings … can you tell me your name, ma'am?"

I looked at her blankly and slowly replied, "It … it's Katelyn … Katelyn Corbin."

"Thank you, Miss Corbin," she said, writing in her notebook, "now this one may be a little difficult for you, but do you know the two people in the back?"

I sat there for a minute, my world continuing to collapse in on its self. I just looked at her with a blank stare as her question slowly penetrated the haze of my mind. I thought about it, I knew the answer, but I didn't want to voice the finality of it out loud. Then I looked down and once again saw all the blood covering my hands and arms, smeared on my jeans and the front of my shirt, I began shaking as I slowly looked up at her again my emotions beginning to crumble once more.

"It's alright Miss Corbin," she spoke softly, "take your time."

I covered my face with my hands, the tears flowing freely again, as the sobs wracked through me. I slowly lowered my hands, and feeling as if I had transformed into a lost little girl, looked at the officer, and, sobbing through my tears, sounding like a small child I slowly nodded and simply said, "Yes ma'am, they're my Mommy and Daddy …" and I broke down again. The last thing I remember about the store was her taking me in her arms and holding me while I cried on her shoulder.

I don't remember much about the rest of that day except that I left the store in an ambulance. I felt so alone and scared as the paramedics and police lifted me on the stretcher and began putting the straps over me. I did remember the paramedic's name that was riding with me though, a young girl named Casey, and probably not much older than I was. She had me sitting up on the stretcher with my back against the pillow. She was so nice to me and talked to me telling me everything she was doing. She was gentle and easy with me as she worked. She told me that she was going to give me some oxygen to help make me feel better as she gently placed the tubes over my ears and carefully set the end just inside my nose. The oxygen felt pure and clean as I breathed it in, I could almost immediately feel it beginning to clear up my thinking. Then she added a little plastic thingy on my finger and told me that it would monitor all my vital signs and not cause any pain. She continued talking kindly to me and occasionally lightly patting my arm as we rode together and I began to settle down just a little.

When we arrived at the hospital, Casey swung into full action, staying right with me as the stretcher was rolled into the emergency room. I heard her call out that she had a possible trauma victim in shock. The rest all happened so quickly it was a blur. I was surrounded by medical staff, all talking and checking me at the same time. Someone said that they were going to give me some medication; that I would feel a little sting, and I would take a nap. I looked at Casey and she softly patted my shoulder and told me that I was going to be alright now. I felt the quick sting of the needle and as I watched the bright lights above me, I smiled as they quickly turned gray. The last thing I remember was Casey beginning to fade slowly away as a curtain of total blackness settled over me, thankfully blocking out all the hurt and pain.

When I woke up and felt like I could talk again, I asked someone where I was and what was happening. They told me I had been brought to the Windy Hill Hospital for treatment and observation. Someone must have given me a bath while I slept because I noticed my hands and arms were clean now and I had on a new hospital tee shirt. My parent's blood was all gone now … at least visibly. I spent the remainder of the day and night in the hospital, mostly sedated and constantly watched. I didn't realize at the time, but due to the tragic events of the day, they had placed me on a suicide watch. Every time I would wake up, the horror of my parents death, and the sight of them lying there in all that blood rushed in all over again, closing in on me until the drugged sleep forced it away.

The hospital staff was all familiar with my parent's store since it was close by the hospital. Some of them even knew me from having shopped there. They were all nice, and kind to me, helping me get through that first day of tragedy, comforting me and constantly asking if they could do anything for me.

The nurses were finally able to get me calm enough by evening to talk to them without bursting out into uncontrollable crying. One of them even came in and brushed my hair for me, talking softly as she did trying to make me feel a little better. By evening, I was sitting up in the bed, my back leaning against the pillows. I had pulled the sheet all the way up to my neck and had my knees pulled up to my chin. My arms were wrapped around my legs, holding them, in a futile effort to keep the world away.

I continued sitting that way, silently staring out the window, across the tops of the close by buildings and into the distant trees. My thoughts were filled with my parents and how much I missed them. I recalled in vivid detail our final words and quick good-bye's when I left home this morning. It never entered my mind that it would be the last time we would ever see each other or that I would never get to speak to them again. I thought about all the things that had been unsaid and all the things I would never get to say. There was a hollow place in my chest, filled with a vast emptiness, and an abject loneliness that was quickly closing in tighter around me.

My thoughts were interrupted by a soft knock on the door of my room and my friend, Billie Jo, a nurse, quietly eased into the room. She loved her job and was well fitted to it because she was tender hearted and cared so much for others. I saw the tears welling in her eyes as she still tried to smile for me. I had known Billie Jo, or BJ as I called her, since I was a child. She was a regular in my parents' store and had taught the basic first aid class last year at school. We had grown to be friendly with each other over the years as I grew. She was very pretty, about my mom's age and had become like a second mom to me. She was always the one that I would go to with my 'girlie' questions that I just didn't feel comfortable talking to my mom about. Then during my teen years when I first started dating and other, more important questions began to come up, she was always there for me to offer her advice and guidance.

"Oh, Katelyn," she began slowly as she came toward my bed, "honey, I'm so sorry about your parents." She carefully sat down on the edge of the bed, and opening her arms to me, I folded into them, feeling safe and protected in my friend's embrace. My tears started again, slowly running down my face as I looked at her, still unable to voice a single word.

"Sweetie," she said in her gentle, caring voice, "I know that you are hurting, but we have to talk about someone who can care for you now. We need to call someone to come and see about you. Do you have any other family members, any aunts or uncles maybe that are close by?"

"The only family I have left," I whispered slowly to her, "is my Aunt Michele and her husband, Uncle John, they live up in South Carolina, somewhere close to Charleston. Their name and number are in my phone ..." I looked around confusedly for it as the tears began again, "but I don't know where it is."

"We have your phone," she smiled reassuringly at me, "I will go and make that call for you, then I'll be right back so you won't be by yourself." She stood, kissed my forehead, lightly stroked my arm, and made her way out of the room.

I felt a little better just knowing that there was someone close by that cared for me; but more importantly, someone that I knew and trusted, and that knew me. I started to stretch out in the bed, safe in that knowledge. I don't know how long she was gone because I fell back into another restless sleep, but when I woke up again, she was sitting in a chair at the side of the bed just like she said she would.

My entire world seemed to be crumbling around me after that day. Those two men not only murdered my parents, but also, in the end, they stole my life too … my home, my friends, and my school … they effectively destroyed everything I loved and held dear. I had to move away, leaving my old life behind me and, looking to heal, recover, and begin a new life, moved in with my aunt and uncle.

I was so blessed to have my Aunt 'Chele to help me through that tragic time. She came to Atlanta as soon as she received the call from the Marietta Police. There was so much that had to be done and Aunt 'Chele was right there with me through the entire ordeal. She actually became the go between for me and everything. She made a very difficult time a lot less stressful. She was quickly joined by Uncle John and they stayed with me, helping me plan and arrange the two funerals. We mingled my parent's ashes together in a large bronze urn and buried them under a huge oak tree in a private funeral at the Georgia Memorial Cemetery, not far from our home in Fox Run.

After the funerals, Aunt 'Chele stayed in Marietta with me while Uncle John went back to South Carolina. Having to sell my home was just so much more pain added to the injury I felt. However, I did have my doubts about being able to ever live there by myself. With her help, I listed the store and our home for sale; both of which quickly sold. She was invaluable to me, helping with the house and everything else that had to be taken care of. All I had to do was point out what I wanted to keep and she arranged for packing and storage, and then took care of selling all the rest.

Even with aunt 'Chele there with me, it didn't feel like home anymore. Now it was just a large empty house, quiet and lifeless all the time. Every time I would walk by my mom and dad's bedroom, or pass by dad's office or mom's computer room the wounds opened up fresh again bringing new pain with them. Regardless of where I was, kitchen, den or living room, their memory was always there. Then when the nightmares began, every night, I knew I had to leave … I had to get away.

The store was a little different; I was able to part with it somewhat easier than I had with my home. It had originally belonged to my Dad's parents and he and Mom had worked hard for most of my life to make it successful so they could give me a better life. They had planned on it being their retirement. In the end, there were just too many memories in both places. I didn't think I could handle the emptiness of either place … and I certainly never wanted to go back into the store again.

So with my aunt and uncle's help and advice I had taken the money I received from the insurance company, the sale of the store and our home, and at their insistence, had tucked it away safely for my future. After settling my parent's estate, paying for the funerals and clearing up the small amount of debt they had, I was left with almost five hundred thousand dollars which should provide a really nice beginning for me after graduation.

Aunt 'Chele told me that while she could never be, or take the place of, my Mother, she would always be there for me both as a friend and as a mother when I needed one. Although, since she is my mom's identical twin, she will always be a constant reminder to me. It was her and Uncle John who suggested – or more like insisted – that I move back to Summerville to live with them and finish my last year of college in Charleston. Aunt 'Chele thought it best that I take the rest of the year off and start back to school in January. They had both said that taking care of me until I finished college and had gotten started on my own was the least they could do for my mom and dad. They were the one remaining solid foundation of what my life had been so I clung desperately to them. I felt that with them I could soon start rebuilding my life again.

However, before I could begin my new life in Summerville, I had to wrap up a couple of things in Marietta, specifically, I had some good-byes to say. I had spent my final week in Atlanta staying in a hotel, in order to finish all the legal paperwork relating to my parents estate. Aunt 'Chele had insisted that it would be better for me to stay there – easier for the attorneys to meet with me … and to be far away from Fox Run and my previous home.

I had spent my last night in Marietta having dinner with my best friends Beth and Tiffany in the hotel restaurant. It seemed like it had been forever since I had last seen them, but in reality it was only about a month. In fact, that was the day, right after we had finished lunch at The Marietta Diner that I had returned to the store and discovered my parents murdered.

The three of us had been friends throughout childhood, school, and into college. We had lived in the same subdivision, cheered together, danced together, and generally shared our lives together. Still there was a tenseness in the air when we met for dinner. I'm not sure either of us knew what to say … and it was a given that none of us wanted to talk about the eight hundred pound gorilla sitting at the table with us. Instead, we talked about school, our plans, and what I wanted to do when I got to Charleston … and of course we all promised to keep in touch with each other. Still, we tried to make the best of it, eating and occasionally laughing, while we sat together.

The next morning while I drove, I thought absently about our dinner, recalling the better details. Now my next and final stop was at The Windy Hill Hospital to say good-bye to Billie Jo. I had called her at home last night and she promised to meet me at the hospital before I left. When I got there I parked and went to a stone bench in the meditation garden to wait for her. I didn't have long to wait, she popped her head in through the gate, and wearing her usual colorful scrubs, came toward me with a huge smile and a happy wave.

"Hey baby girl," she said using my little girl name, "I thought I might find you here. How you doing today?"

"I suppose about like I have been for the past month or so," I answered with a sigh, "not good, not great, but maybe not as bad as I was a month ago. But today's moving day, and that means everything's going to get better from here … or at least as good as it can get … right?"

She took a seat on the bench beside me and silently put her arm around my shoulders. I had to close my eyes and take a deep breath to keep from bursting into tears again.

"I suppose that's a good thing for you," she answered, "but are you sure you want to … do you really have to go?"

"Yeah, I really do. I need the new start … after everything that's happened … after my parents di … you see, I still can't even say it … I just don't think I can really begin to heal until this entire city … and maybe even the State is in my rearview mirror. You know what I mean?"

"Sure I do," she smiled, "you're not the only one that's ever had to put the old behind you and have a new start."

"But BJ, I wouldn't have survived any of this without you," I said, a tear running down my face, "and you know that I know that, right?"

"Oh baby girl, I didn't do anything special," she smiled shyly.

"Yeah, you really did. You were there for me at the beginning, when no one else could be. Or would be. Afterward … after my parents … when I could barely move you held me. When I couldn't even speak, you listened. You heard my heart crying out when it was crushed. I knew you'd be there every time I woke up screaming. You're amazing, BJ, so yes, you did do something special."

"You're pretty amazing yourself, girlie," she smiled, "so are you still having those horrible nightmares you told me about?"

"Every night."

"It'll get better, I promise."

"Yeah, but when," I asked.

"No idea, but it will. Your folks raised you right, you know. They really did. And their final and lasting gift to you is that they made you strong enough to survive anything … even them being gone."

I wrapped my arms around her and cried shamelessly on her shoulder.

"You're gonna do great in Charleston you know … and I expect an invitation to your first art show," she whispered in my hair, "I'll be there with bells on … the first in line to buy a Katelyn Corbin original."

I released my hug and sat back to look at her, "You know I haven't painted since … that day …"

"Don't worry, you will. When a gift that's as wonderful as yours wanders off, it never goes too far. You'll find it again … it'll be there when you are ready for it … and I'll be there to see your first show."

"I know you will," I chuckled.

"You always remember baby girl, me and you, we're as tight as two peas in a pod. But you better go along now girl … I have to go back to work … and before I break down blubbering and crying like a spanked baby … and I don't want you to see that," she said, her voice breaking.

I stood up to walk away, took her in my arms for one last hug and without looking back walked toward my car. Before I got to it, I heard her, with tears in her voice say, "I'll always be here for you … no matter what … you remember that Katelyn."

Since moving from Marietta I have been living with Aunt 'Chele and Uncle John and they are the best any girl could ask for – trying to help me rebuild a crumbling life, adjust to my new surroundings, and almost doting on me since they never had any children of their own. They have made a lot of sacrifices for me and made me feel extra special since I moved here. Sometimes, though, I really feel kind of bad for them, too, because their life has changed almost as drastically as mine. If the circumstances were different it would almost be funny.

They are both in their early-forties, suddenly have a daughter in college, having to take a crash course in parenting, and honestly doing all they can to learn how to be good parents. I try to be as cheerful and outgoing as I can when I'm around them. But sometimes, when the terrible memories come roaring back, I fall into a deep brooding and withdraw inside myself. They are always there for me though, and often ask if they can help. Still, they are always willing to give me the room I ask for to try to work through my tragedy. I know that either or both of them will always be ready to talk whenever I am. I try to let them in as much as I can and do frequently open up to them talking about how I feel. After all they have done for me, I would never want to hurt either one of them by totally blocking them out of my feelings.

The Georgia Bureau of Investigation quickly made two arrests. They charged both of the men with assault, murder, armed robbery and several other related offenses. It seemed that both men had been in trouble just about all their lives. They had been in jail several times for various charges but this was the first time they had ever been charged with murder. Now these two creeps are locked away and waiting on a trial which, it seems, I will have to go back to Atlanta to attend. I will be forced to relive the events of that terrible day all over again; testifying about what happened when I found my parents. The most difficult part by far through will be to have to sit and listen to each of those men tell what they had done that day in the store. I know it will be a difficult experience but worth it when they are found guilty and go away forever so they can never inflict this same kind of pain and hurt on anyone else.

My plans for this upcoming semester include living on campus and getting a job in Charleston during the week. I think I can probably get a good job as a waitress or a hostess somewhere downtown to provide me with enough extra spending money to get me through school. I'm an Art History major, so all my classes this year are related to that subject and since I'm a senior they should be pretty easy, too. But, after discussing it with aunt 'Chele, we both thought it better if I only took three classes and put off graduation until after the fall session. That would allow me time to slowly work back into a normal routine and continue my healing process at the same time.

Besides, I want to try to give aunt 'Chele and uncle John a little extra breathing room, too. This has been such a huge change for them and they are still getting used to having a third person around the house. Aunt 'Chele seemed to be alright with the idea of a job, as long as I kept it part-time and didn't let it interfere with my studies. But she quashed the idea of staying away too long and easily lured me back home on the weekends with the promise of doing my laundry and cooking for me. I have to admit it's a little hard to turn down a deal like that.

Chapter Three

I will be attending The College of Charleston, and the school has assigned me a roommate and 'Student Hostess', her name is Alexis Gordon. She is supposed to be my guide and help me handle all the details of registering for classes, getting settled in the dorm, and generally making a smooth transition from my old school. Being new here, I also have to start all over again building friendships. So I hope that Alexis will become my first new friend, I really need more than just a guide to get started.

I'm excited about the possibility of a completely new set of friends, too. Since Charleston is such an old and romantic city, somehow, I'm sure it has a lot of adventure in store to offer me. Besides, I'm really being offered the opportunity to start over again. At least that's going to be my take on it. It's going to be a little strange at first being 'that new girl' on campus though. Thankfully the College of Charleston is a happy medium between large and small. It's large enough to still have fun but not so huge that maybe I won't get lost in the crowd.

I'm supposed to meet Alexis this afternoon at the book store – which is actually a combination of study area, snack bar, and school store all in one – and get started. When I had my first tour of the school after moving to Summerville the guide told me that it is the center of activity for all the students and faculty. The book store is located in an old building on campus, and as usual looks pretty crowded. So, all I have to do now is try to find someone in this crowd, like me, that looks like they are looking for someone too. No need to make this an easy thing, I guess. After making my way through the crowd for a few minutes with no apparent luck I finally spotted a likely candidate sitting over against one wall. She looked like she was searching the crowd for someone, too. So I decided to take a chance and walk over and introduce myself.

"Excuse me … hi," I said smiling, "my name is Katelyn. I'm new and looking for Alexis Gordon, she's my student hostess and I'm supposed to meet her here this afternoon. Do you know her?"

"Oh, hello Katelyn, I'm Alexis, and I've been looking for you too," she said with a smile and a tinkling musical voice, "it looks like you found me first … how did you know it was me?"

"I guess I got lucky … and you kind of looked like you were searching for someone too! I hope I'm not too late. I actually took time to go up to the room and drop off my clothes and things. I kind of figured the bed without any sheets was mine so I just piled everything on it," I laughed and added, "I really hope I didn't keep you waiting too long did I?"

"No, actually I just got here about five minutes ago. In fact, I was afraid I might have missed you. I had a class that ran a little late today – you know how it is, start of the semester and trying to get everything running smoothly. And, of course, the Registrar's Office didn't provide me with your phone number so I could text you if I needed to. Anyway, we've found each other now. I know that you have a lot of things to do to get settled in, so do you want to get started?"

"I suppose so," I said, "can we start with the books?"

"Sounds good," she answered, "the book store is just over on the other side of the snack bar. C'mon, let's go round this way, I'll show you where! Oh, and by the way, all my friends call me Lexi," she added with a big smile.

I took a really good look at Lexi as she bounced up, like a ball of energy, out of the chair she was sitting in.

"The introduction certainly went well," I thought with a smile, *"She seems like a pretty cool girl, too. She actually reminds me a lot of Tiffany with all that energy … wow, Atlanta suddenly seems so far away now. Lexi's a lot smaller than Tiff though … probably doesn't weigh an ounce over ninety-five pounds soaking wet and she's tiny, too … I'm guessing she might be all of five feet nothing. But she's so cute that she's really pretty and she knows how to dress stylish, too. Those jeans are expensive and a perfect fit. They're just tight enough to look good … and I like the way she has that cute little top covered with an open Oxford. It looks classy but still comfortable."*

"I love her hair … cut short at her neck … I wish I could cut mine like that … it would be so much easier to take care of in the morning. It gives her a really cute pixyish look with the dark blond and the lighter highlights mixed in. And her eyes … soft

brown, friendly and inviting … now those are bedroom eyes … and I pity whoever her boyfriend is when she turns those on him – he doesn't stand a chance – he'll be buying her anything she wants! Combine those with that knock-out smile and wow, she is a real beauty."

"Lord help Katelyn, you sound like you're 'girl-crushing' on her … but still anybody that's that pretty and that full of energy has got to have a great social life going on. Maybe she will introduce me to some of the hot guys she knows. I think maybe I'm glad we are going to be roommates … Charleston just might not be so bad after all."

The two of them walked into the book store with Lexi leading the way. While Katelyn started browsing the textbooks, Lexi stepped away and, leaning against a bookshelf, quietly appraised her new friend, *"I can't believe this is the girl they told me was transferring here from Atlanta. I'm not sure just what I was expecting but I do know this isn't it. She has got to be the most beautiful girl I have ever seen … why in the world is she coming to Charleston and not going to some big city like L.A. or New York? She's certainly going to be the big fish in this little pond from now on … and she's going to be my roommate. Yes! Thank you, God! My senior year just might not be so forgettable after all!*

Of course as pretty as she is we may have to get some guards just to keep all the boys away from the dorm! Wait … what are you thinking, Lexi … no … no guards! I mean with all that beauty she's sure to attract a lot of boys. I hope maybe she'll introduce me to some of them, too!"

"I can't believe how tall she is … she has to be almost six feet … and she's wearing flats … and a good portion of that is legs … long and pretty … so much for sharing clothes, I guess. I bet

she doesn't weigh a pound over a hundred twenty-five either … and what I wouldn't give to have a perfect tan like that, too. It has to be all natural … it's too perfect to be store bought. I'm guessing I know where she likes to spend her spare time."

"That dark hair makes her eyes really stand out too … they're so blue, I wonder if they are contacts … nah, probably not, everything else about her is natural so her eyes probably are, too. I wish my hair was that long … it's full and thick … and almost half way down her back and lying in waves."

"I just cannot believe how absolutely perfect this girl is … and she's not even wearing makeup. She's the kind of girl that everybody stops and notices when she walks in a room … and I'm going to be her wing-girl, oh yeah, life is definitely good! She has style, class, and elegance all wrapped up in one package. I'll have to ask her to teach me some of her beauty secrets …"

I heard Lexi softly chuckle in the background and thinking maybe I had missed something important turned quickly around asking her "What is it? Did I miss something … what's happening … where do I need to look?"

"Oh, no," she replied softly chuckling, "it's nothing, really. I was just thinking about what a great year this is going to be. I guess I just got temporarily lost in my own head. Sorry 'bout that! Anyway, you got all your books, now?"

"Yeah, I think I've got everything I was supposed to buy … c'mon … do you have time to grab a coffee and sit in the study area and chat for a while?"

"Yep, I've got the rest of the day," she answered, "all my classes are over. I guess that you'll get started tomorrow morning?"

"Yeah, I have 'Middle Age European Art History' first

thing. Do we have any classes together?"

"Yep, we have 'Modern Asia' together, over in the afternoon."

"Cool, that's my last class of the day," I said smiling, "how about you?"

"Yep, me too … so would you like to get in the quick tour of Charleston after we finish classes for the day?"

"I would love to, you can show me all the cool spots," I said with a big smile, and then added, "do you think there's any possibility of getting any good seafood in Charleston?"

"Hummm … good seafood … in Charleston … I don't know if that's even possible … but we'll certainly try," she winked and laughed.

We both bought a large coffee, found a table and sat down together to begin laying the foundation for a great new friendship. I peeled the top off my cup and took a tentative sip.

"Whoa, straight up black … you're pretty serious about that coffee thing aren't you," Lexi commented.

"Uhhh, you don't even know the half of it … I call this is my 'anti-nightmare elixir' …" I answered with a laugh.

"Your anti-nightmare elixir," she questioned, cocking an eyebrow.

"Yup … if I drink it, it keeps me awake, and if I'm awake, I'm not asleep, if I'm not asleep, I don't have nightmares … and if I don't have nightmares, I don't have to see my parents bodies all covered in blood again … so, my 'anti-nightmare elixir," I smiled innocently.

"Okayyyy then …" she answered slowly.

"I promise, I'll tell you all about the nightmares and what caused them later," I reassured her.

"Yeah, I read some of that story when I Googled you,"

she relied sheepishly, looking down and lightly biting her bottom lip.

"You Googled me … really," I asked, "why for pity's sake would you do that?"

"Are you kidding me … it's the twenty-first century … and we're going to be living in the same room … so I had to find out if you were, like, pure evil, or a Goth Girl, or something worse like maybe infected with 'The Bieber Fever'," she chuckled, "but seriously, you're a lot hotter in person than your pictures!"

"Well, thank you," I smiled, "and when it comes to music, I'm more old school … mostly Southern Rock … you know ZZ Top, Lynyrd Skynyrd, Foghat, .38 Special, and The Allman Brothers … got that from my parents."

"Well, at least they had great taste in music …."

"Ummm … you said 'had' … as in past tense," I interjected, "so I guess you read more than just a little of the story?"

"Yeah, I did … and that must have been horrible … I just can't imagine …" she trailed off.

"Thank you," I said, "But, honestly I'm glad you Googled me. Saves me from having to relive my parents' murder for the billionth time. I kind of came here specifically to not have to do that anymore. If I can help it. It's gonna be bad enough when I have to go back to Atlanta for the trial."

We talked and laughed for over an hour, like we had known each other for years. The time just flew by, while we sipped our coffees. I told Lexi that I was originally from and grew up in the Atlanta area and that now I was living with my Aunt 'Chele and Uncle John up in Summerville. I told her the whole story of how I had come to be here in Charleston … the articles on-line left out a lot. I also told her that if I woke up in the night crying – I didn't dare mention the screams – it was probably just one of the nightmares and I hoped I wouldn't disturb her. She seemed really sad to hear about the tragedy that had taken my parents. She was very attentive to what I said and offered to help me anyway that she could. I told her that meant a lot to me and that we would probably talk more about it later, I really didn't like to linger on it for too long. She smiled and said that she understood.

She told me that she was from Savannah, and had lived there all her life.

"Oh, and you know what's just too cool," I tossed in trying to lighten the mood, "look at us … two Georgia Peaches together … do you think Charleston has any idea what it's in for now …" and we both broke up laughing.

Lexi continued that she was a History major and loved the Low Country because of all the historical places that were close by. She just wasn't sure yet what she wanted to do after graduating though.

"I would love to be able to go to Europe and continue studying, maybe get my Masters, and then come back home. I suppose I'll probably have to teach at some point. But my real dream is to become a museum curator more than anything. I mean, if you really want to see me happy, toss me in a big room full of dusty old books, tell me to find something, and close the door on your way out. I really love doing research and finding important things that otherwise would have been lost to history," she said.

We kept up our friendly chit chat and after a little while, Lexi slowly leaned back in her chair, stretched a little, smiled and almost in a whisper spoke softly to me, "Don't look up right now … but it seems like you might have caught the attention of Mr. Dubois! I've seen him look over here at you twice. That's him sitting across the room in the tan leather chair reading."

I glanced up, quickly looking back down, and asked cautiously, "Who … or what … is Mr. Dubois … professor … grad student … what?"

"Oh no, he's a whole lot more important than that," she answered with her quick, sweet smile.

I glanced up again, taking a better look at him this time and saw a very handsome man, sitting comfortably, deeply absorbed in a book. It was difficult to judge his age, but most probably early to mid-twenties. He had delicate features and an easy smile as he read; his face was smooth with no discernible beard shadow, something unusual in most guys his age. He was very stylish, nicely dressed in what were obviously very expensive tailored slacks and a long sleeved turtleneck; even his leather shoes looked expensive. He sat easily in the chair, comfortable, as if he was right at home.

He looked healthy and strong, nicely built, probably tall with long legs that were crossed and with a book sitting comfortably propped on one knee. If he had been dressed differently, I would almost have thought he worked in the outdoors. But his hair was what caught my attention, I suppose because the style was unusual; long, and lying easily along the top of his shoulders, it appeared more European than American. It was dark brown and very thick with a light curl in it. There was no doubt that he was a cultured man with a good education. Everything about him spoke of great wealth but in a nicely subdued manner.

"Wow! That is one hottie with a body," I whispered, and then added a little laugh, "he's so fine he could read the ops manual of my new laptop to me and I would pay pretty close attention to him … I mean … stay intently focused on the material."

No sooner did those words come out of my mouth than I heard a soft voice float through my head saying, *"Be very careful, Katelyn, those kind of thoughts are more dangerous than you know and could very well lead you into things you're not yet ready to experience."*

I looked over quickly to see if he had maybe overheard me and said that, but he hadn't so much as moved, still concentrating on his book.

"Yeah, I know … he's definitely a biscuit I'd butter and eat whole," Lexi whispered back "he is really dreamy and just look at that hair … there's not many guys around that can pull off that style successfully."

"Uh huh," I said "but he sure does, and good, too!"

Then suddenly, there came that voice again, soft and gentle as it passed through my mind, *"I told you, Katelyn, tread carefully, your thoughts are dangerous, you're playing with fire and don't even know it."*

"Did you hear that," I asked Lexi.

"Hear what," she asked looking at me.

"Oh, nothing it must have just been my imagination," I said looking back across the room at him, "so if he's more important than the professors, what exactly is he?"

"He's … well it's hard to say exactly *what* he is …" she began, "I think he's a patron of some sort of the school, nobody really knows. He just sorta showed up around here a few years ago."

"So what's he doing hanging out with the students," I asked.

"I wouldn't say he hangs out with us. It always looks more to me like he's … well, you know how people get in cages to swim with sharks?"

"Sure," I smiled.

"Yeah, well, at least to me, he comes across as a shark

in a cage surrounded by people … whether you actually notice it or not, he's always watching … like he's measuring everyone around him," she proposed quietly.

"You know, for some odd reason, and I don't know why, but that makes sense."

"But as to why he's here, I dunno … maybe he gets tired of rambling around all alone in his plantation."

"Plantation? Really? As in Gone With The Wind, huge oak trees, Spanish Moss, big house with tall white columns kind of plantation?"

"Yup, that's the kind …" she continued, "He owns and lives out at Whitehall Manor between here and Hollywood; it's down between Highway 162 and Wadmalaw Sound going towards Savannah. It's been in his family since the beginning of time … I've heard he completely restored it a few years back."

"What is Whitehall Manor," I asked curiously.

"It's this huge old plantation, supposedly one of the first built in the state and it dates back to the early 1700's. It was originally one of the old land grant plantations from the King of England. And according to my research, until somewhere around the end of the nineteenth or early twentieth centuries, it was *the* place for Charleston society to gather."

"Well that sounds pretty cool … and like a place I'd like to visit! I bet there's some really nice artwork out there," I replied, looking him over again, "but I doubt it could get any better than what's sitting over there!"

"Katelyn, consider yourself warned young lady, I've told you those are dangerous desires you are having and they ~will~ get you in trouble my beautiful little orphan."

There was that strange voice again, still floating around in my head, very distinct, but nothing like I had ever heard before. I shuddered all over as a sudden cold wave passed right through me, *"This is just too weird,"* I thought to myself.

"Yeah, well, don't plan too hard on visiting there anytime soon," Lexi continued, "nobody, and I mean *nobody,* goes anywhere near Whitehall without a personal invitation from him … and that's not too likely to happen for a couple of regular students like us."

Lexi continued right on with her overview of history, "So anyway, historically speaking, his place is way past cool, for sure. I would love to see it too, but unfortunately the closest I've ever gotten was passing the drive-way turnoff. Now, though, I dunno, it's just this amazing, kind of legendary estate. It's crazy-old, older than the country we're sitting in, I mean. It was part of the chartered Province of Carolina."

"Okay, you lost me with that one," I grinned and pointing at myself added, "Art Major, not History … remember?"

"Well, like I said, it began as a land grant from King Charles to some Dubois ancestor. Basically, the King gave the entire Carolina Colony to eight of his best friends in 1663 …"

"Wait … are you saying King Charles … gave these guys a colony?"

"Yup … now go ahead and guess what it was called …" she grinned.

"Charleston …" I asked, raising an eyebrow.

"You're close, I can see the gears working … keep trying," she chuckled.

"Wait … do you mean the old Charles Towne … and it became Charleston?"

"Ding Ding Ding … you win … and you done it without the internet," she laughed!

"So you're saying that his family was one of the Originals … that's pretty neat … bet he wouldn't have any problem getting into the Sons of The American Revolution!"

I did another once over of him and mused, "He sure is one nice looking man … wonder if, or why, he's still single …" I softly whispered and quickly added, "oh please … tell me he's not gay … that would be such a waste of a fine piece of beefcake!"

"No, I'm pretty sure he's not gay," she answered with a girlish giggle, "the rumor around campus is that he's a widower … a very wealthy widower, by the way. Besides, I've seen him paying pretty close attention to some of the girls …"

"Well, he could pay pretty close attention to this girl and she wouldn't argue one bit about it," I chuckled.

"Yeah, I do know what you mean … because that wasn't subtle at all … by the way, that includes you and a bunch of other girls, too," she chuckled, "but you may have an inside track … the word is that the Art department is his favorite, closely followed by the History department, and he has made several large gifts to each. He even set up a couple of hefty endowments that have helped more than one student finish their course work. If this were the middle ages, he would be a De' Medici, but in the here and now, he's pretty much a fixture in the study area, I'm sure you'll see him around here a couple or three times a week."

"That's certainly something to look forward to … Charleston *really* might not be so bad after all," I smiled as I took another quick look at him.

"Yeah, but keep in mind he never really has anything to do with anybody though, he usually comes in to buy a book and then, if he stays, just sits and reads all afternoon. He has spoken a greeting once or twice to me, but just in passing. He has a very soft Charleston accent, but I'm guessing he must have spent some time in England, too, because I think I can hear just the lightest touch of a London accent in his intonation."

"But I think maybe he has some kind of health issues though, sometimes when he comes in he looks kinda pale, like he really could use some time in the sunshine. Then, at other times, like now, he looks pretty healthy."

"Yeah," I said, with a sly grin, "from here he looks pretty healthy to me, too."

"Katelyn … Katelyn … Katelyn … why must you be so strong willed? You just won't listen will you?"

"Well, it does give us something to think about, anyway," I said, as we slowly went back to our drinks, and other topics about school.

Chapter Four

I was still vaguely aware of Mr. Dubois' presence while Lexi and I continued to sit there idly chatting. It was more of a subconscious acknowledgment of his being there that lingered around the fringes of my mind, but I was not really paying him any more attention. I was more attuned to Lexi and our chatting with each other and trading more girlie secrets about the school and some of the students.

Our conversation kept up and became more detailed as we warmed up more to each other. I was actually beginning to feel as if we had known each other for years. We were so engrossed in our talk that neither of us was aware of anyone anywhere close to us when we were jerked back to reality by a sudden and unexpected interruption.

"Good afternoon, Ladies … might I please introduce myself," a soft and silky smooth voice spoke right in front of us. We both looked up, startled, at the same time. In fact I actually jumped at the sudden shock of his closeness. He must have seen my reaction at the unexpected surprise. In return, he flashed a perfect smile and quickly added, "Oh, please do excuse me, I did not mean to frighten you."

I found myself looking up into the most intensely gorgeous emerald green eyes I had ever seen. They were deep and inviting like a pool of cool water on a hot day. They actually glimmered as I found myself being drawn into their depths … so comforting, so mesmerizing … I wanted to just sink right into them. Just as suddenly, and with no warning, they changed and I got the profound feeling that they were searching back, into the very depths of my soul. I literally shivered in my chair at their sudden coldness even though I found myself unable to look away.

I tried to remember my manners, *and* how to talk, but replied with a low, strained, 'Hi'. I couldn't believe myself, the hottest, most perfect man I had ever seen was standing right in front of me, asking if he could talk and all I could do was stammer. I quickly thought to myself, *"Geez, Katelyn, really … you couldn't do any better than 'hi' … you go girl, that's certainly going to make a great first impression with him … how lame can you possibly be …"*

A soft smile played teasingly about his mouth as he continued standing there, revealing perfectly straight, white teeth, his eyes still intent on me, "My name is James Thomas Dubois, of Whitehall Manor … and you are?"

"I … I'm sorry," I stumbled over my words again, "good afternoon, sir … " I said, trying to quickly recover my senses and not look like a total idiot to this dream standing so comfortably in front of me. I swallowed quickly and started over, trying to smile, "my name is Katelyn … Katelyn Corbin," I said, offering my hand, "and this is my friend, Alexis Gordon," I said indicating Lexi.

"It is indeed my pleasure to meet you Katelyn Corbin," he continued smiling at me and taking my hand in his. "You must be new here, I do not recall having seen you on campus before, welcome to Charleston."

"Thank you, sir, it's a pleasure to meet you," I replied, "and I am new, I've just moved here from Atlanta, today's my first day of school."

When he touched me, taking my hand so gently in his, I noticed how very cool and soft it felt. I was still absolutely mesmerized looking into his eyes, unable, and un-wanting, to look away, and with the added sense of touch I got the impression of a tangible connection between us and it was pulling me even deeper into him. It was as if time simply stopped as he continued to stand there, smiling, softly holding my hand and looking into my eyes.

I was suddenly overtaken with a peculiar desire … one that I couldn't explain … I had the strangest feeling that I wanted to stand up and let him take me in his arms … I wanted to feel his arms around me, his body against me, and I wanted to get lost in the aura of strength that seemed to surround him. I was again speechless … and I felt almost … helpless.

Then deep inside me there came a sudden, unexplained flash of fear, and for a split second I knew how the prey felt looking into the eyes of the predator. The sudden fear disappeared just as quickly as it came and was replaced by a comforting wave of peace and safety that seemed to wash over me, settling all around me. I was immediately and completely at ease.

"I assure you Katelyn, the pleasure is all mine, and I

do hope this isn't the last time we meet," he said still gazing into my eyes and continuing to smile softly as he released my hand.

Then reaching inside his pocket he took out a small silver case, opened it and handed me a card saying, "This shall ensure your safety and protection anywhere you may find yourself in the Charleston area. Please keep it close to your person in case you need it and present it to anyone you might have issues with. I wish you a pleasant stay and a good afternoon. May you be at peace, and above all, stay safe."

"I hope it isn't the last time we meet, either," I whispered softly, almost to myself.

Then, still smiling, he nodded his head to each of us, turned and walking swiftly away, he was gone just as suddenly as he had appeared.

I blinked and suddenly felt like I had been shaken out of a dream. I felt slightly dazed as I looked askance at Lexi, "Wow, Lexi ... what in the world just happened ... that was so insanely intense ... and why didn't you jump in and say something?"

She took a short, deep breath and slowly exhaled, as if she too were being shaken awake before softly replying, "I'm not exactly sure Katelyn ... I felt ... mesmerized ... it was almost like I couldn't speak and I'm not too sure I could have moved either. How did he do that? He was sitting in that chair stone still and then suddenly standing right here in front of us ... did you even see him move? And please tell me I saw him bow when he introduced himself?"

"I didn't see him move either, of course I wasn't really paying that close attention to him. I was too busy chatting with you, and, yeah, I think he did bow, maybe just a little. Humph, it seems our Mr. Dubois might be a real life gentleman. He even talks like a gentleman … very proper … in fact," I smiled remembering his easy words, "He certainly looks young enough, but he talks like I would imagine some of the old traditional gentlemen of the European aristocracy to speak."

"Honestly, Katelyn, that is the most I have ever heard him speak to anybody," she said, "he never engages in conversation with any of the students. I've been here and seen him off and on for over three years and I've never gotten much more than just a quick nod of his head in passing or the occasional 'good day' from him."

We looked blankly at each other, still puzzled over what had just happened. Then I remembered the card in my hand and looked down at it. It was an elaborate and expensive, textured, bone colored parchment card that was heavily engraved:

And turning it over in my hand, I saw one line written on the back, in a beautiful, flowing, bold, script:

Protection and Safe Passage, J.T.D.

"What'd you think that means … and what'd you think he meant about keeping me safe in the Charleston area," I asked still looking down at the card I held.

"Well, duh Katelyn, let's see … besides being really handsome … he's obscenely rich … he's well known … and he has good connections … so tell me, what do you think he meant," she laughed.

"I think I'm gonna go with a 'get out of a speeding

ticket free' card," I laughed as I looked at the card in my hand, "you think it would work for that?"

"Katelyn, you've got forty foot legs … those would get you out of a speeding ticket," she answered laughing, "that card on the other hand would likely get you out of a murder rap … but either way, I think I would do like he said and keep it close to you just in case."

She and I were both still in shock over what had just happened, we talked some more, trying to figure out what to say about the whole situation. Finally, with no real answer to explain it, we decided it was time to head back to the room and call it a night.

Later, back in the dorm, and still unable to sleep, I lay restlessly on my pint size student bed, thinking about Mr. Dubois. My introduction to him had indeed been the strangest incident of the day. I had found most of the men I talked with to be a little intimidated of me. They shied away as if they were scared of me, not that I am a frightful person, but Mr. Dubois had dominated the introduction and our small talk. That was different for me because usually it was the other way around.

He had such a profound effect on me … one that I couldn't explain and didn't understand. I know it sounds weird, but the thing is, when he walked away from our conversation, he left me feeling very pleasant and relaxed … in fact, I had felt almost as if I had just had sex … really good sex … and I had enjoyed it.

There was something else about this man – besides being handsome, tall, and charming – that seemed to be so out of the ordinary … it was almost as if he radiated a persona that marked him as … as different. He looked as if he was so confident of himself; it gave the impression of his self-confidence just pouring out of him. I was intrigued, and unquestionably had more than just a passing curiosity in him. I wanted to know more about him … who was he … what did he do … and what things interested him.

I continued to dwell on how he had made me feel … it was as if the entire world had disappeared when he looked into my eyes … there was nothing, nobody, except him, looking at me, and me looking back at him … my heart had sped up in my chest when he took my hand in his, my skin tingled all over as I struggled to know what to say to him. I felt like I wanted to talk to him, like I wanted to be close to him. There came a deep settling in me that we would meet again. I relished the thought of that time, hoping it would be sooner rather than later.

I realized there was something special, something unique that attracted me to him more than I had ever been attracted to another man before. It was almost as if there was some drawing force, pulling me toward him, and I liked it. Truthfully, I enjoyed the thought of being close to him again.

But, as I lay there, I just could not shake the feeling of his eyes as they looked into mine. They were the most memorable thing about him. They were so intense, so alluring, I felt so peaceful looking into them. They made everything alright … my past … my present … and my future … were all there, absorbed in those beautiful, deep green eyes.

I don't think I had ever seen anyone's eyes glimmer like his. They were such a perplexity, so full of warmth and light but with an unexplained cold darkness behind them at the same time. During those few seconds that he held my hand and looked into my eyes, I felt like all of my entire life's secrets were laid bare for him to examine. I couldn't hold anything back, and I didn't want to hold anything back, from him. In fact, if it hadn't been so peaceful and calming, it might have been more than a little frightening.

Finally, in the early hours of the morning, when I had examined our meeting from every angle, sleep began to leisurely creep in upon me. I struggled against it with all that was in me, knowing that so often it brought with it the terrible nightmare. Unable to stop its insidious crawl, I gradually surrendered, step by step and almost fearfully, to the alluring pull of the darkness. When I could fight no longer, knowing that I was about to tumble into the frightening depths of untold terror and endless horror, my eyes closed and I drifted off into the hands of the waiting darkness.

But this night was different. I slept soundly and peacefully for the first time in months, and thankfully, there were no screams to rip me out of the depths of my slumber … because this night, there were no nightmares. Instead, I dreamed peacefully about his eyes, and each time the dream was the same, those bright, emerald green eyes … soft, deep pools, comforting and inviting as they looked into my soul, protectively watching over me, keeping the terror of the night safely at bay.

Chapter Five

The huge grandfather clock in the outer hall slowly tolled the midnight hour. The deep resonant sounds of its Westminster chimes resonated throughout the lower level of the house. I sat quietly in the main parlor, the sound of the chimes echoing through the darkened house while I meticulously reflected on the events of the day.

I found myself absently listening to the slow tick-tock of the old clock when I realized that the sound of the silence that surrounded both the house and the grounds at this hour, for some strange reason this night, seemed unusually loud and weighed heavily upon my soul. I was attempting to relax, the fresh blood I had taken earlier in the afternoon from that luscious co-ed I had marked out at the end of the last semester, was slowly absorbing into my system, refreshing and strengthening me, but my mind was too preoccupied with the events of the day to make relaxation a firm reality.

Instead, I was engrossed in considering the course of my life and the role that Fate has played therein, accepting that for whatever reason, Providence has often intervened in my life. Its first intrusion, in 1748, began with the deaths of my beloved wife and newborn daughter. Afterward, in 1753, it then led me on a journey to England where, consequently, I had met Charlotte Ann and received an incredible gift at her hands.

It was in that spring of 1753 that I was born to second life and subsequently discovered the true meaning of the Fountain of Youth, and forever to have the appearance of the twenty-eight year old I was when I first drank from her veins.

Finally, this very afternoon, in January 2012, some two hundred sixty four years after its first appearance, Fate had once again reared its head in my life. The affairs of earlier, as often times have happened when Destiny steps in, left me momentarily confused, but even more so, curious as to its desired end result.

The day began as nearly any other day, the only difference being that it was the first day of the spring semester at The College of Charleston, and, as was my habit, I made my appearance on campus concealed in the guise of the wealthy patron of the school that I have successfully cloaked myself in since just after my return to South Carolina near the end of the nineteenth century.

The mortals think that it's a family tradition running back to my great grandfather since they have no conception that I am or could be, an immortal ... a vampire in their terminology. I often wonder, if they were to actually discover my secret, whether or not they would continue to accept the large amounts of money I donate to the school that allows me free access to the campus for feeding. After allowing myself a chuckle at the thought of the looks on the faces of the Board of Regents were they to uncover that colossal truth, I resumed my pondering of the events of the day, interested as to exactly what would be the end result of this latest intervention of Providence in my life.

When this present intrusion of Fate began, I had been sitting comfortably in a chair in the student union pretending to read but in actuality listening closely to the chatter of conversation on all sides of me. I had learned by now to identify the presence of Fate whenever it arrived on the scene, and this particular appearance began when I heard my name mentioned not once, but twice, in a whispered conversation. I quickly tuned out the hum of the surrounding noise and honed in on it, focusing my attention on the two girls who had decided to make me the topic of their afternoon discussion.

I cast my eyes across the room and found myself looking into the face of a most attractive young girl, one with truly penetrating and lovely electric blue eyes like none I had seen in nearly three hundred years. They were so stunningly gorgeous as to have almost taken my breath away.

A second look revealed that she was also strikingly beautiful … her tanned skin was smooth and clear … she had long, thick, dark brown hair framing her face and covering her shoulders like a cowl. I could easily see the deep blue line of the carotid artery running up the side of her neck pulsating with her young life, beckoning to me, just one blindingly swift bite away.

A closer examination revealed her face and features to be perfectly symmetrical, with the exception that the corners of her mouth were both slightly upturned, resulting in a semi-permanent smile that gave her just an added touch of mystery, thus making her all the more enticing to me. She was without doubt, the embodiment of perfect human beauty. While I continued to watch, the blood lust flashed intensely through me, leaving behind the gentle tingle of my fangs preparing to extend.

That particular girl, a new student on campus, had introduced herself as Katelyn Corbin from Atlanta, and she had quickly become the precise reason for my current musings, and was indeed a conundrum. On the one hand she was absolutely delectable, when I had introduced myself, the scent of her blood had covered me like a cloud, reaching to the very depths of my nature and pulling me toward it.

I had breathed in her heady scent, and found myself salivating at the thought of taking this young girl … the fragrance of her youthful life was so intense that I found myself also quickly becoming physically aroused at the thought of taking her blood. There was no doubt the taste of her blood, like a perfectly aged vintage wine, would be joyously rich and delectably satisfying … and it was literally all that I could do to restrain myself from snatching her then and there. There was no doubt that had I done so, I would have taken more than just a drink of her blood … I would have taken her life also. It was a life and blood that I felt sure in a manner like none other before it, would for the time being at least, satisfy the immortal thirst.

But on the other hand, when I had looked beyond her brilliant blue eyes and into her soul, I quickly discovered a complexity of hurt the width and depth of which only Death itself can leave. I had easily recognized the trauma and scars she carried hidden away because they were dreadfully similar to the same ones that I had carried for so many years in my own mortal life.

I had no inkling the cause of her grief, yet knowing first hand from my own experience how difficult it is for one so young to have to bear the pain and agony of such loss, my empathy for her momentarily overtook my nature. That single moment of compassion was, in actuality, probably all that saved her life. Once my nature had been forced to shift its focus, I was further intrigued to also discover that she was a very powerful telepath … a gift that she obviously had no knowledge of as demonstrated by her completely unbridled thoughts that were focused in my direction.

Yet in spite of all this, there remained one other perplexing event that made my afternoon experience so much the stranger … while I had continued to examine this young girl, I had been unexpectedly overcome with a desire to tell her about myself and my nature … all of the secrets … not holding back anything. I could not understand why, but all of a sudden, it became extremely important to me that *she* know *me* … it was very nearly a driving force within me to completely open up to her … I felt as if I wanted to sit with her and explain in detail my entire life … from the beginning until now … something that for nearly three hundred years I had never desired to share with a mortal.

My silent deliberations were suddenly interrupted when I realized that I was no longer alone. I looked up and around for the presence that unexpectedly filled the room – a presence that I was incredibly familiar with – even after the passage of over two and a half centuries – that of my wife. Her spectral apparition, while not frightening to me, did add to my bewilderment of the day's events being as this was the first time I had seen or felt her presence since the events of my birth to second life.

She stood perfectly still and silent before me as if she were examining every feature of my face. Finally she slowly reached out her hand toward me, and I was overjoyed as once again the gentle touch of her delicate fingers soothingly caressed my cheek. Her eyes contained a glint of joy when she slowly smiled at me, a special smile that had always been reserved for our most private moments.

"Mary Beth, my darling wife," I began slowly, happily, "it's wonderful to see you again ... to what do I owe the pleasure of this visit?"

"James, my beloved husband, my first and only love," her delicate voice floated softly through my mind, *"do you not remember my words when last we spoke?"*

"Indeed I do," I answered carefully, "you told me that at some point in time, I would find someone else ... an immortal mate ... and I have heard those words repeated over and again nearly every moment of every day since you uttered them."

"Your immortal memory is as good as your mortal memory ever was," she smiled again, *"and that point in time has finally arrived. Though you didn't know it at the moment, you met her today and she shall change your life in ways that you could never have foreseen, just as you will change her life, restoring love and happiness in her soul while at the same time, fulfilling both your destinies."*

"Are you referring to the young girl ... Katelyn ... the new student ... the one that I had so desperately to struggle against taking this afternoon?"

"Indeed I am ... why do you think you were so conflicted ... so hesitant ... so unable to simply take her like all the others before her ... it's because Fate has laid his hand upon her, just as he did you, and now, the two of you are predestined to explore eternity together ... as time passes and you grow in unison, you will take some from her, she will take some from you, and each of you shall become stronger becoming one with the other, forming an unbreakable and eternal bond between you."

"But what of you my love," I questioned, "what shall

become of you?"

"I have watched over you James, ever since the first day we were parted," she whispered softly, *"and now that your eternal mate has entered your life, there is no longer room for me outside of a memory. I will go now and join our daughter Mary, and the two of us shall live for eternity in our realm just as the two of you shall live for eternity in your realm."*

"I love you Mary Beth …" I whispered, "and I shall always maintain a special place in my heart for you … and I hope, whatever realm you live in, that you will also keep my memory alive in your heart."

"You have been in my heart since long before I crossed over," she smiled happily, and feeling the soft brush of her lips on my cheek, she continued, *"and I have no doubt that you will always remember me."*

"Forever …" I answered.

"But now my love, your mate needs you … quickly … go to her and begin your watchful protection over her until the time comes when you are joined together."

I watched, broken hearted as she began to fade away, and felt tears that I knew were filled with blood begin to trace their way slowly down my face.

I stood motionless for a few moments staring at the place where only a moment before the spiritual likeness of my mortal mate had stood … then like a clarion bell in the night her words rang through me again, *'your mate needs you … quickly … go to her'*, and like an unseen force, they plucked strongly at my soul.

I quickly envisioned the student dormitories at the campus and, in a twinkling of time, translated myself there. When I arrived, having spent an untold number of nights over the years within the various rooms of the building, I knew immediately where I was and how to find my way around. I shielded myself from the view of any wandering mortals that might be awake and about at this late hour, and began my search for Katelyn's room.

The memory of her scent was so intense that it filled my nostrils and was very nearly a visible trail to her door. I quickly located her room on the third floor, at the far end of the hall on the right. I once again melted into the darkness and reappeared on the other side of the door. I looked around and found that her room was very much like that of any of the other co-eds, there were posters pinned to the walls, books and clothes littered the floor and every available shelf had something on it. The two beds were both occupied, Katelyn in the one furthest away, next to the window, and her roommate in the one closest to the door. I stepped silently across the short distance and stood beside her bed watching and listening to see what it was she needed.

I noted that she appeared to have just been overtaken by sleep and was slipping deeper into it by the moment. Her descent seemed to reach a certain point, just short of peaceful rest, and there it stopped. I listened as her breathing increased, becoming ragged, her brow began to crease with pain, and her heartbeat sped up precipitously, filling the air around her with the scent of fear.

Earlier in the day, when I had momentarily taken her hand, I had encountered a terrible nightmare, like an evil monster, lying in wait in her subconscious. I knew it had come again to assault her dreams, vividly replaying the day she had discovered the bodies of her murdered parents. She began to thrash about mumbling words that quickly turned into a vulnerable whimper, *"Noooo … please, please don't make me go any further … I don't want to keep going … I want to stop now … please just let me stay here in the dark … I don't want to see what's ahead … I don't want to see them that way … please don't make me look at it again …"*

I reached out, carefully touching her hand and silently whispered to her mind, *"Peace Katelyn, pass the night pleasantly and serenely.'* I repeated my admonition a second time and watched as her brow began to smooth out, her breathing and heartbeat both settled to a low, steady rhythm, and I knew that she was sleeping soundly, undisturbed by the awful night terror. Her face became completely relaxed as she now continued to drift deeper into sleep.

I very carefully reached out and brushed the hair away from her face with my fingertips and silently leaned over her. I breathed in her delicate fragrance, one that was soft and clean, committing it forever to memory, and then ever so lightly touching my lips to her forehead, spoke once again to her mind, *"I shall stay and protect you until the morning, and when I leave, I shall take the night terrors with me. After this night you shall never again be bothered by the horrors that lurk in the darkness, now sleep peacefully my love and take your rest."*

I closely examined her as I began my continued protective watch over her, wondering at what force in the universe it was that had brought us, two complete strangers, born two and a half centuries apart, one mortal and one immortal, into each other's lives.

While she peacefully slept, the scent of her blood, still retaining a surreal element of innocence, one that I didn't often encounter in the co-eds, floated above her, surrounding her like a protective veil. My nature flared up inside, reminding me of just how vulnerable she was lying there, and how luscious she would taste were I to take her.

Quickly turning my thoughts from an incessant nature, I noted instead that during the initial stages of the nightmare she had kicked her covering to the end of the bed. She lay there completely exposed, clothed only in a pair of scanty lace panties and a loose, thin, tee shirt that had worked its way up to the bottom of her breasts.

The man that I am certainly appreciated to no end the work of beauty that nature had fashioned in her … I saw nothing about her that was not perfection personified … not unlike a flawless sculpture of a Greek Goddess … her skin was as smooth and clear as alabaster … her dark hair was splayed out fanlike on the pillow revealing her perfectly formed neck that was so inviting to my nature. Her shoulders looked soft as they tapered into long delicate arms, and hands that were slim and graceful with beautifully formed fingers and perfectly manicured nails. Her breasts, though small, were equally proportional to her build. Her stomach and flanks were flat and taut, flowing into and forming the shallow valley at the bottom of her belly. I smiled at the slight protrusion of her hip bones and noted that, like so many others of her age, she had a tattoo, this one a winged Fairy, which perched delicately atop the right side. Her legs were long and elegant, with feet and toes that were as perfectly formed and impeccable as the rest of her body.

I once again fought against my nature, resisting the desire to allow my fangs to extend and take her. However beautiful she was, lying there uncovered, unclothed, and her life at my mercy, the gentleman I was raised to be overcame the physical man's immortal lusts, and reaching out I gently pulled the sheet back over her nakedness, covering her to her shoulders.

Then I straightened up and stepped away, back into the dark shadows, between the window and corner of the room, just across from her bed. Drawing the darkness around me like a cloak, I stood there for the remainder of the night, silent as a crypt, and motionless as only an immortal can.

While the hours passed away and I continued my vigil, I began to sense a disturbance in the center of my being. It was a sensation I had not experienced in over two centuries. It continued to stir, and finally coming to the forefront, I realized what it was ... it was love for another person ... and that person was lying peacefully in front of me.

As this realization sank home to me, I willingly surrendered my will to that of Fate. I pondered where Fate, this time, would lead, not just me and her, but both of us. As the dawn of a new day, in more ways than I could have ever imagined, crept closer, I continued to watch and consider Katelyn, and as I did so, my perception of her, as that of a possible mate, changed hour by hour.

The only disturbance of my watch came when her roommate, the one with the tiny musical voice, stirred and woke, walking drowsily to their bathroom and then returning to her bed and immediately falling back asleep. Katelyn began to stir an hour before dawn and just before she opened her eyes I disappeared from her room, returning to Whitehall, where I began to prepare the estate for its first mortal visitor in more than a century.

Chapter Six

The next day, after classes, Lexi and I met up in the commons area again to study and compare our notes from the lectures and then plan something to do. We talked about our various options and finally decided to take the afternoon and evening off. We agreed to go downtown, she offered to drive, and find some fresh seafood for dinner instead of eating on campus.

Lexi has the most awesome car, a fully restored, bright red, 1965 Mustang convertible that her parents gave her for high school graduation. So she drove us downtown to a small but really nice and comfortable restaurant on King Street called the Old Towne Grill. We wandered in and were able to find a seat right away in a booth about half way to the back. It had a welcoming and comfortable family diner feeling to it. The smells from the kitchen filled the air with a mixture of seafood, strong herbs, and other spices. We both ordered a glass of red wine and sipped on it while we checked out the menu. Everything looked and sounded so good it was impossible to choose a single item. So we did the next best thing, we split one of their seafood platters and had white wine for our dinner.

The seafood was outstanding and lots of it, too. There was a good selection of shrimp, scallops, oysters, a couple of fish filets, and some calamari. We chatted with our waitress while we ate and when she found out that I was new in town she insisted we try their Low County Shrimp and Grits.

Lexi and I looked at each other and hesitated a bit. So our waitress agreed to bring us a sampler order on the house if we would try them. We did … and they were to die for good! So to show our appreciation we ordered dessert – a chocolate truffle mousse and it's a good thing we were splitting it because it was way more than enough for one. We really enjoyed ourselves but afterward realized just how much we had eaten.

"Lexi, that was absolutely wonderful," I said as we left the restaurant, "probably the best seafood I have ever eaten … much better than what we have in Atlanta!"

"Well duh," she answered with a happy laugh, "maybe because we have the *sea* that the *seafood* comes from!"

"Yeah, good point … and the wine here isn't bad either," I chuckled.

"Yup, it's pretty good," she agreed, "and with that said, do you want to let's walk off some of the shrimp and grits you ate? And crab? And flounder? And hush puppies … dang it, lady, we ate a lot!"

"I know, right … and if you keep taking me to these

kinds of places and I keep eating like that, it won't be long I'll be putting on my 'Freshman Fifteen' and then some! So yeah, let's go walk … besides it'll be good to get the city under my feet. Get to know her a bit."

We both laughed happily and decided we would take our walk down King Street to work off some of the meal. It was a nice evening out and starting to cool off a little. When I stepped out on the sidewalk and into the cool air I realized that after two glasses of wine, I probably did need the walk. Besides, it was certainly better than going right back to the dorm room.

I was glad for our decision, too, because I wanted some alone time, with nobody else around, to talk with Lexi. We began checking out the windows of some of the stores while we walked. Since most of them were already closed for the day all we could do was look, which also ensured we couldn't do any damage to our bank accounts, either.

After a couple of blocks of easy strolling I broke the silence, "Lexi … I've been thinking …"

"Let me guess," she smiled happily, "it has something to do with a tall, handsome man with green eyes?"

"Oh so you're a mind reader too," I grinned back, "just another of your many talents?"

"If only you knew of many talents," she laughed uproariously.

"But yeah … you're right … it does … the problem is I don't really know how I feel about him. He made such an incredible impression on me. But, I can't decide if he's mysterious, dangerous, or just plain wonderful."

"But Katelyn, what if he's all three," she asked looking at me with an impish smile.

"Now that would be an interesting combination, wouldn't it," I commented, "but, do you know anything at all about him other than what you told me about yesterday?"

"Nothing, except that he's very private. In fact, no one seems to know much about him," then she added with a grin, "but I have a feeling that you are going to try and take a peek behind that curtain of mystery and see what else you can find out about him, aren't you?"

"Well," I laughed, "since I can't get him out of my head, I might as well see what else there is to know. But, Lexi, I just can't get over his eyes. They were so … I don't know … different. I felt like he was looking into my deepest self and seeing all my secrets. But it felt good, too. Anyway, seriously, I really would like to hear from him again, soon. I bet that if nothing else he would be a fun date!"

"Ummm … define fun," she smiled looking up at me.

"Well … you know …" I laughed.

We both shared a friendly chuckle over that and continued with our walk. After a few more minutes of silently walking, Lexi looked over, and with a mischievous grin said, "I just had an idea … want me to take you and show you something really big … that is if you think you'd be interested. It's something all the native Charlestonians brag about and not many people know what they are looking at when they see it."

"Alright, you got my interest," I laughed back, "is it close by or do we have to drive?"

"It's your first night out in Charleston, you deserve to see it in style Hot-Lanta," she laughed, "let's splurge … we'll take one of the horse carriages and really enjoy the evening."

"That sounds like fun," I said, "but aren't we supposed to be walking off our dinner, not having it walked off for us by Clydesdales or … or whatever those horses are. I've never actually met a horse before."

"Yeah, but we have walked almost three blocks. That's should be good for forty or fifty shrimp, easy," she smiled.

"You certainly didn't miss your calling by choosing history over math, did you missy," I laughed.

"Probably not," she grinned broadly, "but I can balance a checkbook … if I have to … come on … my treat … you're going to be blown away when you see how big this is."

"Okay, I'm game … I saw one of the carriages back at the top of the block, let's go see if he's still there."

We caught the carriage and Lexi told the driver we wanted to go down King, circle around White Point Gardens, and make a short stop at the battery before returning. She paid the driver and then we sat back in the seat and enjoyed the ride. It was my first carriage ride and I let my imagination roam, quickly becoming a princess in a royal coach. It was really an adventure for me and soon between the slow clip-clop of the horse's hooves and the sound of the iron wheel bands rolling on the cobblestone and brick street, I started getting heavy eyes. Combined with the big dinner, the two glasses of wine, and the cool evening air, I quickly found myself edging closer to sleep.

As we rode along down King Street, I looked over at Lexi with a big smile, and yawning said, "If this keeps up you can just wake me when we get where we're going."

"Oh no you don't Lady …" she laughed pushing playfully at my shoulder, "no sleeping … you have to stay awake and enjoy the whole experience … besides … we're almost there."

"Sorry … blame it on the shrimp … and the wine! It's really lovely out here," I answered drowsily, "but I sure don't want to miss something big.

Even in the late dusk the Gardens were a thing of

beauty with the huge old live oaks planted all along the edges of it. I could see the sculpted walking paths and some monuments from the carriage. The air around us was filled with the smell of the salty harbor water mixed with the scent of some early blooming magnolias wafting all around us. There was a big white gazebo in the center of it with a small band set up in it, the sound of their music carrying softly on the breeze. Along the waterfront stood the old cannons still pointing across the harbor at Fort Sumter. I made a mental note for us to come back during the day sometime soon and have a picnic.

When we got to the battery and stopped, Lexi grabbed my hand, and jumping out of the carriage with me in tow, said, "C'mon, sleepy head, you have got to see this to believe it!"

I was suddenly wide awake again and excited about whatever the big attraction was she wanted me to see. I followed her to the railing along the edge of the water where she stopped and extended her hand out over the harbor.

"There it is," she exclaimed with a flourish and a laugh.

"There what is …" I asked slowly, a little confused, "It looks like Charleston Harbor to me."

"It only looks like the harbor to you because you're a foreigner!"

"Hey, I'm not a foreigner, I'm from Atlanta," I laughed back.

"I rest my case …" she giggled happily, "I'm kidding … but look, there, on your right is the Ashley River …"

"Okay, I see that," I said turning and looking up the river.

"And in the other direction, to your left, is the Cooper River …"

"Yeah," I said nodding and looking back at her, "I see that too."

"And this," she continued pointing out in front of us, "is the exact point where the two rivers come together and continue out past Fort Sumter to form the Atlantic Ocean," and she burst out laughing, "you see, I told you it was big!"

"Oh dear Lord," I laughed loudly as the realization of her joke sank in, "tell me again … how much wine did you have?"

"Only two glasses … just like you," she chuckled.

"Yeah, but you got a smaller package to put it in," I answered hugging her as we stood there laughing. Then turning back, leaning casually on the railing, we stood there together, two friends quietly looking out over the harbor, each of us lost in our thoughts. After a few minutes I glanced over at Lexi, who was still smiling like the Cheshire Cat at her joke and thought to myself, *"It's so wonderful to be out again and to enjoy it with such a great new friend."*

On the drive back to campus, Lexi was telling me all about the many things to do, and places to visit, in the Charleston area. She pointed out several sights along the way and told me a little about each one. I slowly began to realize how tired I was from such a full evening and started thinking about how good it would be to get in my little bed tonight. I laid my head on the back of the seat and closed my eyes for a couple of minutes to think.

When I opened my eyes again I looked over at Lexi and very seriously said, "Lexi, thank you so much for this evening. You can't possibly imagine how much I needed to just get out with a friend and clear my head. I am just absolutely worn out tired and looking forward to a good night's sleep."

She looked back at me with a smile that only sisters

can share and said, "Yeah, Katelyn, that was kinda the plan all along. Just don't get too tired on me, because I have a couple of other plans in mind, too."

"Does it consist of some more of that yummy seafood like we had tonight," I asked with a huge smile.

"I'm sure there will be plenty more of that," she answered, "but first, how would you like to maybe take a ride down to Folly Beach this weekend? It's really nice this time of year. We could get our toes in the sand, soak up some sunshine … and maybe check out some of those fine guys, too!"

"Hmm … that sounds like fun … yeah," I smiled, "I'm in … let's plan on doing that. I could get used to Charleston, you know … seafood, the beach, good company … and you did say hot guys, right?"

"Smokin' hot and lots of them," she laughed.

"Great," I laughed, "but I need to call Aunt 'Chele first, just to make sure she isn't expecting me home this weekend."

We were still laughing and giggling about our night out when we went through the dorm doors into the lobby. Just as we started up the stairs I turned to Lexi and quickly asked, "Hey, did you check our mailbox today?"

"Seriously … you mean like envelopes and letters and stuff like that," she laughed, "Do you really still get snail mail?"

"Uhhh, yeah, I still get snail mail," I grinned.

"Well, how properly old fashioned of you," she chuckled, "I haven't checked the mail since like, I don't know, 2005 maybe."

"You should check it, you might have won the

Publishing Clearing House," I laughed.

"If it isn't in e-mail, I don't pay it any attention," she chuckled and added, "by the way, do you use text messages or do you still use carrier pigeons?"

"Yeah, Ha Ha, you're funny … besides carrier pigeons are extinct … I'm checking the mail anyway," I said.

I opened our shared box and found a slip inside that instructed me to check at the dorm desk for a delivery.

"See … there is something there," I crowed, waving the slip around.

I handed the girl on desk duty the slip and asked what kind of delivery I had. She handed me a note and a single long stem red rose. My name was hand written in a beautiful script on heavy parchment and closed with a red wax seal. The paper exactly matched the card I had in my purse so I guessed who it was from before I even opened it. I looked at Lexi and she was looking at me with a huge grin that said she thought so, too.

"Hmmm … wonder what this could be …" I mused playfully.

"Bet I know … and who it's from too," she smiled.

"Truth time Lexi," I said as I passed the rose under my nose and flipped the noted around, "Do you think he's mysterious … dangerous … or just plain old fashioned romantic?"

"Well I suppose he *could* be all three," she began slowly, "and honestly, not trying to be a Debbie Downer here, but if I had to bet, I'd probably go with dangerous … I just don't know how dangerous and to whom. But at the same time, you gotta admit the rose and note is pretty romantic."

"Well, why wait, let's find out," I said as I broke the seal on the note and began reading it … and a smile began spreading slowly across my face.

Katelyn,

I would be honored if you and your friend, Alexis, would join me at Whitehall Manor this Saturday afternoon for a late lunch. Perhaps 2:00 pm, if that would be convenient for you. Please present this note to the Gate Keeper and he shall grant you access to the estate. I look forward to your company. Until then, I remain,

Sincerely,

JTD

I was utterly speechless as I stood there holding the note and the rose. I could not believe what I was seeing. I sailed through mixed emotions … all good ones … excitement that he had invited me … well, us … to lunch … anticipation at getting to actually visit Whitehall … and happiness at the thought of getting to see him again so soon.

"Well will you look at this …" I grinned huge.

"What is it, Katelyn, what does it say," Lexi asked, her eyes lit up with excitement.

"It seems that he's invited me to Whitehall Manor for lunch this Saturday."

Lexi looked astonished and maybe a bit numb before finally saying, "Oh, my God! Katelyn! You got a personal, handwritten invitation to Whitehall for lunch! It would seem that you did make quite an impression on him. But are you going to accept it … are you really going to go way out there? All alone? It's almost an hour's drive away … I don't know if that's safe. You know you can't be too careful these days and even if –"

"He's invited you to come along too," I smiled at her.

"Oh … Okayyy … well in that case we obviously have to go," she smiled, trying unsuccessfully to hide her happiness.

"Silly duck … you're ridiculous," I chuckled.

"Yeah, absolutely … but we're still going, right? Right? We're going," she almost begged, "Please say 'yes', we just have to go. I want so badly to see Whitehall after all I've heard about it. I have so many questions and, heck, my thesis could get published because of this visit! I mean no one has been in there in … I don't know … ever! So … please say we're going."

"Yes Lexi, we're going," I smiled patiently at her.

"Oh Katelyn – thank you … thank you … thank you," she laughed happily and danced around.

"I'm going to assume that you're happy about this," I grinned at her.

"You don't know how happy … you've made my career … thank you … thank you … thank you," she bubbled and then standing on her tiptoes she grabbed my shoulders and kissed me on the cheek, "I can't believe it … we're actually going to Whitehall!"

"Of course we're going," I said with a smile, "besides, according to you, it seems that just everybody doesn't get an opportunity like this … and I did tell you I would love to visit out there and see the … umm … artwork," I added with a little chuckle.

I silently handed her the note to read for herself. I stood there for a moment, while she reread the note, soundlessly remembering Mr. Dubois. I saw him again in my mind, so handsome, so mysterious. I just couldn't forget his vivid green eyes and how they seemingly peered into the depths of my soul. Then somewhere, again deep inside, I suddenly had just a touch of uneasiness edging toward fear. I just could not put my finger on what was causing it yet. It felt almost as if I knew I should stay away, just crumple the note up and forget about it, but, like the forbidden fruit in the garden, I just had to have a closer look.

I did look forward to the trip, but after the sudden mixed feelings, I just could not seem to get as excited as Lexi about it. Finally, I decided that I was being impractical about the whole thing. Maybe because I had such a dark past I was simply afraid and didn't want to face anything new and unknown. I wanted to feel completely safe in my own little world, someplace where I could never be hurt again. I realized I was going to have to make a real effort to shake the past and move on with my life. I knew that's exactly what my parents would have wanted me to do, too.

"Besides," I thought to myself, *"you're getting exactly what you wanted … a chance to see him again and spend some more time with him … make the best of it, enjoy the opportunity … after all he is pretty wonderful … at least at first sight."*

So I turned to Lexi again and with a smile said, "Of course you know, this means we'll have to wait until Sunday to go to the beach."

"Oh, that's alright" she answered quickly, her eyes sparkling with happiness as the excitement lit up her face, "We can go to the beach anytime! I still can't believe we actually got a handwritten invitation to Whitehall. This is so fantastic! I've heard so much about it, I can't wait to get out there and see it for real! And, uhhh, you think I could have the note … to put in my scrapbook."

I looked at her with a laugh and said, "I'll even give you the envelope too … my, my here I thought I was the one all excited about wanting to see Whitehall and its 'artwork' now just look at you!"

"Yeah, but that was before I ever thought we would get the chance to really visit," she laughed.

We went up to our room and as we got ready for bed, we sounded like a couple of girlie girls, letting our imaginations run wild about what we could expect this weekend. Her exuberance over the invitation was contagious and I soon forgot any of the reservations I might have had to begin with and drifted off to a peaceful, dreamless sleep.

Chapter Seven

Saturday morning finally arrived, after what seemed like an endlessly long week, and Lexi and I left campus for Whitehall; this time it was my turn to drive while she gave directions. We traveled going south out of the city and picked up an old back road with only two lanes. She told me that it used to be the main route from Charleston to Savannah until the big interstate came through and by-passed it.

The scenery along this route was just beautiful, like nothing I had ever seen in the concrete jungle that's Atlanta. The countryside along both sides of the road was flat and looked sandy with sea and marsh grasses growing all along the road. I saw several old stores here and there that were closed and boarded up, some beginning to crumble, victims of the interstate I supposed. Occasionally there was an old house, built up off the ground, the lumber on it was gray and fading, with an old man or woman sitting on the porch in a rocking chair. They all waved as we passed, I suppose they were amazed that any traffic still came this way.

We continued making our way southward for a little over an hour, when Lexi pointed up ahead to a spot on the side of the road that was the turn off to Whitehall's driveway. I turned into it and began up the short drive to where I saw the gated entrance. It was flanked on either side by a brick wall constructed of what appeared to be repurposed brick but truth be known was likely original to the property.

The two tall black iron gates were huge and gave the impression of being heavy, solid metal. They were typical of gates I had seen in the historic section of Charleston. They were elaborately decorated with intricate scroll work. The whole was topped with a high arch connecting the brick walls and the name WHITEHALL worked into the iron – and they were shut. I began to get a sinking feeling as I pulled up to them and then, surprisingly, they began to open – all on their own.

When I had passed through the gates and continued up the drive the first thing I saw was a long double line of imposingly gigantic, old oak trees surrounded by a thick carpet of lush green grass. These easily had to be the biggest trees I had ever seen. They lined each side of the lane, meeting and melting together at the top. I didn't know much about them but I did know that these trees had to be a couple of hundred years old. Their black bark looked thick and rough; their roots had grown up out of the ground surrounding each one like a protective barrier.

The roots, lower trunks, and large sweeping limbs were partially covered in a thick carpet of green tree moss.

The limbs were thick and gnarled and many of the heavy elbows and upper limbs were dripping with gray Spanish moss. Some of the massive lower limbs had actually bowed with age and nearly touched the grass on the outer sides of the drive. The huge upper limbs almost completely blocked the daylight; the small amount of sunlight that did filter through was quickly absorbed by the dense black bark of the trees. The drive looked like it stayed in a perpetual state of twilight, only here and there did a sunbeam actually break through all the way to the ground. And there appeared to be no end to them as they curved away out of sight. I had the strangest feeling again of being a princess … only this time I was looking into the dark, enchanted forest.

"Wow, isn't this just classic," I said pulling myself back to reality and turning toward Lexi, "it looks like it came right off of some *'Gone With The Wind'* movie poster, doesn't it?"

"This is pretty awesome," she replied, "I've never seen anything this beautiful … and just listen … it's so quiet and seems so peaceful … it makes me want to just stay here forever."

The driveway itself was covered in a mixture of sand and crushed oyster shells that had been raked smooth. I started moving slowly up the drive, when an older man stepped out from behind one of the trees. He lifted his hand up in a small welcoming wave, but at the same time blocked the lane. I eased to a stop and he stepped quickly around to my side of the car. With a kind smile and a soft voice he asked, "Good afternoon, may I help you, please?"

"Good afternoon sir," I answered him with my own smile and handed him the note I had received, "We have an invitation from Mr. Dubois for lunch."

He scanned the note, handed it back to me with a

friendly smile, and said, "Thank you Miss Corbin, welcome to Whitehall Manor, please follow the allee straight ahead, it will be almost a mile to the house. You may park in the front, by the fountain. Mr. Dubois will meet you there. I sincerely hope that you and Miss Gordon have an enjoyable visit."

I started on toward the house and glanced in the rear view mirror and saw … nothing … the man had disappeared just as suddenly as he had appeared. The drive was empty all the way back to the gates, which I noticed were now swinging closed again. I looked over at Lexi and said, "That has to be some of the best concealed security I have ever seen."

"What do you mean," she asked "He was probably just one of the grounds keepers."

"You think so," I replied, "did you happen to notice he called both of us by our last names?"

"Yeah, I heard that, so?"

"Lexi, neither one of our last names are on that note anywhere," I said, "and I don't think a regular grounds keeper would have known them."

"Oh, you're right, I hadn't thought of that. I guess maybe he was more than just a nice old man."

When we reached the end of the allee we passed through a low rock wall with two older capped gate columns on either side. Each of the columns had a huge white marble eagle perching atop them. The drive, now lined on either side with thick green grass, continued a short distance, ending in a circle surrounding a low walled pool with a massive marble fountain sitting serenely in the center of it. The fountain was three tiers high, looked to be at least twenty feet tall, and had a spray of water shooting straight up from the center, and then bubbling quietly as it spilled its way from top to bottom.

There at the end of a wide walkway lined with bright red azaleas, sat the quintessential Southern plantation house. It was absolutely huge, built in the Greek revival style with six giant white fluted columns, topped with elaborately carved Corinthian caps, supporting a huge pediment that stretched the entire length of the house. The house itself was built of white stone with tall windows each flanked by black shutters on either side. There were long wings with matching windows added on each side of the house to make it appear even bigger. On either end of the wings, ivy covered the walls and surrounded the windows there. The porch and front entrance was elevated with four steps leading up to it. The front door itself was actually two doors with side lights half as wide as each door and the whole was capped by a fan shaped top light made of glistening stained glass. There was a small railed veranda that sat above with French doors leading out from the second story.

I parked by the fountain, looked over at Lexi and said, "Wow! Will you look at that …"

"Yeah," she whispered, "Wow is right! Just look at the size of this house, its enormous. Do you think Mr. Dubois lives here by himself … you don't think maybe he has his own Scarlett O'Hare hidden away in there … do you?"

"Well, we're about to find out," I said as he stepped out the front door onto the porch.

He was dressed in a pair of tan casual slacks with a long sleeved, black turtleneck, both of which looked to be tailor fitted. He had his hair tied back at the nape of his neck, with a black ribbon, making a short ponytail. As he stood at the top of the steps waiting for us, I noticed for the first time how tall he actually was, probably a couple of inches over six feet. Even at that distance I could see and feel his eyes on me.

"Daaaammmmmmmnnnnnn girl … will you just look at that tall drink of coooool water," I added with a soft chuckle to Lexi.

"It's looking more like 'Gone With The Wind' by the minute," Lexi commented under her breath, "so, are you ready for lunch at Tara?"

"As God is my witness …" I answered with a thick Southern drawl, "I will never go hungry again."

"Yeah maybe not … but right now something tells me you're pretty thirsty girl," she giggled quietly, then added, "you okay over there?"

"Yeah … I think so … I don't know … not sure," I answered.

When I looked across the short distance back into his eyes a cold chill slowly made its way through me. I shivered as I realized that I could sense something strange … not necessarily evil, just something different … something I was completely unfamiliar with … something I wasn't exactly sure whether or not to be afraid of or to be comfortable with. The chill lasted only a few seconds before it passed through and out of me … and was immediately replaced with that calming voice I had heard in my head the other day when I first saw him saying, *"Relax, Katelyn, you are absolutely safe here, no harm shall come to you."*

I shook my head just the tiniest bit. Still unsure if the reassurance was my own inner voice or something else. I took a deep breath and started walking across the drive to the steps. I looked up at the beautiful top light above the door and noticed that made into the framework of the stained glass was the word 'Whitehall' and the date '1720' centered under it. I took in a short breath realizing just how old the house really was.

Lexi and I reached the top of the steps together and he

greeted us with a smile and a silky smooth, "Good afternoon, Ladies. Welcome to my home! I trust you had a safe and uneventful trip today?"

I smiled and offering my hand said, "Good afternoon, Mr. Dubois. Thank you so much for the invitation; you certainly have a very impressive home."

He took my hand lightly in his, again it felt cool to me, just as it had the first time I met him. His skin was soft and his nails perfectly manicured. Then, as he easily held my hand, all of the anxiety I had harbored just seemed to melt away. I was suddenly relaxed and felt peaceful.

"Please", he replied, still holding my hand, with an easy smile and a light sparkle in his eyes, "my friends call me James. I would be honored if the two of you would do likewise. Please come inside, lunch is set on the rear veranda. I hope you like a more healthy selection. I ordered fresh fruit, some spring herbs and fresh greens for a salad and had a white wine brought up from the cellar."

"Thank you so much for lunch, that sounds delicious," I smiled at him.

"It sure does," Lexi added with a grin, "and Katelyn just mentioned something about being really thirsty!"

He grinned and chuckled softly at her comment adding, "Perhaps we shall be able to find you something to quench your thirst."

We walked through the front door and found ourselves in a very large central hallway. I looked around at it, realizing that it was easily twenty feet wide and ran the entire width of the house from front to back. The ceilings in this majestic room had to be nearly thirty feet high and were open all the way through the second story of the house. It was the grandest foyer I had ever seen.

The side walls were divided by a wide chair rail. The

wainscoting beneath it was red and white cedar; the walls above were a continuous painted country scene rolling from one end to the other. The ceiling was a beautiful sculpted white plaster with gorgeous wide moldings. And hanging in the center was a huge cut crystal chandelier that sparkled brightly in the afternoon light. Even the floor was spectacular, being a highly polished red oak that reflected the light of the front and rear doors. It was so perfectly polished I almost felt like I needed to take my shoes off just to walk across it.

Toward the back of the hall was a giant double staircase on either side winding upwards, meeting at the top and forming a balcony across the back of the space. The balcony covered the entire rear wall and led to the second floor rooms. The delicate looking banister railings were each anchored by a beautifully carved newel post, and ascended the stairs, flowing across the top forming the front rail of the balcony. The rear wall behind the balcony was a series of cut glass panes forming a huge window that allowed the sun in and lit up the entire space with bright natural light. At the back of the main hall under the balcony was a double French door that was at least eight feet tall, again flanked by wide sidelights, opening to the rear veranda.

There were several doors along the side walls which I assumed led into other parts of the house. I glanced into one as we walked past and saw an immense formal dining room. There was a huge table set with twelve places, in what I could only guess was antique China. Two large silver candelabras, each with five tall white candles sat on the table.

Behind another was what appeared to be either an office or a library and study. The walls that I could see through the partially opened door were lined with floor to ceiling book shelves. There was an impressive fireplace with a carved wood mantle and a huge mirror set above it, and several comfortable looking chairs scattered throughout. The windows in both the rooms I could see were tall, reaching from floor to ceiling, making the rooms bright with the natural light that was beaming in. They were hung with thick velvet drapes, tied back and pooling on the polished floor. Each room seemed to have its own color and theme. I was amazed at how everything about this house was so plush and luxuriously immense.

We walked through the rear doors onto the porch which was almost as impressive as the front, again with columns, only smaller. It looked out onto a beautifully landscaped rear garden with low sculpted shrubs lining the walkways though it. There was a central, rectangular fish pool made of granite with a single fountain head spraying up from the middle of it and lily pads floating in it, serving as a shade to the swimming fish. The flower beds were perfectly kept and on either side of the yard stood a mammoth old Magnolia tree.

The porch was set with a buffet table on one end and off to the side. The area there was shielded from the sun by thick Bougainvillea growing on trellises. Tiny little green and red hummingbirds flitted in and out around the pink, purple and red flowers looking for a sweet treat. There was a large selection of tropical fruits and various greens arranged on the buffet to make a salad – it really did look mouthwatering. Just beyond the buffet sat a small round table with a neat little floral centerpiece and three chairs waiting for us.

James held the chairs for each of us, and when we were seated, he turned to the buffet. He prepared three salads and sat one at each of our places. He then poured three glasses of white wine, and took a seat at his place.

The three of us chatted, making small talk, about various things while we ate lunch. I tried to watch James as close as I could without being too noticeable. He had a smooth, soft voice that could have talked you into … or out of … as the case may be … anything, and his beautiful green eyes were just as compelling. With the two combined he could probably have asked and gotten anything he wanted from anybody, myself included. He seemed to get more comfortable and relaxed with our company as lunch went along. I suppose we were all trying to get to know each other better. After we had finished lunch he leaned back in his chair, crossing his long legs and weaving his fingers together in front of him.

"This man is absolutely breathtaking," I thought to myself as I glanced over at him, *"wouldn't it be wonderful if he were to actually ask me out on a real date. I could easily get used to that idea."*

I watched as he slowly smiled at me, a twinkle lighting up in his eyes. I began to let my thoughts wander as I sat there, looking out at the gardens. I felt like I had stepped through a portal to another place and a time where life was so much easier. It was a feeling that I found genuinely satisfying, and easily let my imagination roam, wondering what Whitehall had been like in those far away days.

"I understand that you are a history major Lexi," James' voice cut easily through my thoughts, as we continued sitting at the little table, "Do you have any plans for after graduation? What would you like to do with a History degree?"

"I'm not real sure just yet," she answered, "although I would like to go to Europe, if my money holds out, and maybe get my Masters before coming back to the States and starting a career. My dream though is to work in a museum somewhere and maybe become the curator."

"A noble undertaking, preserving our past, that certainly sounds very interesting," James replied with a smile, "I enjoy studying about the past, too. It's always interesting to read and consider what modern scholars think of it. I think some of them have no idea what it was really like. Although some of them do have interesting perceptions of what they *think* it was like."

"Do you mind if I ask what your degree is in," she asked uncertainly.

"Certainly you may … and I don't mind at all … I began my education at Harvard and afterward continued my study in modern business at Cambridge … although due to events beyond my control I was unable to complete my course of study there," he smiled in answer.

"Wow, what an absolutely perfect smile," I thought to myself.

"Well then, should you decide to pursue the European program please let me know. I have some very influential friends at universities in London, Paris, Berlin and Milan. I feel very certain that any one of them would be more than willing to assist a promising young historian like yourself to begin her career," he smiled warmly at her.

Her eyes and smile said it all when she bubbled, "Oh James, that would be so fantastic! I could just see myself teaching and studying at one of the major universities in Berlin … nothing would make me happier! I promise you, if the finances work out on my end, I will be asking you for an introduction."

"And what about you, Katelyn, you're art history I believe," James asked, those gorgeous greens looking right into me again.

"I've had a couple of ideas, initially I wanted to be an elementary school art teacher, but I really haven't given it much thought lately. I've had a particularly tough year and have had a lot of issues to work through. My parents both were murdered last April, and there has been a lot of legal issues and paperwork that has taken my mind off of a career. I finally have the estate settled though so I suppose I probably should start to refocus more on the future. I've only got about a year until graduation and that will go by in a hurry."

I noticed the heavy silence that suddenly seemed to settle over us and I quickly added "I'm so sorry … I said too much … I didn't mean to spoil our lunch …"

"Oh no, Katelyn, nothing like that, you should know that it's our past that makes us what we are and often times gives Fate the opportunity to guide and shape our future. We must think of life as a trip through time. Often times when one event happens, it makes way for something else that would not have happened otherwise," he smiled reassuringly and leaned forward to lightly touch my arm.

"Take for instance," he continued, "and I know it's a sad trade off, but had your parents lived, you would in all probability still be living in Atlanta and I would not have had the pleasure of your acquaintance or of the two of you having lunch here today."

"Never concern yourself about what has happened, sadly we cannot change the past, but fate always seems to work its way out in our lives. I assure you everything will be quite alright. And should you find yourself in need of any further legal assistance with the estate, again I have many contacts, and more than a few of them are lawyers. I'm sure that any one of them would be more than willing to offer any guidance you may need," he smiled, his cool hand resting lightly on my arm. I felt a wave of relaxing comfort flow through my entire body.

"That's strange, but it sure does feel good," I thought and then answered, "Thank you for your kind words, they're a comfort."

I continued basking in the sudden easiness flowing through me. It was so calming it could almost make me forget my surroundings. Lexi spoke up breaking through the contentment and asked, "James, what do you know about the history of Whitehall? Do you mind telling us about it?"

"Certainly," he answered smiling, "Whitehall has a very long and full history attached to it. In fact, it has been owned by a Dubois from its very founding and is named for the ancestral home in England. I'm descended from French Huguenots who settled in the English countryside after fighting on the side of William the Conqueror."

"Whitehall was given as a land grant from King Charles the Second to one of my ancestors in 1678 and the initial grant, which is framed and hangs in the main parlor, was for nine thousand acres. Of course over the years it has dwindled to the current four hundred seventy-eight acres of the estate proper and another two thousand acres of wooded swampland surrounding that ... land that due to it being what it is, modern developers have no interest in attempting to develop it ... and land that I, as the current owner, have no desire to part with ... so everyone concerned is happy."

"My first ancestor in the colonies arrived in South Carolina – then it was only known as Carolina – in the early 1680's, and armed with the land grant began to carve out a new living for his family here."

"The original house was built in 1690 and added to and enlarged over the years as the family grew. It burned after a lightning strike in 1715 and the current house was rebuilt on the site in 1720 and, like the original, has been added to and improved over the years."

"Whitehall was in the beginning, a very successful indigo, then rice, and later cotton plantation. In the early part of the war for independence my family remained loyal to the King. However, they soon changed sides and fought with the Patriots after learning of the terrible atrocities committed by the British commander and his troops in Charleston and the back country areas."

"It survived the War Between the States unscathed, although nearly an entire generation of the Dubois family died in fighting for Southern Independence. It fell into disrepair in the 1870's due to most of the family moving away, although it never passed from our ownership. I purchased it from the remnants of the family several years ago while I was living in London and began a complete restoration. My goal has been to return Whitehall to its original splendor of the 1740's in every way possible. And that," he said smiling, "is the short history."

Lexi and I were both leaning forward on the table by this time listening as James continued his story. He knew so much of the history and he presented it almost as if he had been there himself. When he had finished, Lexi leaned back in her chair and said, "Wow, I can just imagine all the people that have walked these porches and gardens. That is such an amazing story, so much history in one place."

"Yes, it is," I added, "and you have certainly done an excellent job restoring the house and grounds. I feel just like I have stepped into the past sitting here this afternoon."

"Then I have accomplished my goal," he smiled happily, "which is to make each and every one of Whitehall's visitors feel like they are experiencing it as it was. It is indeed an amazing story, you can't imagine how much more there is to it, and I have only just begun to scratch the surface."

"Nonetheless, I realize it's beginning to get late and I'm sure both of you would like to get back to the campus before darkness settles in completely. The low country and its back roads get very dark at night and all kinds of unsavory creatures come out to play; many of whom I'm sure you would not want to shake hands with in the dark.

"Oh, but I have a 'Protection and Safe Passage' card that someone gave me in case of trouble," I chuckled happily.

"Indeed you do … and I'm pleased that you took it seriously. But since it is late afternoon, perhaps if I offer a full tour of the house and grounds in the near future it will provide you with an ample incentive for a return trip."

"That would be great … and maybe there would be a chance to see the hidden art that's locked away in the family vaults," I spoke up quickly and easily.

"I promise," he said with a soft laugh, "just for you a special tour of the family art!"

"Humm … I can't wait … I hope this time it's a private tour," I thought quietly to myself.

James smiled at me again as he walked with us back through the huge hallway we had come through and out the front entrance. At the top of the front steps, once again taking my hand in his, and looking into my eyes, he said "I have avidly enjoyed your company this afternoon. I hope that you have a peaceful evening, please drive carefully on your return, and stay safe."

He seemed to be saying so much more than just a casual so-long. Almost as if there was some hidden meaning, something he was trying to say directly to me. This was twice he had looked right in my eyes and said 'stay safe'. Each time it had been with such feeling and seriousness. I didn't understand what he was trying to communicate, and it certainly raised a question in me. However, for the time being I was just too tired to give it much thought. It would have to wait, so I tucked it safely away to come back and examine later after I was rested and could think clearly.

"Oh girl you are so in it," Lexi laughed, interrupting my thoughts as we started the trip back to campus.

"I know right! I mean he's just dreamy and mysterious and …"

"Rich as all get out …" she chuckled.

"I prefer 'refined' …" I answered with a fake air, "but do you think he's "in it" too?"

"I'd wager all the money in my bank account on it …" she laughed, "of course right now that's only like eighteen bucks and change, but still the thought counts."

We were absolutely overjoyed at the day's experience and continued to chat happily about our day for the hour plus trip – which seemed to pass in only a few minutes. Both of us were still in awe at the immenseness of Whitehall as we got back to campus and settled into our small room for the night.

When Katelyn and Lexi had passed through the front gates and were safely on their trip back to campus I returned to the parlor to sort through my thoughts on the afternoon. I found myself smiling as I recalled Katelyn's many carnal thoughts that had been directed at me during our lunch. I wondered if that was a trait of all modern young women, or if, because she was so attracted to me – perhaps in part by the draw of the immortal – it caused her thoughts, amplified by her strong telepathy, to be so pronounced.

Either way, I became thoroughly convinced that passing a night in her bed, or better yet, her passing a night in my bed at Whitehall … and what a novel thought that was indeed … would be very nearly as pleasurable as feeding from her. Especially since my bed had, to this point, only been shared in the past by other immortals. The first, toward the end of the nineteenth century, and not many years after my return to America, had been Gale. Then in the first quarter of the twentieth century, after a long and romantic relationship, I had shared my bed with Sarah. Then finally, after her move to America in mid-century, my bed has been shared exclusively with Charlotte Ann, my maker and first immortal love.

One thing however was abundantly clear, shared bed or not, if Katelyn was indeed to become my mate I had many plans to make and things to set in order. I would have to begin preparing to bring her over, but quickly decided that I would not just summarily change her, as had happened to me, instead I would use her telepathy as an ally and begin planting thoughts and questions in her mind. She would have to come to the realization, on her own, with a little coaxing from me of course, about my immortal nature. Then and only then would I offer her the gift of second life. And if that were to come to pass I would need to know her much better than what I currently did.

My desire was not to simply manipulate her mind, but to know *her*, as a person. So I decided the best manner in which to get to know her was to be around her and observe her … and not necessarily when she knew I was present. So for the next two weeks I spent every possible moment watching her. I spent nearly every moment of every day on her campus, leaving only to feed at another close by campus, then returning to her. I attended classes with her, shielded of course, until I grew weary of the instructors and their abysmal lack of historical perspective. I watched her in the student union, when she left campus, and in her room. During the nights, while she slept, I whispered thoughts into her mind, replacing her previous night terrors with pleasant dreams of myself and Whitehall Manor as her home.

However, during all this time, I began to notice that, with the exception of attending classes, she was never outside the company of Lexi. I watched amazed as the two of them grew closer, day by day, until they had not only formed an inseparable bond, but actually became nearly blood kin. I soon realized that if Katelyn did indeed accept my gift and become an immortal, I would have to come up with a plan to separate the two of them for a time until she became acclimated and comfortable with her new life.

Chapter Eight

When we got back to the room I immediately called Aunt 'Chele before it got too late. I was so excited about my trip out to Whitehall and everything I had seen and heard. I had to describe the house and its beautiful gardens to her in detail. But when I started telling her about James, instead of the adult woman that I am, I once again felt like a high school girl talking about her first love. I gushed and bubbled all about what a great person he seemed to be. I even told her about the first time we had met in the book store and what an impact his presence, especially his eyes had on me.

"James is just so wonderful, aunt 'Chele," I continued telling her, "I don't know what it is about him but anytime I'm around him I feel so safe and protected ... it's almost like there is a wall around me to keep the bad things away. I'm actually totally comfortable and at ease. He makes me feel like I could just sit with him, doing nothing, and be completely happy. I've never felt that way around any other man. In fact, I look forward to seeing him again soon. He even promised me a tour of the family art collection the next time I come out."

"Aunt 'Chele, when he looks into my eyes I just can't seem to look away, his eyes are the prettiest green I have ever seen. They glimmer softly and it feels like he is looking right into my soul. He makes me want to open up and reveal my deepest secrets to him, there's nothing I wouldn't be willing to share with him."

"When he talks to me his voice is silky smooth and comforting with a soft Charleston accent with just a touch of a British inflection. His words flow over me like a waterfall, calm and relaxing. I want to hang onto his every word, to find out more about him and what he's thinking. I think I could listen all day, enthralled, I've never felt anything like it."

"Then when I'm talking to him, he is attentive to every word. He makes me feel like what I'm saying is important to him, like he wants to remember every word I say and keep every thought I have. It's strange but I feel like I've known him forever, like he's been a part of my life. I don't know how to explain it but he makes me feel like he's the one that can help me close my deepest wounds and move on with life."

"He is such a perfect gentleman, Aunt 'Chele, unlike some of the other guys I have dated. He treats me like a lady, like I'm special, and that's a nice feeling. They just don't make men like him anymore. It's almost like he has stepped right out of the past, and if I had to describe him with only one word, it would be charming. I guess living in that big old house, that's probably filled with ghosts from the past, and surrounded with all that history, it must have rubbed off on him. He's almost too good to be true!"

Aunt 'Chele listened attentively to me as I went on telling her all I could about him, how tall he was, his long European style hair, and his nice clothes. She chuckled a little and said, "James sounds like a really nice man, and, sounds too, like you might have fallen hard! But sweetie, how old is this man, the way you describe him I wonder if he's old or just an old soul?"

"Actually, I'm not sure how old he is ... I'd guess certainly no more than his mid-twenties," I answered thoughtfully, "but with his gentlemanly demeanor, there's no doubt there's an old soul banging around in there somewhere!"

"Well, Katelyn," she said, "he sounds nice, and you deserve a good man. But please don't get too deeply involved without building a good solid foundation first. Darling, you've had too much hurt to be as young as you are and I certainly wouldn't want to see you get hurt again. You've had more than enough of that for one lifetime."

"Aunt 'Chele, thank you for being concerned, for loving me and for being there for me to talk to," I said with a smile in my voice, "you sound a lot like my Mom. And I mean that in a good way. I gotta go before I start crying ... Lexi and I are going to the beach in the morning but I'll try to call you later in the week, love ya, bye!"

I clicked the off button on the phone and did shed a single tear knowing that she cared enough about me and my life to offer her advice ... and helping me to not feel completely alone in the world.

The next morning Lexi and I got up early, stuffed our swimsuits, beach towels and big floppy hats into a bag and headed over to Folly Beach. I had a brand new pink bikini that I just couldn't wait to wear. I wanted to work on my tan so I needed to get as much sun as possible on my body.

We spent the morning, walking the beach and playing in the edge of the water like a couple of kids. After one or two failed attempts at building a sand castle we finally decided to find a suitable spot and spread our towels out. We sat back watching the surf and soaking in the sun. There was a lot of interesting scenery that walked by, which we thoroughly enjoyed watching and commenting on. Of course the two of us put some pretty impressive scenery out there as well and certainly drew our own share of attention, too!

There was a lot of girlie talk on that beach! We talked about everything and everybody we knew. The time just flew by and before long the sun was starting to get lower in the sky. We finally decided we had had enough sun, were kinda tired and more than a little hungry so we quickly slid into some cut-offs and short tee's we had packed to wear off the beach. I suggested seafood, again, because since I moved here I just couldn't seem to get enough of it. The seafood in Atlanta had been alright, but terribly expensive, and nothing like here where it was fresh everywhere and mostly affordable.

As we drove off the island, Lexi spotted a little place called Th' Crab Shack that looked promising, so we decided to try it out. It was sitting just off the beach and was surrounded by open decks with umbrella covered tables. We went in hoping to find a good place to sit and actually got a table on the deck where we could sit and look out across the dunes and the beach to the ocean. It was crowded but really laid back, with that 'beachy' feel to it. They had beach music playing in the background and I recognized the sounds of The Tams, The Swingin' Medallions and The Beach Boys. The place smelled wonderful … I couldn't wait to eat! After checking out the menu, we started with a shrimp cocktail for each of us and then decided to split a bucket of steamed crabs and oysters. And I had to have a side order of fried green tomatoes. We topped it all off with a tall glass of cold, fresh sweet tea.

While we sat there and sipped on our tea I started to notice that some of the customers began to move a few of the tables around. They soon had cleared out a large area of the deck and made it into a dance floor. In just a short time several of the couples began to move out and started dancing. When the light began to fade, one of the waiters came out and lit the Tiki torches that were placed around the deck railing, the music was turned up loud and everybody was up and dancing.

A couple of those fine guys we saw earlier on the beach came over and asked us if we wanted to come join the party and dance with them. We both looked at each other at the same time and with a big smile we let the boys lead us by the hand onto the dance floor. We danced off and on for the next couple of hours, stopping only to drink more tea, and having the time of our lives. We finally had to say our good-byes to our new friends and started back to campus. It was the perfect finish to a perfect day!

Lexi drove us back to campus and our conversation quickly turned to what we had to look forward to the coming week. I had a paper coming due and she had a test on Wednesday. So we decided we had better settle down, get busy and probably stay close to school for the rest of the week.

"I think I'm going to go home this weekend, Lexi. I haven't been up in a couple of weeks and I miss aunt 'Chele. It'll be nice to get away from school for a couple of days and try to relax. But, you know, if the opportunity were to present itself, I wouldn't mind maybe going back out to Whitehall again Friday before I go home," I offered hopefully with a smile. "I could just get a little earlier start … maybe get home Friday evening instead of waiting until Saturday morning."

"That sounds like fun, but if it happens I'm afraid you'll have to do Whitehall by yourself," she looked over at me and with a quick girly giggle added, "now be careful there Scarlett and don't cry any big ole crocodile tears that you'll have the entire afternoon, all alone in that big old house with that wonderful man."

"Why, Lexi," I drawled out, "I would never in all my days allow such thoughts to enter into my head!"

We both guffawed at my fake Scarlett accent.

"Seriously, though," she added, "I think I'm going to just run on down to Savannah for the weekend to see my parents, too. I haven't been home in a couple of months and I really miss them a lot. Since I've got an early schedule Friday, I can leave before lunch and probably be back Sunday afternoon before supper."

So with our week planned, when we got back, it was straight to the room and showers … it's amazing the places beach sand can get into … then settling into something comfortable. I have always been a pajama girl when I'm relaxing at home, but in the dorm, its tees and boy shorts for both of us. It's just more comfortable, and provides us both with an easy excuse not to go out.

Chapter Nine

The rest of the week was nothing to brag about, just classes as usual. But then, on Wednesday evening, Lexi and I stopped by the commons to get a snack before going back to the room. And walking through the study area I looked up and saw James coming out of the book store. He was carrying a couple of books that he appeared to be concentrating on.

"Alright," I thought to myself, *"I am so glad we stopped in this evening! Talk about great timing!"*

I leaned over and quickly whispered to Lexi, "Look Lexi, there's James, he's just coming out of the book store!"

Just then he looked up and saw both of us, and with a smile, started walking toward us. "Good evening, Katelyn ... and Lexi ... how are you ladies this evening?"

He again easily took my hand, actually just the tips of my fingers in his, and smiled at me. I noticed that his hand was warm this time, and he was absolutely glowing all over as if he had been in the sun all afternoon.

I of course sank into those beautiful green eyes and swam in that silky smooth voice trying to recover my own voice and answer him.

"I'm good," we both answered at the same time, then looked at each other and smiled at our timing!

"It's good to see you again, James," I said unable to control my big smile, "what brings you up here in the middle of the week?"

"There are two things actually," he smiled his perfect smile, "the first is that a couple of the art professor's had new books released today. I thought I would come and pick up a copy of each. I try to support the art and history departments as much as I can and while I was here thought I would have a quick afternoon snack."

"Oh, what kind of snack … what do you like to eat … you know there's good seafood all over Charleston," I interjected with a girly grin.

"I'm usually not too picky," he smiled back, "most of the time just whatever I can pick up quickly."

"Cool, I like not picky … especially if there's shrimp involved … so now, what are the books about," I asked pointing at them in an effort to keep the conversation going.

"The first one is about seventeenth century Italian artists and the styles they used. The other one covers eighteenth century American art and how it played off the earlier European influences," he explained showing me the covers.

"The second, and most important reason, is the two of you," he continued looking back at each of us, "I was thinking about both of you earlier today and I had hoped that we might meet this evening. Do you think perhaps you would like to come back out to Whitehall again, say Friday afternoon when you finish classes? I could give you the full tour I promised earlier."

"Wow, he has got to be a mind reader," I smiled to myself.

"Do you think maybe I could get a rain check on the offer," Lexi answered sounding heartbroken but quickly added, "I would love to come visit again and take the full tour, I really would, but I haven't seen my parents in a couple of months and was planning on going home Friday morning to spend the weekend with them."

"Please my little friend, don't look downcast … perhaps you will be free for the next time … and I promise you there will be a next time. And to give you something to look forward to when you do return – since you are a historian – I shall allow you, at your leisure and undisturbed, to peruse Whitehall's extensive and private library."

I watched as her face lit up, a smile spreading across it, her eyes lighting up at the thought as she answered, "Oh I can just imagine the treasures hidden on those shelves."

"It contains one of the largest and foremost first edition collections in the country," he smiled further whetting her appetite, "but, in the meantime, I hope you have an enjoyable visit with your parents."

"It will be like being in my own personal heaven," she mused quietly at the thoughts of Whitehall's library opened to her.

Then turning his smile back to me, continued, "How about you Katelyn, while I realize that it may not be proper for a young lady to visit unaccompanied, I assure your safety, and you are welcome to visit again if you would like."

"I would love to," I said quickly, trying to contain my excitement and not sound too enthusiastic, "I have a morning class at eight and will be finished at nine thirty. I can come out when I finish that class. I probably could be there around noon, would that be a good time?"

"Certainly, and I shall have you a lunch prepared. I look forward to your visit. Until then," he smiled, and took my hand in his again, "stay safe."

There was that 'stay safe' again. I swear every time he touched me and said that there was a wave of easy comfort that passed right through me. It was like nothing I had ever experienced. I just could not explain the feeling it gave me. I felt like nothing in the world could or would hurt me then … I was safe and totally protected … and it really felt good, too!

I was so excited about the visit that the rest of the week just couldn't go by fast enough for me. I called Aunt 'Chele Thursday evening to tell her about the weekend.

"You sure do sound like you're on top of the world tonight," she said when she answered the phone, "is there anything new with this fellow James you met?"

"Not really," I began, "I did run into him in the book store yesterday but that's the first I've seen him since last Saturday. But he invited me to come back out to Whitehall tomorrow morning. I was thinking that since I only had the one early class I would go out there and then, if I don't stay too late, I can come on home tomorrow evening instead of waiting until Saturday. But either way, I'll call you and let you know what I'm doing."

"That will be wonderful, sweetie, I can't wait to see you again! Do you have anything special you want to do while you're here," she asked.

I chuckled and said, "Laundry, maybe!"

"I remember being in college so I'm sure you have plenty of that," she laughed big and added, "I think we can take care of that."

"That's really good to hear because you know, and I'm not real sure why, but when I lived at home, I'd just always put my laundry in the basket and it magically reappeared … washed, folded and hung up in my closet," I chuckled.

"Amazing how that works isn't it," she laughed drily at my joke, "but how about after *I* wash, fold and hang up *your* laundry, maybe I can find time to throw in a side order of some pancakes and bacon to go with it."

"Oh yummy … that sounds delicious," I answered happily.

"We'll plan on it … and I'll tell John you're coming. We'll both just be tickled to have you around! Katelyn, the house just seems so quiet again when you're not here."

"I'll try to liven it up a little by telling you all about James when I get home. I gotta go now, love ya aunt 'Chele!" I said as I touched the end button on the phone.

I rolled over on my bed and looked at Lexi with a big smile on my face. She put her book down and smiled back at me, "You really like him, don't you," she asked.

"Yeah, I sure do," I said, "I really enjoy being around him. There's just something about him, especially when he touches me. It's nothing electric or anything like that, just something … different … a soothing that makes me feel good. When he looks at me I feel like he's looking at me for me … for who I am. He makes me feel … comfortable … and not like he's just trying to take my clothes off."

"But my money's on you'd probably let him do that too," Lexi said, looking at me with a knowing smile and biting her lower lip.

"That's a very real possibility," I answered with a nod

and a happy smile, "but of course the timing has to be right … you know, like when the first opportunity presents itself."

"Oh, of course, naturally … it's all about the timing," she snickered, nodding her head, "but seriously, I think he believes that you're pretty special, too. I see how he looks at you. I don't see how you can survive those wonderful eyes …"

"It ain't easy, and besides, who said I wanted to," I laughed again.

"Hummm, be careful there girl … that sounds like it could be dangerous … but fun … anyway, I hope you have a great time out there tomorrow," she smiled and picked up her book again.

"Good night, Lexi," I said, clicked off my bed light, and rolled back over to go to sleep.

While I lay there waiting on sleep to cover me and take me down for the night, I started thinking about all that had happened recently. My life seemed to have turned a corner, finally. School was going well … I had found a great friend and roommate in Lexi … and I had met a wonderful man that I couldn't wait to be around.

Suddenly, I realized that I had not woken up screaming from my nightmare since the first night I had met James. The nightmare had been almost a nightly occurrence for months, and now it had been almost two weeks since I had it. I wasn't sure I understood why but I certainly hoped its absence would continue. I smiled at that newly discovered freedom as I drifted off into a peaceful and comfortable sleep.

Chapter Ten

The next morning I woke from a really deep and restful sleep. I usually have very vivid memories of my dreams, but this morning, I could barely remember them. I vaguely recalled some small bits of the nightmare, but it never became fully developed, and this time it didn't wake me up. I lay there sleepily pondering this new development when suddenly I snapped fully awake and remembered James' eyes.

I had dreamed of them again, the deep green wells of peacefulness. In my dream they were keeping a watch over me, holding the darkness of my night terror safely at bay. I didn't remember seeing him or even his face in the dream, just his eyes, glittering as they pierced deep into the darkness. Every time the horror of my nightmare had started to intrude into my sleep I had heard his soft voice saying, *'stay safe Katelyn, sleep peacefully, my love.'* Then the terrible nightmare would slink away, back to its awful hiding place. His eyes were just a dream, but it was a good one … one that had been so real I could almost feel his presence around me in the room.

I had slept in just a tee shirt and the warm morning sun coming in the window was falling across me and warming my bare legs. I stretched lazily, soaking in the warmth as I continued to lay there recalling his words from the dream. I didn't want to get out of bed, it felt so good lying there, like a blanket of contentment had settled over me. But, I knew that the sooner I got up, the sooner the weekend would start.

"Besides," I thought to myself, *"there's not much chance of seeing James while I'm lying in bed … at least not this bed,"* I added with a little giggle. I forgot all about the nightmare as my thoughts began to wander off in more pleasant directions as I continued thinking about him … those inviting green eyes … his strong build … the way his hair just touched his shoulders … I felt a pleasant warmth begin building and spreading out from the center of my body … passion began to burn stronger and hotter in the bottom of my stomach. I raised my knees and slowly began to open my legs. My skin tingled electrically as my fingertips began to slide their way gently across my bare thighs and tummy, reaching toward the top of my panties, *"Ummm … you better stop that, Katelyn,"* I quickly thought, *"before you get yourself all worked up and frisky … besides you really don't have time to pet the kitty this morning … you've got class …"*

So with one more lazy stretch and a wonderful new excitement coursing through me, I kicked the comforter off my feet, rolled out of bed, pulled on some old sweats, twisted my hair up in a ponytail and quickly ran out to class.

When I returned after class, I took a long hot shower and looked over my clothes trying to decide what to wear. I figured I might as well show off my assets a little bit. I wanted to look really nice for James, something he would remember. So I picked out a pair of my best low-rise jeans that fit perfectly, just a little revealing but not too tight, and paired them with a brightly colored sleeveless short shirt that showed off just the right amount of tanned mid-riff. Finally, I added a pair of flat sandals, and then brushing my hair to a lustrous shine, I pulled the sides back just slightly and added a small bow at the back. I smiled as I looked in the mirror, turning around, checking every angle, now I was ready.

I was in a hurry, grabbing my laundry bag, car keys, and starting for the door when I happened to see a note propped up on our desk. It was from Lexi and she had written a quick good-bye in her tight little scrawl that said:

Katelyn,

Hope you have a great afternoon – now don't you do anything I wouldn't – ha, ha! ;-)! Drive careful, see you Sunday night.

Luv ya, Lexi

I smiled as I read it and then thought about how we had grown to be such close friends in the last few weeks. We were both supposed to graduate soon, her at the end of the summer session, and me at the end of the next fall session. The thought of us going our separate ways passed through my mind and made me feel sad to see that day come. I could already tell I was going to miss her badly but believed that we would stay in touch and continue to be lifelong friends.

I arrived at Whitehall just about noon as I had expected and turned up the long drive toward the house. I noticed this time the gates were already open and there was no security to meet me, but I somehow thought that my presence on the property was already known.

The huge oaks were so impressive that I actually took a minute to stop, sit quietly and look down the allee, admiring their majesty. That's when the inspiration hit me that I should do a painting and preserve them on canvas forever. My painting talent had lain dormant for months as I tried to put the pieces of my life back together. Suddenly, now seemed like the right time to pick up that particular piece again. I felt the desire begin to rise in me to paint and it was as strong as ever. I would be sure to mention the idea to James and ask his permission to come back out soon and begin the work. I felt sure he would allow me the privilege. I slowly took one more step on the long path toward my return to a normal life.

I parked near the front fountain, just like last week, and sat for a moment. I let my eyes wander over the big house, taking in all the details, actually looking at it as one huge work of art. I was still so impressed with the enormousness of Whitehall. I just could not imagine what it must be like living in such a grand old house with so much history attached to it. Although, as the idea quickly sailed through my mind, I didn't find it to be such a completely unattractive thought.

I started up the steps just as James came out the front door to meet me. He looked wonderful as ever, wearing a pair of khaki Dockers and a pink golf shirt, his hair was pulled back and tied with a tan ribbon that matched his shirt. He smiled approvingly, looking happy to see me, as he quickly appraised my outfit. His eyes nonchalantly passed over me, lingering for an extra moment at my throat and nearly bare shoulders, then moving down my arms, stopping at my tanned tummy and the top of my low-slung tight jeans before returning to my eyes.

"Oh, you done good, girl," I thought to myself, *"he likes what he sees!"*

I gave a small, hopefully shy, wave and said with a smile "Hey there, how are you today?"

"Very good," he said still using his proper English, "it's a pleasure to see you again, Katelyn. May I," he asked as he opened an arm toward me and wrapped it lightly around my shoulders giving me a small hug.

"You may hug me anytime you wish," I replied happily snuggling closer to his side, and thinking how good his arm felt, like it belonged there, resting lightly on my shoulders, and silently added, *"and hold me for as long as you want!"*

We walked into the house and I reached up to pat his hand as it lay on my shoulder. Although normally cool to my touch, his hand was actually cold today. *"Humm, that's strange,"* I thought, *"I wonder why his hand is so cold, it's really warm out today,"* and I made a mental note to try to ask about his health if the opportunity presented itself. He looked oddly at me and, with a quick smile, easily removed his arm from around me, almost as if he had read my thoughts.

"I must apologize if my hands seem cold, but sometimes I can be just a tad bit anemic ... although I attempt to control it as often as possible. But, minor health issues aside, I believe the last time you were here I promised you a private tour of the family art collection," he said smiling, "would you still like to see the paintings or perhaps something different?"

"Well I can think of at least one other 'something else' I

wouldn't mind doing with you, but for now I suppose it doesn't matter what we do as long as we do it together," I thought quickly, but then pointing at myself with a grin said, "Art Major ... remember ... and that's just what I've looked forward to, I can't wait to see your collection! I'm sure there are some real treasures hidden away."

"Just some old paintings," he said with a smile and continued, "but before I subject you to dusty old artwork, I've taken the liberty to have some lunch prepared for us, it's ready on the rear veranda, if you're hungry," he offered.

"That sounds good," I said with a little smile, "I actually stayed in bed a little longer than I should have this morning and didn't take time to have breakfast before class."

We continued through the house to the back porch. Just like last week there was a small table but with only two chairs this time. There was set on it a small platter arranged with some finger sandwiches, a plate of freshly baked oatmeal-raisin cookies, and a pitcher of fresh made lemonade.

Smiling and using the most fake Hollywoodish version of a southern accent I could imagine and waving my hand like I had a fan in it said, "Oh, goodness, my favorite cookies, how-ever did you know?"

Laughing in return at my girlish play acting, he bowed deeply at the waist, with a hand flourish and an exaggerated accent of his own answered, "My dear sweet young lady ... I was under the impression that a beautiful Southern Belle such as yourself would always be partial to lemonade and oatmeal cookies."

"Thank you for the compliment James, I really appreciate it," I said with a shy smile as I looked down and felt myself blush deep red at his praise.

We chatted and made small talk throughout lunch. As

I finished the last of the lemon-aid, he asked, "Well Katelyn, what are your plans for the weekend, will you be going home or returning to campus?"

"Yeah, I thought I might go home. I haven't been home in a couple of weeks and I really miss my family," I replied, "and since Lexi has gone to visit her parents, I thought there was no need to stay in the room all alone all weekend. We're both planning to be back on Sunday evening. But what about you, do you have any special plans for the weekend?"

"I was thinking about a quick trip up to New York. I called a friend that lives in the city and suggested that she and I spend an evening together at the theater and then share a meal afterward. I plan to return home Sunday afternoon also, so nothing special really," he said smiling.

"Oww … that sure did sting … how could I have not considered the possibility of a woman in his life … I guess I should have known … he is just too handsome … too gentlemanly … too … everything … not to have a girlfriend. Besides, she lives in New York City and has to be wealthy like him … not to mention young, pretty, and from a well-connected family so I couldn't possibly compete with someone like her … I just can't believe that I could have ever fooled myself into thinking he was single and I had a chance with him."

"Oh … I see … a significant other," I said dejectedly, my heart falling as I tried not to let my disappointment be so blatant. I felt silly that I had just never considered the possibility of a woman in his life.

"Oh, she's just an old friend," he said with a knowing smile, "I am not currently romantically involved."

"Me, Me, pick me … I'll be your companion … you can be romantically involved with me," I thought quickly to myself.

Just then my little inner voice unexpectedly spoke up,

softly saying, *"Now Katelyn, are you really sure that's what you want? You don't actually know him, his nature, or his lifestyle … are you ready for all that a life with him would entail? You should be sure of your choice before making it … some choices have no going back."*

I shook myself back to reality as James added, "Perhaps one weekend soon you might be able to join me on one of my short trips?"

Suddenly my heart was back in my chest and the universe was all good again at that thought.

"Sure, I don't see why not. I think I'd enjoy a few days away with you," I answered around my smile.

"Well then, it's settled, but until then I'm sure your family would like every minute they can get with you, so I suppose we had probably better get started with our tour, besides I wouldn't want to be the cause of you getting home too late," he smiled at me and my heart skipped a beat, again.

We visited several rooms on the lower level of the house and there were at least two framed oils in each one. The house was a bona fide museum with oils from many eighteenth and nineteenth century European masters. I saw works by artists that I had only seen mentioned in books including Bouchor and Canaletto. There was a Renoir, a Monet and an actual Blake manuscript. The quality and value of the art alone was astounding to me. But the most shocking painting I saw came as I was preparing to leave. I peeked into a room that was only partially open as we walked back toward the front and I gasped loudly, "Oh … my goodness!"

James stopped short and asked, "What is it, Katelyn?"

"The paining of that couple over the fireplace … that's you isn't it?"

"It couldn't possibly be," he smiled disarmingly, "but it is my namesake ancestor and his wife. Come, I'll show you," and he pushed the door the rest of the way open and led the way into the room.

I looked at the painting and it could easily have been James and standing next to him was a very beautiful young woman. Only the dates on the nameplate, which was engraved 'James Thomas Dubois, 1725–1753 and wife Mary Elizabeth Johnson, 1729–1748', belied the fact that it was indeed James.

"Oh my," I said, still in shock as I examined the painting. "She was so young, only nineteen, and pretty too. I wonder what happened to her."

"Yes, she was indeed a very attractive woman," he said wistfully, almost as if he had known her, "she died during childbirth. That happened a lot during those days. The family lore has it that he later died of a broken heart."

"What a romantic love story," I mused quietly, "I wonder what it would be like to have a man that loved me so much that if I died, he would grieve himself to death also."

"I feel certain Katelyn that you would have that effect on any man who truly loved you more than he loved life itself," he said sadly. He looked back up at the portrait and suddenly seemed very sad. I had an unexpected desire as we continued to stand there together to reach out and put my arm around him. Then he caught himself up, looking a little surprised, and said, "I have done a lot of family research, and sometimes it feels as if I have a personal connection to them."

We turned to leave, and I saw him quickly glance back at the painting and smile just so slightly. My mind turned to my own parents and how much I missed them as I began thinking about the trip up to Summerville.

"Katelyn," he said, as we stepped out to the porch. I turned to look at him and suddenly his eyes looked distant as he continued, "thank you for taking an interest in my family history. I don't often get to share it with others. I hope you have a very enjoyable visit with your aunt and uncle," and taking my hand, he kissed the tops of my knuckles and said, "I hope I shall see you again soon."

"Thank you James, I would like to see you again soon, too. I hope you have a pleasant trip and enjoy your weekend," I smiled and started to get in the car to leave when I remembered my painting idea.

"By the way, I think I would like to start painting again. I haven't practiced in several months since ... well, since before my parents died ... but I was suddenly inspired earlier today when I arrived. Do you think I could come out sometime and start with a still of the oaks down the allee?"

"I'd be glad to have you come out, what about Monday morning? I can talk to your professors and take care of your classes for you."

"That would be wonderful," I said, "I'll gather all my supplies from storage while I'm home this weekend. So, I'll see you Monday morning, around ten maybe?"

"I shall look forward to seeing you Monday. Until then," he said smiling, "stay safe."

I started down the long drive towards the highway and I glanced up in the mirror. The last thing I saw as I entered the first curve was James still standing at the top of the steps, his hands resting on his waist, his gaze fixed solidly on me.

The trip up to Summerville seemed to fly by as I

thought about my afternoon with James and all he had showed me. My thoughts lingered on the painting of his ancestor and I wondered at how such a strong family resemblance could be passed from generation to generation. I was also excited and looking forward to beginning my own painting again. I smiled as I wondered if my artwork would endure that many years.

The weekend at home was wonderful. Aunt 'Chele and I spent most of the day Saturday, enjoying our time together, doing some shopping and catching up with each other. Afterward, we met Uncle John downtown in the evening for supper at a restaurant called Breck's.

Then Sunday came and the weekend was quickly over. I was still excited about the special time I had had with aunt 'Chele and uncle John. At the same time, I was also looking forward to getting back. I was ready to put paint to canvas. Truthfully, I'm not too sure if I was more excited about painting again or just getting to spend more time with James.

When I got back to school Lexi was already in the room. She told me all about her trip to see her parents and how great it was just to be with them for a little while. I shared all the details about my weekend and the planned trip back out to Whitehall in the morning.

"Wow!" she said with a little giggle, "it sounds like you're getting a three day weekend. I hope you have a great time tomorrow."

"I'm sure I will," I said with a big smile, "after all, I'll get to see James again!"

"Katelyn, you got it bad, girl! But, maybe if you get back in time tomorrow evening we'll go downtown for dinner."

"I'll make it a point to be back in time just for you," I

said sleepily, "good night!"

"You, too," she said.

Chapter Eleven

When I had seen Katelyn safely off and on her way to Summerville, I telephoned and notified my pilot to be standing by to fly to New York. I hurriedly placed a call to Charlotte Ann and asked her to meet me for an evening out, specifically a play at the Met and a meal afterwards.

My Gulfstream landed at LaGuardia after a short and uneventful flight from Charleston, and there I found a car and driver that my pilot had arranged to be waiting at the hanger to take me on to the Waldorf-Astoria. I called Charlotte Ann from the lobby – my suite was in use and unavailable to me on such short notice – and told her that I had arrived and would meet her on the sidewalk outside.

While I waited for her, I stepped out of the front entrance of the lobby, and patiently watching the rushing vehicles on Park Avenue, noticed that the night air was unseasonably warm. The traffic made a steady noise in the early darkness of the evening and that was the one part of the city that I didn't really care about. Still I couldn't help but appreciate how much the city had changed since 1875 when I had first came here. It had grown from a busy city to a bustling metropolis. New York had always been busy, even then, but now it seemed to never rest, to never sleep. The lights of the surrounding buildings had turned Park Avenue into a perpetual daylight. I smiled and chuckled softly as I compared it to the relative peace and quiet of Charleston.

I was alerted to Charlotte Ann's presence when she stepped through the revolving door of the main lobby and started toward me. I turned and smiled broadly at her, admiring how well she had acclimated to the city. I noted the manner in which she carried herself, looking around with the eyes of a predator, carefully noting her surroundings, fully aware of all that was going on as she continued toward me, leaving no doubt that she absolutely belonged here.

She was as beautiful as the first time I had seen her in Cambridge in the spring of 1753 … young, only in her early twenties, and extremely pretty with a beautiful smile that lit her face with a happy glow … barely five feet tall with thick dark brown hair cascading around her shoulders and framing her face … albeit she was dressed a bit more contemporarily now, with a short, tight pencil skirt and a silk top for the evening. A beautiful diamond choker and matching bracelet that she wore glittered in the evening light. Her returned smile reflected lovingly in her soft brown eyes. She quickly crossed the space between the doors and where I waited, and melting into my arms, we shared a deeply passionate and lingering kiss, not caring who saw us or what they might have said as they stepped around us.

"James … good evening my handsome gentleman …

it's so wonderful to see you again, you're as handsome and desirable as always. I was so happy when you called, it's been too long since we spent time together," she said looking up at me with a smile that only a real lover, one who knew the secrets of my soul, could give. I took her hand in mine as she cuddled against me, easily interlacing our fingers together, and again lightly kissed the top of her head.

"I have missed you so much Charlotte Ann and I apologize that I've not called sooner. I've got no excuse except that the months and years pass by so quickly and life so often gets in the way of my good intentioned plans."

I smiled again, my love for her shining in my eyes, and wrapping my arm around her, pulled her close as we began to stroll away at a casual pace along the sidewalk.

"I'm so happy you agreed to meet me Charlotte Ann," I began slowly, "I've needed desperately to talk to you about the current situation I find myself in … and I knew that you would understand … you've always guided me when I needed it, and I value your advice very highly."

"James, you know that good counsel has often gone both ways over the course of our friendship," she answered with a grin.

"Yes, we've experienced numerous things and countless places together and I don't recall a single regretful one. Although it's been a while since we spent time together … what's it been now, almost ten years … so it's past time that we rekindled our friendship … let's enjoy a play, and then go hunting afterwards just like in the old days."

"Ah, my dear friend, you know me too well … wine me and dine me … and I'll give you anything you want," she laughed, her brown eyes sparkling with delight, reflecting the light all around her, as she looked up at me.

"Anything," I asked mischievously, grinning at her.

"Anything … and you know it … but I sense that you have much more than just carnal pleasure on your mind this evening … besides, you can get that in Charleston any time you wish," she quietly chuckled, "why don't we walk to the Lincoln Center? It's only a couple of miles from here. We can go up to 59th, cross to Broadway and be there in no time. It will be a nice easy walk for us and allow us time to talk. Perhaps after the play we can go down to Times Square and search out our meal."

The two of us began walking in silence up Park Avenue as I tried to gather my thoughts, looking, I'm sure to anyone around us to be a couple of star crossed lovers out for an evening stroll while enjoying the pleasure of the others company.

"I'm going to assume from your silence that you've found someone, haven't you," she asked casually breaking the quietness after a few minutes of noiseless walking.

"Yes, I believe I have … and the more I'm with her, the more sure I become. I think about her continually, always looking forward to the next time I can see her. It's been so long since I've had a companion Charlotte Ann, but the prospect of it becomes more appealing to me every time I see her."

"And since she isn't with you shall I assume that she's a mortal …"

"Yes, and so very thoroughly so too."

"Then you know I must ask … does she know yet … about you I mean," she asked quizzically, raising an eyebrow, "you know that is a pretty big secret you carry."

"I think that somewhere, in the deepest part of her being, she knows what I am, but it hasn't as yet became a reality to her. But she does have good intuition, and so I am not trying to completely hide it from her. I still would rather not just tell her outright, so instead I have been planting some small thoughts in her mind, just enough to raise a few subtle suspicions. I would prefer for her to put the pieces together and come to the conclusion on her own."

"Presuming of course that you plan to bring her over, do you think she is strong enough … our lives entail a plethora of changes … will she be able handle all that the change brings with it?"

"I think she will be able to acclimate to it easily enough."

"Then when do you plan to change her," she continued.

"When, and if, she agrees to accept the gift," I answered matter-of-factly.

She stopped walking and looking up at me in an almost shocked tone asked, "Do you mean to tell me that you intend to give her the *choice* of being mortal or immortal … to actually decide whether or not she wishes the gift?"

"And why shouldn't I," I continued slowly, choosing my words carefully, "I didn't have any choice … of course neither did you … but times were different when you and I became immortal … do you think either of us would we have accepted the gift and taken the same path if we had been given the choice."

"Fate had already chosen our paths for us James, so there's no need to think in 'what if's', had it not been for the gift, you and I were far too separated in time to have ever met otherwise. And while it is different and almost unheard of to give one the choice," she mused approvingly, "it's that difference that has always made you my gentleman."

"Viva la Difference," I smiled cheerfully, "and I'm very thankful that you made me your gentleman."

"Fate brought us together James, and we built a

relationship that both of us needed at the time, one that we both shall remember forever. I still hold very fond memories of all the years we spent together."

"As do I … you made me what I am Charlotte Ann, then you taught me how to love again when I thought that was impossible for me … and I'm eternally grateful to you for that. But over the years, you and I have grown so much closer than just the lovers we began … we have a connection that is much deeper than that. We are a part of each other, body and soul, bonded forever."

I drew her closer to me as we continued walking, looking down at her with a smile and again gently kissing the top of her head.

"James, love, you and I have had over two hundred and fifty years to talk about us … but tonight you have me truly fascinated," she prompted with a smile, "please do tell me more about this intriguing young girl that has captured your heart."

"Her name is Katelyn, and she is the most beautiful girl I have seen in years. She is very lady like, educated and worldly but still retains a certain amount of innocence about her. I met her at the college one afternoon when I went down for a meal. Charlotte Ann, when I saw her, she rattled me to the center of all that I am. I have never had a mortal look at me the way she did. Her look penetrated my soul and stirred something I haven't felt since Mary Beth first touched my heart. I knew almost immediately that she was the one I have waited so long for and I wanted desperately for her to know me. I struggled to restrain myself from taking her at once and sharing my life with her. But something deep inside would not allow me to just do that to her. I had to first find a way for her to know about me, my nature, this life I wish to offer her, and to then become comfortable with that knowledge."

"And how do you think she'll react when she finds out the truth about you and your nature?"

"I'm not sure just yet, but I do hope for a positive reaction. I've discovered that she is a strong telepath but is unaware of her gift. She speaks a great deal in her mind that she doesn't know I hear. Judging from her thoughts, I believe that she has as strong an interest in me as I do in her. In fact, she was somewhat downcast when I mentioned seeing you for the weekend. I had to quickly reassure her that you were only an old friend and not a ... what did she call it ... 'significant other' I believe was the term she used."

"If she only knew just *how* significant I was in your life," she chuckled happily, "but do you think she will remain as strongly interested when you reveal your true nature to her?"

"It's difficult to say for sure, only time will give me that answer."

"You know that from the very beginning I've always wanted nothing but the best for you," she began, softly patting my arm with her free hand, "and I hope you get what you want, you deserve to be happy. However, should she reject your offer of the gift, and you wish to leave for a period of time, you know that you are welcome to the house in London for as long as you may wish."

"Thank you, I do appreciate the offer, but I sincerely hope that I don't have to accept such an offer, instead that she and I will remain together and build a life at Whitehall."

"I'm sorry, I shouldn't have interrupted, please do continue James, I must know more about this incredible young lady who has had such an impact upon you."

"Katelyn's nearly as tall as I am; her hair is brunette, a little darker than yours, and long, about half way down her back. She has the prettiest blue eyes that just absolutely light up when she smiles. She has impressed me to no end. And though she isn't, and never will be Mary Beth, there are times Charlotte Ann when her bashful smile and innocent blush stir up the memories of her and makes me want her that much more."

"She's extremely intelligent, and very modern in her thinking, too. She visited me earlier today, and had absolutely no qualms about spending the entire afternoon alone with me. Why in my day a lady would never have been unaccompanied with a gentleman in his home for the entire afternoon."

"Allow me to inform you that your day is long in the past James, and we ladies will now spend our days … or evenings … and nights, anywhere and with anyone we wish … much as you and I once did," she laughed as she snuggled close against me.

"I suppose times have indeed changed … and she is always completely relaxed when she is with me, and trusts me implicitly, as she should, which of course makes it so very easy to read her. As I said, she has her own brand of innocence, but unfortunately it has been deeply wounded. Her parents were both brutally murdered last year, something she is still working through and coming to grips with, so for that reason I do not wish to reveal too much to her too quickly. I would rather bring her along slowly and not overwhelm her with new ideas."

"Probably a very wise decision," she nodded in agreement, "but do you think you will have to wait very long before she gets suspicious and begins asking questions?"

"No, I don't think so … it's coming soon," and with a smile added, "I'm seeing to it that she is starting to have some very pointedly specific questions. But I have already placed her under my protection."

"Oh … how so," she asked cautiously.

"She has the most graphic nightmares of her parents murder … it was she who discovered their bodies. The first time I took her hand I discovered the nightmares lurking in her subconscious mind. I have since stood watch over her on several occasions while she slept, speaking peace to her and settling her mind, keeping the night terrors away so she could rest peacefully."

"Again, another wise decision I think," she nodded in agreement.

"She's very strong Charlotte Ann, but at the same time she is still young and tender. She cares greatly for those around her. I have tried to warn her away several times … to give her some subtle cautions … just to see if she could be scared away. But she just keeps coming back … as if Fate is indeed drawing us together … she's proven to be extremely strong willed … actually in many ways she's very much like you."

"Well, you always did have excellent taste in women … at least I thought you did," she laughed softly looking up and still smiling, "She sounds wonderful James, and I'm very happy for you."

"I feel so different when she is near me, Charlotte Ann … the years seem to fall away and I'm youthful once again. It reminds me so much of the spring of 1753 when you and I first met, and then our first summer together. I want to spend every minute possible with her, the same as I did then with you."

"I told you this day would come, that you would find an eternal mate."

"I have been alone for a long time Charlotte Ann, but

since I've met her, I relish the idea of a companion again. I think I've forgotten what it is like to share my life with someone. I've been at Whitehall for so long that I have just become comfortable with my life there. But since I've met Katelyn, I find myself making excuses to go to the college to look for her, and to spend just a few minutes with her."

"I find that I'm happier than I have been in years when I'm with her. And when she visits Whitehall, it's such a pleasure to see her bright smile and her eyes light up when she sees me and to hear her happy laughter ringing through the house. I enjoy the time we spend together and our conversations. She has taught me how to laugh again, how to enjoy my life all over again … and I want her to be a part of that life and share it with her."

"James, it sounds to me like you have already fallen in love with her and she sounds like a perfect match for you. If you really think she's the one, you need to pursue it, begin to make plans and preparations. Remember, if she accepts the gift that you wish to offer her, the first month is going to be the most difficult for her. You know what has to be done and the preparations that must be made."

"Charlotte Ann, I want so much to give her the gift, but even more, I want her to want it, and to be able to fully appreciate it. And should she accept the gift it will only compound everything about her that is beautiful, both inside and out. I hope that she chooses to accept it, but if not, I'll not force it upon her. Still, if she chooses, then I can look forward to the day that the two of you meet, and become friends."

"Well you know of course, that even more than friends, in the strictest human sense, she will be my granddaughter … and I've waited nearly three hundred years," she chuckled.

"And I have a feeling, in the strictest human sense of course, that you will spoil her to no end," I grinned.

"You don't know the half of it," she laughed cheerfully, "it will be absolutely great to have someone to shop – and hunt – with … ahhh … we shall have such adventures, she and I. We will come to thoroughly know one another's traits and habits."

"You know of course," she continued happily, "if she accepts … and when she has changed … that I shall be happy to come to Charleston to assist her with becoming accustomed to some of the new changes that will take place in her life."

"I knew that I could depend upon you and I'm sure she will appreciate having you there to field some of the more difficult questions that only another woman can answer."

"Then the issue seems settled … and you and I have some preparations to make and shopping to do," she continued, "we shall begin with a visit to Vickie as soon as she opens her shop in the morning. There are many details, some larger than others, that must be taken care of between now and then, some of which will take more time than others. When you return home, continue the direction you have chosen, and of course, allow her to make her own decision. James, you are very wise, I know that you will handle the situation in the correct manner and then make the proper decisions."

"I knew I could count on you, now as then, to guide me and give me good advice Charlotte Ann. Now, let's go inside and enjoy the performance, just like old times and old lovers."

"James … darling … you know I love you … but you have got to be careful how you use that 'old' word …

regardless of my age, I'm still a woman," she laughed as we walked arm in arm into the Lincoln Center. We settled in my private box, the big gold curtain just to the right of us, still happily smiling and chatting as the house lights began to come down.

After the play ended, we retraced our path down Broadway to 59th Street and then 7th Avenue to Times Square. Once there we began our hunt in earnest and quickly found a small alley leading away from the main entertainment area, and, laughing like two very excited lovers, we ducked between two ne'er-do-wells standing ideally on each side of the entrance and disappeared into the narrow passage. They of course followed us until the glare of the lights faded away and we were surrounded by near darkness, then tried to accost us, one of them flashing a huge knife and demanding our wallets.

"Well now … doesn't this just remind you of that night in London in … when was it … 1853 … or thereabouts," I asked with a smile, eyeing the two would be thieves.

"I suppose it is similar, there were two of them there as well," Charlotte Ann laughed, "but it also reminds me of the time in Le Havre in 1750 … I wish you had been with me then … you should have seen the look on that old salt's face when he realized who he had crossed!"

"Just shut up and give us your wallets and jewelry before I gut you," the one with the knife snarled.

"Oh listen, he even sounds like the old sailor …" she took a stance as if she were holding a knife and laughingly mimicked, "'I'll spill yer guts, Lassie'."

I chuckled at her play acting and then asked calmly, "What do you think, dear, shall we change it up a bit this time, as I remember you disarmed the one in London, would you allow me to do the honors this time?"

"Oh, by all means," she chuckled, raising her hand to her forehead in distress, "I shall play the damsel in distress and you may defend me with their lives!"

The one with the knife took a step in my direction and began, "You think you can take …" and before he finished his sentence I had grabbed his arm, twisted it behind his back, breaking his wrist and dislocating his elbow and shoulder in the process. I took the knife from him and slid it into the waistband of my slacks.

"Yes, as a matter of fact I do think I can … and in fact … I know I can," I laughingly answered the struggling malefactor. Then pulling his head back, bit into his neck and his blood exploded forcefully into my mouth. I then began to leisurely feed, drawing his life out of him.

The other fellow stood in shock for a moment before turning and attempting to run.

Charlotte Ann reached out and grabbed him, then flashing her fangs, laughed coldly, "Nun-uhhh … don't be in such a hurry to leave … it's your turn now, your partner there has crossed the Styx and is waiting for you to join him on the other side … however, I have decided to be gracious and give you a choice … so tell me, how's this going to end … I mean you're going to die … that's a given … but would you prefer quickly … or slowly … your option."

He was too frightened to speak after watching me kill his partner so she answered for him, "Oh very well, slow it shall be … besides I shall enjoy it more that way!"

And in an instant she grabbed his shirt, pulling him to her, bit into his neck, and taking her time drained the life out of him. When she had finished she quickly searched both of them and found a total of eighteen dollars between them.

"Just as I thought … nothing … no jewelry … no

money to amount to anything … not even a subway token! Meh, they're probably the type that would jump the turnstiles anyway! You know, I really miss the days when the brigands, rogues and charlatans that we fed off of were more industrious and carried their spoils in gold coins," she commented drily, then stood up, looking at the money in her hand and shaking her head sadly, snapped her fingers and flipped the meager bills into the air and watched as they fluttered to the ground.

Then turning back towards me and holding out her hand she said, "Knife please."

I handed it to her and, grabbing each of the dead thieves by the hair, she bent their heads back and swiftly slit their throats so severely as to have nearly decapitated both. We made our way out of the far end of the alley and after walking a couple of blocks, hailed a cab to return to the Waldorf and home.

Chapter Twelve

After returning to the Waldorf and passing a night of very passionate immortal lovemaking, something I had not enjoyed since the last time I had seen Charlotte Ann, nearly a decade past, we began Saturday morning taking care of some of the details in preparation for my bringing Katelyn over to second life. She suggested that we begin our day by calling on our mutual friend Vickie at her emporium. I agreed and added that I wished to make a couple of stops of my own afterward. I wished first to call upon Weissmann's to have a special necklace made for Katelyn and then stop to see David and Donna Feldman, the current owners of Dmitriy & Co. custom furniture makers, an establishment that I had conducted trade with since its founding around the turn of the twentieth century.

I planned to have a coffin prepared for Katelyn to use for those periods of rest she would require in the first two or three weeks after her transition. While the coffin was strictly a traditional thing, and I was anything but traditional, it was not necessary. However, it would be much simpler than attempting to completely secure and close off an upstairs bedroom which would require both light and sound proofing to ensure her undisturbed rest. At the same time, the coffin would provide her a place of complete peace and seclusion during those times when she would need to sleep while the change completed its work in her and she became acclimated to her new life.

"James darling, would you give me your hand for a moment," Charlotte Ann asked as we prepared to leave the apartment, "I would like to see Katelyn and get an idea of her sizes. I have a special gift in mind that I would like to purchase for her but wish to insure a proper fit."

She reached, took my offered hand in hers, and I sensed her gently step into my mind, passing quickly through my thoughts. She released my hand and stepped back saying, "My, she's much more beautiful than you described … and I wager that she will make a strikingly elegant and attractive immortal. There's no doubt that her beauty will be the main draw on her prey … and if she accepts your offer of immortality … I look forward to the day that I can actually meet her and she and I can share a hunt together."

"I almost pity the prey that the two of you would draw," I chuckled.

"You should … because they will not stand a snowball's chance in Hades once we select them," she answered as we left the apartment.

When we arrived at Vickie's she met us as old friends, "Good morning Charlotte Ann, it's so wonderful to see you and James together again!"

"Good morning Vickie," I answered smiling, "it's good to see you again, too."

"It's been too long … I wonder why it is that I've known you both for over twenty years … and yet we only manage to meet about once or twice a decade," she gently chided.

"That may be true but we do at least manage to make regular, and large, deposits to your bank account," Charlotte Ann laughed.

"And I appreciate that, more than you know," Vickie laughed, then added, "and just look at the two of you … neither of you have changed a bit since the last time I saw you. One of these days Charlotte Ann you're going to have to tell me your secret of staying young … and after I use it, I'm going to insist that all of my models use it too!"

"Oh, I can tell you what the secret is Vickie," I chuckled, "but are you sure you want to know it?"

"Of course I do James, please by all means tell me …"

"It's really simple … it's just good healthy eating," I laughed.

"Oh poo … I live in New York City … where pizza, street vendor hot dogs, and cannoli's abound," she laughed, "but at least now I know why you stay in Charleston!"

"There's a new and even better reason for me to stay in Charleston too … her name is Katelyn."

"Ohhhh really," she smiled, "and here all along I thought you and Charlotte Ann were a couple …"

"Now Vickie, I've told you that he and I are just life-long friends," Charlotte Ann spoke up.

"That's right … and next you're going to tell me it's a totally platonic friendship too," Vickie chuckled.

"I never said any such thing," Charlotte Ann laughed, "you don't think I would keep him around this long just to have someone to take me to the theater do you … besides, I do occasionally enjoy having someone that can take me to paradise too … but the real reason we are here today is that James' new love is soon to become his mate."

"Then I offer my sincerest congratulations James," she said, "and that means I should get serious … so, how can I help you this morning?"

"I would like to purchase a gift for her," Charlotte Ann smiled, "something special that I can send back with James. I was thinking about black silk … perhaps maybe a pajama negligee set … oh and it must have a matching robe and slippers."

"I can easily supply that … now, tell me about her … I need sizes … the extent of my magic is limited only to needles and thread you know … although I wish it did extend to mind reading."

"Stick to needles and thread Vickie," I interjected with a laugh, "you probably wouldn't like what you found inside most people's heads."

"I suppose you're right," she sighed and turning to Charlotte Ann asked, "Now, about Katelyn …"

"She's tall, probably only a couple of inches shorter than James, so I would say almost six feet … and she's slim … I would say she appears to be about a hundred twenty or twenty five pounds … can you make do with that," Charlotte Ann asked, perfectly describing Katelyn.

"Absolutely, in fact she sounds a lot like most of my models … and I think I have just the thing … please excuse me and I'll be right back."

When Vickie returned she had exactly what Charlotte Ann had described … the entire set was black silk, trimmed in black satin with ebony buttons … and it made me look forward to seeing Katelyn wearing it. After Charlotte Ann paid for the ensemble, we took the specialty box and left

Vickie with a promise not to wait another ten years before returning.

When we had reached the sidewalk, and turning to walk down 5th Avenue, Charlotte Ann nodded toward the box I carried, "The reason for that is it will eventually be a comfort to Katelyn. The first time she spends the night with you … and from our talk last evening I'm assuming she hasn't yet …"

"No she hasn't …" I answered and quickly added, "yet."

"Well, when she does, please see that she wears it the next morning … and on all other subsequent occasions when she stays," she continued, "she needs to wear it as often as possible in order to have it thoroughly saturated with her human scent. Then, when she makes the change, you should dress her in it before she awakens to second life. It may at first be off-putting to her, but it should retain just enough of her lingering human scent to serve as a thing of comfort and familiarity to her as she enters a new and confusing world."

While we talked we covered the distance to Weissmann's little shop in the diamond district and entered to find him occupied at his work bench.

"Good morning Mr. Weissmann," I smiled as he looked up from his work.

"Well, Mr. Dubois, it's such a pleasure to see you again … and Miss Erickson … good morning to you both … I hope you are in good health," he answered, standing and removing his magnifying hood, "and how can I be of service to you today?"

"I need a medallion and a heavy necklace to hang it on," I began slowly, "all in pure gold of course … I would like the medallion to be about two ounces … with my family crest on the front and on the reverse please engrave 'To Our Eternal Love'."

Weissmann nodded his head, and closing one eye and rubbing his chin mumbled quietly to himself.

"Now that I've described what I want, please tell me what you can do with it," I chuckled.

"Oh it's not a difficult thing …" he answered, "not a difficult thing at all. Actually, I'm thinking I will render the pendant itself in fine gold just as you ask. At two ounces it should be just under an inch and a half around and twice the thickness of a double eagle. But rather than cast it I shall hand carve the crest and the inscription. I would however, suggest one small change though, the chain would be stronger were I to use twenty-two carat instead of fine … does that meet with your approval and sound like what you have in mind."

"Ahhh, Weismann, you have a gift," I chuckled, "it sounds perfect. I shall be returning to Charleston in the morning, do you mind if Charlotte Ann comes by to pick it up when it's ready? She will arrange to have payment transferred from my account at the same time."

"I always look forward to seeing Miss Charlotte Ann grace my shop with her beauty," he smiled, and turning to her continued, "You may pick it up any time the day after tomorrow."

"Again Mr. Weissmann, thank you so much for your service," I said as we turned and left his shop.

We walked the few blocks from Weissmann's down to Chelsea and West 25th Street. When we entered the front showroom of Dmitriy & Co., I gave the secretary my name and asked to see David. After a very short call, she escorted us to David's private office and closed the door behind us.

"Good afternoon Mr. Dubois," David greeted us with a smile, "it's a pleasure to see you again."

"And you as well," I answered, "I hope you and your wife are well."

"Yes, very good," he answered.

"David, as you know, your family has designed and built furniture for my family for over a century," I continued, "and I find myself in need of your very best services."

"I think I can provide anything you have need of Mr. Dubois," he answered.

"I'm sure you can … and that's why I'm here," I began, "I need a coffin …"

"A coffin …" he repeated slowly.

"Yes, and it must be your very finest work, none other like it, and of course as usual, I shall spare no expense."

"I'm so sorry for your loss Mr. Dubois … I shall have it completed as quickly as possible."

"I'm not in need of it immediately … but soon … probably the next few weeks," I answered slowly.

"Shall we begin a drawing," he asked pulling a sketchpad from under his desk.

"I wish it to be completely unique … something like an Egyptian sarcophagus found in one of the royal tombs … and made with some kind of exotic wood. It must be a bit larger than usual … I don't wish her to feel cramped … and gold trim, as close to pure as you can work with …"

"That doesn't present a problem, I can do as you wish," he answered as he began sketching.

"I would like a full couch design … and it must be feminine … please line the inside with velvet … I would like the top and pillow to be embroidered with red roses using silk thread … and please put a soft, comfortable mattress inside … she of course won't be using it for very long, but I would like for her to have the utmost in comfort while she does."

"If you will allow me a few minutes to work on my sketch I think I can have a preliminary draft for you to see," he commented, still looking at his pad, drawing quickly. In a few moments he turned his pad around and invited me to join him at his desk. Charlotte Ann and I both stood to peer at his drawing.

"My initial thoughts," he began, "is to use African Blackwood, we call it Mozambique Ebony, it is the most exotic wood in the world. I shall design and cast Seraphim in gold, bowed in prayer at each corner with their wings wrapped to the sides and stretched along the bottom of the lid thusly. The handles shall be constructed of black onyx, with gold embellishments, and each attached to a rectangular golden plate. The plates will be heavily scroll engraved, finished in a high bas relief funerary scene with the words "Just Sleeping" engraved into them. The top will be highly curved in this manner, and the whole carefully hand polished to a deep black. All of the golden trim will be rendered in eighteen carat. An alloy mix of eighteen to six, gold and nickel, will give the trim a slight shine, more so than pure, and make it hard enough to withstand a slight bump. Finally, every seam and joint will be accented with decoratively carved molding."

"Then for the interior, to give it the feminine touch you asked for, I shall acquire the finest handcrafted pink cashmere velvet from northern India, and the embroidered roses will be hand stitched with natural Tibetan silk. I assure you this shall be as close to what you would find in a royal tomb as possible. Finally, I shall construct it ten percent larger than usual."

I smiled silently as I admired his drawing, nodding slightly in approval, but added one last touch, "I would like you to do one other thing … here in the center of the top …" I pointed, "please add a plate in fine gold, deeply engraved with roses and inscribed in a beautiful script, 'My Beloved Katelyn, Forever Young'." I watched as he added that final note.

"Well James, since you are doing all that why not just have air conditioning and cable television installed for her too," Charlotte Ann chuckled.

"That would be an interesting touch wouldn't it," I smiled in return, "but I think she can repose without it."

In an effort to remain decorous, David coughed and quickly looked down at his sketch adding a note to the drawing before looking up for my final approval which I gave with a short nod and added, "I would also like an accompanying catafalque for it to rest upon."

"Shall I have it transferred to a particular funeral parlor for you," he asked.

"That will be unnecessary," I answered, "when both are completed, please notify my courier service, they shall handle transportation and delivery. I shall have it picked up and full payment transferred to your account."

"Thank you again for your patronage Mr. Dubois, and again, I'm sorry – but pleased – that you would call upon me to provide such a service for your family. I shall have it ready for delivery in about seven to ten days … will that be sufficient?"

"That will be perfect," I answered and with that Charlotte Ann and I turned and left his office.

"And you accuse me of being absolutely incorrigible," I laughed when we had gotten out to the sidewalk, "*'Well James, since you are doing all that why not have air conditioning and cable television installed for her too'* … you realize David almost bit the tip of his tongue off to keep from laughing?"

"Yeah, and did you see the look on his face … priceless," she answered as we turned our steps toward the hotel.

When we returned to her suite in the Waldorf I began to gather my things to return to Charleston and Whitehall. When I scrolled up the number to call the pilot to file the flight plan, she reached and plucked the phone from my hand and smilingly melted into my arms.

"James," she began, looking up into my eyes, "you are the first and only one I have ever sired … and now you are preparing to sire a mate … you cannot imagine how happy I am that you are passing the gift … and to a mate no less. I don't begrudge that … but when you take your mate, you and I shall necessarily have to redefine the nature of our relationship. We have had something special for the last two and a half centuries … and we both knew that had Ferdinand came back into my life at any time during our relationship, you would have been honor bound to step aside for him … now, it is I that am honor bound to step aside for Katelyn when she becomes your mate. After this weekend we will never again have the same physical relationship we have had and enjoyed since the beginning … our affiliation will change and we will develop a friendship that shall be deeper and more lasting than ever before. But before that happens, I would like for us to have the remainder of the weekend together … please stay here with me … you can return early Monday morning and then begin your life with your new mate."

I took her in my arms, kissed her deeply and said, "I am here because of you Charlotte Ann … you are my maker, and for now my lover, and you know that I will do anything you ask me to do."

Chapter Thirteen

I arrived at Whitehall early Monday morning just like James and I had planned. I had my canvas, easel, oils, and other painting supplies that I had brought down from aunt 'Chele's after the weekend. I was so excited about painting again. I actually felt more like me than I had in a long time. I couldn't wait to set my things up and get started. It seemed almost like it had been an eternity since I had last painted. In reality, it had been months since I had even thought that I might ever want to paint again.

I drove slowly up the allee, looking at the individual trees and trying to get a feel for them. I recalled B.J's words before I left Atlanta … *'When a gift that's as wonderful as yours wanders off, it never goes too far. You'll find it again … it'll be there when you are ready for it'*. As I approached the end of the drive, I could feel the old stirring in me when there was something I really wanted to get on canvas.

"Good morning, Katelyn," James greeted me as he started down the steps toward me, "how was your weekend?"

"Wow," I thought smiling up at him, *"just look at him will you … I guess two can play that 'show off my assets' game!"* He again had his hair tied back at his neck and was dressed in a dark green, silk shirt that complimented his sparkling green eyes. It was cut to fit his body and finely tailored with single French cuffs and gold cuff links. That alone would normally be amazing but he had coupled it with a pair of nicely tight fitting black jeans. The entire outfit highlighted his wonderfully masculine build. He flashed his brilliant white smile at me and I had to swallow quickly because he was literally making my mouth water. I smiled back, appreciating what I was seeing.

"It was really good," I answered quickly, trying not to choke on my words. Then giving him a quick overview of the events asked, "and how about you, did you enjoy your trip?"

"My trip was very enjoyable and quite entertaining," he began, "I went to New York and met with my friend I mentioned to you. We haven't seen each other in some time so we rekindled our friendship. She and I attended a performance at the Metropolitan Opera where I maintain a private box. Afterwards, we finished our evening by enjoying a meal together in a little out of the way alley just off of Times Square."

"It sounds like you had a great time," I smiled, "and those 'little out of the way alley' places usually have the best food … I just know the two of you enjoyed yourselves."

"We did in fact have a wonderful time … and you are

more right than you know about those out of the way allies … this particular one indeed had a fine offering, with a very unique spice to it, not too much so, but still very delectable to the palate."

"Actually Katelyn, you were a large part of our evening's conversation," he commented casually as he helped me unload my painting supplies from the car, "I have always enjoyed her companionship; we've known each other for a long time so we're able to talk freely about anything together."

I smiled, quietly happy inside, knowing that I had been the topic of conversation on his date, and wondering just what they had talked about.

"Possibly the next time I go up you will be able to accompany me. I know that your presence would make my trip all the more enjoyable and memorable," he smiled, "perhaps then you and I can share a meal together."

"I hope so, that would be really nice and I would love to see a performance in person at the Met," I said with a big smile.

"Then we shall plan on it," he said smiling, "just a matter of working out the details. Now, is there anything I can get you before we set your things up and I leave you to paint?"

"Thanks, but I had breakfast at school, so I'm not really hungry. I think I would like to paint from just over there," I said, pointing at the right side of the yard, "I can set up under that small tree and get the view I want. Those are some of the most impressive oaks I have ever seen down the allee and I really want to try to capture their strength and essence."

"Those trees are indeed a big part of Whitehall's history," he said as we began walking toward the place I had indicated, "according to all accounts they were planted in 1740 and usually have a life span of over six hundred years... in fact, there's one such very impressive tree like those further out on Johns Island, it's called 'The Angel Oak', and it is believed to be in excess of six hundred years old. I believe that you shall successfully capture the full impressiveness of these trees. I will leave you here with them for now. I shall be up in the house working on some research. Should you need me, just call out."

"Thanks," I said smiling at him and started laying out all my things, anticipating passing the beautiful morning in deep concentration. I began mixing paints on the palette as I turned to watch him walking slowly across the lawn back to the house.

"He sure does have a nice butt ... and those black jeans show it off wonderfully ..." I smiled to myself as he walked across the grass and toward the front steps, *"I wouldn't mind getting him on canvas ... or better yet on a set of silk sheets ... hummm ... and maybe not necessarily in that order ... anyway, they're both good ideas ... I think I might have to pursue one if not both of those options."*

I chuckled softly to myself as he disappeared into the house taking my romantic thoughts with him. I smiled once more at my thoughts as I picked up a brush, sat down to face the canvas, and turned my full attention in that direction.

I stood in the parlor watching Katelyn through one of the tall windows and smiled as I once again wondered what she would say if she knew I was able to hear her most secret thoughts and desires. But most importantly, I found myself experiencing feelings of tenderness toward her that I had not felt for another woman in over two hundred sixty-five years.

There was no doubt in my mind that I had grown to love Katelyn, and now I found myself wanting to share everything I had with her … my life, my home, my very existence … much the same as I had felt when I first saw my Mary Beth. I smiled as I considered how both women, one in one life, the other in another, could have the exact same effect upon me.

After watching her for nearly an hour, all the time considering what was happening in my heart and soul, I turned away and busied myself inside the house, peeking out at Katelyn once or twice over the next couple of hours. She seemed to be happily lost in her thoughts and the painting she was working on so I retreated to the library to read. I had settled comfortably in my chair and began reading when I suddenly sensed someone watching me. I looked up and unexpectedly found a woman standing in the room appearing to intently scrutinize me. I realized that she was a spirit and so smiled at her while she continued her inspection of me. I couldn't help but notice that she strongly resembled Katelyn and she smiled before finally speaking.

"I wished to meet you Mr. Dubois," her voice floated gently through my mind, *"my name is Melissa Corbin, and I was Katelyn's mother."*

I nodded slightly before answering, "I am James Dubois, the Master of Whitehall Manor, welcome to my home Mrs. Corbin."

"I know that you and my daughter are romantically involved with each other," she continued straightforwardly, *"I also know that she doesn't know yet what you are … but I do … and I also know of your plans to make her an immortal like you. If she loves you Mr. Dubois, and gives her consent, I shall also give you my approval, but please remember she has no one left except my sister and her husband to call family. I ask only that you treat her well and take care of her … while she does present a tough and*

independent façade to the world around her … she's much more fragile and more easily broken than you can possibly imagine … so please don't hurt her … she has had more than enough of that in her young life …"

"Mrs. Corbin, I have waited over two hundred fifty years for your daughter to come along … I swear to you that I will not force my gift upon her without her consent and I will never harm her."

I saw a sudden look of unconcealed fright cross her face and she looked around sharply and said, *"Please Mr. Dubois … it's not Katelyn's time yet … do whatever you have to do, but save my daughter's life at all costs …"* and she simply disappeared again.

It was such a nice sunny day that I had decided to wear a pair of short shorts. I had thought maybe I could get a little spring sun on my legs, improving my tan, as I painted. I settled on the short stool James had brought out, and kicked off my sandals so my toes could wiggle in the soft grass as I painted. It was so peaceful and calm here. The sun was playing through the branches of the small tree above me, warming my legs as I sat there.

I smiled as I realized that my talent was indeed waiting for me … right where I left it. I must have spent the better part of two hours just getting the general shape of the allee done. Then I started working on the individual trees. For the first time in over a year, I actually got lost in my work, totally oblivious to my surroundings and the passage of time.

Then all of a sudden with no warning, I was interrupted by an unexpected rustle and a precipitous commotion in the branches over me. Before I could even look up to see what it was there was a heavy thud on the ground next to me followed by a loud buzzing sound. Then something hit me so hard on my upper thigh that I was knocked completely off the stool I had been perched on.

I had grown up living in the North Georgia pine lands so I knew there was only one creature on earth that made that kind of sound – an angry rattlesnake. The next few seconds happened so fast they became a complete blur. All in one instant it seemed, I saw a huge brown Diamondback, lying in the grass, still buzzing but now moving in the opposite direction away from me. The excruciating pain in my leg and blood on my thigh told me what had happened … and probably what was about to happen … and I screamed.

My scream was the classical movie type shriek of fright, one that I didn't even know I had in me, only the screams of my nightmare came closer. Then, as fear started creeping over me, I felt long streamers of pain beginning in my leg and quickly burning their way upward as the venom moved through my body. The pain spread quickly into my right side and soon my face felt like it was on fire.

I tried to scream again, hoping to get James' attention but all that came out was a low, hoarse moan. While I lay there in pain I heard and felt my heart racing in my chest and I realized it was rapidly pumping the venom through my system. My leg and right arm was already numb and I couldn't move either of them. The fire of the venom now spread into my left side, down my arm and began to fill my leg. My toes tingled before bursting into flames as the venom reached them.

I tried with everything in me to move … if I could just get to James he could get help for me … but my body refused all of my efforts to make it function. There was nothing else I could do, so I began to cry thinking how unfair my now shortened life had been to me. I was afraid and the thing that scared me the most was that I was going to die … and I was going to die all alone with no one to even hold my hand while I did.

I lingered just on the very edge of unconsciousness while everything began going gray. I knew I was about to slip away when I heard my name. I opened my eyes and saw my mother standing there looking down at me and she was smiling.

"Katelyn … Katelyn … baby don't you give up … you must fight this for just a little longer … you can do it … you're strong … you must keep fighting … you must keep living, it's not your time yet."

"Oh Mama …" I whimpered, "it hurts so bad … my whole body is on fire."

I tried to reach out to her, I wanted desperately to touch her, to feel her soft hands on me again, but I was unable to move.

"Just fight it a little longer Katelyn, I have help on the way," she smiled again and vanished.

I lay still on the grass, unable to move as the darkness of death began to spread faster and faster over and through me, finally extinguishing the fire of the venom. The last thing I saw was the beautiful blue sky above me and then it too began to dim as blackness thankfully overtook me. I finally gave up the fight and passed out as the cool shade began taking me down, deeper and deeper into death.

I knew it was almost over when I again heard the comforting words that Aunt 'Chele had spoken to me so many times when I was locked in the throes of an inescapable nightmare. Only this time it wasn't Aunt 'Chele and I wasn't in my bed, but I was locked in a terrible nightmare.

"Katelyn … Katelyn … I'm here darling," I heard a voice tearing its way through the terror. I struggled to barely open my eyes, now blurred with the pain, and I saw James kneeling over me.

"You will be alright, my love, I promise I shall not allow you to die," I heard him say as he lifted my now completely limp body in his arms and began carrying me. I must have passed out then because the next instant I was lying on a bed in one of the upstairs bedrooms.

Everything seemed like my nightmare, gray and cloudy, swirling around me. I could hear James saying something but I couldn't make out the words. I didn't feel any pain now, or for that matter, my arms or legs either. I thought in those few minutes, *"death is so much quieter and easier than I had thought possible."* I heard James again saying something to me. I tried so desperately to force myself to focus on him and concentrate on what he was saying, but all I could make out was "anti-venom" and "drink this." I closed my eyes again, waiting on death to wrap its arms around me.

I laid her on the bed and taking a silver trophy goblet from one of the shelves, opened my wrist to the deepest artery and began filling it. When it was nearly full I closed the wound in my wrist and went to her side. I lifted her head and softly spoke, "Katelyn, my love, I know that you can hear me … this is anti-venom for the bite … you must drink all of it … it will kill the poison inside you and help bring about healing."

I lifted her head and holding it to her lips began pouring the blood into her mouth and forcing her to swallow. She almost gagged on the flow, but I kept pouring saying, "It's almost over, you only have a little left to drink."

When she had taken it all and I wiped her mouth, she opened her eyes the tiniest bit and I heard her thoughts, *"My knight in shining armor … trying to save my life … so sweet of him …"* then she faded away again into darkness.

"Katelyn," I began slowly, "I must get the remainder of the venom out of your leg, this will be painful but I will be very careful and try not to hurt you any more than necessary …"

She groaned in response and tried to open her eyes again but still couldn't hold them open. I quickly bit into her leg, just where the snake had struck, and the remaining venom, bitter as gall, shot out of the open wound and filled my mouth. I knew the pain of my bite was intense and so was not surprised when she passed out, but I continued my work. Once I had the wound open and the blood flowing, I opened my wrist once again and poured a couple of ounces of my blood into it to kill any residual venom, seal it up and heal the surrounding area.

I next took a soft bandage, wrapped it around her leg and taped it in place. Finally, I undid her shorts, which were covered in her blood, and slid them down and off her legs. I bathed her legs, feet and hands to remove the last vestige of her blood, then tossed the cloth and her shorts into an open fireplace and burned them … I didn't need anything with the lingering smell of her blood lying around … especially if I wished to save her life and not turn her.

When I had assured myself that my "anti-venom" was working and she would be alright, I sat back for a few minutes to watch her. I looked up in time to see her mother once again, this time standing on the far side of the bed. She looked at Katelyn, smiled, and then at me saying, *"Thank you for saving my baby … we both knew it wasn't her time …"*

"I promise that I will take care of her and see that she heals and fully recovers," I said.

"What about the blood you just gave her ... will it make her like you now?"

"No Mrs. Corbin, it won't," I began, "in order for that to happen, I must first take her blood, nearly all of it, allow it to mingle with mine, absorbing the vampiric gene from it, and then give it back to her ... that will bring about the change, making her like me ... but she isn't ready for that yet ... she must first learn of me and my nature ... and she isn't ready for that either."

"Very well ... then for the time being, I'm going to leave her in your charge ... she may soon become like you and when she does, she will also be your mate ... but please remember that she'll always be my daughter first ... please take care of her." Then she disappeared again.

Chapter Fourteen

After ensuring that Katelyn was sleeping and in no further danger, I returned to the yard and began searching for the snake that had caused all of this trouble. I intended to find him and kill him … all of the predators in the area surrounding Whitehall, whether natural or supernatural, large or small, knew to keep a respectful distance from me and my property. If one ever crossed that line, as this one had, they paid with their lives … and they were all well aware of the penalty.

I quickly found the snake, an Eastern Diamondback, resting in a sunny spot about a hundred feet away from where his attack had taken place. He was a large one, a bit over seven feet long, and obviously old. I walked up on him and he alerted to my presence but due to my slower heartbeat, about thirty-five beats a minute, making my body temperature close to seventy-eight degrees, much lower than that of a mortal, he was unable to positively locate me. He swiftly coiled his body into a striking position, shaking his rattles in an attempt to warn off whatever had invaded his space, weaving his head and flashing his tongue in an effort to lock onto my scent and location.

"It won't do you any good," I spoke, letting him know exactly where I stood, "you not only crossed the line into my domain ... you struck my mate ... and in return I shall kill you for it."

I watched as he zeroed in on where I stood and drew back his head in preparation to attack. He was strong, and fast as forked lightning, knowing he could take any natural threat, so I allowed him to strike. When he did, I quickly side stepped and caught him in the air, mid-strike, just behind his head, and looking into his beady eyes said, "I'm faster than you are too ... now allow me to show you what it feels like to get bitten by a predator."

He had attempted to wrap his body around my arm, but the shock of my bite hit him like a thunderbolt and he immediately went limp in my hands. His rattles began to rapidly slow and I knew he was dying, but not yet dead, so I twisted his head off and threw it into a small creek that flowed toward the river at the rear of the property. When I returned to the house with his body, I placed it in a trash bag and then into one of the unused food freezers. I would have one of the grounds-men tan the skin and turn it into a nice trophy gift of some kind for Katelyn.

When I returned to the room in which Katelyn lay, I continued my watch over her until she began to stir about. I knew the vampiric blood in her system was at work killing the venom as well as any other virus that may have been lurking in her body. She mumbled several names but the one that was most often and most clear was that of Lexi, her roommate. I took her phone from the bedside and scrolled through to find Lexi. I was a bit surprised at the lack of contact numbers – there was mine, Lexi, her aunt and uncle, some girls from Atlanta – Beth, Tiffany and Billie Jo – and sadly, there were still numbers for Mom and Dad, and no one else. So I placed a call to Lexi.

"Hi Katelyn," she answered cheerily on the second ring, "how's your day going with James … are you behaving yourself?"

"Uhhh, hello Lexi … I'm sorry it isn't Katelyn … this is James at Whitehall …"

"James …" she asked slowly, "what's going on … where is Katelyn … why are you calling from her phone?"

"Katelyn's alright," I reassured her, "but she's had an accident …"

"Oh my God, is she okay, what happened?"

"She's fine … now … and resting … but she was attacked and bitten by a rattlesnake."

"Are you sure she's alright … where are you … which hospital did you take her to?"

"I promise you she's alright … and she's right here at Whitehall … I administered some anti-venom, bandaged the bite area, and she is sleeping right now … but she has called out for you several times … I was hoping perhaps you could come out and be here when she wakes?"

"Yes … yes, I'll leave right away … I can be there in about an hour … maybe less … does she need anything?"

"Perhaps you should bring her a complete change of clothes … there was a large amount of blood from the bite so what she was wearing was mostly ruined."

"I'll bring something for her … anything else?"

"I'd suggest something to sleep in too … I don't think she will be up to leaving tonight."

"James … can … can I stay there with her … please?"

"Yes, by all means, you are welcome to stay with her as long as she stays."

"Thank you so much … I'll leave right now and see you soon."

"Lexi, once again, she will be alright, so please drive safely," I said ending the call.

I floated in and out of consciousness, seemingly half way between life and death, just barely aware of some movement around me, but not really knowing exactly what was happening or where. When I was lucid, I felt … strange … my entire body was tingling all over with tiny pin pricks. Then I suddenly remembered what had happened, the big snake, the pain of the bite, and James giving me some kind of medicine. I slowly opened my eyes as I felt myself beginning to rise out of the fog, and saw James standing beside the bed, talking on my phone.

He was barely speaking above a whisper, but I was able to hear him clearly as he talked until he ended the call and turned to look at me, "How do you feel," he asked smiling, "better, I hope?"

"I … I thought I was dying," I said.

"You would have if I hadn't heard your scream and gotten to you. That was one big snake, you know, he was almost seven and a half feet long; and he emptied his venom glands when he bit you. I brought you in, administered some anti-venom to prevent you from dying, and removed the remaining venom from your leg."

"You … had anti-venom … here," I asked, questions

starting to fill my still cloudy mind.

"Of course, one does not live out here on the edge of the wild without some kind of defenses," he answered with a smile, "but, back to my question, how do you *feel*?"

"I'm … strange … I'm not sure how to describe it … my whole body is stinging. My skin is burning all over like I have a bad sunburn or something."

"That's a good sign; it means the anti-venom is working."

"I can barely keep my eyes open … the light from the window is hurting them it's so bright … and I swear I think I can hear cars passing out on the highway … that can't be though, that's over a mile away."

"That sounds like more of the side effects of the anti-venom. It especially heightens your senses for a short time as it works. It should wear off and pass out of your system in about three or four days. I think you will be just fine then," he said, "but, for now, you are still very weak so just lie still and rest, let it continue to do its work. Lexi will be here in about an hour to help tend you and stay with you until you have recovered."

"I thought I heard you talking to her …" I whispered hoarsely.

"Indeed you did … you called out to her several times in your delirium so I knew you would like to have her close."

"Thank you for calling her for me … I really would like for her to be here with me."

"It's my pleasure," he said, "now you need to rest until she arrives. You should begin to feel much better by the morning, and then you can call your aunt and tell her what happened."

He walked to the window and closed the blind, then

as he reached the door he turned and with a cold smile and an even colder hardness in his eyes said, "Oh, and by the way, your new snakeskin day planner and desk set should be ready in a couple of weeks … he knew better than to hunt in my domain and he paid for his indiscretion."

I suddenly realized what he had meant when he had said that it *was* a huge snake. Then he turned out the light and walked out, closing the door behind him. I closed my eyes and slept a fitful, but peaceful and dreamless rest.

I waited by the front door for Lexi to arrive and when she did, she ran into my arms, and burying her face in my chest burst into tears. Then with her voice trembling and full of fear she whispered softly, "James … is … is Katelyn going to be alright … she's the only real friend I have at school … please tell me she's not going to die … please don't let her die?"

I held her in my arms for a few moments and releasing a wave of comfort and reassurance toward her, lightly kissed the top of her head then cupped her cheek in my hand before answering, "Lexi, I can assure you that Katelyn is going to fully recover … the anti-venom I gave her is very strong and will do what it is supposed to do … she's only sleeping right now … and should wake again before long … I promise that your friend isn't going to die."

I could feel the fright pouring in waves off of her as I gently wiped a tear from her cheek, and, with my arm still around her shoulder, ushered her into the main parlor to explain what had happened to Katelyn, and to describe, in very vague terms, what I had done for her, and to once again reassure her that Katelyn would be alright. When she looked up at me, I saw an expression of complete helplessness, eyes brimming with tears, while she listened to what had happened.

We went upstairs where Lexi immediately took a seat beside the bed, and reaching out took Katelyn's hand, and sat quietly waiting on her to wake again. I noted that every so often she would snuffle back the urge to cry, but even so an occasional tear still escaped and ran shamelessly down her face. I took a box of tissues, and putting one in Lexi's free hand, set the remainder of them on her lap.

She nodded slowly in somber acknowledgement and turned her face back toward Katelyn and her sentinel … and what I observed as she sat there intrigued me to no end. Although I didn't know Lexi very well – I had only really looked at her a handful of times over the course of her college attendance – she had never appealed to me as one I would take … she was tiny, almost elfish in her appearance … and her voice was small and childishly musical in its tone. Perhaps the fact that she was very much like an adolescent was what had kept me from taking her in the past, being that a steadfast rule in our world is that we do not take children or innocent blood. While she may have been an adult in age, she still had a strong childlike appearance and the scent of her blood had the complete innocence of a newborn.

However, what little I did know about her, from the few times that I had seen her before Katelyn's arrival on campus, is that she was usually alone. She didn't take part in any social events, she had no friends that I knew of, and she seldom even came into the student union. In fact, she was much like me in many ways, she kept to herself except when she had to leave her dorm room. But now I watched as she sat beside Katelyn and began to discover a Lexi that I had never seen, never understood. She was kind hearted and tender, her deep friendship and love for Katelyn was very evident … and I admired those traits as she sat there completely silent, never taking her eyes off her. She sat her vigil for the next hour and a half until Katelyn slowly opened her eyes and looked over at her.

The next time I opened my eyes, Lexi was sitting next to the bed, holding my hand. She saw me look at her and burst into tears saying, "Oh, Katelyn, I was so scared for you! When James called and told me what had happened I thought the worst. I had to come right out. Are you alright … how do you feel … can I do anything for you?" Then she climbed onto the bed beside me and put her arm around my shoulders and hugged me close.

I smiled back at her and weakly said, "James seems to have taken pretty good care of me and he seems to think I will be alright soon."

James was standing at the foot of the bed looking at me in a concerned manner and again he asked me, "How do you feel, now?"

"About like I did," I slowly replied, "although I'm beginning to feel some strength in me … the feeling is beginning to return to my arms and legs … and I can move my fingers and toes again … in fact, now that I think about it, I really feel incredibly strong right now, almost like I could run."

"Well, I wouldn't attempt that just yet," he said with a smile, "that's still the side effects of the anti-venom you're feeling. Let's allow your leg to heal first then you can run the marathon. You'll feel better in the morning, maybe even able to walk around a little by then. Don't remove the bandage from your leg just yet, let it finish healing. It should be completely healed by tomorrow or the next day and we'll take it off then. Get some sleep, if you can, for the rest of the night. I will check on you again in the morning. Should either of you need me in the night, just call out, I'll be close by."

I felt safe now knowing James was close by and Lexi was lying beside me. I stretched out in the bed and turned toward Lexi, cuddled closer to my best friend and we both drifted off to sleep with our arms wrapped protectively around each other.

I turned and left them together, returning in a short while to find both sound asleep, cuddled in each other's arms. I smiled and covered them with a light blanket to ensure they slept warm and retreated to my study downstairs.

Later in the evening, between midnight and dawn I went to once again check on them as they slept. When I silently entered the room, I was surprised to see the spectral apparition of Mary Beth, her back to me, watching over them.

"Mary Beth, it's good to see you again," I spoke softly ensuring that no human ear could hear.

"Not Mary Beth, Father … just Mary," she answered, her soft voice floating through me, and turning toward me, I saw my daughter smiling at me.

"It's a pleasure to see you Mary, it's been a very long time," I commented.

"It has … but I desired to come see your new mate," she smiled, *"Mother likes her and is happy for you … and she has told me all about her."*

I was rather a bit taken aback to discover that they had talked about us, Katelyn in particular, but supposed anything was possible.

"She's beautiful Father, just like Mother said she was … I remember how you held me in your arms as I made my transition … the strength and depth of your love for me was incredible … and if you love her the same way, she will be yours forever."

"I do love her Mary … much more than I ever realized possible … she has touched my soul like only your Mother ever could."

"And Katelyn loves you Father … much more than you can appreciate right now … she looks forward to a life with you … although she doesn't yet know just what kind of a life it is predestined to be."

"I promised her mother that I would take care of her forever," I smiled.

"I'm sure you will … and at the same time, do not discount the little one lying there beside her … she too is special in many ways and is ultimately destined for second life as well."

"What … Lexi … when … how?"

"The time isn't yet … and you are not to be the giver of the gift … but you know the giver … and you shall have known her for a time and a half time before the gift is given," she answered and disappeared, leaving me standing alone in the room silently watching the two girls sleeping peacefully beside each other. I turned and returned to my study where I quietly pondered Mary's seemingly prophetic words concerning both Katelyn and Lexi as the remainder of the night now passed slowly away.

James must have come in during the night because when I opened my eyes the next morning I noticed that both of us were covered with a light blanket. The window blind was open again and the sunlight stung my eyes so much I wasn't sure I could keep them open. And then, rather than hearing him, I sensed his presence, somehow I knew that he was downstairs in the main hall. I closed my eyes and softly breathed out his name, barely above a whisper, trying not to wake Lexi who was still sleeping peacefully beside me.

When I opened my eyes again, he was standing beside the bed. He placed his finger over his lips for me to remain quite, and then spoke so low that no one else could have heard him, "You're going to be alright, Katelyn, I'll explain everything that's happened to you later."

"Can I get out of bed," I asked, trying to untangle myself from Lexi without waking her at the same time.

"Katelyn, are you alright," she asked sleepily.

"I'm fine," I said looking at her with a huge smile, "I just woke up and I really, really need to pee!"

She looked questioningly at James and he nodded and pointed, "Please, by all means … the bathroom is over there."

I sat up on the side of the bed and then slowly stood up. I was surprised that there was no pain at all in my leg. I walked across the room toward the bathroom with Lexi right beside me holding my arm. When I had finished my business I returned and sat back on the side of the bed with Lexi still hovering close by ready to offer a helping hand.

"Do you feel like taking a quick walk around the room with me now," James asked with a smile.

"I'm not sure about quick … but I think I can try," I smiled back at him as I stood up, making sure to put my weight on my good leg. Then with one arm around my waist and the other holding my arm to steady me, he walked slowly around the bedroom with me. As I walked, I literally felt myself getting stronger, almost as if nothing had ever happened to me. I felt a sudden new strength begin surging through me. Then as I looked all around me, I noticed that everything in the room was so much clearer than I remembered, so bright and sharply defined. I started to feel confused about myself and looked questioningly at James.

He simply smiled again and said "It'll all be gone and out of your system by the end of the week, then you'll be back to your normal self again."

He laid his arm lightly around my shoulders again in a gentle hug and once more there was a wave of unexplained comfort passing through me. I had to remember to ask him how he did that, and then I thought of all the other questions I had been storing away and wanted to ask about.

Without warning I heard the voice in my head speak up again saying, *"Katelyn, darling, all of your questions will soon be answered, just make sure you really want to know the answers before you ask the questions."* By now I recognized the voice and chalked it up to my inner self, but I still wondered where it had come from and why now.

James said that it was time to change the bandage on my thigh, which he refused to let me watch him do, saying I didn't need to see my leg just yet but that it seemed to be healing very quickly. So I lay back on the bed, with my fingers interlaced together behind my head, as he slid my pajama bottoms down past my knees. I quietly looked up at the patterns on the sculpted ceiling, more than a little chagrined as I thought to myself, *"Well, this is not even close to the scenario I had in mind for the first time he undressed me … and certainly not with Lexi watching!"*

He was a perfect gentleman, but I still felt a little embarrassed lying there with my pajama bottoms around my knees and his cool, silky smooth hands moving around on my upper thigh as he carefully removed the old bandage and taped the new one in place.

When he was finished he gently pulled my bottoms

back in place, his fingers sliding lightly across the bare skin of my thighs, causing them to tingle just a little. I realized with a quick smile and an abrupt blush that those same cool, silky smooth fingers had also produced another, completely unexpected, but very pleasant tingle elsewhere in me at the same time.

We spent the rest of the day on the rear veranda. James and Lexi both insisted I wear my pajamas and stay relaxed. I called aunt 'Chele about noon and told her what had happened. She immediately wanted to come down but I talked her out of it. I told her that James was taking good care of me here and promised that if I started feeling bad again I would have James or Lexi drive me home.

She made me promise to call immediately if I started getting sick and then told me to hand the phone to Lexi. I did, and the most surprising thing happened, I could actually hear both sides of the conversation. Aunt 'Chele made Lexi promise to bring me home so she could take me to her doctor if anything happened to me. Then she asked to speak to James so Lexi handed him the phone and I heard her ask, "Mr. Dubois, is Katelyn really alright? Please, she's our daughter now, we love her very much and she's all we have left. Is there anything I need to know or do to help out? Please tell me everything?"

"May I please call you 'Aunt 'Chele' …" he asked softly, reassuring her with a calm voice, "thank you … yes ma'am, Katelyn is perfectly alright. As she told you, I administered some anti-venom and have been closely watching her to ensure that she recovers from both it and the venom completely … in fact, I'm going to ask that she and Lexi remain at Whitehall another night."

"But what about school," she asked, "will it be alright for her to miss those classes?"

"Yes ma'am, and to insure there will be no issues with the school, I will contact their instructors later this evening and explain the situation fully to them."

"Thank you so much Mr. Dubois, and please call me if Katelyn needs anything or I can be of any assistance."

"Please don't be concerned Aunt 'Chele, I will continue to take excellent care of her and I promise to contact you immediately if she needs you … yes, here she is …" and he handed the phone back to me.

"Oh, Katelyn, sweetie, I feel so much better after talking to him. You do like he says and get your rest tonight, then call me tomorrow and let me know how you are doing. And please try to come home this weekend; I want to see you so badly. I love you so much baby and I'll talk to you then." She hung up the phone and was gone.

Chapter Fifteen

We stayed again that night at Whitehall but only Lexi slept. It wasn't that I couldn't, I just didn't have any desire to, in fact, I wasn't the least bit tired. I felt like I had so much energy zooming through me. My whole body was still tingling and I still felt strange but in a good way. It was like everything in me was being renewed … and I still had that urge to just get up and run. I noticed, too, that even with the lights out and the blinds drawn, I was still able to see everything in the room in sharp detail. The darkness had no effect on my vision.

Just like the night before, I was again acutely aware of James in the house throughout the night. I could actually feel his presence wherever he was in the house. I knew every move he made but I never actually heard him. I thought to myself that if this was the side effects of the anti-venom what would happen when it began to wear off. Would I be so tired that I would have to sleep for a couple of days? I suppose that was a question … another one … that I would have to file away to ask.

I stayed in bed, lying still, until Lexi woke up because I didn't want to disturb her rest. Just as she was waking up James knocked lightly on the door and eased into the room. Strangely, I knew he was there before he knocked. Somehow, I think I had actually felt his presence coming closer to me as he came up the stairs, although he never made a sound. It was so peculiar, like we were somehow connected by a cord. I wondered if perhaps he knew what I was experiencing.

"So how is my little patient this morning," he asked with a smile, looking into my eyes, searching into their depths as if looking there for the answer to his question.

"I feel pretty good," I answered, "except my eyes are still a little, well, actually, a lot, sensitive, but I think I'm ready to get up and move around a bit."

I reached out my hand to him and he gently took it, slowly wrapping both of his around it. When he did, I felt something physically pass between us. I somehow sensed that I shared a part of his life. There was a secret that I didn't fully understand that we now held between the two of us. I smiled back at him knowing he would explain it all in due time. He winked at me and nodded. With no further explanation needed, I knew that he knew what I was feeling.

"Very good," he smiled back, "I think you are close to being fully recovered and ready to get back to normal. So, let's take your bandage off before you get dressed and see how your leg looks."

I looked hesitantly at him and asked, "Do you think it's going to leave a really nasty scar … I mean I've always considered my legs to be my best asset … well, them and my butt!"

"I don't think there'll be a scar," he chuckled and winked, "but let's have a look and see."

This time I sat on the side of the bed, and James took a seat on a short stool in front of me. He reached and very carefully began to slide my pajama bottoms down to below my knees while I quietly thought to myself, *"And once again Lexi watches as he takes my pajamas off … this is just wrong on so many levels!"*

He seemed to be taking his time as he gradually removed each piece of tape from my leg, carefully loosening the bandage. While he continued I noticed again how satiny smooth his fingers and hands felt, gliding softly across my skin, gently caressing my thigh as he slowly worked removing the tape. The longer he took removing the bandage the softer and silkier his touch seemed to get until he finally began to gently lift the bandage itself away.

"Ummm, there's that incredible tingling again," I thought quickly, *"and if he can do that with a casual touch, just imagine …"*

James looked up at me, winked and flashed a quick smile as he took the bandage completely away. I felt a hot flush go over me as I noticed the coincidence of my sexy thought and his smile … at least I hoped it was coincidence. I looked down at my leg and exclaimed, "Oh! … Wow! … Look at that!"

I jumped up in my excitement and my pajamas slid easily the rest of the way down my legs and pooled around my feet. But, I didn't bother to think about that as I looked at my leg where I had been bitten. It was just as smooth as it had been and the skin around the bite area was just as soft and tanned as it always was. There was simply no sign of the bite or even the tiniest hint of a scar. I was shocked to say the least, but very happy, because, well, if I can be accused of any vanity, it would be my legs. They are my best asset … long, shapely, and beautiful … they more than make up for my small chest … and I know it too, so I keep them smooth and tanned. There, I admitted it I am more than a little proud of my legs.

"How is that possible," I asked, "there's not even a sign that anything happened!"

"I injected a little of the anti-venom into the bite area before I put the first bandage on. It's very strong, but certainly good at what it does," he smiled back at me.

"Mmmm, Katelyn," Lexi began, pointing and struggling not to laugh, "you … uhh … might want to look down."

I looked down and saw my pajama bottoms lying pooled around my ankles … but then I realized what she was talking about … and my jaw dropped open and I was suddenly very embarrassed as I realized I had been standing right in front of James wearing only a short tee and my panties … and his face was only inches away from my tummy … and my girly parts!

He looked up at me, winked, and with a mischievous grin and a little chuckle said, "You can pull your pajamas back up now … or if you would prefer, I can put them back in place."

My temperature shot straight up, heating my entire body. I felt a sudden hot flush beginning at the base of my neck, quickly spreading upward across my face and all the way to my hairline. My face and neck flamed bright red at the unexpected embarrassment. I stood silent, my face on fire, trying to decide if I wanted to laugh or cry at the situation.

"I'll go and get some fruit and juice ready for breakfast, the two of you can come down when you finish getting dressed," he smiled as he stood and chuckling softly to himself as he walked out of the room added, "Oh and Katelyn, that's a very pretty little Fairy you have there, and now that I have had the opportunity to *closely* inspect her, I can honestly say that she's quiet colorful and very lifelike."

And unable to restrain herself any longer Lexi guffawed loudly and happily with laughter at my embarrassing moment.

While I got dressed the questions were flying full speed around in my head. It seemed like there was so much I wanted to know. I just didn't understand everything that had happened in my life recently. There was something, very vague, but it was there none the less, playing around on the edge of my thoughts, I just couldn't put my finger on it. I felt like I knew the answer but just could not pull it into full focus. It was like trying to remember the answer to a test question, it was in my mind and I knew it, but I just couldn't pull it out. I resolved to think it through over the next day or so and come to a firm answer.

Lexi and I went downstairs where James had a light breakfast prepared and waiting for us. The fruit and juice were all fresh and tasted good, but as I ate I realized that I wanted something else, something different. I just didn't know what. My breakfast was just not satisfying an unknown craving inside me. I continued to think about it as I ate and finally, the only thing I could think of was … a bowl of warm tomato soup?

"What's happening to me …" I thought to myself, *"why do I feel this way … my breakfast isn't good … and I love fresh*

fruit and juice ... I don't even like tomato soup ... why am I craving it?"

I looked up at James and he was studying me with a modest smile, almost as if he knew what I was thinking, and he asked, "Are you alright, if you don't feel you are fully recovered you're welcome to stay as long as you wish."

"I'm feeling pretty much back to normal I think. I really enjoy being here, it's so peaceful, but I have to get back to school. I can't stay away much longer," I answered.

"Very well, then," and he turned to Lexi and asked, "Would you mind if she rides back with you? I'm not sure she's ready to drive just yet."

Then looking back to me continued, "Katelyn, I shall have your car delivered to the college for you later this afternoon."

We finished breakfast and prepared to leave. James walked with me to the car and opened the door for me. I turned and hugged him, pulling close to him, and said, "Thank you so much for all you've done. I *really* owe you my life. I hate to think what would have happened if you hadn't been here."

I saw a world of sincerity in his eyes as he looked at me and spoke softly, "Katelyn, darling, I'm glad that I was here when you needed me most ... at least I was able to prevent *you* from dying ... I will see you again soon."

He took me in his arms and held me close as his arms slid lightly down my back and rested around my waist. I thought for a moment that he was about to kiss me ... and I was suddenly conflicted ... I wanted him to kiss me ... right here, right now ... but at the same time I didn't want somebody – even if it was Lexi – to witness our first kiss. I felt that our first kiss should be ours – mine and his – and not shared by anyone else.

Suddenly there was that comforting wave that felt so good washing over and through me again. I also quickly noticed that his closeness and the comfort it produced suddenly felt so much stronger than it ever had in the past. Whatever it was, I liked it.

We started down the long drive and I leaned back, closed my eyes and relaxed for the ride back. Then my little inner voice quietly spoke up again, *"Katelyn, consider well the questions you think you may want to ask. The answers are there and ready for* you, *but are* you *ready for the answers?"*

"Yeah, I really think I am," I said without realizing it.

"What did you say," Lexi asked quickly.

"Oh, nothing, really, I guess I was just thinking out loud," I replied, and continued, "Thank you so much, Lexi, for being here for me the last couple of days. I really appreciate you helping James nurse me back to health. I'm so glad you are my friend!"

"Katelyn, you don't know how much your friendship means to me … and I hope we are going to be friends for a long time," and with a big smile she added, "besides we wouldn't have wanted James to have had to nurse you back to health all by himself now, would we?"

Chapter Sixteen

After Katelyn and Lexi had departed I returned to the library to read and await the arrival of early evening to begin my nightly hunting. I picked a book off the shelves, settled comfortably into my favorite chair and began reading when my telephone rang … it was Charlotte Ann.

"Hello Charlotte Ann, it's so good to hear from you," I began as I touched the answer key.

"Hello James, I hope I'm not interrupting anything?"

"Nothing at all, Katelyn just left and I'm preparing to go hunting," I answered.

"Good, I'm glad that you are by yourself … I didn't wish to intrude while your little human was around."

"Now Charlotte Ann, be nice … my 'little human' as you refer to her is soon to become a full-fledged member of the family," I said quietly.

"Oh, is that so … then she has agreed to accept the gift?"

"Not yet … but her curiosity is mounting and beginning to get the best of her, so it's coming," I continued, "most likely the next time she comes to the house … at least I think we shall have the conversation about it then."

"That's wonderful news and I look forward to her joining the family," she chuckled, "when she does, you know that I will fully accept her and be there to assist her in acclimating to her new life … but until that happens, she's still human … and that makes her *your* little human and *I* shall keep my distance."

"I understand your reluctance to be around mortals," I laughed softly in response.

"Well, as far as I'm concerned, they *are* only good for one thing …"

"Oh, and is that only what you thought of me," I asked chuckling.

"What I thought about you isn't important … besides, you know she could never do for me the things that you did for me … anyway, that was a very long time ago … but dining choices aside, that isn't why I called … I thought I would come down and deliver the pendant you ordered from Weissmann last week," she said.

"Excellent, if you come down this evening we shall go hunting together …"

"And you can fill me in on everything that has happened since we were together," she laughed, "I'll see you in an hour or so … good-bye for now."

True to her word she arrived in just under an hour, joining me in the parlor, she melted into my arms and I greeted her with our usual passionate kiss.

"You know, I'm going to miss you doing that when

Katelyn makes the change," she smiled up at me, "But no matter, I'm thrilled that you are soon to have a mate."

"Thank you Charlotte Ann … and I too shall miss our romantic times, however I do look forward to Katelyn joining me."

"You should be … and when you do, the romantic times that we have shared shall pale in comparison to what a mated relationship will be … trust me – I know – and you shall soon find out. I know that you love your Katelyn … I also know that she will be well taken care of by you …" and slowly breathing in, she added, "and I must add, she smells absolutely delicious. But speaking of smelling delicious, I must ask, why is there the scent of another human girl lingering in the air? I know it can't be Katelyn … in fact, it's much like the scent of a child – purely innocent."

"That my dear would be Lexi," I smiled in answer, "and you are correct, she does smell incredibly tantalizing … however, she is Katelyn's roommate and has spent the last two days and nights here … with Katelyn."

"Oh, and why is that … I mean, I would expect Katelyn to be spending the nights here … with you … and besides you are not known to have visitors, especially mortals at Whitehall."

"Unfortunately, I had no real choice in the matter. Katelyn was attacked and bitten by a large rattlesnake a couple of days ago. Her life was saved only because I gave her my blood to drink, but during her delirium she called out several times to Lexi, so I called and invited her to come out and stay with Katelyn until she was recovered."

"I see … well this Lexi, whomever she is, smells incredibly luscious … and since you have Katelyn, may I have her?"

Her playful teasing triggered the words that Mary had spoken about Lexi … '*she too is destined for second life and you are not to be the giver of the gift … but you know the giver …'*

"You may not," I answered quickly.

"Oh James … please, please, please," she giggled playfully.

"This is one time I have to say no Charlotte Ann … and you know it's not because I'm opposed to you having any human you want … any time … any place … just not *this* human. Katelyn and Lexi are the next thing to blood kin … one would almost think they are sisters … they are always together … where you find one, you will find the other … and were something to happen to Lexi it would devastate Katelyn … and I just can't have that at this time."

"Oh very well," she surrendered, and slowly sniffing the air one more time continued, "but she really does smell wonderful … it's not often one finds an adult whose blood is filled with the purity and innocence of a child … I'm sure that she would make a memorable little morsel to say the least."

"Perhaps so … but I'm sure you will be able to find others," I chuckled, adding, "and probably just like her."

"Maybe, just not in the city … they mature so early there," she laughed, "Oh well, that's really not why I'm here in the first place … here is the pendant you ordered … and I have to admit, Weissmann did a wonderful job … he is outstanding at his craft."

She reached into a small purse she carried and handed me a wooden box that I immediately recognized as Weissmann's handiwork, it was beautifully aged teak wood, carved to perfection and he had even added my crest emblazoned into the top of the box. I opened it and there nestled in rich red velvet lay my promise gift that I intended to give Katelyn upon her acceptance of the gift of second life. As usual the work was exquisite, the hammered gold shimmered in the late afternoon sunlight pouring in through the tall windows, highlighting the details of my crest, two English griffins standing and holding a shield that was divided into four sections by a cross. The shield was topped with a King's crown, and the family name was inscribed in a ribbon at the bottom.

I gently lifted it out of its nest of velvet and hefting it in my palm was more than satisfied with the weight of the gold. I slowly turned it over and saw that he had deeply engraved two lines in a flowing script on the reverse …

'To Our

Eternal Love'

I allowed the chain, which was also weighty and solidly made, to flow through my fingers. When I had completed my inspection, I smiled with pleasure, seeing that Weissmann had once again exceeded my wishes in his creation.

"I must agree with you Charlotte Ann, I think perhaps Weissmann outdid himself as usual. I can hardly wait until I fasten it around Katelyn's neck."

"I'm sure that once she realizes its significance, she will not only treasure it, but wear it proudly … and if the truth be known," she looked up into my eyes with a loving smile, "I look forward to seeing her wearing it as much as you do."

I returned it to its box and closing the lid, placed it in the drawer of a writing desk that sat in the parlor. Then turning back to Charlotte Ann, I kissed her forehead and smiled, "Now, we shall hunt …"

We disappeared from the parlor and in a matter of a few seconds reappeared on Broad Street, a short distance from The Blind Tiger Pub. It was a busy night, the tourist and college crowds were both out in force making the pub an ideal spot for our hunting. We walked the few steps to the entrance and, once inside, we split up … Charlotte Ann going toward the bar on the left, and I toward the courtyard straight ahead, but before I did so, I watched her for a moment or two.

Charlotte Ann has always scouted out and chosen what she calls 'the pretty boys' in a pub … she claims that in her opinion, they taste better … and it didn't take her long to choose her latest victim. He fit her description of a pretty boy just perfectly. He appeared to be young, probably fresh out of high school, and just beginning his first year of college. I must admit that in my opinion he retained the angelic purity of a youth rather than the handsomeness of a mature young man … and likely had the same purely innocent scent that she had commented on at the house.

I'm sure he filled the bill just perfectly for her since she was only interested in a quick drink and not the carnal pleasures that she no doubt suggested in her thrall. Besides, in his youth he would not have had the ability or the staying power that she sought in a lover. I watched amused as she wasted no time in charming him with her immortal beauty. Before he knew what was happening she had placed an arm around him and closed in, expertly sinking her fangs into his neck for her first little drink of the evening.

I smiled at her quick success and continued my trek towards the courtyard located just outside the back of the building to search out my own meal. I glanced around the crowded area and my eyes settled on a young co-ed that was sitting alone on the right side, under the tin awning towards the back. I quickly appraised her and decided she was exactly what I was hunting. She was one that not only would provide a drink, but, in another place and time, I would have treated her, and myself, to a night in her bed.

She was quietly sipping on a glass of wine, and appeared to be waiting on someone … although I doubt she expected that someone to be me. I walked up as if I knew her, captivating her as I spoke, and taking a seat beside her, began making small talk. While we talked, I continued deepening my thrall of her, quickly drawing her into me.

The moment her will bent and shattered to mine I leaned in to her, lightly kissed her lips, and gently brushing her hair aside, bit swiftly into her neck. I was rewarded with an unexpected, yet utterly delicious drink. Her blood was filled with the spice of adventure and a quest for the unknown. I decided to take an extra-long drink from this one, and enjoy the surprising lusciousness I had stumbled across, while at the same time taking the liberty of searching her mind as I did. She offered up memories of hiking, swimming, boating and even a parachute jump, and all of those daring exploits combined together to produce an intensely powerful and provocatively peppery taste to her blood.

Unfortunately, after several mouthfuls, I had to stop or else this young girl would have no further adventures. Still, I felt that a small payment of some kind was no doubt in order for such a wonderful drink. I dug a bit deeper into her subconscious, discovered her deepest, darkest, most daring fantasy, and planted within her the courage to not only carry it out, but to enjoy it as she did. I left her sitting where I found her, her eyes a bit glazed, as if perhaps she had had one glass of wine too many, and knowing that she would be weak, but fully recover in a day or two.

When Charlotte Ann and I had returned from our hunt later in the night and settled into the parlor, I broached a question to her that I had been mulling over about an unexpected situation that had recently revealed itself.

"Charlotte Ann … might I impose upon you for a favor," I began.

"After taking me out for a meal like I just had, of course you may … and it's not an imposition at all."

"Perhaps not, but you haven't heard what it is yet … I would like for you to remain in Charleston … possibly for some time to come … an issue has revealed itself and it needs to be handled, but due to my preoccupation with Katelyn, I am unable to provide my undivided attention to solving it."

"That does sound … interesting … what kind of an issue are you talking about?"

"It would appear that another immortal, a vagabond from all appearances, has taken up residence in the area … and with the upcoming transition of Katelyn … I would like him gone."

"That certainly doesn't pose a problem … it fact it sounds easy enough … do you know anything at all about him?"

"Very little … except that he kills … often … he is responsible for several – shall we say, recent disappearances – in the area … and I am unable to continue to clean-up behind him … besides I don't need that happening in my backyard … especially now. I have followed him on a couple of occasions and he has not, so far, detected my presence. He displays traits of one who was turned and then cast adrift, and he dresses like a ragamuffin. Unfortunately, at the present, all of my time and attention must be focused on Katelyn, so I am unable to deal with him … hence my asking you to settle the matter."

"You know that I will do anything you ask and remain as long as you wish," she smiled.

"I knew you would, and I thank you … and since I don't know how much of your time it will take, and being as you probably don't wish to be at Whitehall when Katelyn shows up – which she does on a regular and unscheduled basis now – I will arrange for you to lodge downtown in the Presidential Suite at The Mills House for however long it takes to settle the issue."

"I like The Mills House," she chuckled, "there's always a very good selection of, shall we say, dining partners … not to mention their wine list is exceptionally remarkable. Now, how should I handle this rogue immortal … simply encourage him to move along … or just eliminate him … either way, problem solved."

"I would think the elimination of another immortal, regardless of their indiscretions, should be the absolute last option. Why don't you scout him out, discover as much about him as possible and then we can take care of the situation whenever and however circumstances demand."

"As you wish Lord Dubois," she answered with an exaggerated theatrical bow and a laugh.

"Stop that Charlotte Ann … you know I detest titles," I grinned.

"Ah, that's right, you Colonials and your aversions to aristocratic English titles," she continued chuckling, "still, like it or not, you *are* the reigning immortal authority in America."

"Perhaps, but I shall defer to you m'lady, both as my maker and the firstborn of the English subjects in our world … as such, I shall grant you full authority to handle this situation in any manner you may choose."

Chapter Seventeen

I spent the next four days after returning to school, relaxing around the room and getting back into my normal class routine. Lexi and I only went out together a couple of times to grab a quick snack and then right back. She stayed busy working on a mid-term paper that had to be finished. I began to notice that the anti-venom seemed to be wearing off and I quickly began returning to normal again. I still felt renewed and strong, but my vision wasn't quite as clear or sharp as it was. My energy level was still increased but I could feel it beginning to diminish. I even lost that strange craving for tomato soup. I started sleeping again, very peacefully, and thankfully, still without the nightmares.

The one drastic change however, that had not weakened, was my thinking and reasoning skills. They were suddenly sharper and clearer than they had ever been. I was able to retain with total recall anything that I read in a book or looked at on-line. Of course that was a tremendous help as I continued researching, trying to sort through all the questions I had concerning James that were swimming in my head. I spent most of my time thinking about the things I had seen, heard, and felt before and since the snake had bitten me.

The voice that I kept hearing in my head was the strangest thing of all. It seemed to me as if somebody was trying to tell me something, pulling me toward an incredible truth, but at the same time warning me and trying to push me away. Whatever it was, it wanted me to know something, but still not as badly as it wanted to keep it hidden. Whatever that truth was, I somehow knew that it was right in front of me.

Every time I thought I had come up with an answer though it just didn't seem plausible. Everything added up, but the answer still stunned me. I went back to the beginning and kept analyzing the questions from every angle, but each time the answer always pointed in the same direction. I just could not wrap my head around what I kept coming up with … it wasn't real, it couldn't be … even with my new reasoning skills my brain just could not, would not, process what the facts were pointing to. I decided that I must still be having some side effects of the anti-venom and just not looking at things from the right prospective, with a completely clear mind. That had to be it, because the answer that I kept coming back to was just not acceptable, it just could not be what all the evidence pointed to.

I had almost decided to take the conclusions I thought I had come to and go talk to James about it. I really needed him to sit and listen to me. I knew if he did then he would break into that little smile, laugh out loud at my silliness, and all the questions would simply fade away.

My thoughts were interrupted by my phone buzzing on the desk. I smiled when I looked at the screen and saw it was aunt 'Chele.

"Thank goodness," I thought quickly, *"here's a chance for some sanity to push all this out of the way."*

She and I had talked at least once every day, and sometimes twice a day, since I had gotten back to the dorm. I was happy for this interruption, I really needed to take time to clear my mind and then start all over again.

"Hello, Aunt 'Chele," I answered the phone with a smile, "how are you this afternoon?"

"Katelyn," she began slowly, and I could hear the tears in her voice, "I need you sweetie ... can you please come home right away?"

Suddenly my heart skipped two beats and fell right into my feet, I knew something terrible had happened.

"Is everything alright," I asked, beginning to panic, "did something happen to Uncle John ... is he okay?"

"It's nothing like that, but a letter came today from the GBI," she continued slowly, "one for each of us and it's pretty important."

"Oh, well, just a letter," I thought, *"that can't be too bad, can it?"*

"OK, Aunt 'Chele," I answered her plea, "I'll leave right now and come on up, I can be there in an hour or so."

"Please be careful and drive safely, baby, I'll see you when you get here ... I love you so much," she said now crying.

"I will and I love you too, bye!"

I told Lexi that I had to run home, a letter had come for me from the GBI, "It's still early enough, I may be able to get back in time for dinner if you want to go out."

"That's what you said the last time you started out too," she said with a deadpan look and then broke into a huge grin.

"I'll try to do better this time and watch out for snakes, I promise."

"I'm going to hold you to it," she laughed as I started out the door.

I rushed home as fast as I could, not so sure about the safe driving part, but I got there anyway. I went straight in and Aunt 'Chele hugged me close to her. I could see that she had been crying again. She wordlessly handed me an official looking letter and I went to the couch and sat down to read it. As I read the words on the paper I could feel my life being ripped apart again, the tears began flowing unchecked down my face. It was just so incredulous I could not believe what I was reading. When I finished, I had to reread it just to be sure that I wasn't imagining things.

"Noooo … NO! NO! NO!" The news hurt so badly I wailed like a wounded animal, "It can't be, this has to be a terrible joke … this can't be happening! How could they do this? It's so not right, it's unfair!"

The letter was from the Victim's Affairs Office of the Georgia Bureau of Investigation. It was a notification that the men who had 'allegedly' robbed and killed my parents had been released and all charges dropped. I could not believe what I had just read. In fact I read it a third time just to be sure. It seemed that some low level bureaucrat somewhere had put the wrong information on some form and their court appointed attorneys had used it as an excuse to get them off.

I was strong and I knew it, but my youth and the experiences of my short life had just not prepared me to face all that I had faced over the last year. I had endured the shock of my parent's murder. I had endured having to relocate and completely restart my life. I had endured nearly dying from a snake bite; and now the ones directly responsible for it all had just been released and were totally free. I simply could not endure any longer, I was not physically or mentally able to handle this. I could feel my world beginning to crumble around me again. I felt like all of my wounds had been reopened … what little bit of healing I had experienced was completely ripped away.

It seemed that the entire weight of the world was and had been on my shoulders for the last several months, and suddenly, I just could not bear it any longer; this was the final straw – the one that broke the camel's back. I once again became a lost little girl … I was frightened … my parents were dead … I was left all alone in the world … and the big bad wolf was nipping at my heels. I just could not believe this was happening to me. I took the letter and started for the door.

"I have to go," I said through my tears, "I can't deal with this right now! Tell Uncle John I'll be back in a couple of days, I'll call once I settle down …"

"But, Katelyn, where are you going, what are you going to do, sweetie?"

"I don't know what I'm going to do … and I'm not sure where I'm going to go … but I have to get away and think. I promise I will be alright. I love you both more than anything," I said and was out the door and in my car in a flash.

In reality, I knew exactly where I was going and who I was going to see as I drove away in the dark. There was only one person who could help me through this and tell me what to do. I was going to Whitehall, to James, and this time without an invitation. I knew inside that he would understand and forgive me for just showing up. I also knew he was the only one who could help me with this.

I drove the almost two hour trip to Whitehall in just under an hour and half, crying most of the way. I drove without even paying attention to the road. I just let my instincts guide me to my destination. I kept thinking over and over, *"James, please be there … please, please be there … I've got to see you … you have to be there … please don't be out of town tonight!"*

I reached the drive and started the mile trip up to the house. Before I could get there I saw the front of the house lit up like it was daylight. "Oh, thank God," I breathed out softly, "he's here! He'll know what to tell me to do!"

I parked in front and started running for the door. Before I could get half way up the steps James had the door open and was standing on the porch.

"Katelyn," he exclaimed, "what's the matter, are you alright, has something happened, why are you out this late?"

I ran into his arms and burst into tears as I hugged him, "Oh, James, I'm so glad you're here, I was afraid you would be out of town, and I just had to see you! I knew that you could help me and would know what to tell me to do about this."

"Katelyn, darling, please settle down, take a breath, and tell me what's happened. Whatever it is it will be alright, I promise," he answered me.

I stepped back and without saying anything else simply handed him the letter I had received. He read it over, then reaching out, easily wrapped an arm around my shoulders, and guided me toward the door.

"Come, let's go inside, I need to consider just what kind of action is most suitable for this situation," he said.

He assisted me to a seat on one of the couches and

pouring a snifter of brandy, placed it in my hand and instructed, "Drink this while I read, it will help settle you."

I sat on the sofa, feeling broken and downcast from the news I had received. My body, shaking with fear on the inside, was shivering on the outside from the dampness that had penetrated my clothes. I began to sip the golden liquid, quickly sensing its warming glow as it begin to flow through my body. I watched him as he reread the letter and saw that his mouth was set in a hard line, his green eyes were flashing fire and looked cold as a winter snow. I had seen this look once before and I actually felt almost frightened. He lifted his chin just a little and began lightly tapping his lips with the tip of his finger as he thought. Then looking down at the letter once again, his lips began to curl up into a sinister grin and a soft chuckle slowly rolled out of him as he muttered slowly and softly, "Yes … yes, I believe that will work … and it would be most appropriate."

Then with his eyes softening again to their regular green, he looked at me with a curious glimmer and a smile, and speaking with a voice full of menace, one that was hard and stern, more so than I had ever heard from him, said, "Katelyn, I think I know the perfect way to take care of this situation."

"James, before you say anything, can I ask something real quick," I pleaded.

"Anything my dear, what is it?"

"The letter says that the case against the two murderers had been 'Dismissed with Prejudice', what exactly does that mean?"

"In a legal usage, it means the case is closed and can never be brought back to court," he answered slowly.

"So then … my mom and dad are dead … and the two men that killed them will get totally away with it," I whispered softly, taking a sip of the brandy I still held in my hand.

"Katelyn, I promise you, this will all come right. These two shall not escape the recompense due them in this matter. I give you my word, one way or the other, they will not go unpunished and you will receive the justice due you."

"I hope you are right … I would so hate to know my mom and dad died for nothing," I whispered.

"I have seen Karma, both good and bad, at work in people's lives, and I can assure you that she will catch up to these two. However, due to the seriousness of their crime, it may take a little time, but then again, please know that revenge is always a dish best served cold."

"Oh thank you James," I said draining the remainder of the brandy and setting the empty snifter on a table, stood back up and tentatively stepped toward him and back into his arms again, "I knew you would know what to do … I knew you could fix it."

I snuggled close to him, my hands resting against his chest as he wrapped his arms around me with a smile, drawing me to him. I turned my head, resting my cheek against his shoulder, so I could look into his eyes as he began to gently pet me. I heard his soft breathing, and felt the coolness of his hands through my shirt as he lightly stroked my back, caressing me, soothing me. I felt myself, between the brandy and his gentle touch, begin to calm down as a peaceful relaxation rolled over me in wave after wave.

I cuddled in closer to his chest as I slowly slid my arms around him, holding him close. I looked up into his eyes, and without a second thought or the least hesitation, I kissed him, pressing my body even closer to his. I felt his entire body tense in my arms for just the barest fraction of a second. I moved my hand up, sliding it under his hair, resting it on the back of his neck and pulled him into my kiss. His stance relaxed and he kissed me back.

"Wow! His lips are so soft and kissable," I thought to myself as I closed my eyes and continued to kiss him. His returned kiss was full of passion and sent a nicely unexpected quiver through my body. *"Ummm … that felt so good,"* I thought to myself. Then my tongue shot into his mouth and I pulled him even closer, not wanting to let him go.

Suddenly we were kissing passionately, our arms locked around each other. He darted his tongue into my mouth, gently touching mine as we pulled closer together. We kissed each other, long and deep, our tongues slowly exploring the other's mouth. When we broke the kiss, I felt his breath as it softly caressed my face. I looked into his deep green eyes and slowly whispered, "Woooow … that was good!"

He pulled his lips away from mine, then with one hand on the small of my back and the other around my shoulders he pulled me against him and began to lightly nuzzle at my neck … and my knees began to go weak. My neck has always been my 'turn me on, lock the door, turn off the lights' weakness … and he went straight for it.

I softly moaned again as I pressed my body into his … I wanted him … I needed him … like I had never wanted or needed another man … I wanted to feel him close to me … I wanted to feel him inside me. His kisses … his caresses were the most intoxicating thing I had ever felt in my life and I didn't want them to ever stop as he brought his lips back to mine.

Then I kissed him back … long and slow … lingering … my tongue hungrily exploring his mouth. I clung tighter against him, molding my body to his, as our kissing became deeper and more intense. His arms tightened around me and I felt his own need, now pressing strongly against my body, as he drew me even tighter against him. I shuddered with pleasure throughout my body and a low moan rose slowly out of my throat.

"Katelyn, dear sweet Katelyn," he breathed out my name, "I so desperately want you … I want to take you and make you mine … right this minute."

He began to once again trace the tip of his tongue along my collar bone and the base of my neck … and it was like throwing gas on a flame as he slowly licked upwards toward my ear … my smoldering passion exploded into a roaring open flame. No man had ever made me feel what he was making me feel right now … I had never felt anything as deeply passionate.

"Yessss … please …" I breathed out, "take me … make me yours … I want you to … right now."

I turned my head upwards just a little, trying to expose as much of my neck as I possibly could for him. It was the most sensual feeling I had ever experienced. His lips felt wonderful, like the finest silk as they moved easily on my skin, his cool breath flowing over me like a stream. I wanted to stretch my neck even further for him, the pleasure he was producing in me was absolutely incredible – like nothing I had ever experienced.

He abruptly stopped and pulled away, shaking his head and saying, "No … not like this …. not this way … this isn't right … oh Katelyn … dear, dear Katelyn … you have no idea what you just asked for … both of us are playing with fire … we are about to cross a line from which there's no going back."

Suddenly my little inner voice spoke to me again, *"Katelyn … please … these desires are more dangerous than you realize, you are taking the first steps into a brand new world that you know nothing about."*

And for the first time, in my head, I directly answered it back, *"I believe I know more than you think I do … and I really don't care anymore … I've lost everything … my parents, my home, my friends, my world and all that I hold dear … I've got nothing else to lose so let it lead where it will …"*

I looked into his eyes and breathlessly kissing his lips again, pleadingly whispered to him, "James, please … let me stay here tonight … with you … and I'll cross whatever that line is … just … please don't ask me to leave … don't send me away … not tonight … I don't want to be … can't be … alone … not tonight … please I want you to hold me … and make love to me."

He smiled as if he were looking into my very soul with his beautiful green eyes. I had never in my life been so strongly turned on by anybody. I didn't understand what was happening, I felt like I was being pulled into him, drawn in and lost in his presence.

I suddenly squealed and laughed unexpectedly as he swept me off my feet and into his arms. He easily carried me up the stairs, kissing me as he did, and into his bedroom where he slowly began to undress us. His touch was light and easy as his fingers glided softly over every part of my body. He told me how beautiful I was as he continued gently kissing, his lips touching everywhere his fingers did. When he had completely undressed me he held me in his arms, his hands continuing their gentle caresses making my skin tingle with excitement. I kissed him passionately, my tongue darting in and out of his mouth, my own hands searching his body with desire.

When we settled into his bed he gently took me in his arms and held me close. I snuggled closer against him, our bodies felt so wonderful together as we wrapped our arms around each other. We continued kissing, petting each other heavily. Our hands eagerly exploring heretofore hidden parts of the others body as he kissed me again and again.

My fingers glided slowly across the cool naked skin of his body, our kissing becoming even more passionate as we continued. He touched my ears and my neck again with his tongue, gently licking them and I began to moan in pleasure. The familiar tingle he had briefly caused before began to roar through me like liquid fire. My desire for him and my own passion became more intense with each soft kiss and every gentle touch. I wanted so badly to feel his exquisite body close to me … inside me … and I wanted to return the same pleasure to him that he was giving me right now … I let my lips wander lazily across his neck and shoulder, and back again to his sweet, soft lips. We continued our playful petting as our hands carefully explored every inch of the other's body.

James looked into my eyes, and I shivered with delight, as his soft hand slowly moved over my shoulder, lightly touching my breast, continuing down my side, sliding over my back and across my leg. His soft touch sent little tickling shafts of blissfulness, radiating out from the center of my body. I felt the tingle out to my fingertips and even down to my toes as he slowly drew his satiny smooth fingers back up the inside of my thigh and touched me. Little arrows of pleasure shot through me as his fingers gently stroked my body making it tingle throughout.

His kissing continued, his lips searching out every part of my body. He moved easily down my body, his lips resting for only a moment on my breasts, his tongue lightly teasing each of my nipples. His fingers lightly touched my stomach, gliding like silk across me. I opened my legs invitingly to him as his tongue traced lightly along the ridge of my hip bones and into the flat shallow valley of my tummy. I lost myself in the pleasure that went ripping through me when his tongue lightly touched the tender skin there. He gingerly kissed the inside of my thighs, his soft lips like the tender kiss of a butterfly.

My body started to tremble all over, my insides quivering like jelly, at the anticipation of what James was about to do. I began to breathe harder, my breath catching in my throat as he gently kissed my uplifted knees. I quickly sucked in a breath as he began trailing the tip of his tongue along the inside of my legs. I moaned in pleasure at the light touch of his velvety soft tongue on my thighs, then cried out in unexpected delight as he teasingly nipped at the tender skin on the inside of my legs. He made his way to the top, pausing to playfully lick at the little hollow place at the top of my thighs before passing his tongue over me letting it play teasingly around the sides of the tenderest and most private spot of my body.

He slowly raised his head and gently ran his tongue around my navel, dipping inside it, and then trailed downwards, back to the center of my body. My breathing became heavier, my groans louder as he continued moving his tongue deftly around my body. I was moaning louder now in pure delight … the more I groaned, the more he seemed to enjoy what he was doing. He continued for several minutes, over and over again, painting me with his tongue, letting it glide over me from bottom to top and back again.

James licked me like a little kitten and it felt so delightful I thought I would explode! My body literally shuddered all over when he finally slid his tongue inside me. I was burning with desire and every nerve was standing on edge as I lifted my hips against him, another small moan escaping my lips. I was suddenly having a very difficult time controlling myself as he slid his hands under my butt and continued playfully licking at me.

My entire body began shaking as intense pleasure vibrated through me, "Ohhhh … God … James …" I panted out, pleasure beginning to wash over me as the first waves of an orgasm began to build deep inside me, "please … don't stop … it's sooo good … ohhhh, please … please … don't ever stop … Oh God … I've never felt anything so wonderful … I can't stand it anymore," I cried out, my body jerking up against him, as my orgasm broke, rolling in waves over and through every inch of me … and I lost myself in the unbelievable ecstasy of it.

When my orgasm began to recede he slowly made his way up again, covering my body with his. I opened myself to him, my entire body tingling like never before, every nerve in my body felt like it was on fire with expectation as he gently and easily slid into me. I moaned softly, sucking in a breath as he filled me and we melted together, becoming one with each other. The feeling of completeness in me was indescribable as our bodies came together making full contact with each other. I felt like I had actually become a part of him. I arched my back and pulled my knees up, tightening my legs around him, holding him, gripping him, not wanting to let him go. He gently wrapped his strong arms around me, pulling me tight against him, pushing as deeply into me as he could.

He kissed me again and this time I tasted myself on his lips and tongue. Everything in me wanted more of him; I just could not get enough. My fingers slowly glided up and down his back and sides, gently stroking him. My breath caught in my chest and I thought I would completely lose control of all my senses as he slowly made love to me … the pleasure was again building stronger and stronger inside me and I knew I couldn't hold back much longer.

Suddenly, with very little warning, I was caught up in the most intense, bone shaking, teeth grinding, orgasm I had ever had in my life! It rolled through me like thunder again and again. I convulsed with pleasure as I was wracked through and through with delight. I couldn't move anymore as my entire body stiffened up, arching upward against him.

I wrapped my arms tighter around him, holding him, pulling him closer against me as groundswells of sheer joy washed over me in what seemed like an unstoppable orgasm. I felt like I couldn't breathe, but I knew I had to. I fought to catch my breath as it became short and fast, my heart racing out of control in my chest, my lungs screaming out for more air, as I struggled to breathe.

Finally, I did the only thing I could … I sucked in a deep breath and screamed in pure, undefiled pleasure … and began bucking wildly against him, thrashing around, trying desperately to hold on as the pleasure continued rocking swiftly through me. I clinched my muscles closer around him, holding him as tightly as I could. I wanted this feeling to last forever as wave after wave of sheer delight continued to wash over me, again and again, releasing and cleansing me at the same time.

As I continued writhing in pleasure, James moaned loudly, pushed hard and deep into me and stiffened in my arms. He groaned uncontrollably and I felt his orgasm break loose deep inside me, throbbing strong and hard as again and again he released his passion. When he finished, his orgasm coming to an end, he slowly thrust into me a couple of more times. I felt so good … so full … so satisfied as he held inside me just another moment. I wanted this intimacy

… this closeness … to last forever. Then he slowly began to pull out of me, dismounting and stretching out contentedly beside me.

I felt as if everything that had been pent up inside me – my parents' death, my anguish, my own near death, and finally my disbelief at the release of their murderers – suddenly was unleashed. All of the pain and hurt that had been locked inside me seemed to flow out of me, leaving me feeling completely drained and empty inside.

When it was over, I snuggled against him, clinging as close as I could, enjoying the feel of his nicely muscled body close against me. I lay wrapped in his arms, looking into his eyes and smiling at him, lightly kissing his lips … there was no need to talk after what he had just done for me. Besides, no words could describe how I felt right at this moment anyway.

I was totally exhausted and weak from the pleasure he had given me. A feeling of complete peace and contentment filled me, resting easily upon me. I felt flush with the heat still on my body from the intense lovemaking and wondered casually at how cool his whole body felt next to mine. I wondered how he could have done what he just did and not break a sweat. I smiled happily as I let my hand move gently across his chest and stomach relishing the naturalness of the two of us lying together.

Sleep came quickly and easily, covering me like a warm comfortable blanket as James lightly brushed his fingers through my hair, delicately caressing my back and shoulders, as I cuddled happily beside him. I slept for the rest of the night curled in his arms. It was the most peaceful and restful sleep I had had in almost a year … complete relaxation … no dreams … no nightmares … just a deep, dark, happily undisturbed rest.

Chapter Eighteen

I held Katelyn in my arms the remainder of the night, continuing to lightly rub her back while she slept, until just after dawn. Then whispering a command to her not to wake until after the sun was fully risen, I slipped out of bed and stood silently watching her as she sank deeper into an impenetrable sleep. I was mesmerized by, and very nearly overcome with her beauty … her face was completely at rest and she appeared more relaxed than I had ever seen her. I had to pull myself away from staring at her and began putting things in order for when she woke. I began by smoothing out the sheets – the finest silk, by the way, since she had so loudly thought that's where she would like to spend time with me – then carefully pulled the duvet up, covering her nudity.

I continued moving silently around the room, moving a chair and placing it within easy reach of the bed. I took the black silk negligée, robe and slippers that Charlotte Ann had purchased, and, placing them on the chair, carefully arranged them for her. Then I placed a note on top of them asking her to join me at her leisure for breakfast, and as a final added touch, I placed a single long stem red rose on top. I exited the room, leaving her sound asleep, peacefully dreaming, and went to the veranda to begin putting in place my plan for her revenge.

While she continued sleeping I telephoned a Warlock in Atlanta to collect on a debt of honor he owed.

"Voodoo Shoppe, this is Jonathan, how can I help you today," he answered on the first ring.

"Hello Warlock … are you still pedaling all those roots, herbs and fake spells to the mortals," I chuckled without identifying myself.

"Ah, James … my friend …" he laughed nervously then quickly continued, "at least I hope you're still my friend … I really wouldn't want you to be angry with me."

"To that point, I can agree whole heartedly with you," I answered.

"I'm sure you didn't call just to chat over your morning coffee, did you … and by the way … you're not in Atlanta … are you?"

"No, but I could be in just a short time if I need to …" I answered playing to his fears, "do I need to?"

"Uhhh, no … I don't think so," he stuttered.

"Why don't you relax a bit Warlock," I began again, "the reason for my call is to inquire if perhaps you would care to square the debt you owe me?"

"What are you asking me to do," he asked cautiously.

"Just a small favor …" I began, "I'm going to give you a couple of names, please write them down …"

"Alright … I'm ready," he responded, "who are they?"

I read him the names of the two murderers from the letter Katelyn had brought with her last night.

"Wait a minute … I know those two names," he interjected, "I read about them in the Journal-Constitution … aren't they the ones that killed that store owner and his wife over in Marietta last year … the story is that they got off the charges because of some SNAFU in the court system."

"That would indeed be them …" I confirmed.

"And what exactly am I supposed to do to them," he asked slowly.

"Nothing at all … at least not *to* them," I answered, "you may leave *that* little detail to me …"

"And do *they* owe you a debt also," he asked slowly.

"They don't owe it to *me*, per se, but, they do owe it to a very dear friend … and it shall be collected," I answered.

"Dude, I'd hate to be in their shoes right now," he mumbled under his breath.

"Perhaps so," I answered, letting him know I had heard his comment, "but you needn't concern yourself with that … I would however, greatly appreciate it if you would find out where they live, keep a close eye on them, and perhaps cast a keeping spell of some kind, something to tie them to their house so they are unable to wander too far away from it … see, nothing too difficult … at least not for someone as powerful as you."

"If I do this … will it square my debt to you?"

"Totally and completely …" I laughed, "and you can even discontinue wearing those useless turtlenecks too … they're a bit outdated … and wouldn't stop me anyway!"

"How did you know about that," he sputtered.

"Jonathan … you disappoint me … you should know by now that I have eyes and ears everywhere," I laughed, "so, am I able to count on you to do this for me?"

"Consider it done … I'll call you when the ward is in place and give you the address."

"Very well … and I shall call you when the debt is erased … have a good morning," I said ending the call and sat back to await Katelyn's awakening.

I sensed when she woke and felt a momentary flash of fear pass through her as she wondered why I had left her alone and where I might have been. I smiled as I listened intently to her thoughts and discovered that she was more than satisfied with our lovemaking the previous evening. In fact, she was still entertaining some rather frank and straightforward carnal thoughts about our night together and what she would have done had I remained in bed this morning, causing me to look forward to the next time.

In short order she began to move around the room and I heard the shower come on and knew it wouldn't be long before she joined me. I continued listening to her thoughts as she showered, there was no doubt that she certainly had a thorough thought pattern, and chuckled to myself when they suddenly turned to the possibility of her becoming pregnant with my child. I would be sure to settle that thought in her mind and assure her that she had no worries about bearing a child … after all, it was she who was to become the child.

When she came out to the veranda … she was the vision of a goddess … her beauty was almost indescribable … her face was clean and bare without any makeup … her hair, freshly washed, was lying in waves around her face and shoulders … the small amount of Cherokee blood remaining in her made her tan absolutely perfect … and it was indeed fortuitous that I do not wear pajamas or jogging pants because I had a swift and very carnal reaction to the sight of her in the negligée.

Chapter Nineteen

When I awoke the next morning, I was a little more than disappointed to find the bed beside me empty. Suddenly the memory of the previous night flooded through me – and I certainly would not have objected to a second round of the previous night's lovemaking. I smiled a happy smile as a pleasantly warm feeling began to spread through my body. The sun was shining brightly through the window lighting and warming up the entire room. Then for just the barest moment a gentle fear started to creep into me because, unlike the last time I was here, I couldn't sense James' presence in the house. It passed just as quickly because I knew he wouldn't leave me all alone, he was more of a gentleman than that.

I looked around at the bed I had spent the night in ...

it was obviously an antique … and massive, like everything else at Whitehall. This was truly a colonial style bed; the headboard itself was a magnificently carved work of art. The top was framed with an equally beautiful white canopy and supported by four tall and intricately carved posts. There were matching white sheer curtains for each side and the end; all tied gracefully back on the tall posts. And of course James had pulled the sheets and comforter carefully over me when he had awakened and gotten up.

I stretched comfortably under the silky sheets, relishing their soft coolness against my skin and wishing I could stay in bed, but reluctantly knowing that I had to get up. I sighed and smiled happily as I lay there for a few more minutes, thinking about him, delighting in the sun's warmth, and savoring the wonderful memory of his lovemaking.

I continued to dwell on last night and all that had happened. I have to admit I've had sexy thoughts about James almost since the first time I saw him. Physically, he's everything a girl could wish for, but add in his kindness, and the way he treats me, then taking into account his caring and tender treatment of me while I was convalescing after the snake bite, and it makes him even more desirable. The thoughts of the two of us having sex had definitely been in the front of my mind lately, and especially so since the last time for me had been right before my parents died, just a little over a year ago. So I was ready … *really* ready, but last night had been completely unexpected and spontaneous. There was no way I could have anticipated or been prepared for what happened.

I came to him, hurting and in shock, seeking his guidance and advice as my life once again seemed to be crumbling around me. He had unintentionally ignited my passion as he had comforted me, petting me and holding me close to himself. I hadn't realized just how much I wanted him and I quickly surrendered to the passion of the moment allowing it to completely overtake me.

I smiled happily continuing to think about last night … I cashed my 'V' card a long time ago, and I have slept with more than one man but I have never had a man make love to me like James did … it was as if he had awakened something deep inside me … and in return I had made love to him with complete abandonment, unlike any I had ever made love to before. While I do have some experience, and that doesn't mean there's been a revolving door of lovers through my life, James was so … different … to the other lovers I have slept with … his lovemaking was, without compare, the best I have ever experienced.

The lovers I had known in high school and later in college, had been purely physical … all about the sex … for me and them … it was fun and I enjoyed it. I had wanted it and allowed it to happen otherwise none of them would ever have gotten me out of my jeans in the first place. But the sex last night with James had been … oh so different … like nothing I had ever experienced in the past … the orgasms he had produced in me had been of epic proportions … he had not just had sex with my body … he went beyond that and made love to my soul … and it was so much more satisfying than just a physical act. I had given him my body but he had gone even further … delving deep into my soul … touching both body and soul … and I had sensed his unending love in every touch … every kiss … every gentle caress … it was as if he knew exactly what and where, inside and out, all of my 'turn-ons' were to be found.

Our bodies, like two pieces of a puzzle made for each other, had fit perfectly and tightly together … and he had made me feel more complete than any other man before him.

He was gentle, slow and methodical, pleasing me again and again with just his soft touch. He had seemed to not care about himself, concentrating solely on me, pleasing me and meeting my needs over and over again. He acted as if he had all the time in the world. If only he had stayed in bed for a little while longer this morning … I would certainly have returned his favor.

I started to get out of bed and remembered that I didn't have anything on and I wasn't real sure just where my clothes were either. I looked around for something to wear and noticed a chair had been set beside the bed. It was draped with a long, black silk robe, folded and placed on top of it was a pair of black silk pajamas with matching slippers set out for me. Lying on top was a note, written in his beautiful script, along with a single long stem red rose. I reached over, picked up the rose, enjoying its fragrance for a moment and then read the note:

Dearest Katelyn,

You will find fresh towels laid out in the bathroom for your use. Please join me at your leisure for breakfast on the rear veranda.

James

I smiled at the note and his thoughtfulness, then slid into the robe and slippers, and carrying the folded pajamas, went into the bathroom to take a long hot shower and wash my hair. I turned the water on and waited for it to get hot then slowly stepped into the shower. I lifted my face to the nozzle and allowed the hot, steamy water to flood over me, refreshing and reinvigorating me. I was completely lost in the warmth of the shower and my thoughts of last night as I began slowly soaping my body.

All of a sudden I remembered that I hadn't used any kind of protection last night … and neither had James. I had always insisted on protection but last night's passion was so emotional, so sudden and intense that the thought had never even crossed my mind. I quickly thought about my cycle and where I was in it. I was due in less than a week so it was possible that I got lucky. I did not want to get pregnant right now. I needed to finish college and get a job before I could even think about a family. Although having a child with him was not the worst idea in the world, still I didn't want or need a child in my life right now. I supposed I would just have to be anxious for the next week … and remember to be more careful next time, no matter how intense the passion at the time.

When I finished the shower, I stepped out and grabbed one of the towels James had put out for me. It was a big, thick, cotton terry-cloth towel and it quickly soaked up the water on my body. I wrapped it around myself and stood in front of the mirror while I dried and brushed my hair. Then I put on the pajamas, which fit as perfectly as if I had bought them myself, slid back into the robe and slippers, and luxuriating in the feel of the soft silk sliding against my bare skin, started downstairs with a happy smile.

James was sitting on the veranda at a small table with a glass of juice and some fresh fruit at my place.

"Good Morning Katelyn," he smiled, "I hope you slept well."

"Good Morning to you, too, and yes, I did, thank you," I replied happily as I sat down and took a sip of the juice and a bite of fruit and smiling warmly at him continued, "And thank you so much for the pajamas, and fresh towels, and the rose was beautiful, it was so thoughtful of you."

He watched me closely as I ate and drank, a small smile playing around his mouth, then in a soft, gentle voice he began, "Katelyn, I think perhaps we need to talk about what happened last night."

I looked over at him with a hurt look and felt a lump of fear begin to form in the pit of my stomach and I thought *"Oh, no … not him … he's better than that … he has to be, I know he is …"*

"Oh, Katelyn, darling, please don't look distressed," he said, "I want you to know that last night was very enjoyable, more pleasurable than you can possibly imagine."

"I don't know about that, I've got a pretty good imagination," I chuckled, quickly glancing up at him.

"Perhaps so … still what happened last night can also be very dangerous to both of us … we're playing with fire."

"Yeah, I got the fire part … no problem there," I said with a huge grin, "but dangerous … the only danger I can think about is that neither of us used any kind of protection whatsoever last night …"

"Please Katelyn, allow me to put that fear to rest … there is no possibility that we could produce a child together … at least not in that manner."

"Oh James," I almost whimpered, "I'm so sorry, I had no idea that you …"

"No Katelyn, it's quite alright … it doesn't preclude us from producing a child if you wished … just not in the usual method … so please don't allow the thought to bother you … but, as I was about to say … you do things to me …"

"Uhhh, yeah, I certainly hope so," I interjected with a smile, "and if you had stayed in bed this morning, I would have done more things to you."

"Indeed I'm sure … but when we are together, you make me feel things I haven't felt in a long time. Last night, I lifted you and carried you in my arms up the stairs … but you … you lifted me in your arms and carried me to a height of pleasure that I haven't enjoyed in a very long time. And knowing my passions and my desires as I do, I was afraid to really let myself go … I was afraid of getting too caught up in the ecstasy of the moment."

"Oh God … James … if what you did for me last night was constrained, I don't know if I could stand you really letting loose," I giggled with happiness.

"Perhaps soon we shall be at a point that I am able to fully release my passions … still I want you to understand that I may not be the man you think I am. I would never intentionally harm you and I watch myself very carefully when I'm with you. I give you my word, I will concentrate on controlling my passions, but I felt that you should be aware of the danger you could be in when this happens again ..."

I sat back in my chair and began to relax again, a gratified smile spreading quickly across my face. *"When ..."* I thought happily, *"he said when, not if …"*

"So from the look on your face I'm to understand that you enjoyed last evening as much as I?"

"This is where I get to say more than you could possibly imagine," I grinned impishly, "not to mention looking forward to a repeat and you allowing your passions free reign!"

"Perhaps, but I'm only concerned for you Katelyn … my desires and passions are a very strong and driving force within me, and I have been known to lose control of them. Should I allow that to happen … as I very nearly did when we first kissed last night … you could be hurt … and I assure you I would never intentionally hurt you."

"James, I don't often play rough … I don't really like it that way … I prefer slow and intense … like last night … but if I ever did decide to play rough … you would know just how far to go … and no further … I assure you … still it's very gentlemanly of you to be concerned, and I know that you would never hurt me on purpose. Last night was the best night I have had in a long, long time, both in terms of restfulness and … otherwise … so please don't worry about me. I'm a big girl and I know how to take care of myself."

"Very well," he said at last, "I just thought it was something I should mention."

"Well," I laughed happily, "there's something I should mention too, and that's that I have to go get dressed and leave, I'm going to miss another day of classes and …"

"Don't fret about that," he smiled, "I'll call your professors and explain the events of your legal case and ensure that your absence has no affect upon you."

"How do you do that," I asked curiously, "you just pick up the phone to the instructors, and they do whatever you wish."

"Well, there's one of my questions out in the open," I thought quickly to myself, *"now if I just had the guts to ask all the others."*

"You soon will," I heard my inner voice answer back.

"You have to understand dear, and please don't think me a braggart, but I have donated a considerable amount of money to the college, and in return they don't mind doing a favor for me – or someone I care deeply for – every now and then," he smiled.

"Alrighty, if you say so … but I still have to go up and get dressed … Lexi was expecting me back in the room last night."

"And given the choice," he grinned innocently, "where would you have preferred to spend the night?"

"Where do you think," I answered, leaned in and

quickly kissed his lips … then turned and darted up the stairs laughing as I did.

After I had gotten dressed, he met me at the foot of the stairs and we walked to the front of the house together. As I started to leave, he said "Drive carefully, Katelyn, and please call me later this evening," then he gave me a quick kiss on the cheek and added, "stay safe my love."

"Nun-uhhh lover boy … ohhhh, no … I hope you don't think you're going to get by with just a peck on the cheek do you … especially not after last night … I know how good you can uh … kiss," I chuckled playfully, and I put my arms around him and kissed him … deeply and passionately. I felt his arms slowly encircle me as I held him there, lingering for a couple of minutes as we kissed ardently again and again. I also felt his immediate and lascivious reaction that my kiss had upon him.

"Now that's more like it …" I slowly purred with happiness as our embrace broke, and, reaching down, gently massaging the bulge in his jeans, I stepped away and laughed, "and I think I had better go now … from the feel of things, if I don't leave, we will likely have a repeat of last night sooner than either of us thought … but I'll call you later tonight … I promise!"

I started hurriedly down the steps before I decided to stay, but quickly added, "Maybe we can get together again soon. I would really like for us to sit and talk about some things I have had on my mind."

"You have my word, we shall do that soon," he said smiling happily.

As I drove down the shaded allee, still smiling contentedly to myself, my little inner voice unexpectedly spoke up again, *"Please, Katelyn, you are about to ask some potentially life changing questions … you need to be absolutely sure you want to know the answers before you do."*

"I do," I reassured myself quietly, "I really do … I have to know the answers … if only for my self-satisfaction."

I knew exactly what questions Katelyn wanted to ask, so I surmised it was best to give her a couple of days to build her nerve and prepare herself for a reality altering conversation that would finally confirm for her what she already knew deep inside. I also had to prepare myself … this conversation would be the moment of truth … for both of us … the moment she confirmed her suspicions regarding my true nature … the moment she either chose mortality or immortality … the moment she would choose to become my mate … or the moment she would turn her back and walk away from me forever.

I knew that I would need to bolster myself for Katelyn's hopefully upcoming transformation, so to further prepare myself, I spent the next seventy-two hours in Savannah, hunting out of Gale's loft. I utilized the time … sometimes with Gale, other times with Sarah. It was a very successful time for all three of us. Additionally, when an immortal is needing to build strength for whatever reason, in this case a potential transformation, the taking of a victim's life is much more strengthening than just a quick drink, so it is needless to say that I killed numerous times during my visit. When the end of the third day came I was glutted with blood and much stronger than I had been in a very long time. I was now ready, if she chose, to bring Katelyn over and make her my mate.

The act of taking a mate in our world is an extremely private and personal thing and usually is never talked about until after it has been accomplished. The exception in this case, being my discussing Katelyn with Charlotte Ann which further illustrates the complex and profound nature of our relationship, and not just that of maker and child, but also the depth of our love for each other. Although I didn't think it necessary to explain to either Gale or Sarah why I was feeding so much, I believe Gale may have suspected, even so, she never alluded to or brought up the subject of my sudden, but brief, visit.

Chapter Twenty

Lexi was lying comfortably curled on her bed reading a book when I walked into our room. She turned toward me and smiled, "Well, look who's back … good thing I wasn't very hungry last night," she said with a laugh and a wink.

"I don't remember telling you just *which* evening I'd be back …" I laughed happily, glancing at my watch, "besides I'm back early enough for dinner *this* evening."

"Alright, guess I'll have to give you that one," she grinned, "but still that must have been some letter for you to decide to spend the night at home."

"Well, actually Lexi, I sorta didn't stay at home last night," I replied with a big smile, "you see … I kinda ended up spending the night at Whitehall."

Lexi looked blankly at me and as understanding suddenly filled her eyes, she shot straight up in the center of her bed and grinning hugely shouted, "Oh … my … God … Katelyn Corbin! You and James … you did it … you did the deed!"

"Yessss …" I said with a coy little smile, and a quick laugh, "*we* did the deed … several times in fact!"

"Oh, you have got to tell me all about it … how did it happen? Was he good? Great? Out of this world wonderful?

My eyes lit up and with a huge smile I said with a happy laugh, "He was all three, Lexi … my God, it was the most amazing sex I have ever had in my life … I didn't want it to ever stop!"

"Details, girl, details, you are my best friend you know," she laughed happily, "I need to know … you have to tell me these things!"

"I feel so wonderful this morning … not as good as I did last night mind you," I quickly added with another laugh, "but, wow, was it good …"

"Oh, Katelyn, I'm so happy for you! I can't believe you actually did it! Wait a minute, what am I saying? Of course I can! The way the two of you look at each other, I knew it was just a matter of time until it happened!"

"I mean that's not really why I went out there last night, I didn't go intending for it to happen, it just sort of did …" then taking a seat on the edge of her bed and starting with the phone call from aunt 'Chele I recounted the entire evening in minute detail to her.

"Wow, Katelyn, that's awful … I mean the first part … but that last part sounds like it would be kinda fun," she chuckled, "so what do you think he's going to do now?"

"I hope he does it again … and soon," I giggled.

"Not that, silly," she laughed, "I meant the first part."

"Oh, that … I really don't have any idea," I answered, "he just promised it all would be made right. He said it might take some time, but that revenge was a dish best served cold."

"Well, he does seem to have a lot of influence with a lot of people," she said, "I guess you'll just have to be patient and give him some time to do whatever it is he does."

"Yeah, I guess you're right … c'mon, let's go get something to eat, I'm starving … after all I did have a pretty vigorous work out last night," I laughed as we started out of the room, then turning back to her, and raising one eyebrow grinned, "Oh … and did I happen to mention that it was the *most* phenomenal sex I have ever had in my entire life …"

"Hummm … let me see … yeah, I think you might have mentioned something about that in passing …" she grinned.

"He did things to me that no one else has ever done … I'm talking about orgasms of *epic* proportions again and again!"

"Oh, now I really want to hear all the dirty details," she snickered hilariously adding, "so it was really that good, huh?"

"Yeahhh, Lexi … it was *that* good … let's just say that I'm not, and never have been, a screamer … moaning, yeah, lots of loudly moaning … but last night … I had such a difficult time breathing … the sex was so passionate and the orgasms so powerful … screaming was all I could do!"

"Really," she grinned asked, "so did he …"

"Oh yeah," I smiled happily, "from my nose … to my toes … and *everything* in between!"

"WOW!" she exclaimed, "and what about …"

"Oh girl please … he did that *really* good," I laughed.

"Well, I gotta ask," she smiled sheepishly, "is he …"

"Perfectly fulfilling … fits me like a dream … and more than satisfying in every way that you can possibly think of!"

She chuckled at my answers.

"Lexi, trust me girl, it was everything you could possibly imagine and more," I chuckled as we continued on our way out.

We went to a small restaurant, ordered dinner and then sat and talked – mostly girlie talk about the previous night, with a lot of added details. We both tried to keep it light to help keep my mind off the letter I had gotten. But still, deep inside me, there rested a reassurance that somehow, some way, James would make it right. I just believed that he cared that much about me.

When we got back to our room and ready for bed I picked up the phone, hoping it wasn't too late, and called James like I said I would.

"Hi!" I said, trying not to sound anxious when he answered the phone.

"Good evening Katelyn, did you have a pleasant afternoon," he asked.

"Pretty good," I said, "I'm sorry to call you so late …"

"It's quite alright, I don't often sleep much."

"I would have called earlier but Lexi and I went out for dinner and the time got away from us," I said beginning to ramble, making excuses to keep talking. I wanted so badly to ask him to let me come back out, but I wasn't sure how.

"Before you left this morning, you mentioned wanting us to have a talk of some kind, would you like to come out to Whitehall Saturday morning and do that," he asked, quickly solving that problem for me.

"Yeah, I think I would, if it's alright with you that is."

"That will be good," and I heard the smile in his voice

this time, "I look forward to hearing what you have on your mind … shall we say around noon?"

"That sounds good, I'll see you then," I said, relaxing at the easiness that was in his voice now, so with a little giggle I added, "until then, stay safe."

"No, *you* stay safe," he said suddenly seriously, "sleep well my love and pleasant dreams, good-bye for now." And the call ended just that quickly.

"Hum, well that went pretty well," I murmured softly.

"Do you have another date," Lexi asked from her bed.

"Yeah, but this time it's going to be a little more serious," I said.

"Are you kidding … just what could possibly be more serious than what happened last night," she chuckled.

"Well, this time I'm just planning on talking … although plans can change," I smiled, "but you know that he and I have been spending a lot of time together lately … and we've grown a lot closer."

"Really … ya think," she laughed, "like *real real* close?"

"You could say that," I grinned, "but I've had some questions about him that have really been bothering me. I just need to have a long talk with him to try to, I guess, clear the air and settle my mind before this thing goes any further."

"Katelyn, I'm going to be very honest with you. James seems like a pretty awesome guy so try not to get too serious, too soon and scare him away," she warned carefully.

"Somehow Lexi, I don't think I have to worry about scaring *him* off," I yawned, "I may actually be more concerned with scaring *me* off … G' night … love ya girl," I said and clicking off the light rolled over to go to sleep.

But as I lay there in the dark, wide awake, looking out the window at the trees, a quiet uneasiness began to move over me at the thought of all the questions I wanted to ask. A knot began forming again in the pit of my stomach when I thought about the direction in which the answers all pointed. I still just could not allow myself to think that it could possibly be true. I knew I was just being silly I told myself. Finally, in the early hours of the morning, sleep crept slowly over me and I rested.

Chapter Twenty~One

The remainder of the week seemed to fly by with classes and preparing for mid-terms. Then as Saturday drew closer I began to get more apprehensive as I thought about the pending conversation with James. Although I was anxious to finally get the chance to ask all the questions that had been troubling me almost from the beginning, there was a dark fearfulness resting in the pit of my stomach. I wanted to ask them … I had to ask them … but I still couldn't believe *what* I had finally decided to ask him. Still at the same time I wanted James to listen and hoped that he would simply burst out laughing at me. Then I could put all this silliness behind me and get on with this … relationship? That's the first time I had really allowed that term to enter the equation, although I knew it was quickly heading in that direction … at least for me.

"Maybe," I quietly pondered my situation as I drove in the morning sunshine, *"the other night wasn't just something that happened because I was so emotionally distraught. Maybe there is more than just a casual friendship developing. Oh, great, and here I may just screw up the best thing that has ever happened to me because of some inane questions. Way to go, Katelyn, you really need to think this thing through!"*

But in reality, I had thought it through, and there was no way I was ever going to be happy unless I got my answers and put the whole thing to rest. As I continued on, getting closer to Whitehall, I tried to list the questions in my mind and decide how best to put them out there. I was still wrestling with the issue when I arrived and turned up the lengthy drive toward the house.

I stopped the car just inside the gates and looked down the long shady drive, pausing to take in the huge oaks, remembering with a contented smile the last time I was here. Suddenly the thought crossed my mind that one way or another, today, like the last time I came here, could very possibly be one of those days that I would remember in clear detail for the rest of my life. I drove slowly the rest of the way up to the house.

"Good morning, Katelyn," James smiled warmly at me, hugging me and gently kissing my forehead, "how are you today?"

"I suppose I'm alright," I answered with a soft sigh.

"I have a small brunch set out on the veranda for you," he said tenderly, "Let's go out there and we can have that talk you've wanted to have."

We walked silently together through the door and as we started down the large hall, my tiny silent voice spoke up, *"So, you've made your decision … you do know that from the beginning this conversation really was going to be inevitable … and that's a good thing … so please you shouldn't feel badly about it … after all it's been building since the very first day."*

"Yeah, I know, but I'm just not sure how to begin it, and the thought of having to talk to him about my suspicions frightens me … what if he confirms them and really is what I think he is … or worse yet, what if he tells me I'm crazy and chases me away?" I thought back to it.

"I don't think he will do that," the still voice continued, *"after all, the questions you are harboring are serious … and you do deserve your answers … they will finally make everything crystal clear for you."*

"I'm just so afraid of what those answers might actually reveal to me, I know that what I suspect couldn't possibly be real … I don't think … but if they do confirm what I think I already know, they could actually change my entire life," I continued my silent dialogue.

"While that is true, you must understand that life itself is nothing more than a journey through time and that journey is filled with constant change, often times when you discover something new, it makes way for something else that would not have happened otherwise," it replied.

Suddenly I thought to myself, *"Oh, great! It just gets better and better Katelyn … now you are having detailed conversations with the voice in your head!"*

When we got to the veranda we sat at the little table that was quickly becoming a fixture of our visits. James watched me, smiling, as I picked at my food. I didn't have much to say, I just simply wasn't sure about how to broach this thing.

Finally, breaking the heavy silence, he spoke up, "I suppose the best thing for us to do is simply put everything out in the open, so I will begin … Katelyn, I have become quite fond of you in the last few weeks, I care for you more than anyone I have known in a very, very long time and as such I do not wish for there to be any secrets standing between us. So please don't be afraid to ask me anything you want, I will not withhold anything from you."

I glanced up at him, just on the verge of tears, and nodded ever so slightly as he continued, "I know that you have some concerns and some serious questions regarding things you have seen but do not understand. You know by now that I am a very private and secretive person, but because I care so much for you, I give you my word I will answer all of your questions and will not laugh at you regardless of how senseless you may think the questions are, I promise. Now, perhaps the answers are not what you may expect ... some of them may shock you ... and some may even surprise you ... still you will have your answers ... and I hope you are prepared for them."

"Thank you," I smiled sheepishly, "there are just so many things I want to ask that I'm not real sure where to start."

"Katelyn, I want you to know ... everything ... all of it," he prompted, "so why not just start at the beginning ... once you ask the first question, it will be as if a dam has broken and the remainder will follow ... and to be completely honest with you, I have looked forward to this opportunity to answer your questions as much as you have wanted to ask them."

"James, since I met you my life has changed in so many ways," I slowly began, "you've been good to me ... and good for me, too. You've helped me, perhaps in some ways you don't realize, to begin healing from my parent's murders. You seem to always be there for me at just the right time ... with just the right thing to say when I need it most ... our second meeting in the bookstore, when I wanted so badly to come back out here – you were there … then when I was here and got snake bit – again you were there … and it was you I came running to the other night when it seemed that my world was crashing down around me again. Sometimes I almost feel like there's this invisible connection between us … something … some powerful force … that's drawing us together."

"Perhaps that force as you call it is known as Fate," he answered smiling.

"Maybe that's a good name for it …" I answered slowly, "and possibly it knows more than either of us. Still, I have to wonder what it's doing in my life … your life … and dare I say, our lives."

"I believe that Fate is what one is meant to be," he slowly began, "and Destiny is what guides one into their Fate. I would say that together they have a master plan … which includes both of us … and they're working it out to their satisfaction," he answered.

"I suppose that's as good an answer as any," I agreed, "but James, the morning after I stayed here the first night, you told me that you may not be the person I thought you were, and while that is possible, I am so afraid that you may be the person I have come to believe you are … and if you are … that frightens me to no end."

I looked across the table into his eyes, took a deep breath and continued, "You always seem to know what I'm thinking and often times I've sensed that you are able to look into my mind and read my thoughts. Sometimes when I look at you … I almost, for just a fleeting moment, catch sight of another man … a man that is hiding a huge secret … a man that vanishes before I can get a clear picture of him … you seem to be a man out of place … almost as if you actually walked across time from some distant place to the here and now. There's no doubt that Whitehall is your home and, if what I suspect is true, it has been for more years than I can possibly imagine."

He sat smiling, quietly watching me, listening to me, and nodded in agreement.

"I have heard you say things about people or places that sound as if you had those experiences years ago, long before you could possibly have been born. Sometimes, when I look at you there's an almost unfathomable depth of life in your eyes and then I wonder if you are in fact as young as you look, and if you're not, how many years you've actually lived. You are so perfect, too perfect for someone your age … such a proper gentleman … always right where I need you … when I need you … and you have a way of making all my concerns simply evaporate … until the next question surfaces."

His eyes narrowed just the tiniest trace, flashing bright green as he looked at me across the table. Nearly imperceptibly he tilted his head, raising his chin, and then he slowly smiled at me, as if he knew what my next question would be.

My heart began to sink in my chest as I took a deep breath, swallowed hard, and thought to myself, *"Okay, Katelyn, here's where you throw it all out the window …"*

"I'm so afraid to ask you this …" I whispered slowly.

"Katelyn … look at me please …" he softly said and casually reaching across the table, took my hand in his, I slowly looked up again, "you mustn't ever be frightened … not of the question … not of the answer … and certainly not of me … but if you want to know the answer … the secret as you call it … then you must ask the question."

He released my hand and I withdrew it back across the table, as I continued, "But I'm so scared I already know the answer …"

"I think you do too," he spoke softly, "you just have to come to grips with it."

"Normally, this wouldn't concern me, but there are a lot of things that have raised questions in me … like for instance, sometimes when I touch you your skin feels cool … and combined with all the other little things … I have to ask …" I began explaining, pulling on the very last reserves of my courage … but then I dodged the big question one last time, "are you one of a kind … or are there others like you James?"

His eyes locked onto mine and with a little laugh said, "I'm sure there are, but, in exactly what sense do you mean 'like me'?"

I looked directly into his eyes, with both fear and uncertainty … of him … of my next question … and of the unknown.

"James … this is going to sound so stupid … but …" I swallowed hard, took in a deep breath, and finally just blurted out, "are you … a … a vampire?"

I cringed all over when the big question had finally escaped my lips … and then closing my eyes, covering my face with both hands, drew up into the fetal position in my chair and whispered, "Oh, no! Oh, God, no! I did not just ask you that! Please tell me that is not what just came out of my mouth! How could I be so stupid? I'm so sorry James, I know I'm over-reacting! I've been searching for answers on my own and have looked at a lot of weird websites! Please, please forgive me for being such an idiot!"

I drew myself up as small as possible wishing I could just disappear into the cushions of my chair. Suddenly the tiny little hummingbirds hovering in and around the Bougainvillea sounded so loud in the heavy silence that followed as time seemed to slow to a stop. After a long minute I slowly opened one eye, peaking at him through my fingers, and then bravely opening both eyes I sat there as he watched me from across the table. His beautiful green eyes were sparkling in the afternoon light and there was just the faintest trace of a smile beginning to play at the corners of his mouth as he began chuckling softly, "Hummm … so that's it … that's your big question … and just as simple as that … you've asked … but I suppose it could have been worse, you know … I could have been a werewolf."

I looked unbelievably at him, my jaw dropped open and I broke out with laughter, "James … that is so not funny … besides, I've seen you naked … you don't have enough body hair to be a wolf! I knew I was being silly and I don't know why I thought that or even why I entertained such an idea at all."

"It couldn't be helped Katelyn," he said very seriously looking right into my eyes, "you are a very intuitive young lady, you pay very close attention to details and you saw evidence of things you did not understand. You took all the little pieces, all the hints … many of which I gave you by the way … and you came to a logical conclusion for yourself. It just took a little longer for it to sink in and for you to actually accept the possibility of my being so."

"Wait a minute … stop talking … don't go any further … just stop right there," I choked out unbelievably, staring at him across the table, "are you actually telling me that … that you really are a … a … a vampire?"

"Yes," he replied simply, "I am, and I have been for well over two and a half centuries."

I sat and stared at him dumbfounded. Suddenly all of the questions, the doubts, the oddities, everything just fell in place. It all clicked and now made perfect sense … he was crazy. I looked at his beautiful green eyes again, thinking how wonderfully handsome he was, and slowly shook my head, not knowing what, if anything, I could possibly say in response.

"Great!" I suddenly exclaimed, "Just when I think that I am the luckiest girl in the world, have found the best – dare I say boyfriend – any girl could ever want, then he turns out to be crazy and tries to tell me he's a vampire … just freaking wonderful! And I thought I was the crazy one talking to voices in my head!"

"Are you quite finished now," he asked calmly.

"I don't know … you tell me … am I," I snapped, still trying to process his calm, simple answer.

"Katelyn, I want you to pause for a moment and think seriously about the last few months since you allowed me into your life. I believe that you have not only suspected, but deep inside, maybe even known what I am, almost since the first day we met. You started having doubts and questions from that very first introduction. You figured this out on your own, but only because I allowed you to do so. I gave you hints and clues to my nature knowing that you would come to this conclusion. I did it because I wanted you to know me and know my nature."

"Think back for a moment about the light touch of fear that you had deep inside you the first time you looked into my eyes. Recall for a moment your reaction when you received my first invitation to come to Whitehall, how you felt that you should just stay away. Think about how sometimes you still get just a quick flash of fear when you get too close to me. Although I am not, never have been, and never will be, a danger to you, all of those feelings are your natural reaction to what you know deep down inside that I am."

I sat in stunned silence, listening as he continued.

"You know that little voice you have been hearing in your head … the one that you have so recently begun answering and talking back to? That has been me all along, talking to you, trying … at first … to warn you away, and by the way, I was more than a little surprised when you started to answer me. So, no, you are not crazy because you are having conversations with the voice in your head. You were talking to me, you just didn't realize it."

I thought quickly back at all the times I had heard the voice. "It really was you, wasn't it," I asked sluggishly as I recognized now that indeed it did sound like him and suddenly the light came on and it all made perfect sense.

"Yes, Katelyn, darling, it really was me," the voice in my head whispered quietly. I looked at him and he was smiling at me like the cat that had just eaten the canary, *"and you can answer me this way if you wish,"* it floated through my mind, *"you have a very powerful gift of telepathy inside you … a gift that you have been using all along, even before you met me, but you were blissfully unaware of it."*

"I don't think I'm ready for that just yet," I answered hesitantly, still in shock, slowly shaking my head, "at least not knowingly."

"I apologize if this is too much for you to process right now," he said, "but you did ask the question, and all I am doing is supplying the answer. If you remember, I have spoken to you several times and told you to be absolutely certain that you wanted to know the answers before you asked the questions."

"Yeah, but I *had* to ask the questions … especially *the* question … because I knew you were somewhat out of the ordinary … but I didn't really expect you to confirm that you are … so different," I answered as the tears began to well in my eyes again. My world was suddenly spinning out of control; its axis had been completely shifted in the last few minutes. But I was determined if, as he said, all this was really true, I could, and I would, deal with it. Somehow, even with this new information, I would bring my world back right again.

"Please … give me a minute to try and think this through … I need to sort this all out, and try to accept that you are telling me that you are a … a completely different kind of person."

"Vampire, Katelyn, I'm a vampire, and it's quite alright for you to use the word around me, after all, it is what I am and what I have been since the spring of 1753."

"Mmmkay … I think I can say that … you, James Dubois, the man I think I am falling in love with, is a vampire … there I said it … no, wait … did you say 1753 … as in before the American Revolution 1753 … I mean … I know you said two and a half centuries … but the year puts it so sharply in perspective … and it still doesn't make it any easier to process, not yet anyway."

"It's like any new idea," he said, his easy smile returning, "It just takes a while for you to accustom yourself to the thought and get used to it. I assure you, it will get easier as you get more comfortable with the concept."

"But James … I knew you had a secret … but a *vampire,*" I muttered quietly, "you're admitting to being something that I thought was only a fictional creature in movies and books."

"I had to become comfortable with the idea of it in the beginning, too. There were a great many changes to which I had to adapt. Fortunately, I had a very good teacher to help me adjust and become familiar with what I had become. Everything was new to me and suddenly I had an eternity in front of me in which to live with absolutely no fear of death.

But most importantly Katelyn, I learned to enjoy my life, I am happy with what I am, and I wouldn't go back and make changes even if I could."

"Think, if you will, for just a moment about my life and the enormity of immortality … I've bore witness to history as I've lived across the centuries … I've seen Kings and Empires rise and fall … I've seen mortals at their very best – and their very worst. It's astounding when you consider the things I've seen and done … the many places that I've been … the number of years I've lived … and yet for all practical purposes, I still live my life day to day just the same as you do … only with some minor differences in diet and sleep patterns."

"Yeah, 'bout that sleeping thing … it's the middle of the day, and the sun is shining, how are you … is *awake* the right word?"

"I can see myself in a mirror and I even appear in photographs, too," he chuckled in answer, "too many weird websites, Katelyn, you said so yourself. You see, day or night really doesn't matter, it's just a superstition … and there are many other superstitions that don't apply either. I can live and transact business in the daylight just as easily as the night."

I quickly thought back to the first night I had spent at Whitehall … alone … with him … in his bed, "Well, then I suppose the next question would have to be have you ever, uhh … you know … uhh …" I trailed off and with the first two fingers of my right hand opened into a 'V' just pointed to my neck.

"Are you asking if I have ever bitten you … fed from you … drank your blood?"

"Yeah … that."

"No, I haven't … honestly … and I would tell you if I

had … although *you* have drunk my blood," he said matter-of-factually, "and rather a goodly amount of it too I might add."

"Ewww, yuck … nun-uh … not me … oh James that is just beyond disgusting … I would never do anything like that, besides I think I would remem …" I started to say, then abruptly stopped short as a sudden realization struck home, "wait a minute … the anti-venom … was it … is *that* what it was?"

"Yes, it was," he answered simply with a smile, then continued very seriously, "I gave you my blood in order to save your life Katelyn. Otherwise you would have been dead in a matter of minutes … and I would *not* have allowed you to die that day."

"Wait … do you mean … you would have …" I slowly trailed off as I suddenly understood the implication of just what he meant when he said he would not have allowed me to die that day. I took in a deep breath as I sat there, looking straight at him.

"Yes … that's precisely what I mean," he answered seriously, "Katelyn, had I seen any sign of your eminent death that afternoon, I would have immediately changed you to prevent your dying. I've lost one mate to Death, and I could do nothing about it … I wasn't about to allow Death to cheat me out of another one. That's why I watched you so closely and asked so often how you felt. I had never given my blood to a human before. I knew it would work because our blood will destroy any poison. I just wasn't too sure of the effect it would have on you."

"Well then," I said, taking in a deep breath, "I suppose perhaps this would be a good place for me to maybe say thank you for saving my life."

"You're most welcome," he smiled disarmingly at me.

Suddenly, with just that simple exchange, the atmosphere seemed to relax just a bit and didn't seem as strained as it did a few minutes ago.

"Ohhhh … alright," I sighed slowly, "let me try to recap this so far, internalize it, and breathe a minute before I attempt to continue … you are a vampire … we can communicate telepathically … you have not fed from me … but I have drank blood from you … that pretty much sum it up?"

"I think you have it, so far," he answered with a smile.

"Oh, God, how did this happen," I said shaking my head to try to clear it.

"That's a fair question," he said soothingly, "will you please allow me to try to answer it for you?"

"Sure … why not … at this point I think I'm beyond shock, so go ahead, I'm listening," I said, my mind still too boggled to think straight.

"Let me try to put this in perspective for you. Humans are initially drawn to other humans because of their beauty, are they not?"

"Yeah, that's usually the way it works," I agreed slowly, then grinned and chuckled, "at least until they discover the beauty is only skin deep."

"I am by nature a predator Katelyn, and so I do have a certain amount of beauty that enables me to draw prey to me. Humans, my prey, are drawn to me because they see something beautiful. Think back to the very first thoughts *you* had of me. My kind are drawn to beautiful humans in order to feed. So you see it works both ways … humans are drawn to me because of my immortal beauty and I'm drawn to humans because of their mortal beauty."

"I chose you, Katelyn, I was drawn to you like a moth to a candle because you are without doubt the most stunningly beautiful girl I have seen in the last hundred and fifty years or so …"

"Humph, now that has to be the most original pick-up line I've ever heard," I said, still trying to lighten my mood.

"Perhaps," he smiled and continued, "but very much the truth. Our first meeting in the bookstore was not an accident. I don't, as a rule, have casual conversations with students."

"So I was told," I nodded.

"As a predator, it was your physical beauty that initially drew me to you. I wanted so desperately to feed from you, so I started watching you, gauging you. Then, when I realized that you didn't act like other girls your age that are blessed with such beauty, I saw you as out of the norm and that became just as strong of a draw. I stopped to consider just exactly what you were. I knew you weren't a vampire, and I also knew you weren't a member of the immortal world, but at the same time you didn't act like a regular human either."

"So there are others like you, and you are able to pick them out," I replied interestingly, more statement than question.

"Yes, again you are correct," he smiled, "anyway, I sat there and listened to the conversation you and Lexi had concerning me …"

"Hold it … you heard that," I asked, "All of it?"

"I really don't mind reading to you, Katelyn, but can it please be something besides the ops manual to your new laptop," he grinned, "those things are so terribly boring!"

"Yeah, they really are," I answered, unable to stop a short giggle at the memory of that comment.

"Katelyn, I can hear any conversation I choose to tune into to anywhere, usually within several hundred feet of me.

Do you recall telling me that you thought you could hear a car out on the highway the day you were bitten?"

"Yeah … are you saying … I actually did …"

"Yes, you see, our blood, when used medicinally, has an immediate, although temporary effect, on a mortal. Remember the increased vision you had, and the sensitivity to light? My blood actually linked us together, how else could you have had the sense of my presence anywhere in the house and every move I made? Likewise with you, I knew when you slept, when you woke, I knew that you were awake the entire second night. Then on the third morning, at breakfast, when you were craving tomato soup … that was my blood in you calling out for more … but all you knew was that you were craving something thick, red and hot … and as a mortal the only thing you could relate it to was tomato soup."

"So then, I wasn't just imagining all that …" I asked, "but, is that what it's like all the time? For you, I mean?"

"Absolutely, remember I am a predator, and all the increased senses go hand in hand with that," he continued, "but, as I was saying, after I got over the initial attraction your beauty had on me, I quickly discovered that you were also extremely intelligent and very strong-willed, but deeply wounded and that increased my intrigue even more. I could not understand how one so young and with so much worldly beauty could have such a deep wound, until I heard you tell Lexi about your parents. And I knew that was our point of commonality … we had both lost someone we dearly loved and had to carry the scars of that loss inside us … the kind of deep scars that only Death can leave behind."

"It was at that point that I made my final decision to meet you, and look further into your life. You actually drew me to yourself, so I suppose you could say the predator became the prey. I wanted to see if I could somehow help close the open gash in your soul. I wanted to make you as beautiful on the inside again as you are on the outside."

Then all of a sudden alarm bells began going off in my head, "Wait … wait … wait … wait … you said that you are a predator … *what* were you doing in the campus bookstore that day … or do I even *want* to know the answer to that question?"

"I do have to hunt and feed Katelyn, and the various campuses in the area offer me a wide and varied selection to choose from," he answered indifferently as if he had only been inspecting an assortment of steaks.

This was suddenly way too much information. I bolted up from my chair saying, "I'm gonna to be sick!" and I made it to the railing, leaned over and violently lost everything I think I had eaten in the last day and a half. James was there as fast as I was trying to rub my shoulders and back. Between heaves I managed to choke out, "Don't … you … dare … touch … me … right … now!"

He carefully sat a glass of water on the top rail then he backed away and sat down in his chair again. I heaved a couple of more times as I clung desperately to the porch railing for support, although by now there was nothing left in me to come up. I tried to steady myself, then rinsed my mouth with the water and staggered slowly back to my chair.

I looked at him, still with watery eyes, and a trembling voice said, "I'm sorry I did that … it's so embarrassing … James, I don't know why this makes sense to me, perhaps because of my feelings toward you, but … I think I can deal with the idea of you being a vampire … it's just that I suddenly could not deal with the thought of you killing someone that I might know all because you look at them as … as some kind of macabre 'Happy Meal'."

"Katelyn, often times humans find new concepts, things they don't understand, to be repulsive. You're better than that," he began slowly, "please try not to respond in such manner. Look at me … please … am I not still the same man that you have known all along; the man you have trusted and asked advice of; the man who saved your life; the man you made love to with such abandon. The only thing that has changed between us is that now you know what *kind* of a man I am, my true nature."

"While I can see and understand your point of view," he continued, "I didn't mean for you to misinterpret what I said. I have killed in the past, that's true enough, and I will again in the future, it's my nature. However, I do not have the need, the driving force if you will, to kill anymore, and I haven't for a long time. Nevertheless, I am more than capable of doing so, and would if the circumstances called for it. But most of the time I only take enough from my victims to sustain me. They never know it, never remember it, and I leave them alive."

Somehow, there was the tiniest little bit of settling in me, but I still had a lot of uneasiness and felt like I was on the verge of maybe throwing up again … if there was anything left.

"Enough … James, please," I said weakly, "I don't think I can take anymore right now. I came to you with questions, questions I should never have allowed myself to even consider, and you have candidly answered them, more so than I could have ever imagined. You have shown me a side of the world that I only thought existed in folklore and fairy-tales, a side so dark I could not have fully conceived it a week ago."

"So I suppose that only leaves me one final question

…" I took a deep breath, suddenly feeling like the rabbit looking at the fox, "how does this affect us James … our relationship … now that I know your secret … do you … do you have to eliminate me as a threat to that secret … does my knowing that you are a vampire mean that you have to kill me?"

James sat thoughtfully, his fingers tented in a steeple under his chin, his mouth in a tight line, finally answering, "Of the available options … that is one …" he began, and my heart fell into my feet, "although it's certainly not my first choice."

I think I audibly breathed out and said, "That's good, I'm not too in love with that one myself."

"Katelyn," he continued, looking in my eyes and smiling, "first of all, let me reassure you once again that you are completely safe with me and that I pose no danger to you. I didn't save your life just to take it away. I would never hurt you. I care much too deeply for you to even consider that as an option. I told you, you know my secret because I allowed you to know it … because I wanted you to know it. In almost three hundred years I have never wanted anyone to know everything about me and my nature as desperately as I wanted you to know it … from the very first moment I laid eyes on you."

I began trying to seriously consider the situation I was in, and hoping for a way out. I began to believe that I might actually leave Whitehall this evening in somewhat the same condition, physically, if not mentally, as when I arrived.

"You're shielding your thoughts," he said, looking at me, "I can't read what you are thinking right now."

"Good," I retorted, trying my best to sound confident, "I don't want you in my head right now, and since I don't know yet how to get in yours, what is another option?"

"There are a couple more options," he smiled, "one being that I simply wipe away your memory of me and our relationship."

"Oh God, no … please James … not that … please, there has to be a way that I can keep what we have … my memories of you are special to me … you have been such a help to me. You said there were a couple of options," and as pure fright crept slowly over me, I whispered, "*what* other option remains?"

"The only other option, and my personal choice, is for me to change you," he said simply.

"Change me … you mean … you want to make me a vampire … like you," I asked shocked.

"That's correct," he answered calmly, "that's the real reason I allowed you to figure all this out … the reason I chose you … because I want to offer you the gift."

"Gift," I exclaimed horrifically, "That's what you call it, a gift? You're talking about taking away my life … and you call it a gift?"

"I'm only talking about life as you know and understand it," he continued with a smile, "there is so much more that you don't know about, a life that is so incredible as to be nearly inconceivable to the mortal mind … you have no idea of what lives in the world around you. There is an entire other world Katelyn, one that contains many more created beings that you are unable to see with your human eyes. But, if you think about it for a moment, there are times when you come so close to it that you can actually feel it on your skin. Please trust me when I say that humans and vampires are not the only beings who reside in this world."

I looked up at him and grinning sheepishly asked, "Werewolves?"

"Yes, those too," he answered with a smile.

"But … I've just begun to live my life James … I don't want to die … I'm too young," I slowly whispered fighting back tears. I sat back in total disbelief, my mind racing, and closed my eyes.

"You're not going to die Katelyn, you will merely change, genetically, and become like I am … and I'm certainly not dead as you well know …"

"Yeah, don't I know that," I said peeking at him with a smile and trying my best not to snicker at his humor.

"What you will do is live," he continued with a chuckle, "and experience life, and love, like you have never imagined. So please, Katelyn, be who you are, consider my offer with the openness you have always had, then should you decide to accept it, you will soon come to understand that it really is a gift."

I slowly sat back in my chair, and shaking my head, closed my eyes.

"Oh God, James, I am so totally overwhelmed …" I thought to myself, *"I don't know what to think, what to say, or what to do here … I just wish I could turn back the clock a couple of hours … I want so badly to ask you to hold me, to comfort me and tell me everything is going to be alright and that it will all work out."*

"You just did," I heard him whisper in my head, *"come to me, Katelyn, my dear, let me comfort you and ease your mind."*

My eyes flew open and I looked across the table at him. He was smiling at me as if nothing had happened and quietly said, "You forgot about your telepathy, your gift projects strongly, and when you relaxed you threw open the door to your thoughts and I heard you plainly."

I slowly stood up, my mind still swirling with all that had just taken place, and making sure my legs were steady enough to hold me, never taking my eyes off of him, I carefully made my way around the table to where he was sitting. He extended his hand to me and I slowly sat down in his lap, wrapping one arm lightly around his neck. I suddenly felt like a lost and confused little girl again, as I looked to him for peace and comfort. He took me gently in his arms, carefully wrapping them around me, moving slowly so as not to further frighten me. I sensed a familiar wave of comfort and security radiate out from him and shimmer through me. I cuddled into his chest, tears flowing freely down my face as I looked up at him and sobbing through my tears softly asked, "Now … do we have to do it right now … today?"

"You're not ready yet Katelyn," he answered softly, and lightly kissed my forehead, "we must first make some plans, prepare for what lies ahead, and then, only when *you* are ready, I will bring you over."

Chapter Twenty~Two

Wave after wave of the most blissful peace radiated through me as I sat there, cuddled against James' chest, wrapped lovingly and securely in his arms. It soothed my trembling body and settled my troubled mind, as he held me in his arms. I sensed his love as it washed over me, knowing he would do me no harm. He quietly stroked my cheek, his tender touch adding to my comfort. My eyes grew heavy and I soon fell asleep, sitting in his lap, resting peacefully in his embrace.

When I awoke, the sun had set and it was fully dark outside. I was lying in the upstairs bed where we had first made love. I was alone in the room and James was nowhere to be seen or felt. I lay there, looking around the familiar room, comfortable in a place I knew all too well. I considered my situation and began to think about all that had happened this afternoon and how my life was soon to change so drastically because of it. I was more than a little frightened, again having to face an unknown future. I turned over in my mind all the things James had confessed to me … how my fairy-tale suspicions had turned into cold hard facts. At the same time, I was intrigued by the thoughts of all I had learned today … that an entire other world co-existed with mine. A world that, it would seem, I was about to become a part of. A world, until now, that I had no comprehension of … one where vampires lived … and if vampires were real, then what else could be real and living in that world, too. I slowly got off the bed, still a little shaken with all my new knowledge, and started downstairs to find James. I needed to know what was going to happen next. I found him standing in the huge library, paging through a book when, a little hesitantly, I slowly walked in.

"I heard you wake and come down the stairs," he said looking up and smiling at me, "please, let me get you a glass of wine, it will be good for you. You've endured rather a shock to your sensibilities today."

"Humph … yeah, that's an understatement if ever there was one," I muttered quickly to myself.

He stepped over to a small table, poured the wine, and returned with a glass in each hand. He handed me an elegantly engraved, fluted crystal wine stem filled a little over half way.

"To the love of a beautiful woman," he said touching the rim of his glass to mine, then taking a sip and smiling at me.

The wine, a deep dark red, looked warm and delicious, still I looked suspiciously at it before I gingerly lifted it to my lips and took a small sip.

"Wow … that's good," I spoke softly as I slowly took another tentative sip, "really good … what is it?"

"It's French, a Thomas Barton Claret from the Bordeaux region," he answered casually, "this particular one is a 1764 vintage. I brought it up from the cellar while you slept."

"But, that makes it almost two hundred fifty years old … and probably very expensive," I said slowly as I held the glass to the light and looked at the rich red wine.

"It is indeed, but do you like it," he asked with a smile.

"Yes! It's probably the best I've ever tasted," I answered.

"Then for you, it's worth it … besides, you must bear in mind that I bought it the year it was vined so it wasn't so very expensive then," he chuckled, "but what's important is that you relax and enjoy it. Anyway, I have several more cases of it in the cellar. Katelyn, I understand that today has been demanding for you, but realizing and accepting a new truth is always the first and most challenging step."

I took a deep breath and exhaled as I started to feel, and was thankful for, the warmth of the wine as it began to work its way through me, helping me to relax and begin to feel more at ease again.

"I hope that you slept well and rested," he continued, still gazing into my eyes, "please tell me … how are you feeling … and more importantly … what are you thinking?"

"I suppose I am trying to make an honest effort to contend with a lot of new information," I said still sipping slowly on the wine, "and considering that my boyfriend just confessed to me that he is a vampire … and that he wants to make me one too … I suppose you could say I'm a little traumatized … but at least I haven't run screaming in terror out the front door … not that I've totally ruled that option out … yet."

I looked over at him and took in a long breath as I slowly continued, "I thought that I was ready for a long term commitment in my life. But what you are asking me to commit to is something that is so far outside my realm of understanding that I'm still not sure I fully comprehend the entire concept. I'm still trying to get used to the idea of having to become like you, wondering what it will be like, and what will happen to the me that I, and others, know when I do."

Looking into my eyes, he said softly, "I love you Katelyn, and I wonder if you understand just how much? I would never force the gift upon you … you do not 'have to become' what I am. If I had wanted to force you, I could have taken you and changed you the very first day we met and no one could have done anything about it. But I didn't do that because I wanted you to have the choice I never had … I wanted you to want the gift as much as I wanted to give it to you. I wanted you to be able to freely make your own choice and to be fully comfortable with it. I wanted you to know me and know my nature, in hopes that we could share a true and genuine love together."

"James, there are so many more questions I have now. Besides you, my entire world consists of my Aunt 'Chele and Uncle John. Will I ever be able to see them again … and what about Lexi? She's more than just a best friend to me, we are like sisters to each other … how will I ever explain all of this to the three of them?"

"Katelyn, darling," he said as he crossed the room to me, taking me in his arms again, "You don't have to take the slightest thought about any of that. I will take care of all of those issues and guide you through everything that we must do, but only after you are ready. Perhaps in time, you will be able to see your aunt and uncle again. While it may be difficult at first, perhaps there are ways, later on, in which we can have Lexi remain a part of your new life if you wish."

"However, because of my deep love for you I have been considering other avenues while you slept. There is one other option available, one that would be very hurtful, at least for me. I could quickly and easily step out of your life, just as quickly and easily as I entered it. Whitehall is indeed my home, but I have other residences in other places and I can readily make any of them my home in short order. You could remain here ... I would even allow you the free use of Whitehall should you desire ... you could build your own life and memories here. I would, of course, ensure your safety, happiness and financial security. Then, in seventy-five or eighty years, I could return again to Whitehall and take up my life just as it is now."

I stood there in his arms, his love more tangible than ever, as I realized how much he was willing to give up for me. Suddenly the idea of not being forced into his world, but given a choice about it became more appealing to me. With my own free will and a choice of my making, I could become what he was, doing so willingly, and being with him forever. I closed my eyes and relaxed in his arms, cuddling closer to him as I made a truly life altering decision.

"James," I began, taking a step back and looking into his eyes, "what you've just offered is not really another option ... that's just a rewording of the wipe away my memory of us option that you offered on the veranda earlier this afternoon. Do you honestly think, after all that has passed between us, that I could stay here, in your home, and build a life and memories without you as a part of it? You would be in my every waking thought ... whether I was here in the parlor, or sitting on the rear veranda … or attempting to sleep in our bedroom … your presence permeates this house and it would surround me all the time and in everything I did. At this point, my life will not be complete without you in it … I could never be happy without you … and I want you to be happy as well, so I believe the only way we can both be happy, and both of our lives be complete, is for us to be together … and the only way we can really be together is for me to become like you."

"Our lives are already connected, we have become so intertwined, such a part of each other that I have no choice but to follow you, we have to see this thing through to its completion. So I've made my decision James … of my own choice, I willingly and freely accept your gift to me. Now, I've taken the first and most important step … the next step is up to you … take my hand Caesar … lead me across the Rubicon … and onward to our destiny."

"Very well, my love," he smiled at me, "let's begin our walk together. I will guide you and take special care of you as we go through this. We have some arrangements that need to be made …

"Does that mean I need to make 'Final Arrangements'," I grinned mischievously.

"In this case, not so much *final* arrangements as, shall we say, *initial* arrangements … but I compliment you on having a very pointed sense of humor my love …"

"I know, believe me, I've been called a smartass more than once … but do you think my 'pointed sense of humor' will carry over into my new life," I asked seriously.

"I assure you it will," he confirmed, "and probably become even more pointed!"

"Good, I like having a sharp wit," I laughed, "and since I'm making 'initial arrangements' instead of 'final arrangements', I suppose that means I don't have to order a coffin?"

"You needn't worry yourself about such things," he answered cutting his eyes sharply at me, "because after about two weeks, unless of course you just happen to wish to, you'll never sleep again."

"Well, that's certainly a trait that would have come in handy for all those tests and finals over the years!"

"Perhaps so, but now you don't have to be concerned with those either," he chuckled, "unless you just want to return to either high school or college."

"Let me think about that one for a second … uh, no thank you … I'm so done with all that drama," I quickly replied.

"But Katelyn, I must ask, during the next few days and weeks, will you trust me enough to do the things I ask, even if you don't fully understand them at the time?"

"I'll trust you, James, so long as you make sure that none of those I love gets hurt. They should not have to get pulled into this new world because of me and the decision I've made for my life."

He smiled at me and said, "I assure you that no harm will come to any of those you love Katelyn, you have my word on it. Now, would you like to return to school tonight, or do you wish to stay the night and return in the morning?"

"If I stay the night, will you tell me about your life and how you came to be like this," I asked smiling up at him.

"I will tell you everything about me, whatever you wish to know, withholding nothing from you," he said, and gently leading me to one of the small loveseats, continued, "I don't wish you to be frightened Katelyn, but now that you know what I am, I want you to see me as you've never seen me before … I want you to finally see that other man, the one you said you have often been able to catch a glimpse of for just a fleeting moment … I want you to see the immortal that I am … please wait here while I set the room in order, and prepare to allow me to take you on a journey down a very long memory lane. I shall rejoin you in a moment."

I watched as he began to move quickly and quietly through the large parlor, lighting every one of the long white candles in the room. When he had done that he turned off all the modern lighting and my eyes quickly adjusted to the dimness. I looked around in awe, the beauty of the room was now illuminated like never before in the dancing shadows that were cast by the flickering light of the candles. He turned and began walking back toward me carrying a large silver candelabrum.

I sat in astonishment, silently staring at the most stunningly magnificent man I had ever seen in my life. He looked like what I always thought an angel would appear like. When he fixed his eyes on me and smiled, I had to remind myself to breathe. I watched mesmerized by his beauty, as he continued to make his way back to where I was sitting.

He appeared to glide silently in the shadowy light of the candles and I was completely captivated with him, unable to move or speak at what I was seeing. His eyes, those beautiful green eyes, had taken on a faint glow as they reflected the muted light of the candleholder he was carrying. His hair, now loose and touching his shoulders, had an incredible shine to it; his skin, though not pale, had taken on a lovely luminousness. Had I not known he was an immortal, I most certainly would have known he was more than human.

My eyes followed his progress back to where I was sitting. He carefully sat the candlestick on a side table and joined me on the couch. Then without a sound, his eyes still resting on me, he put his arm around my shoulders and drew me close against him. I cuddled as closely as I could, sensing his love sweep over and through me, comforting as a warm summer breeze.

"Look around you my dear Katelyn," he softly whispered, breaking the silence. I followed the sweep of his hand as he indicated the room, "This is how I saw this room in my human days … two hundred and sixty years ago."

I couldn't believe how romantically beautiful the room had become as he settled in closer to me and began his story …

Chapter Twenty-Three

I toed off my shoes, folded my legs under me, and cuddled against him on the sofa. He smiled and lightly kissed my forehead as, just above a whisper, he began to relate a marvelous story to me. I listened attentively, often awestruck, for the next two hours, only occasionally interjecting a thought or asking a quick question.

"I was born in this house, in fact, in what is now our bedroom, in 1725 and grew to maturity here, learning to be a planter, like my father and grandfather before me."

"It's almost unthinkable that I am sitting here, wrapped in the arms of a man that was alive more than two centuries before my grandparents were born," I remarked, looking up into his eyes, "and yet he still doesn't look a day older than I am … and it's even more incredible to think that

I have fallen so deeply in love with that man."

"I have lived a truly astonishing life Katelyn, but a life that has been lacking and unfinished … and soon you shall make it complete, fulfilling all that has been deficient," he smiled, kissing the top of my hair and continuing with his story.

"My present life began in the early Spring of 1753, when I was twenty-eight years old. I was studying at Gonville and Caius College in Cambridge as did many of the sons of wealthy planters at that time. My presence though was under very different circumstances since my father had sent me there to recover from my grief. I was a widower of four years, still suffering heavy under my loss."

"I had gone out one afternoon for a leisurely walk along Trinity Street. I remember it being a particularly nice day simply because warm days in England can be such a rarity. I soon became lost in the sun's warmth as I strolled remembering how my dear wife had many times accompanied me on similar walks. I receded deeper into my thoughts, enjoying the memories I so affectionately held of her."

"All of a sudden, my thoughts were interrupted and I forced myself back to reality. I found myself in the path of the most adorable woman I had ever seen and had very nearly stumbled over her."

"This was the kind of woman that one just did not see in the colonies, even in big cities like Charles Towne or Boston. She was striking in her beauty and very alluring. She was wearing one of the latest styles from Paris and as was highly desirable in a lady at that time, she was so perfectly pale, that her skin shown like porcelain. She was very petite, a little less than five feet tall, but she had the most incredible strength radiating out from her. She had the prettiest russet brown hair that was also done in the style of the period. Her eyes were light brown, with long lashes, and the brightest passion emanated from them. When she looked up at me she had the sweetest, most inviting smile. Suddenly, for the first time since my Mary Elizabeth had died, I was stricken by the beauty of another woman."

"Wait ... the lady in the portrait ... the one in the library," I interjected questioningly, "her name was Mary Elizabeth ... so that *is* you in the portrait ... and *she* was your wife?"

"Yes, that is indeed my beloved wife and I, we sat for the portrait in 1746, just a year after our marriage."

"That explains why you became so suddenly emotional when you were telling me about her," I whispered.

"I loved her very dearly Katelyn, she was more than my wife ... she was my life, my entire world, and the center of my universe. Mary Beth was my first love, the mother of my son, and I loved her more than life itself. I was devastated when she died. I couldn't understand why she had left and taken our little girl with her. I thought that my entire existence had come to an end."

I reached and placed my hand on his chest, looked up at him with tears brimming in my eyes and whispered, "Oh James, I'm so sorry for your loss. I can empathize with the hurt and devastation that you felt. When my parents died, I was crushed and thought that my whole world had ended."

"We both have that in common and just as I still hold a special place in my heart for her, you shall always have a special place for them," he said and then resumed with his tale ...

"'Oh, please excuse me, sir,' she said smiling, 'I'm afraid I was lost in my thoughts and did not see you there.'"

"'I'm afraid that I was the inattentive one, and so very glad that I was, else we might not have had this opportunity to meet. My name is James Thomas Dubois of Charles Towne,'" I introduced myself, and hurriedly continued, not wanting this chance meeting with such a beautiful lady to end so quickly, "'Might I be of some assistance to you?'"

"She smiled up at me and I was surprised as an almost forgotten stirring began in the depths of my being. It was as if I had suddenly come awake from a terrible dream and life was now returning to me."

"'My name is Charlotte Ann,' she replied, offering me her hand. I took it in mine and lightly kissed it ..."

"I suppose, however, before I get too far into that story I should go back and start at the beginning," he smiled, "however, please understand that my human life was indeed another life, and it took place a very long time ago. Many of the memories from that life are still hurtful, but for you, I will gladly share them so that you may better know me and my past."

"You recall the short history I related of Whitehall when you first visited. The ancestor that founded Whitehall in the 1680's was my Grandfather," he began, "he and my father had been very successful at planting and due to their hard work, had accumulated a great amount of wealth, making our family one of the wealthiest in the colonies. They had planned my life for me from the very beginning and their plan was for me to be the first Dubois in the colonies to live the life of an aristocratic gentleman."

"I had the best tutors money could buy at that time, and beginning at an early age, studied all the accepted subjects. I learned to speak French, German and Latin; received instruction in the proper usage of English, and even learned a little Spanish. Those are all languages that I retain the use of even today."

"I became quite proficient in math and writing. My geography skills were without compare. I studied all the masters of literature, learning the plays and poetry that had formed the basis of western civilization. When the opportunities presented themselves, I even attended opera's, which planted in me the seed of a deep appreciation of music of all types."

"After the completion of my primary education I was to attend Harvard beginning in the spring of 1741 upon my sixteenth birthday. There I was to polish and complete my education whereupon I would become the aristocrat they had dreamed of me being."

"When I returned to Whitehall after Harvard, during my twentieth year, I met and soon married my wife, Mary Elizabeth. Soon after our marriage, we discovered that she was with child and due in the fall of the year. She gave me a beautiful baby boy, James Thomas Junior. It was through him the Dubois linage has continued. We loved each other dearly and were a very happy couple, learning about each other, growing closer each day and looking forward to a long and happy life together."

I looked up at him, smiling at his evident happiness as he described his wife and son.

"We soon discovered that she was to give me another child and we were again so very excited. As the day for her delivery drew closer we brought in the mid-wife to tend her. Unfortunately, there were complications, as often happened then, and my wife and new daughter did not survive the birth."

"Needless to say I was distraught with grief. Mary Elizabeth had been my first and only love. My entire life had changed in the course of an afternoon. It all seemed so terrible, I was only twenty-three years old and now a widower."

"I spent the next four years working at Whitehall with my father expanding my knowledge of the day to day operations. I threw my whole self into learning the art of being a planter. Everything was about work, I didn't want friends and I didn't want a social life. In the evening I would go to the little family cemetery and grieve for my lost wife and daughter. I just could not get over them. The hurt in me was so deep, but still I tried to cover it with my work."

"My life continued that way until, finally, in the fall of 1751, after three long years of grieving, my father called me into his study one evening. He poured us both a snifter of brandy and told me to sit, pointing out a chair. He said that he had had enough of my mourning, it was killing me, and it was past time for me to put it behind and move on with my life. He declared that I was to go to England, be enrolled at Cambridge and spend a couple of years studying there. It would give me the opportunity to get far away and clear my head. Then upon my return I was to assume the title of 'Master of Whitehall' and take over the operations in order that he could retire."

"Being my father, I did as he wished, and in the early fall of 1752, I boarded a ship in Charles Towne and set sail for England. I stood quietly at the rail that morning, the early mist lying along the surface of the water as the ship began to move away from the pier and out into the harbor. I watched as Charles Towne grew smaller, finally disappearing into the rising morning fog. Little did I know at that time just how much that trip would indeed change my life. It would be almost one hundred and twenty-five years before I returned to Whitehall."

"Then, of course, I met Charlotte Ann and we quickly

became close … especially after she told me that she was a widow and how her husband had been killed in the colonies. We had so much in common and she listened attentively as I told her about my own Mary Elizabeth and the tragedy that had struck our lives. It seemed that we had so much shared sadness in our lives."

"We continued to see each other over the next couple of months. Our friendship quickly developed into a relationship as we seemingly grew closer each day. I quickly fell in love with her, realizing that while she was not completely filling that empty spot in my life, she was at the least making it smaller. Then came the fateful day when she changed my life forever."

"It was a beautiful afternoon and she and I had walked in the park. She asked me to accompany her back to her townhouse that she had something very special she wanted to share with me. She looked so beautiful to me that day as the sun played in her soft brown hair. I, of course, was very excited that she had invited me to her home … and without a chaperone."

"How quaint," I giggled, "no chaperone!"

"When we entered her home she asked me to kiss her, and I willingly took her in my arms. I began gently kissing her soft lips, soon losing myself in the fragrance of her perfume. I was so enamored at the thought of the pleasures she was offering me that I didn't feel her arms encircle me, pulling me to her. I didn't notice how she was suddenly holding me tighter than I could have thought possible. She lightly brushed my neck with her lips and then I felt a sharp pain as her teeth sank into me. I tried to struggle and get free but there was no use. Although small in size, she was so very much stronger than I could have ever imagined."

"I felt the life flowing out of me, her mouth latched

tightly to my neck, the fear of dying covered me, and then a calming wave swept over me reassuring me that I was going to be alright. Just as I thought I was going to die she opened her wrist and held it to my mouth saying, 'Drink, my love, and you shall truly live'. She forced it to my mouth and I tasted the blood on my tongue as it began filling my mouth with its heavy, coppery taste."

"After I swallowed the first time, it became a sweetness that I could not seem to get enough of. I grabbed her arm and held it with a renewed vigor, trying to get more. I closed my eyes and drifted away lost in the ecstasy of it all as her blood flowed into every part of my body, filling it and changing it."

"When I awoke, my human life had ended and a new immortal one had begun. Everything that I had been was now completely changed. Although times have changed and many years have passed, I am exactly now as I was then, in the spring of 1753."

I listened attentively to everything James was telling me, trying to prepare myself for when it would be my time to change. I wanted to know everything to expect.

"What did you do … afterward, I mean, when you woke up," I asked curiously.

"Charlotte Ann took me that day and began to teach me about my new life … what I had become … how I was to live. She became more than just my maker to me … she became teacher … healer … and hunting partner."

"We soon left Cambridge," he continued, "we needed a place where I could hunt and grow and not draw undue attention to ourselves. While I began growing into my new life, I had no desire to return to Charleston or to Whitehall."

"I soon received a letter that my father had contracted a 'swamp fever', probably what is known today as yellow fever, and died. Whitehall and all of its operations had been bequeathed to me. Through the use of her agent, I set up operations in England and ran the business as an absentee landlord. I instructed the agent to hire an overseer and establish a contact in the colonies that would keep me informed of the goings on there. All the while I retained ownership and, as the years passed, kept close tabs on it to ensure that it remained a successful business."

"Charlotte Ann and I traveled extensively through Europe for the next one hundred years. We lived in the wine country of France, a mountain chateau in northern Italy at the foot of the Alps, and even spent time in Spain and Portugal. Finally in about 1850 we returned to her home outside London where we remained until I returned to America."

"Then in 1875, while South Carolina remained under Union occupation, my agent in Charleston notified me that Whitehall was about to be lost due to mismanagement and back taxes. I would not allow that to happen. So, through business contacts in Charleston and London, and posing as a wealthy English 'cousin', I purchased Whitehall and all of its assets for the sum of one thousand eight hundred and fifty seven dollars in gold. I have owned it since, allowing it to pass to myself through the proper legal channels about every forty to sixty years."

"I quickly returned to Charleston to reclaim my home. I was a bit dismayed to say the least when I arrived. The graceful house and grounds that I had left behind was in a shambles. I am sure a lot of the distress that I found was the result of neglect during the recent war between the north and the south. The first order of business I undertook was to have the old overseer's house put in order that I might have an appearance of a place to live while repairs were being done."

"I then hired a small army of carpenters, painters, plasterers, paperhangers, and any number of other craftsmen. I set them to task, supervising the work myself during the day and making plans during the night. It took almost all of three years to completely restore the house to the grandeur you see today. Finally I brought in a number of gardeners to remove, replace and replant the surrounding gardens and grounds to be presentable."

"After all of the restoration work was completed I settled in to Whitehall to live the life of the aristocratic gentleman that my father and grandfather had originally intended for me some one hundred twenty five years previously. Shortly thereafter I dispatched a letter to Charlotte Ann in London asking her to join me in Charleston."

"Did Charlotte Ann come to Whitehall to live with you," I asked, eagerly wanting to hear the rest of that story.

"She did not; she remained in England until I finally talked her into coming to America in the middle of the last century, not long after the end of the Second World War. She visited me of course, and together we traveled the country extensively for a few years. She then decided to settle in New York and remains there to this day. During the last sixty years we have spent some of our time together, each of us visiting the other. However she prefers the large northern cities. The climate there is more like that of England than here in Charleston."

"James, may I interrupt for a moment …" I asked uncertainly, "but is Charlotte Ann the 'old friend' that you went to see in New York?"

"Indeed she is … and I had to see her Katelyn … I was so ecstatic at having met you that I had to go and share the great news and tell her all about you."

"Will I get to meet her soon … and more importantly … do you think she will like me?"

"I have no doubt that she will absolutely love you my dear," he answered, "and you will get to meet her … but not until after you have changed. While you don't understand it now, she doesn't feel comfortable in the presence of mortals. But she is planning to be in Charleston … she is at heart a teacher of sorts, and so will assist you with some of the changes that will take place in your life as you become accustomed to immortality."

"The change is going to be difficult for me isn't it," I asked and probably with a touch of fear in my question.

"Actually, it's very simple and easily accomplished," he tried soothing my concerns, "but what will take some getting used to for you, is being a completely new you in a brand new world."

Then I looked up at him with a strong resolve and absolute honesty said, "But I know that as long as I have you there to guide me, I can do it … James, I believe that with you leading me, I can do anything."

"I have no doubt that you can," he smiled at my self-will, "and now you know my story and how I came to be here. But you have no idea how fortunate I was to be here at the same time that you are. I have waited two and a half centuries for you to come along Katelyn, and now … here you are … and I can only hope that you look forward to sharing my life as much as I look forward to sharing yours."

"But," he laughed happily, "it's no longer late, it's almost dawn, and we have talked the night away. I hope that I have at least partially satisfied your curiosity. I am sure there will be more for us to talk about later."

"Yes, there will be," I smiled, "I want to know as much about this new life as I can and hear more about all those other superstitions that don't apply."

"Pretty much all you've heard don't apply," he chuckled, "once I bring you over, and you become acclimated to your new life, you will simply continue to live your life day to day much as you do now. There shall be plenty of time to talk about that later. It will be daylight soon and you should return to school. Please give me a couple of days to begin to make some preparations for the things we are about to do and I will call you then. In the meantime, think about all I have told you tonight, the impact it will have on your life and those around you, before you make a final decision."

"James," I said looking into his eyes, "there's nothing to think about. I've already made my decision, I want to be with you, whatever it takes and that's final. I've not waited two and a half centuries for a man like you, but I have waited my entire life for you."

"Very well, then," he said and taking me in his arms lightly kissed my forehead, "please allow me to give you a gift, a token if you will, of our soon to be shared lives."

He walked over to a small desk, opened one of the drawers, took out an ornate box, and returned to me.

"Remember the card I gave you the first time we met," he started, "and told you to keep it close to you …"

"Yes, and you had written 'Protection and Safe Passage' on the reverse," I smiled in answer, "I call it my 'get out of a speeding ticket free' card and I carry it everywhere I go!"

"That's a good thing, but in reality that card is a silent signal to every creature in my world that you, and whomever you happen to be with, is known, protected by me, and off limits. This is a visible symbol of that same protection, it says that you have now become family and are forever under my protection. I assure you, that due to my standing in the preternatural world, as long as you wear this, nothing that lives in the world around us will dare to harm you."

He opened the box and took out a necklace. It was a solid gold disk, a little over an inch around, hanging from a heavy golden chain. The disk was engraved with a very ornate coat of arms consisting of two standing griffins holding a shield divided into four sections by a cross, topped with a crown, and the name Dubois in a ribbon at the bottom.

"Welcome, my love, to my family," he spoke as he worked the clasp, easily placing it around my neck and straightening it out. Then with a smile he lightly kissed my forehead again, and stepped back to admire it as it lay glittering in the hollow at the base of my throat, "This is a symbol of 'The Gift' I am soon to give you and your new and eternal life that comes with it. Wear this with great pride, because from now on and forever, you are the only one that can remove it and give it back."

He walked with me to the porch and turning back to him, I moved into his arms again, where I seemed to naturally fit like never before. We kissed deeply and passionately, and then looking into my eyes, he softly whispered, "I love you, Katelyn, so very much."

I kissed him back, suddenly surprised at the thrill his words had caused in me, and never wanting to let him go, I considered just staying with him. I looked into his eyes and for the first time said what I had been thinking for a long time, "I love you too, James … and I always will … now and forever!"

Chapter Twenty~Four

After Katelyn had left for the campus I returned to the parlor and extinguished all the candles leaving the room lit only by the early dawn beginning to leak in through the windows. I had much to think about and so returned to my chair. There was a plethora of issues to work through before I could bring Katelyn over. The most immediate concern facing me, one that absolutely had be taken care of before we could go any further, was her roommate Lexi, and how to get her away from Katelyn and out of her life for a couple of years.

I knew that it would be impossible for me to bring Katelyn over while Lexi remained close by … there would be too many evident changes in her that would raise questions. I also knew that it would take at least two years for Katelyn to become completely comfortable in her new life, and after that length of time, any noticeable changes in her would not be so obvious to someone who hadn't seen her in that period of time.

While I sat there thinking about Lexi and what to do about her, I recalled that during her initial visit to Whitehall with Katelyn, she had stated a desire to one day study and teach in Europe … and an idea began to blossom and soon developed into full bloom. Before I could pick up the telephone to follow through on my idea, I felt a now familiar presence fill the room and watched as Katelyn's mother materialized in the center of the room.

"I understand that Katelyn has placed her life and fate in your hands, and has chosen the path of immortality in order to be with you," her soft voice floated through me.

"Yes, Mrs. Corbin, she has made her choice … and I might add, has made me a very happy man in the process," I answered.

"Does my daughter have to die to become like you," she inquired.

"She will take on an immortal nature, her spirit and soul will remain the same … only her physical body will change … becoming immortal, a body that will never grow old or die …."

She stood silently, carefully studying me before continuing thoughtfully, *"Very well, I did say that if she made the choice, I would give you my blessing …"*

"Thank you Mrs. Corbin," I interjected.

"But please understand Mr. Dubois, I am placing my daughter, the most important thing I had in the natural world, into your hands, so I am trusting you to treat her kindly. And now that I know my baby is and will be taken care of forever, I shall go to my rest. I don't fully understand all that is about to happen to her, but I will leave you in peace as I said I would."

Before I could speak, I sensed another, this time very familiar presence, in the room. I was taken aback as Mary Beth materialized beside Katelyn's mom and taking her arm in hers, spoke silently to her as she looked at me, *"I too am giving up the most precious thing I had in that world … come with me Melissa … we shall talk and I will explain all that is about to happen … in both of their lives."*

I watched astonished as the two of them faded away into nothingness and the air in the room returned to normal once again. I pondered what I had just seen and heard, staggered at a world that seemed to be beyond even my own. I returned slowly to my chair and picking up the phone, called an old friend in Berlin, he picked up on the first ring.

"Guten Tag, das ist Professor Wolfgang," he spoke, his deep resonant voice flowing through the phone.

"Gerhardt! You old wolf," I answered in return, "how are you these days …"

"James, my dear and trusted friend … it's such a pleasure to hear from you … it's been a long time."

"Indeed it has … I suppose that life keeps us both busy," I chuckled softly, "are you still howling at the moon and running through the forests?"

"Every chance I get," he laughingly replied, "but I'm afraid I'm beginning to get a bit long in the tooth and gray around the muzzle. After all these years of shifting, it begins to take a toll on the bones and muscles."

"I'm sure you can still run with the best of them," I chuckled.

"The cubs today have no idea," he answered, "but I'm sure you didn't call just to discuss my running and howling habits … what can I do for you my friend?"

"I need a favor Gerhardt … a big one … I have found my mate …"

"That's wonderful news … and it certainly took you long enough," he interjected.

"I realize that, but she was worth every day of the wait … and she's the reason for the call … or more specifically, her roommate, is the reason for the call … they are both seniors here at the College of Charleston and inseparable. Of course I can't bring Katelyn through the change while the roommate is around … so I need Lexi gone … for at least two years."

"And you want to send her to me," he asked.

"Well, yes, but not just to babysit … I think perhaps she can be an asset to you in return …"

"Is she a member of our world," he continued.

"No, she's thoroughly human … and completely ignorant about our world … but she's a History major and has a long standing desire to study and teach in Europe."

"Humm …" he mused, "perhaps she could indeed be useful … how about if I offer her a two year Master's program in European History … and in return she agrees to accept an associate professorship to help offset any supposed costs that would be incurred. I could then turn over some of my undergraduate classes for her to teach and that would free me up to work on my memoirs."

"Your memoirs?"

"Yes, well they would necessarily be a work of fiction you know … all about a young man born in the middle of the nineteenth century, who, when he is a teenage boy, discovers that he was born with a Lycanthrope gene and his subsequent journey to the full understanding of his nature."

"That sounds like a great undertaking … I would like a signed first printing for my library please … and by the way, how old are you now my friend?"

"I'm old enough that I'm afraid the end of my years may be in sight … I'll see a hundred and fifty eight next

April … but of course none of the humans around here know or could imagine that," he chuckled.

"That sounds like the humans on the Board of Regents at the college here, if they only had any idea what my true nature is and how many years I've passed."

"Well, knowing colleges as I do, I suppose that after the initial shock wore off, they would still find a way to justify continuing to accept all the financial assistance you provide," he chuckled.

"I'm sure they could find a way to get past their shock," I laughed and then continued, "I like the idea of the associate professorship for Lexi … and I think she would leap at the opportunity … let's make that happen … suppose you call me tomorrow and give me a total cost, I shall have the funds transferred right away to your account."

"James, my old friend, you wound my feelings … there is no payment due … any debt that would result was paid many years ago … have you forgotten how that both you and Charlotte Ann took me into your respective homes and gave me shelter and protection in the darkest days of the last century when my kind was being hunted all over Germany and the occupied countries to be used for medical experiments …"

"Neither of us did that for payment Gerhardt … we did it to assist and save the life of a friend in need …"

"Exactly my friend … and now you find yourself in need and I shall do all in my power to alleviate that hardship."

"You are more than kind Gerhardt … and if you wish to do this favor then I shall gladly accept your generosity."

"Consider it done James … and if you would like to do something for me in return …"

"Anything you ask," I assured him.

"When the bells toll for me … I would like very much

for you and Charlotte Ann to transport my ashes to the center of the Black Forrest and there scatter them to the winds."

"We shall respect your wishes my friend," I answered.

"Very well ... and thank you ... now, call me when the young girl is ready to travel ... and you may rest assured that she will be under my complete protection while she is here."

"Thank you so much Gerhardt," I said bringing the conversation to a close, "I shall call you sometime in the next day or two with her schedule."

I touched the end button on the phone and sat back to relax, the first and largest of my issues taken care of for now.

The following morning I placed a call to the Board of Regents to inquire about the possibility of paying out Lexi's remaining classes in order that she could graduate now and make the move to Germany. The quicker she could depart, the sooner I could bring Katelyn over and she and I could begin our lives together. The secretary answered the call and when I had identified myself she immediately transferred me through to the president of the board.

"Good morning Mr. Dubois, this is Robert, how can I help you today," he asked picking up his phone.

"Good morning Robert," I answered, "I hope you are in good health ... I'm actually calling about a possible favor from the school."

"You and your family's foundation have been more than generous to the school in the past ... I shall try to do whatever is within my power ... what do you have in mind?"

"I'm interested in a student ... a senior, Alexis

Gordon," I continued.

"Give me a moment to pull up her records," he replied. I heard him begin typing on his keyboard and waited patiently for a couple of minutes while he brought up Lexi's dossier before continuing, "Yes, I have her information here … what is your interest in her and what would you like to know."

"I have recently become romantically involved with her roommate …"

"Oh yes, that would be Miss Corbin … I believe she is an art major … just transferred in to the school at the beginning of the semester from The Art Institute of Atlanta … a very intelligent young lady," he interjected.

"Yes, that's her," I answered proudly, "but the reason for my interest in Lexi is that she has a deeply held desire to attend school in Europe and teach in one of the universities, which is where I come into the picture. I was speaking to a colleague last evening in Berlin and he has to fill a position for a new two year Master's program in European history that includes an associate professorship. I immediately thought of Lexi for the position."

"That certainly sounds like a wonderful opportunity for her … she definitely has the grades for such a position and title," he commented, "would you like a letter of recommendation from the school for her?"

"That would be very nice of you … but you see the issue is that the position requires her to already have a Bachelor's Degree and is an immediate opening, classes begin in four weeks. I understand that Lexi doesn't graduate until the end of the summer session. I'm wondering if perhaps I could make an anonymous donation to buy out her remaining classes in order for her to take her degree now and be accepted into the program."

"Where exactly is this position," he asked curiously.

"It's in the History Department of the Humboldt University of Berlin … the head of the department, Dr. Gerhardt Wolfgang, is an old friend and will be her mentor."

"Humboldt is indeed a very prestigious university … and you say that Miss Gordon is be an associate professor?"

"She will be teaching some undergraduate classes in order to allow Dr. Wolfgang some time off for writing his memoirs," I said.

"Hummm … well according to her transcripts she has had four semesters of German so it appears that would come in handy," he chuckled.

"How many more hours does she need to graduate and what kind of donation would be required," I asked straightforwardly.

"Her transcripts show that she already has a total of a hundred and twenty-seven hours and since we only require a hundred and twenty-two hours, it doesn't appear that a donation will be needed in this case … you're going to get off light this time," he laughed.

"That's wonderful news Robert, now, how can we make this happen," I asked.

"It's a simple issue … I will submit a letter to the Registrar instructing them to immediately issue her degree, with the stipulation that it's only if she accepts the position in Berlin … then when graduation comes we will call her name at the ceremony and explain that she is absent due to having accepted an associate professorship at the University of Berlin and has already begun her duties there."

"That sounds exactly like what I wanted to happen … I think she will be a huge success for this program … thank you so much for your assistance … and if there's ever any need at the school, please don't hesitate to ask."

"The Dubois family has been a supportive blessing to this school for almost one hundred and fifty years … this is really the least we can do in return," he answered.

"Thank you once again Robert … and I can assure you the school has likewise been an asset to the Dubois family. I hope that you have a pleasant day, I'm sure that we shall speak again soon," I ended the call and smiled at his reference to the generosity of the 'Dubois Family' to the school … if only he knew that I was the family.

Chapter Twenty~Five

There was just a hint of the coming sunrise when I left Whitehall in the early morning hours. The skies were still dark gray but quickly turned to a spreading reddish dawn as the morning sun began to rise out of the Atlantic. Again, I didn't really see the road so much as let my instincts take over and guide me to my destination. Besides, by this time I could have found my way to and from Whitehall in complete darkness.

It usually takes about an hour to drive to or from Whitehall but I had so much going on in my head that my trip seemed over almost before it started. The events of yesterday afternoon, James' revelations to me, and then the story of his own life during the night all fought for their own attention.

When I walked into our room Lexi was getting dressed to go out for the morning. She looked at me, smiled big and said, "Good Morning! Did you spend the night at Whitehall again?"

"Yeah," I said smiling at her, "and I am so tired, we didn't sleep all night."

"Whoaaa …" she laughed, "this is getting big isn't it!"

"Oh … no, I didn't mean it that way," I blushed and giggled, "we actually just sat and talked all night … although, your idea would have made for a wonderful night too."

"Well, that can be fun too … the talking … I mean … so what did you two lovebirds talk about for so long?"

"You wouldn't believe me if I told you," I thought to myself.

"Ah, you know, just usual stuff, his life, where he has been, what he's done and the things he's seen," I answered, being very careful that I didn't accidentally allow even the smallest hint of our real conversation to slip out.

"We talked some about me, my parents, and how their deaths have changed my life so much. I suppose you could call it a night of 'getting to know each other better' stuff."

"Hey, at least you were together though, and having a real conversation, that goes a long way," she said, "and I'm going to assume that nobody got scared off by the seriousness of the whole thing?"

"I was the one that I was worried about scaring off," I laughed, "but, if anything I think in reality we became closer, especially now that I actually know so much more about him. I think there is a real connection between us … one that is going to get a lot stronger and last for a long, long time."

She took a seat on her bed while she waited for me to change clothes for breakfast, and suddenly said, "Wow! Somebody got a new necklace! It looks pretty … can I see it?"

I leaned over and she reached out and looking closer at it, gently took it in her hand, and hefted the weight of the gold.

"Wow, it's heavy … and pretty, too! That's so cool, what is it," she asked as she turned it over in her fingers.

"It's James' family crest, he gave it to me and asked that I wear it," I answered with a huge smile, "because he wanted everyone to know that I am his."

"Oh Katelyn, that sounds so romantic," she grinned big and added, "so is it … like … kind of an engagement ring?"

"I think it's more of a promise of good things to come," I answered with my own happy smile.

"That sounds even better," she smiled as she bounced up from the bed, "I'm so happy for you … c'mon now, let's go get some breakfast … I want to hear all about it!"

I gently rubbed the gold medallion between my fingers, kissed it, smiled and followed her out of the room. The rest of the morning flew by in a daze. I wondered how James was going to handle all the things that had to be done if I was to become a … like him. I still couldn't bring myself to say 'vampire'. I could say it about him, almost easily now, but when it came to me there was a … well, it just didn't feel right, it didn't fit, yet. But, when I allowed myself a couple of minutes here and there to really contemplate it, I was intrigued. I actually found myself looking forward to being changed and able to be with James forever. I wondered what it would be like to see and understand the world around me with an entirely new outlook.

After breakfast and a quick shopping trip to the mall, Lexi and I grabbed a late lunch in the Student Union and I told her I was going back to the room and go to bed. I was so wiped out from last night that I just had to sleep.

"That works," she said, "I have a big test tomorrow, so I'll sit up and study while you sleep."

The next day went pretty much the same except during our lunch break I got a call from James.

"Katelyn, good day," he started, "how are you today?"

"Not bad, I slept really good … and really long, last night … probably because somebody I know kept me up all night the night before … but I'm pretty much rested now. How are you today … I'll bet you haven't slept a wink without me, have you?"

"Very good, thank you … although I feel like I haven't slept in a couple of hundred years," he replied drily, "Nevertheless, do you think it possible that you and Lexi could come out to Whitehall this afternoon when you finish classes?"

""I'm sure we could force ourselves to do that," I answered happily, "but is everything alright?"

"Everything is perfect," he answered, "I have an opportunity that I think Lexi will be very pleased to hear about … you shall see when you get here. I am merely taking care of one of the issues we discussed in order that you and I are able to move forward with our lives."

"Then we'll see you this afternoon as soon as classes are over. I love you, James, good bye for now."

"And I you," he answered in his so proper English, "good bye for now."

I told Lexi that James had called and asked if we could come out after classes. She seemed really excited about the trip.

"I'm happy just to get off campus for a while," she said, "I've been stuck here for the last three days having to study and I'm ready for a little break! What do you think he has in mind?"

"I have no idea," I answered truthfully, "he just said that he had something to tell us. Knowing him, whatever it is, I'm sure it'll be good."

When we arrived at Whitehall, James met me with a hug and I gave him a little kiss on the cheek. He quickly invited us in and seemed to be almost beside himself with happiness.

"Lexi, it's such a pleasure to see you again!"

"Hi James, it's good to be back out again, thank you for inviting me to come along … I just love it here."

"I hope you have been well …" he smiled and continued, "are your studies going well?"

"I'm working toward graduation as quickly as I can," she chuckled.

"I'm sure it'll be here before you know it," he grinned, "do you have any teaching positions lined up for the fall yet?"

"Unfortunately, not yet … but it isn't because I haven't been sending out resumes," she chuckled.

"Yeah, that's the truth if ever there was any," I grinned, "she sits up late almost every night, filling out applications and attaching resumes. She usually has a stack of at least ten each morning to drop in the mail before we go out to class."

"I feel certain the perfect position for you will soon come along when you are least expecting it," he chuckled again, "please, let's all go to the veranda and have a glass of wine. I have some potentially wonderful news to share."

I looked wonderingly at him, trying to figure just exactly where this was going when I decided I would try something.

"James," I spoke silently, *"can you hear me?"*

"Of course I can," I immediately heard his soft reply float through my mind. I looked and saw that he was smiling at me while we walked.

"What are you doing," I continued to ask silently.

"I'm about to take care of one of our issues and at the same time do something very good for Lexi … just watch my love … you are about to see your best friend's lifelong dream come true, and trust me, I believe you will like this as much as she will."

We sat down at the little round table and he poured a glass of wine for everyone and lifting his glass in a toast, said, "A toast to the fulfillment of dreams!"

"Hear, hear," we both answered with girlish laughs, and sipping the delicious red wine, sat back to relax.

"Wow, James, this is really good wine," Lexi commented as she took a second sip.

"And I'll bet it's an old vintage too," I nodded to her and then to James added, "is this …"

"Yes, it is … you seemed to like it the other day, so I brought another bottle up," he began, then turning to Lexi added, "it's a French Claret, vined in the Bordeaux region of France, in 1764 by Thomas Barton."

"Mmmm … I've never had Claret," Lexi commented taking another sip, then sputtered, "No … wait … did I hear you correctly … did you say it's a *SEVENTEEN* sixty-four vintage … as in … the French and Indian War 1764?"

"Yes … that's the one …" he smiled innocently, "do you like it?"

"Like it … I LOVE it," she exclaimed, "you must really have some special news to serve this kind of wine."

"I would say that what I'm about to share is indeed something very special … I believe we spoke of you being a historian with an interest in European history, so as such, I'm curious, do you speak German, and if so, how good is it?"

"It's passable, I suppose," she slowly answered, "it's been a while since I've had any classes or the opportunity to use it so I guess it wouldn't hurt to brush up on it a little."

"You may indeed get the chance to do just that. You see, an opportunity has just come to my attention that I believe will interest you greatly … and you won't have to send out yet another resume. I seem to recall you had said you would like to go to Europe to study after finishing school."

"I did," she answered, "I don't know why, but that has been something I've always wanted to do … but at this point, I may have to wait a year or two and save some more money. I'm just not real sure if my finances are going to be there at graduation to allow me to pursue that or not."

"I don't think you shall have to be concerned about that issue any longer either," he looked over the top of his wine glass at her, "you see, I received an inquiry early last evening from a very good friend at the Humboldt University of Berlin … Professor Gerhardt Wolfgang … and it seems that he is seeking a talented young historian to come to Berlin …"

"Wolfgang …" I questioned silently, *"really … I don't suppose he's a …"*

"Yes, as a matter of fact, he is," he smiled at me.

I was unable to restrain myself and abruptly laughed out loud, then quickly lifting my glass, took a huge swallow to attempt to control the laughter.

"Katelyn … what's so funny," Lexi asked innocently.

"Oh … I guess the professor's name just caught me off guard … Wolfgang … it's just so … I don't know … so

German," I exclaimed, trying to recompose myself.

"Well, yeah … but you do realize that Berlin *is* in Germany … besides, that's a good strong German name … what would you expect … O'Rourke maybe," Lexi chuckled.

"Welcome to your soon to be new world," James spoke silently to me, *"where most things are hidden in plain sight!"*

"Thanks for the warning … I'll try to keep that in mind," I answered.

"Here's what this is all about Lexi," he continued as if nothing had passed between us, "The history department has instituted a new Master's program in European History. It is to be a two year course of study and includes taking an adjunct professorship to help offset the cost of the program. In return the university will provide that talented young historian with room, board, and books, as well as a monthly stipend of fifteen hundred dollars for personal spending. Now, all that remains is for me to assist Professor Wolfgang in finding someone to meet that criteria …"

I quickly took an additional large swallow of wine, successfully smothering another burst of laughter.

"And so Lexi, since you are in the history department, I thought perhaps you might know of a talented young historian that might be interested in such an opportunity," he finished, looking at Lexi with a wry smile.

"Humm … let me think for just a moment … uhh, you did say the Humboldt University, right … the same Humboldt that sits along the Spree River?"

"Yes, that's the one," he played along.

"Well, in that case," she answered smiling excitedly, "I do believe I know just such a person … and yes, I think she would be more than interested in that kind of an opportunity! But James, seriously … do you really think I could stand a chance at being accepted into the program?"

"James, you are so wonderful!" I said, still using my new

found way to communicate.

"Lexi, I assure you, the position is yours for the asking. I only have to make a confirming call to Berlin. However, there is one other small issue."

"Yeahhh," she sighed, "there always is … isn't there?"

"But all things considered, this might not be a bad issue," he continued as Lexi smiled again, "the German class schedule is somewhat different to the American system so the position is an immediate one … new classes begin in four weeks … and it requires an undergraduate degree."

I saw her face immediately fall with disappointment as she thought her hopes were about to be dashed.

"Please don't look downcast just yet, my little friend … you see, thinking that you might be interested, and also knowing that you are not scheduled to graduate until the end of summer, I have taken the liberty of placing a call to the Board of Regents at the college. I have discussed the matter and told them of your desires and this unexpected opportunity. It seems that you have already garnered more than enough credit hours to graduate. So they have tentatively agreed, provided you accept the position, to immediately grant your degree, in order that you fully meet the requirements of the program, they will then call your name at graduation, explaining your absence as being due to the new position," he finished his offer with a sip of wine and a huge smile looking directly at her.

"Oh, James that's such absolutely wonderful news," she laughed joyously, "I'm so stunned I don't actually know what to say! This has been my lifelong dream … a dream that I've held onto for so long … wishing and hoping for it … and now it's suddenly a reality … and served up on a silver platter … I think I'm going to cry!"

"I suppose that means you'll accept," he smiled knowingly at her.

"Oh, yes! Yes! Yes! Yes! Yes! A thousand times Yes! Thank you so very much James," she laughed as tears of happiness began flowing down her face.

"You've just made me as happy as you have her," I spoke silently looking across the table, *"if that's even possible!"*

He turned those beautiful green eyes toward me, winked and with a smile silently replied, *"I did this because she is such a special and devoted friend to you ... and it's for you as much as it is for her."*

"So then Lexi," he continued, turning his gaze back to her, "do you think you will be able to depart in the next two weeks, or three at the latest, for Berlin?"

"Wow! That is so soon and there's so much to do ... but I'm sure I can get everything done. Katelyn, can you help me pack? James, what do I need to take," she asked now laughing excitedly, the tears still rolling down her face.

"Just your personal things," he answered still smiling, "everything else you will need will be in your apartment. Remember, you are moving around the world not across town!"

"Oh, James, thank you again so much for thinking of me! I still can't believe this is happening for me ... there's so much to do to get ready to leave ... and I have to call my parents and tell them the great news! Katelyn, please, can we go now?"

"Not yet," I laughed in answer, "not until you finish that wine ... you can't let half a glass of that be wasted!"

Lexi picked up the glass and drained it in one gulp, then looking at me said, "Now ... it's finished ... com'on ... let's go!"

She stood up quickly and staggered back a step, taking hold of the back of the chair and said, "Woahhh ... good wine ... *very* good wine!"

I chuckled at her and asked, "You want some help?"

"Nah … I think I'm all good now," she responded with a silly giggle, "I just wasn't expecting such a rush!"

"Yeah, well take my arm anyway," I insisted still chuckling, threading my arm through Lexi's. We walked through the house and back to the front porch where Lexi turned and wrapped her arms around James in a huge hug. He took her in his arms and held her close for a moment before breaking the hug.

"Oh, James, thank you once again so much for thinking of me," she exclaimed, looking up into his eyes, "You've just made me the happiest girl in the world!"

"I hope that you make of your dream everything you've always wanted," he smiled, and as Lexi literally bounced down the steps, called behind her, "I'll call you in a couple of days with the itinerary for your flight."

I turned and as I hugged him spoke softly into his ear, "I love you so much and thank you for giving my friend her dream!" And I kissed him quickly before turning to follow Lexi down the steps and to the car.

Chapter Twenty~Six

Lexi called her parents as soon as we left Whitehall ... she was so excited she just couldn't wait until we got back to school. They were just thrilled that she was going to get the chance to fulfill her dream of studying in Europe. I helped her get started packing but since she was really just taking clothes, it didn't take long to finish. The next few days seemed to literally fly away as she began making all the final preparations for her move to Germany.

Lexi and I spent most of the following days together although she did take the first several days to go to Savannah to see her parents and bid them goodbye. It would after all, be two years at least before she saw them again. While Lexi was in Savannah, I began making Whitehall my home, and of course James was obviously proud when I began referring to it as my home. We both looked forward to the day that it would become my permanent home. I have to admit, I amazed myself with the daily planning, dividing my time, almost to perfection, between Whitehall and aunt Chele's house in Summerville. I would leave Whitehall and drive into classes in the morning, visiting aunt Chele and uncle John in the afternoon after classes, and then return once again to Whitehall in the evening to spend the nights with James. Then when Lexi returned, I moved back into our dorm so that we could be as close to each other as possible until she departed.

A day or two before Lexi was scheduled to depart James called me in order to give Lexi the itinerary for the upcoming flight.

"Hello my love …" he said when I answered my phone.

"And good afternoon to you too," I answered, "how are you today?"

"I'm as good as always … still not sleeping much but, it goes with the territory," he chuckled, then added, "Will you put us on speaker please? I have the details for Lexi's flight."

"Hi Lexi, how are you … excited yet," he asked with a chuckle.

"It's a little late for that," she giggled, "I've been excited for nearly a week!"

"Then allow me to add to your excitement … I have scheduled your flight … it seems that one of my investment interests has leased a jet to a businessman in France. Since it was scheduled to leave the same day as you, I thought perhaps you would enjoy it more than a regular commercial flight. You will depart early that morning, and fly direct to Templehof airport."

"Really," she laughed, "a private jet … this just gets

better and better!"

"Oh, only the best for you," he chuckled and then continued, "When you arrive, Professor Wolfgang will meet you with a car and take you on to the University for an initial tour of the grounds and sign you in for classes. He and I talked again last night and presently it appears that you will attend three classes for your Masters and twice weekly you'll teach two undergraduate classes."

I interrupted with a laugh, "So does this mean we have to call you 'Professor Gordon' now?"

"I suppose I can let you continue to call me Lexi," she joined in my laughter.

"And, here's another little detail for you Lexi," James spoke up, "Since this will be a shuttle flight and you'll be the only passenger on board that means you can take extra baggage if you would like. The flight is supposed to take a little over nine hours so the crew will serve you breakfast just after you're airborne, then a final meal and drinks a couple of hours before you land. You'll find it's a very comfortable plane, there's even an en-suite bedroom with a shower located at the rear of the aircraft, allowing you to be fully rested and refreshed when you arrive in Berlin."

"Do you really think I could ever sleep on that flight," she laughed happily, "although the shower does sound like a pretty good idea!"

"Whatever you wish Lexi, I want you to be comfortable and have an enjoyable flight," he replied.

"James, how can I ever thank you for all the nice things you've done for me? This is literally my life's dream, and it's all happening because of you! A 'Thank you' just doesn't seem like enough!"

"Just be successful in your endeavors Lexi ... oh, and reserve me a signed copy of the first book you publish, that will be my thanks," he answered with a small chuckle.

"Oh and Katelyn," he continued, returning the conversation to me, "I'm sure that the two of you are planning to spend your final days together. So I have transferred a couple thousand dollars to your college account for your use … and don't hesitate to ask if you need more. Please go anywhere and do anything you wish and don't be concerned about cost."

"Hummm … we have six more days until Lexi leaves," I began, "that should be more than enough time for us to go down to Orlando and visit Disney World …"

"Yeah … let's go to mouse land," Lexi exclaimed happily.

"If that's what the two of you wish to do, then go and do it," he chuckled, "I want both of you to have fun together and enjoy yourselves. When you return to Charleston, I have made arrangements for both of you to have a special going away dinner at Blossom the evening before Lexi's flight leaves. Please go and have anything you wish, including dessert and drinks, just sign the bill before you leave and I shall handle payment and the tip."

"James, you're so wonderful, thank you so much … for both of us. I can't wait to see you again. I love you so much," I said finishing the conversation and ending the call.

Finally, and sadly, the morning came for Lexi to leave and I drove her to the executive airport on Johns' Island. We were both excited but brokenhearted at the same time. She checked in at the business counter like James had told her and found she was already cleared through Customs. The attendant asked me if I would like to accompany her to the hanger where the aircraft was parked. We both walked out together and there, sitting in the hanger, was not just some business jet, but an Airbus, a huge, beautiful, blue and white Airbus.

We hugged and cried, and hugged some more. Then she boarded the plane and it was rolled out. I stood there in the hanger door, tears rolling down my face as the big jet taxied out and took off. I continued watching as it climbed out and disappeared over the Atlantic … taking my friend to her dream.

After leaving the airport, I drove back to Whitehall, still sad but so happy for Lexi at the same time. I ran into James' arms as the tears started again. He stood there, holding me and petting me, while I cried. I knew it was just temporary but I still felt like I had lost my best friend.

"Katelyn, you will get to see her again, darling, it's not forever, I promise two years won't be long. Soon time or distance will hold no constraints upon you. Remember you can still talk to her while she's there … the last time I checked they did have telephone service in Europe," he smiled trying to lighten the moment for me, "and then when she comes back, the two of you can travel anywhere in the world you wish and have a huge homecoming celebration together."

"James, thank you again so much for what you're doing. Lexi is so happy right now! I wish you could have seen her face when she got on that airplane! I don't understand how you did it, but you've given her the dream that she's wished for and talked to me about almost since we met. I can't begin to imagine what it cost you, but I really appreciate it."

"Katelyn, she's your special friend and it was her dream. Besides, it's just money, and it's not really worth anything unless you're spending it … and I just happen to prefer spending it for a beautiful woman like you," he said with a grin.

"But it had to be so much," I began.

"Actually, according to Professor Wolfgang, the debt was paid for many years in the past. Darling, even if it had cost anything, you must keep in mind that I was born into a very wealthy colonial family to begin with and since then I have had almost three hundred years as an immortal to accumulate even more wealth. I have to admit that the principle of compounded interest is the best accounting tool ever devised … especially when you don't have to touch the account for a century or more at a time. And before long, you too shall begin to amass your own share of wealth as well."

"However, money and finances just isn't important right now," he continued as he held me, "but this is. Your aunt will be calling you soon to tell you about a job offer your uncle has received from an old college roommate. He'll receive a contract for five years that will more than double his salary. They will have to relocate to Portland but all the expenses will be paid by the new company. I've also arranged for a blind purchase of their home, far above market value, as soon as it's listed. Now, will you please try to act surprised when she calls?"

I looked up at him, shocked at what he had just said, "Five years is such a long time," I began, and then thinking more about it added, "that means I'll be … twenty-six before I can even think about seeing them again … that means I'll be almost thirty … and James you know thirty is not a good number for girls."

"Katelyn, I understand that you are still a mortal and as such still think like one," he smiled patiently at me, "but darling you must remember that whether you see them in five years or fifteen years you will be twenty one … just like you are now. Five years is not an extremely long time but it should be a sufficient time before you chance seeing them again. That doesn't mean that you can't still talk to them on the phone or e-mail them, you just can't see them for a while because you are about to have some unexplainable changes take place in you. There needs to be a little time and distance between now and when they see you again so those changes are not as obvious and more easily explained. No one that is close to you needs to notice any sudden changes in appearance that would lead to undue questions."

I stayed at Whitehall with James all afternoon. Later that evening we retired to what had become our bedroom … where I slept and he held me while I did. I spent the evening cuddling next to him in our big bed, my arm and one of my legs draped casually across him. I comfortably drifted in and out of sleep gladly letting him pet me, soothing away my hurt, as he slowly and gently rubbed my bare back and shoulders.

"James," I whispered as I lay cuddled against him, enjoying the smooth coolness of his body, "can I ask you a probably very personal question?"

"You know that I will answer anything you want to know," he answered softly.

"All the time we have spent together," I started slowly, "why have I never seen your … you know … your teeth?"

He grinned big at me showing his teeth and chuckled, "See, they're just teeth … straight and white … the same as yours!"

"That's not what I meant and you know it," I answered trying not to laugh.

"The ones you are referring to are called fangs, darling," he softly laughed, "and it's just something that an immortal doesn't show off. Since their only real purpose is making it possible to feed, it would be a very grave social faux pas to allow them to show. It would be the equivalent of a human man … mmm … how shall I say this … having a visible erection in public."

"Okay, then …" I half choked, half snorted and lost my battle at trying not to laugh at his completely honest but unexpected explanation, "I guess you cleared that right up for me!"

After several minutes of thinking about what he had just explained I decided to keep exploring and ask something else … something extreme. I drew in a deep breath and slowly exhaled before I continued.

"James," I began slowly, "what is it like … for you … when you are with me … you know … my blood … my heartbeat … I know that you can smell it and hear it."

He looked at me with a twinkle in his eyes, lightly kissed my lips, grinned mischievously, and pulling me closer against him so that his lips gently touched my ear, softly whispered, "Katelyn, the scent of your blood and the sound of your heartbeat makes my fangs extend."

This time I giggle-snorted and almost choked laughing at his completely honest and shameless answer.

"Well, thank you … I'm glad that I have that effect on you in more ways than one," I answered still giggling and cuddling closer to him, "but, seriously, is it really difficult for you to be around me?"

He lay there silently for another moment before slowly beginning, "Katelyn, you have been a temptation for me since the first moment I laid eyes on you. Your blood is the most succulent human blood I have ever smelled … it is a distinctive mixture of independence, adventure, and an exceptional style of inner strength that reveals your true character to me. It smells like the very finest vintage wine … crisp, clean and inviting …"

"Better even that your 1764 Claret," I grinned back.

"Not even a comparison," he answered, "but regardless of how alluring it may be, I determined from our first meeting, that I would never take it without your explicit permission."

"Thank you for making that choice … but you know I would give you anything you wanted or asked for," I answered him softly, "and that includes my blood … but would you tell me what it would be like … if you fed from me … what would it feel like?"

"It would very likely be the most enjoyable, probably the most pleasurable feeling I have ever experienced," he spoke softly, "the taste of your blood would be like …"

"Uhh … I wasn't talking about *you*," I commented softly, "I meant *me* … what would the experience be like for me … you know … if you fed from me?"

"Katelyn, you are certainly the inquisitive one," he smiled and kissed my forehead lightly, "you remember the satisfaction you had the first night we shared a bed together …"

"Uh, yeah," I softly laughed, "that's not exactly something I'm likely to *ever* forget!"

"It would be better than that," he said softly, slowly brushing his fingers through my hair, "so much better … I could fill your mind with thoughts and pictures as I fed, making it so extremely pleasurable for you … I could take you to orgasm after orgasm with just my mind as I drank from you."

"Ummm … that sounds pretty good," I murmured, and cuddled a little closer, starting to get all tingly at that thought.

"James …" I purred softly at him, lifting myself up and looking into his eyes.

"No, Katelyn, I won't," he quickly said, knowing where I was headed with that thought.

"But, James, why not," I asked, hurt, "I want you to … I love you and I want to please you … to satisfy you, just like you satisfy me, in every way possible … besides I want to experience what it feels like."

"Katelyn, darling, it's a once in a lifetime experience that you shall have soon enough," he began in a soft tone, "and then we shall have all of eternity to please and satisfy each other. Regardless of how tempting your blood is to me, I am going to bring you over soon, and I do not feel that it would be proper for me to feed from you before you change. After you have changed, you and I shall feed from each other as part of our becoming mates, and I can assure you, when we do, it will be an especially pleasurable experience, and well worth the wait … for both of us."

"Well I suppose if that's how you feel," I playfully huffed, but cuddled back against his side, knowing there was no point in arguing any further. I began casually rubbing his chest and stomach, my fingers slowly exploring his body as we continued whispering softly to each other. I began to feel waves of peace and sleep cover me and knew that my eyes were growing heavy. Then just before I drifted off to sleep, I mentally reflected slowly on the day …

"I purposely wore my cutest, sexiest panties today just special for him … and now I'm about to go to sleep … still wearing them …"

"I shall be more than happy to remove them for you my love … in the morning, after you have slept and rested," I heard his reply float gently through my sleep clouded mind.

I gave a satisfied moan and allowed my body to relax comfortably against his side. I curled closer into him, and now, happily contented, knowing that he would hold me for as long as I slept, drifted comfortably off into my dreams.

I slowly opened my eyes early the next morning just before dawn and looked right into James' beautiful green eyes, shimmering brightly with the second life I was now so used to seeing. I smiled and snuggled sleepily against him for a few more moments, my free hand drowsily stroking his chest. Finally, coming fully awake, and opening my eyes, I smiled instinctively at him.

"Have you been watching me sleep again," I dreamily asked.

"I have," he answered softly, lightly kissing my forehead, "for most of the night in fact. I've said before that you sleep so beautifully and I could watch you forever … even if it's a treat that I shall not be able to enjoy for much longer."

He smiled and leaned in to properly kiss me and I quickly turned my head away and mumbled with clenched teeth, "Nu-huh … morning breath … remember?"

"Katelyn, darling, how often have you woken up beside me," he asked, kissing my temple again, this time just at the hairline, "I promise, each and every one of those times, I have found that nothing about you is offensive to me … even that foul stench you call morning breath."

"James … that's terrible … turn me loose and let me out of this bed … I'm going to brush my teeth and take a shower … I'll be back in a few minutes," I exclaimed, rolling out of bed, and hurriedly dashing for the bathroom. I raised my hand behind me, playfully flipping him a bird as I did.

"That's such a nicely manicured nail … shall I take your message to be a promise of good things to come," he laughed at me, adding, "and if it makes you feel better, you won't have 'morning breath' as you call it, after you change."

"Well, that's certainly another positive to look forward to," I laughed, disappearing into the bathroom.

When I had finished brushing my teeth, I leaned out of the bathroom door and seductively whispered to him, "Now … my breath is all nice and fresh and that 'foul stench' as you called it is gone … and it's time for a special treat … come join me for a morning shower … we can both get clean and fresh together … and I'll give you that morning kiss you wanted …"

I led him by the hand into the bathroom and turning on the shower, waiting for the water to get hot, I turned back, wrapped my arms around him, and kissed him deeply and passionately, "See, just like I promised … all nice and fresh!"

We stepped into the shower together, and when I reached for the soap and he covered my hand with his … "Allow me …" he smiled and taking my body wash and luffa sponge he began to bathe me.

I relaxed against him, enjoying the sensation of his hands on every part of my body, luxuriating in his slow, sexy massage of my neck and shoulders, across and down my back to the tops of my legs. Then wrapping his arms around me, pulling me close against him, he slowly continued with my arms, hands and each of my fingers … finally he moved to my tummy and sides, my legs and all the way to my feet and toes … nobody had ever bathed me like this … when he had completed his soapy massage I felt so clean and fresh. He bathed me from my head to my feet and it was the most erotic and sensual thing I had ever experienced … it was almost as good as the sex we had enjoyed last night … not quiet, but only because it was missing the orgasms. Which I was certain would be coming soon when I slid my body against his, quickly discovering that I wasn't the only one that was turned on by our sexy shower. I turned and wrapped my arms tightly around him, the hot water still cascading over us, our slick, soapy bodies sliding against each other and kissed him once again.

I reached between us, and gently stroking him with my hand whispered against his ear, "Oh my God James … take me … take me now … I can't wait any longer …"

He easily slid into me, pressing me against the shower wall … and I was ripped by an almost instantaneous orgasm. I wrapped my arms around his neck and he held me close, filling me, as I was wracked over and over with the most colossal orgasm. The more he thrust into me the greater the orgasm became … rolling through me like waves crashing on the beach. Finally, when he couldn't hold back any longer, he groaned, pulled me as tight against him as possible and emptied himself into me.

When we stepped out of the shower he took a soft towel and began to dry me off, carefully patting and rubbing every part of my body with it. Then taking my hand in his again he led me back to our bedroom, quickly settling once again into bed. I straddled his stomach, and leaning forward, my hair covering our faces like a damp curtain, looked into his eyes and smiled happily. I kissed him deeply and passionately, happily noting how quickly his arousal responded to my playful attentions.

"Mmmm …" I whispered against his lips, wriggling around on his stomach, "I vaguely recall you promising to remove my 'cutest, sexiest panties' for me this morning … so it seems we both have promises to fulfill … and since age comes before beauty, you first!"

He wrapped his arms around me and, holding me tightly against his chest, sat up, playfully kissed my lips and leaning me back on the bed between his legs, slowly and gently slid my panties down my legs … then lifting me back up, laid back on the bed returning me to my original position straddling his stomach and lying on his chest.

"Mmmm … you did good," I whispered once again against his lips, "that makes it my turn … and it feels like you're more than ready for the promise I gave you, too!"

We were playfully amorous for the next two hours, making love until we were both contentedly happy. Afterwards, lying in each other's arms, softly talking as I cuddled close in his arms, smiling at the enjoyment I had had today I lightly kissed him and whispered, "I wish I could stay right here, wrapped in your arms all day … but I know I have to leave before long …" I slowly began disentangling myself from him, and getting up went to the closet, took out my black pajamas and robe and began putting them on.

"While you get ready, I shall go down and prepare some coffee for you," he smiled as he lightly kissed my cheek, "would you like a French Press this morning?"

"That would be marvelous," I answered stepping back into the bathroom to dry and brush my hair. I joined James on the rear veranda when I had finished my hair and we sat together in the early morning sun while I drank coffee until it was time for me to return to campus.

"You know something," I commented quietly while I slowly sipped the creamy hot liquid, "after I change, I'm going to miss being able to have my hot coffee in the morning."

"You don't have to miss it," he answered softly, "you can still have coffee then, savor it as often as you wish, it will still taste the same … in fact, with your heightened senses, the flavor of it will be greatly enhanced."

"Humm … you think maybe I can change before the next cup," I chuckled, and reaching out for his hand, we settled back into a comfortable silence until time for me to get dressed and ready to leave. We walked together to the front of the house where, delaying leaving as long as possible, we shared one final long, passionate kiss.

"I don't understand everything that is about to happen to me and in my life," I said as we stood there together, "but I do understand that I can't wait until we are together all the time and I never have to leave you again."

"It will be soon my dear, you are at the place that you are almost ready for the change, and I too look forward to not having to be separated from you again either. I shall see you later this afternoon … until then, Katelyn, I love you my darling, stay safe."

Chapter Twenty~Seven

The next morning, Aunt 'Chele called me and was so excited. She told me all about the letter and job offer that Uncle John had received from his college roommate. I told her I was so happy for them and hoped they liked their new home and job.

"You and Uncle John have been so good to me since mom and dad died. You've opened your hearts and home to me, giving me a home and loving me when I thought my world was ending. Now, it looks like something good is coming to you in return. I just know you'll enjoy Oregon," I said as we finished our call.

Now that my family was taken care of I could look unhindered to my future. I continued sitting at the little desk in my room, looking around the empty space that now seemed so small and silent since Lexi had moved out, and was flooded with memories and emotions. I thought back to the day I moved in, the day that we began building a friendship that neither of us could have imagined. In the course of just a few weeks, we were no longer just a couple of college girls sharing a dorm room, instead, our lives had knit together, forming an almost blood kin relationship.

We became the sister that neither of us had ever had and often times we laughed and cried together, sharing our hopes and dreams. It was the one place we could be completely open and honest with each other, holding back no secrets … until the one came along that I had no choice about withholding from her. I glanced around once again and realized that what had been our private little world, was now just a cold and silent dorm room.

I recalled all the good times she and I had had in this little room. We had bonded here, laughing, crying and scheming together … our hearts and souls meshing together until we truly became sisters. For once in my life it seemed that all of the memories, at least of this place, were good ones. I cried silently as the tears ran down my face. So much was happening in my life so quickly now, I had a difficult time keeping up with it all. My mortal life, one that I knew, understood, and was comfortable with, was about to end, and another life, one that was immortal, one that I did not yet fully understand, was about to take its place. So with a final look around at what had been home for the last several months, I decided it was time for me to take the next step on my path to becoming an immortal.

I needed to see James again, to be with him, and ask more questions regarding my upcoming 'transformation'. Besides, the silence in the now empty room was overwhelming with just me. I didn't want to stay here by myself with nobody to talk to or run errands with anymore.

Although I was becoming more and more comfortable with the idea of becoming a … like James … I still harbored some fearfulness of the unfamiliar territory that lay ahead of me. I was becoming more attuned to the realization that my life, as I knew it, was about to end, and that frightened me. I knew that for all practical purposes the mortal Katelyn was going to die, and in her place would be reborn an immortal Katelyn. I had the clear understanding that there would be a completely new me, with an entirely new life, waiting on the other side of that transformation. It was just that unfamiliar region in the middle that still caused me some apprehension.

James called it 'turning', sometimes 'changing', and at others, 'being born to second life', but no matter what it was called, I wanted to know more of what I could expect … what exactly would happen to me, would it hurt, what would happen as I transitioned … and on and on. It seemed that when I got one question answered two more took its place. James had promised me that the change would be relatively simple, over with quickly, and all the questions would then work themselves out for me. My total belief in all he told me was a comfort to me as I continued my walk along this new path I had chosen.

When I arrived at Whitehall and saw James, I flew up the steps and into his arms, kissing him and momentarily forgetting all my concerns. We went to the library and sat together on the love seat and I cuddled against him, feeling the coolness of his body even through my clothes.

"You're cold today … you haven't fed yet. Do you need time alone … to go hunt?"

"I shall be alright," he replied with a smile, "I'll hunt and feed later today while you are occupied with other things. My main concern right now is for you."

"James, I'm so comfortable when I'm with you … it feels like I was born for this time and place … to be right here, right now … please tell me this feeling doesn't change when I become a … well, like you."

"If anything that feeling, and our attachments to each other, will become stronger, in fact, all of your emotions will be greatly heightened. When you love, you will love deeper than you've ever known; likewise, when you hate, you will hate desperately and passionately. Your happiness will be almost giddy with laughter; your anger will become a raging vengeance. Your desire to hunt will be strong, your quest for blood, until you learn to tame it, will be a driving force within you. But there seems to be some other underlying questions that you didn't ask yet … is there anything in particular you would like to know?"

"Yeah, there is … I know the time is drawing close … and although I believe I'm more than ready … I still have some misgivings about it … I guess it's just the fear of the unknown … I know I'm not going to die, but every time I think about the change, that's all I can think about … I just can't help but be a little afraid."

"Katelyn, darling, I don't want you to be fearful, please tell me what I can do or say to lay your fears to rest. You know that I will never force the gift upon you, you have to want it, and you are free to change your decision at any time until the actual change begins."

"Just tell me exactly what is going to happen when I … change," I said slowly, "and I guess I want to know when we are going to make that change."

"I was thinking perhaps tomorrow … or the next day … or next week. There's really no rush, we'll both know exactly when you're fully ready to come over," he smiled softly, "so don't be in such a hurry, you do know it's a one way trip. But in the meantime there are some things I want you to do for yourself, some final mortal enjoyments if you will … it's going to be a long trip … and although it doesn't take long to get there, it does last for eternity you know."

"Alright, I was just thinking the sooner the better though, anyway, tell me what you want me to do and I will go take care of it," I replied.

"Not so much what *I* want you to do, but what *you* want to do," he began, handing me an envelope he had picked up off the table beside us, "I've put a thousand dollars in this envelope just for you … I want you to go back into Charleston, enjoy an afternoon, spend it on anything you desire for yourself … I want you to have a completely human day just for you … because once the change takes place it will likely be two to three weeks before you can be comfortable enough to go back into the mortal world again. So go … have a meal … see a movie … go shopping … do anything you want to do … I want you to have an enjoyable day and evening."

I smiled mischievously and with a laugh said, "I think I might get another tat … how about a Peter Pan to match my Tinkerbell … they can represent you and me for all time."

"That might not be a good idea," he began slowly, "please understand that to the immortal a tattoo appears as an imperfection, and so I'm afraid that Tinkerbell, while cute, will disappear when you go through the change."

"Awww … my Tinkerbell will go away," I asked with mock sadness, "but I've had her since I was sixteen."

"However, I think I might be able to make you forget about it," he smiled leaning in close and kissing me.

"Yeah … I believe that will do it," I answered breathlessly after the kiss.

"Katelyn, you are so very beautiful, and when you turn that beauty will only be enhanced. But remember, when this is over, you will remain as you are when you turn, forever. So, if there is anything you desire to do for yourself – your hair, nails, any kind of beauty treatment – do it now. Then when you get back I will explain to you everything you can expect and we will talk about when to begin, but only if you are ready. There is one other thing," he continued, "Do you have any cuts, bruises or scrapes anywhere on your body?"

"No, I don't think so," then with an impish grin playfully added, "but you are welcome to inspect my body, just to be sure, ya know."

"I would be happy to fix anything I found … or any other small imperfections you may have on your body before the change. But anything larger, such as scars or birthmarks you have will disappear when you go through the change."

I soon left and drove back downtown to have a day of fun. I did all of the things James had suggested. I shopped, saw the latest girlie movie I wanted to see, and then indulged in a treat just for me. I went to Kilwin's ice cream parlor just off the market and had a double scoop, French vanilla in a waffle cone with sprinkles, nuts, chocolate syrup and a cherry on top! Finally I looked for and found a very exclusive upscale beauty salon that specialized in full body makeovers where I could get anything I wanted. I told the girl, whose name was Ashleigh, that I was about to take a long trip with a very special man and I wanted the works. I wanted everything to be perfect for him. She commented that she thought I was already very beautiful so she wouldn't have a great deal of work to do what I had asked for.

"With those kinds of compliments, you won't have to worry about a tip either," I thought happily to myself, but still pleased with her appraisal of me. I know that I'm very pretty and I have been told just how beautiful I am, seemingly by everybody, since I was a little girl. But I have also just never dwelt on it because, until very recently, I always knew the beauty would eventually fade away. Still, it is flattering to hear someone else say it, especially another girl since girls can be so catty.

After several hours of pampering that included a light trim to the ends of my hair, a manicure and pedicure, French nails, a full facial, etc., etc., etc. … I paid the cashier, then turned with a big smile, and put a couple of the hundred dollar bills in Ashleigh's hand and said, "Thank you so much for all your extra efforts!"

I began the trip back to Whitehall, leaving one very happy salon worker behind. While I drove back I had time to think about and linger on some of the questions that had really been on my mind. The biggest question of all soon rose up center stage … when? James had said that he would bring me over when I was ready and we would both know when that was; but how would I know? I was having a difficult time wrapping my head around the fact that I was preparing to die. How would I ever be able to say to him that I was ready to die, ready for this life, a known one, to end and another, unknown one, to begin? How could I ever be calm and relaxed knowing I was about to die? How could I ever say to him 'turn me now, I'm ready'? I finally decided that all those would be questions we would just have to answer together.

Chapter Twenty~Eight

When I arrived back at Whitehall I modeled Ashleigh's handiwork for James. I showed off the two new outfits, complete with shoes that I had bought, recounted the movie I had seen, and with a happy laugh told him about my visit to Kilwin's and the extravagant ice cream cone I had allowed myself to indulge in since I wouldn't have to be concerned with weight gain in the near future.

"I'm so happy that you enjoyed yourself today. I really like what you had done too, it compliments your natural beauty. You are absolutely gorgeous Katelyn, and when you turn, you are going to make the most stunningly beautiful immortal ever."

"You're just saying that because it's me," I winked and chuckled, "but I do appreciate it anyway!"

"Just wait, you'll see," he smiled back.

"Well, thank you, but now, can we please have that talk I wanted to have about what's soon to happen …how my life is going to change," I asked, maybe a little impatiently.

"I'm at your service my love … whatever you wish to know, we shall discuss it."

I want to begin by asking you something personal James … and this means a lot to me …" I began with a timid smile, dropping my eyes and blushing a deep red, "and I know this isn't the most important thing in life but … afterward … when I'm like you … I know that we will still be able to have sex … but what will it be like then?"

He reached, took my hand in his and with a little smile said, "You know Katelyn, sometimes, to be so modern, you can be so bashful … and yes, we will have sex, often and with great pleasure, however, it will be completely different then …"

"What do you mean it'll be completely different … you know how much I enjoy sex with you … I mean … it's the best I've ever had … so will it still be as passionate for me then as it has been?"

"More so than you could ever imagine, like everything else about you, your sense of pleasure and passion will also be greatly enhanced. Preternatural sex will be more passionate and more satisfying than anything you have ever experienced as a mortal. However, because our kind does not procreate in that manner, it will be purely for amusement … for both of us. There will be something else though that will cause it to pale in comparison …"

"I can't imagine what that would be," I interjected happily, remembering not just the first, but every subsequent time we had had sex together and how wonderful it was.

"The kill, and feeding," he said coldly, "That is ultimately how we procreate and as such it will be the most gratifying and most sensuous, thing you will ever experience, nothing will compare to it, especially your first time."

I looked at him soberly and took a deep breath, then said questioningly, "And you will guide me through it in the beginning, I hope?"

"Of course I will, but trust me it will come naturally to you, I doubt you will need very much, if any, of my assistance."

"Alright … thank you for answering that … so I think maybe I'm prepared to handle my next question, please tell me, in detail, what you are going to do to me to make this happen."

"In short," he began, becoming very serious, "when you are at your most calm and relaxed condition we will exchange blood. I will take you in my arms, before we begin, and fill you with a sense of peace and contentment like you have never experienced. As the immortal draws you deeper into itself, you will be able to feel my love for you, more real than ever before. Then I will bite you, just under the left ear where your carotid artery pumps from your heart to your brain … just about …" and reaching out his hand he touched my neck just under my ear, "here … it will be a quick, piercing bite only to open your artery. It's there that I can take the greatest amount of blood in the shortest amount of time."

A sudden shiver passed through me as his cold hand touched me.

"Although I will deaden the nerves in the skin around the area you will probably still feel a sharp, very intense, but short pain ..."

"Humph … can't possibly be any sharper or more intense than that Brazilian I had this afternoon," I blurted out before I realized it.

"That what …" he looked askance at me, "what may I ask is a 'Brazilian', and why exactly would it cause you pain?"

I chuckled softly and mimicking his earlier comment to me said, "James, sometimes to be so versed in worldly affairs and know as much as you do, you can still be so eighteenth century!"

"Well, I am a man of the 1750's …" he started to say.

"And I'm a woman of the 2000's," I smiled, "and since you have surprises for me, I have a couple reserved just for you. I promise I'll explain it to you later. Now, you were saying …"

"The pain of my bite will be very short lived, and I will begin taking blood from you. I will take nearly every drop of blood you have, leaving only just enough to maintain an extremely faint heartbeat. You will pass through an entire gamut of emotions. The first will likely be a touch of fear and then you will feel like you have become sexually aroused – and may even experience an orgasm – but that's just your body's natural reaction to danger. You will sense an extremely euphoric feeling, almost as if you are flying. At that point, we will be able to see into each other's minds, there will be no secrets withheld. And finally you will begin to feel sleepy and your eyes will get heavy as I take you to the very edge of death."

I swallowed hard, looking at him as he talked.

"You did say detailed," he continued, "then when you are at your very weakest, I will open an artery here at the base of my throat, very near to my heart, and place your mouth close to it. After the first mouthful of my blood, nature will take over and you will begin taking blood from me. It will taste thick and coppery at first then it will become very sweet, and you will feel like you cannot get enough. I will let you fill yourself, but take you off at the proper time so that it can begin to work in you. Then, as you begin to regain some strength, I will repeat the procedure again. I will drain you and let you drink three times to ensure that all of your mortal blood has been replaced with my immortal blood, so that when this is over, and you wake up a brand new Katelyn, you will be the very strongest fledgling that you can possibly be."

I took a deep breath, and exhaled slowly, "Then will I have become … a vampire?" The term seemed suddenly to fit and I no longer felt uncomfortable applying it to myself.

"You will be very close at that point but your human body will still be fragile and have to change, to die, if you will. You will go into a deep, almost deathlike sleep. That will be the beginning of the change as my blood flows into every part of you, replacing your human blood and filling your body. It will change and renew every organ and cell in your body. My blood will be very strong in you because I am old and have never made another fledgling, or child. While you sleep, the change will continue working within you. Your body will begin the change by first expelling any parts of your humanity that it no longer needs. As the change continues there will be a little discomfort involved, but you will feel no pain because you will be in such a deep sleep. And please do not fear, I will be with you throughout the entire process. Even when you are no longer able to feel my presence around you, I will be there. During the time you sleep, just before you wake I will wash and clean your body in preparation for you to wake. I will re-dress you, and take away your old clothes to prevent any embarrassment on your part when you awaken."

"How long will I be asleep and what will I be like when I do wake up," I asked.

"Probably no more than a few hours at most and when you open your eyes again, you will have changed. You will no longer be a human, you will have been genetically altered, you will have become an immortal, a preternatural being. Your senses will become more alert – touch, hearing, sight, smell, and even taste – will be at their peak, many times more so than what you remember from your first experience. Your eyesight will be extremely sharp and your night vision will be without compare. Your hearing will become so keen that you can discern any sound from hundreds of yards away. Your sense of smell will also be heightened, being able to distinguish between humans and animals, even male and female. Just wait and see what great things happen when you change."

"You will also develop incredible strength, so much so that no human will be able to withstand you. That will be the result of having gained six extra chromosomes for a total of fifty-two. The normal human only has forty-six chromosomes – twenty-three pair in the regular human you are now verses twenty-six pair in the preternatural being you will have become. You will continue to have a heartbeat but at a much slower pace, normally around thirty-five beats a minute, which of course makes you seem much cooler to the touch. You may breathe if you wish, your lungs will still work, although there will be no need for it. The oxygen for your body will come through the blood you drink. It will supply the needs of your body."

"You may even continue to eat human food, as you have seen me do on several occasions, but there is no real need, because it will no longer have any nutritional benefits for you. Your new system will perceive it as something alien and destroy it when it reaches your stomach. After the first several days or weeks you will no longer need, or have a desire for, sleep. Most importantly you will still have your own personality, the things you enjoy now, you will enjoy even more then. Likewise, the things you dislike now will be even more so then."

"But after this is all over, what exactly will I become to you … will I be your child … a companion … your mate … or just another immortal," I asked still searching for answers.

"As your maker, you will always be my child, which is the strongest bond possible between two immortals. Secondly, you will be my mate and constant companion, which is the second strongest bond between two immortals. But Katelyn, I have waited over two hundred fifty years just for you, I promise you will never be 'just another immortal'," he answered smiling.

"I'm glad to know I'll be that special to you," I smiled and lightly kissed his lips, "now, I want you to come with me … there is something special I want to show you … then I want you to make love to me … not restrained as in the past, but as the immortal you are to the mortal that I am … and when we are finished, we can talk more about tomorrow or the next day or next week."

I took him by the hand and led him upstairs to our bedroom. When we had gotten into bed I moved over against him and pressed myself against his cool body, suddenly enjoying our difference like never before, mortal and immortal, like that of fire and ice. He took me in his arms, kissing me and petting me, his soft hands gently stroking my back and arms and I quickly began responding to his soft caresses, the tingle that he always caused in me quickly spreading to every part.

Suspecting that this might be the final time I would get to enjoy the pleasures of the flesh as a mortal, and not knowing fully what to expect as an immortal, I intended to make the most of this experience. The flames of desire blazed up hotly in me, and I took charge. I kissed him passionately, my tongue darting into his mouth and I felt him expel a breath into me when our tongues touched. Moving to his neck and ears, I let my tongue play across them, my hands roaming hungrily over his body as he began responding to my playfulness. I gently kissed his chest, lightly nipping at and then gently sucking each of his nipples. I looked up into his beautiful green eyes, wrinkling my nose at him, and was almost overcome with the love that I saw emanating out of those emerald depths.

There were so many times that I had wished James had been my first lover, but sadly there was no way to change the past. However, I had decided that today I was going to give him the very last vestige of my innocence. I had one thing held in reserve … something I had never done … something I had never had the desire to do … something so intensely intimate that I had never shared it with anyone … until now. So without a word, I slid under the sheet and began to do a special something that was just for him … and his pleasure alone.

I wrapped my hand around him and softly squeezed, lightly stroking the full length of his manliness. I gently planted little kisses on him beginning at the base, slowly kissing my way to the top, then opening my lips, I began to gently suck on him like a piece of candy. I knew it was physically impossible for me to take all of him … at least in this manner … but I was determined to try to take as much of him as I could. I allowed my fingers to lightly trail along the length of his hardness until I had gotten him nice and wet, then opening my mouth, I gradually began to take him a little at a time. Then slowly and carefully, taking my time, I surrendered everything to him that I had ever held back from any other lover … and he moaned with pleasure. Although this kind of loving was new and different for me … I soon found it to be more pleasurable than I had first imagined it would be and it didn't take long before I lost myself in the absolute pleasure of doing something just for him that I had never done for anyone else.

"Ummm … Katelyn … my love … that's so indescribably incredible … so tantalizing … like nothing I've ever experienced before."

His whispered comments gave me more determination to take this to the finish … this was my special show of love for him … I wrapped my fingers around him, and very slowly, taking only a little of him at a time … until finally, when my jaw and throat muscles relaxed, I leaned forward and took as much of him as I could … and held him there, sucking like a hungry calf would on its mother. Then stubbornly fighting every instinct in me, forcing myself not to gag, I began to pull back, releasing him as slowly as I had taken him. When I reached the end I began to suck on him again, slowly and softly, now massaging him gently with my hand. Now, with my entire concentration fixed completely on pleasing him, I began to take him once again.

I felt the comforting touch of his hand on my back as he quietly spoke and began to lightly caress my shoulders, "Katelyn, my love, I am beyond words to describe the pleasure you are giving me … so wonderful … so intense … I'm afraid … that you are taking me quickly to the very height of pleasure ..."

Then he began to moan again and hearing that, knowing the pleasure I was giving, I once again took as much of him as I could, almost effortlessly this time. I held him for a moment until, with my throat muscles protesting and, in spite of all my efforts, about to gag, I had to quickly come up. I looked up at him with a weak smile. I didn't want to spoil this moment for either one of us ... this was special ... something shared just between the two of us ... and I would finish what I had started. The flames of my own desires roared through me, burning hotter and brighter than ever before as I again slowly and carefully took him, leading him to a new height of pleasure. He moaned again with sheer delight, "Katelyn ... you are ... it feels ... so wonderful!"

I slowly backed off again, holding him just inside my lips, my tongue dancing playfully around the tip, and he began to groan louder. I could feel his tension building, growing stronger in him. I knew he wasn't far from reaching his climax and I could sense it coming closer every second. With a fleeting thought I nervously wondered what would happen when he released himself ... I steeled myself knowing that it wasn't far from happening. I slowly took him once again ... I could finish this ... I would finish this ... just for him.

He groaned loudly again, as I reached between his legs and lightly cupped him with my fingertips. I remained very still, closing my eyes, lightly tickling him with my fingertips, and concentrating on continuing to please him. Suddenly, unable to hold back any longer, his body spasmed violently, arching upward and stiffening all over as he reached the pinnacle of his passion. He went absolutely still, moaning with sheer delight as I took him past his climax, his orgasm ripping strongly through him and bursting into me. His body shuddered wildly as he released himself … so powerfully that I thought I couldn't take it all.

My eyes filled with tears as I struggled, stubbornly refusing my natural impulse to choke at the sudden fullness in the back of my throat and spit it back out. Instead, focusing on breathing slowly, I paused just long enough to allow myself to comfortably swallow again and again to empty my mouth and clear my throat. I once again took as much of him as I could and held him inside until I knew he was finished and his orgasm began to recede. I slowly came up, releasing him, and watching, fascinated, as he began to lose his erection.

When I was sure I had finished pleasing him, I lazily stretched out beside him, cuddling against his body, pressing close to him as he encircled me in his arms. I looked into his eyes and smiled at him, so thoroughly pleased with myself at what I had just done for him.

Although I'm sure my eyes were a little watery and I felt just a tiny bit queasy in the pit of my stomach, I was still thrilled with myself that I had tried – and accomplished – something new. I had discovered an act of love that was so very unique because it was mine and his alone. Knowing that what I had just finished had pleased him … and I held no reservations that he had enjoyed it … made the pleasure of it that much more enjoyable for me too.

As we lay there together, he looked at me with a satisfied smile, his eyes burning brightly and said, "Katelyn, darling you are so very exceptional in every way … in almost three centuries, no woman has ever satisfied me in that manner."

"James, I love you so much that I am willing to give you all of me … to share everything that I have with you and not hold anything back," I whispered in the quiet stillness of our bedroom, "I'm thrilled that I was able to please you … you see, that was the first time I have ever done that, too. You weren't in my life for me to give you my virginity, my body, the first time, so I gave you the only special thing I had left to give."

Without a word he pulled me to him and I lost myself in his deep and intimate kiss. Then I broke the kiss with a mischievous laugh as I looked into his eyes, "First time, huh … in almost three centuries … really?"

"Never," he answered, his lips finding mine again. I couldn't keep up the kiss as I giggled in absolute happiness that we had at least shared some kind of first time together.

"You have no idea how happy it makes me that we did at least have some kind of a first time together," I whispered seductively, and then adding a naughty grin continued, "and, perhaps if you're a good boy you won't have to wait another three centuries for me to do it again … besides, we'll soon have the next three centuries in front of us for practicing and perfecting it!"

"I'm not sure how it could get much more perfect," he chuckled softly.

"Oh, I think I told you once that I have a pretty good imagination," I whispered lightly kissing him. Then taking his hand from my waist I placed it gently at the bottom of my tummy and whispered, "And this, my immortal lover of the 1750's, is a Brazilian!"

I laughed with delight at his abrupt and unexpected response when he discovered my now swollen mound to be as bare and smooth as the day I was born. Suddenly, it was his turn to do things that I had never experienced. He began exploring me, kissing me, slowly making love to my entire body. I felt his smooth lips and velvety tongue on every inch of my skin, then inside me, and finally on my body again. His wonderfully cool hands and soft fingers explored every part of me, searching and feeling, touching, lightly gliding across my skin … and producing sensations I had never experienced. He did things to various parts of my body that brought me to orgasm again and again as he continued his journey from my face to my feet, taking his time, giving pleasure in manners I had never thought a lover possible of doing. Everything he did was so enjoyable, so delightful that I never wanted the pleasure to end.

He slowly made love to me, and carried me to new heights of delight again and again, with great crashing waves of pleasure washing over and through me, this time even better than our first night together! I felt like I was locked in an unending orgasmic cycle … one didn't end before another took its place, rising up from the very depths of my soul. I wanted more and more, not wanting him to ever stop! I tried to get my arms around him and couldn't … finally, trying to get a grip on something, anything … I began grabbing at the sheets, pulling and tearing at them. I was unquestionably being driven wild with pleasure! I couldn't get enough of him … and I still could not believe that anything could be any better than this!

After one final orgasm that literally took my breath away, I lay in his arms, exhausted, but contented and happy, weak from the pleasure we had shared and I smiled happily at him. My passions fully expended, I lay basking in the afterglow of our lovemaking, calmly enjoying every minute of him, wishing again it wouldn't end. He began to softly kiss me again, slowly brushing the hair away from my face, smiling at me as his cool fingers traced lazily along my cheek, wandering down my neck and to my breasts. He began to lightly kiss me and nuzzle at my neck and ear again and the pleasure quickly began to build in me once again. I felt so much a part of him as he casually pulled me closer against him, holding me in his arms. Then as he softly petted me, I looked up into his beautiful green eyes and suddenly found myself sinking into them, lost in their endless depths. He smiled his magnificent smile at me, looking back into my eyes and softly whispered, "I will love you forever and always, Katelyn Corbin!"

I had never in all my life felt so much love as we lay there together, affectionately holding each other. I returned his smile, still lost in his eyes and sighed out my utter love for him. I felt my own eternal and undying love for him shining through my eyes as I adoringly raised my mouth to his to kiss him again.

The next couple of seconds happened quicker than lightning … our gaze broke for only a millisecond and my eyes grew huge as I suddenly caught just the fleeting glance of his extended fangs glistening in the soft light … an image I had never seen … and was not prepared to see. I felt his hand on my cheek as he quickly turned my face away in a final effort to prevent me seeing what was coming … and before I could react to what was happening … he bit me … there was no warning and no numbing of my neck … nothing romantic about it … just a sure and fast strike … followed by a sudden stinging pain that shot through my entire body, all the way to the tips of my fingers and toes as his fangs sank into my neck.

I actually felt his fangs penetrate the skin and muscle just under my ear and puncture the large artery in the side of my neck. He held them there for only a brief moment and quickly pulled them back out. I felt his silky smooth lips lock tightly around the open wound in my neck, the pressure of his lips causing my neck to quickly be completely anesthetized. His strong arms wrapped tighter around me, pulling me closer against him, helpless in his grip as he began drawing my blood out of me.

When the abrupt understanding of what he was actually doing fully dawned in me, my body stiffened in a burst of unexpected fearfulness. Suddenly unimagined terror washed through me, replacing all the physical pleasure that had been there such a short time ago. I arched up against him, my human survival instincts taking over loudly screaming at me to *'get away … get away … you must escape … danger … get away from him'* … but he held me tightly against him, locked in his grip and unable to move.

The sedation that began in my neck continued tingling gently through me, like the numbness of a dentist's nova cane, first in my neck and throat, into my arms and hands, and all the way to my legs and feet … finally, when all feeling was lost, the sedating pull reached my heart. When it did, the incredible pull on my heart stopped being numbing and painful, instead it blossomed out, transforming into the purest, most beautiful, most powerful love that I had ever felt or sensed in my life.

I had asked for this … to be changed … turned to be like James so I could be with him forever. Now it was happening, there was no turning back, and I was suddenly so horrified at the thoughts that were flying through my mind. I realized with clarity that I was going to die … no … not going to … I was dying … I was suddenly so terrified … and there was nothing I could do about it. He continued tightening his grip on me so that I could not move … then, as I felt my life coming to an end, flowing quickly out of me, my eyelids fluttered … trying desperately to hold to the vision of life as I knew it … once, twice … and again … then gently closed on my human life …

Chapter Twenty~Nine

I continued struggling, trying desperately to hold on, instinctively fighting with everything in me to live, as I felt my life being steadily drawn out of me. I could hear my heart beating wildly, rushing at first then beginning to slow, almost to a stop. It barely maintained a beat, becoming almost hushed as I was nearly drained of the life blood in me.

"No, don't stop! You must keep beating," I screamed silently to my heart, *"I have too much life in front of me, I want so desperately to live now! Please don't stop beating; I'll die if you do!"*

It answered my plea with another beat … slowly … deliberately … and then another … each fainter than the other. My heart was empty, but still it struggled in a vain effort to live, trying to push life giving blood that was no longer present through its hollow chambers. I grew weaker, my heart taking longer between each pitiful, desperate beat. I felt so empty inside, a mere shell of what I was, and I began to slip away.

Then the most amazing thing happened … I suddenly became aware of being separated from my body. I knew that I was still locked inside my body; I could feel the confines of it around me, holding me. But some part of me was suddenly free, floating above the entire scene. I looked and saw myself on the bed. James was holding me securely in his arms, his mouth still tightly attached to my neck. I saw my body, tight against his, my arms wrapped around him, holding, gripping. I watched in wonder as my grip began to slip and my arms slowly fell from around him. My entire body, now cold and pale, went limp as I watched my life continue to pour out of it.

His skin took on the most vibrant glow as my blood surged into him. I could feel his mouth on my neck, pulling just so slightly now. He moved his head away from me and I saw the slightest trace of blood, my blood, on his lips.

"No! James! Please don't leave me," I silently cried out in sheer terror, *"I'm still in here! James … please hear me! James … I love you so much … please don't leave me like this!"*

Then a hot wetness unexpectedly exploded in my mouth, filling it, and gagging back, I choked on it. It tasted like copper, heavy and thick. I knew instantly what it was, I remembered the taste. It was blood … his blood, and he was pouring it into me. I knew I had to swallow if I wanted to keep breathing. It filled my mouth over and over as I swallowed again, drinking it in. It coated my throat as it began flowing toward my stomach where it blazed up into a raging fire and shot outwards into my body. My lungs ached as I sucked in air, filling them. Still his blood continued filling my mouth, gushing into me. I was able to swallow easier now, it tasted so good, so sweet, and I wanted more. I couldn't get enough of its goodness.

I felt and heard my heart as it picked up its beat again, slowly increasing, pumping the new blood throughout my body. The empty shell I had become was slowly being refilled. I was able to follow the path of this new immortal blood, tingling and burning, as it reached every part of my body. It felt good as it coursed strongly through me. I lay there, very still, unable to move as his blood moved steadily through my body doing its work, changing me, strengthening me. I watched curiously from above as he watched me. I saw the color return to my body as the blood reached my skin. I had no sense of time as it happened. It could have been minutes or hours, I didn't know. Soon I realized that I could feel again, first the softness of the bed, then the firmness of James' body against me.

Just as I thought I wanted to open my eyes and begin to move, I felt James at my throat again, followed by the sharp sting as his fangs penetrated my skin once more. I wanted so badly to move, but I couldn't, I felt paralyzed, I didn't have the strength in me. I could feel the blood begin to leave my body again as he sucked it back out of me. I recognized the strong pulling sensation as my life seemingly gathered in the center of my chest, and rushed hurriedly out the open wounds in my neck.

"Wait! James, no … don't do that," I pleaded silently, *"it feels so good flowing in me, it's mine now, please don't take it away!"*

I felt like I wanted to cry … it was mine, he had given it to me … why was he taking it away … I was so close to being like him … and now he was taking it all back … had he changed his mind … was he going to allow me to die after all?

My body was soon nearly empty, dying again, my heart slowing once more as the new life that had flooded me, ebbed away, receding back to where it had come from. I listened as my heart began to beat slower, struggling again … once … twice … then a terrible silence as it stopped completely. A dreadful fear filled the sudden deadly quite. I wanted nothing more than to hold on to life as despair filled me, replacing the life in my body. But there was nothing I could do to stop it as it flowed out of me. I felt so helpless, unable to move, as I lay there. I sensed death at the outer edges trying to slip in but something held it back, preventing it from coming any closer and taking me away.

Just as quickly as it seemed to leave me, I tasted fresh blood in my mouth again. This time I was the one pulling, trying to get as much as I could. I was suddenly more aware of James as his blood refilled me. I could hear the slow, steady thump-thump, thump-thump, of his heartbeat now, it filled my head and blocked out any other sound.

Then I heard the comforting sound of my own heart as it started to beat again, slowly, once more pumping new blood and new life into me. I felt myself filling once again with the new life as it once again flowed into every part of my being. I felt myself merging into him, becoming one with him, as our hearts now beat in unison, steady and strong. Then I realized I could see into his mind. I saw first-hand everything he had told me. I watched as his life of nearly three centuries played out like a video in front of me.

I watched him grow from a happy child into a handsome young man. I felt his love for a beautiful and affectionate wife; the thrill at the birth of his son; the devastation and dark depression that surrounded him when she died. I saw Charlotte Ann when she entered his life, bringing with her the end of one life and the beginning of another. I wandered through his mind, picking up each of his memories, holding them, examining them like the personal treasures they were, and then carefully returned each one back to its place. I saw all of the things he had seen, the places he had been. I felt his pain and happiness as if it were happening to me. And all of his memories culminated with me standing beside him. I luxuriated in the moment, knowing we were finally together, forever.

There was a twinge of bitterness when I felt him bite into me a third time and once more begin taking it all away. My life, my blood, flowed out of me again. I was so weak this time, moving closer toward the dark abyss. Then I vaguely recalled him saying that he would take me to the edge three times. I knew deep down inside that when he had finished taking my life this time, he would restore it, then it would be forever, and nothing could take it away again. I readily surrendered to him as he pulled it back out of me, knowing it would soon come back, refilling me.

When I tasted his blood the third time I sucked hard, greedily pulling with all my might to take it all into me. There was a sudden, strong desire in me to drain him as he had done me. I wanted to leave him an empty shell. His hot blood came roaring into me and thundered through my body like a runaway freight train, exploding into every fiber of my being. It was life, sweet life, and this time, it was mine, forever, and nothing, not even him, could ever take it away. His strength and energy filled me like never before, blazing through me, making me tingle throughout my body.

It soon became just too much for my human body, now weakened after the trauma of the initial bloodletting, to endure any longer. I felt exhausted, like I had exerted myself beyond my limits. I wanted desperately to sleep, to simply close my eyes and rest.

I quickly and easily slid back inside my body, I felt it slowly constrict around me, holding me, wrapping me tightly in its grip. I became aware of my heartbeat again. I listened and counted as it began to pick up speed once again … five … ten … twenty … thirty … finally settling at its new, steady pace of thirty-five beats a minute. I felt my breathing stop and knew that my body was beginning to die, the change had begun … and resting peacefully, I descended downward into a deep, still, darkness …

The darkness that surrounded me was thick and heavy, seemingly weighing in on me from every direction … until it wasn't … and I suddenly realized that I was now standing in a place bathed in light. I looked slowly around me and quickly recognized the area surrounding the South Chickamauga Creek … a place that was special to me, a place that held wonderful memories of my childhood. My family had owned a lake house here in the North Georgia Mountains, not far from Ringgold Gap. We had spent our vacations and many of our weekends here when I was growing up. I smiled silently as I picked out the strip of sandy shoreline, that we had called 'The Beach', that ran along in front of the house.

My mind was filled to overflowing with the happy memories of my childhood in this place, and I wondered for a moment how I had gotten here … and why this place, why now. While I dwelled on that question, my thoughts were interrupted by something softly but incessantly pushing against my ankles. I looked down and was astounded to see two cats rubbing their way around and between my feet. It was Mr. Tibbs and Mr. Whiskers. Tibbs, a gray Maine Coon, had been my first pet when I was a child – he had died of old age when I was six. Then, not long afterward, I had gotten Mr. Whiskers. When I got him he was a tiny, little orange Tabby kitten that grew into a fat, loving cat that had slept at the end of my bed, cuddled at my feet every night until I was a senior in high school when he was suddenly taken by feline diabetes. It had broken my heart when he died and we buried him in the back yard next to Mr. Tibbs.

Yet strangely, here was both of them, alive and happy it seemed. I stooped down, and smiling hugely, called each of them by their name and began petting both, rubbing their ears, patting their heads, and stroking their backs … they were soon purring loudly at my accustomed ear-rubbing. Mr. Tibbs contentedly continued his circular path around my feet, rubbing my ankles with his nose, while Mr. Whiskers flopped down in front of me and rolled over for a belly rub.

"It looks like they are happy to see you again and telling you hello in their own way," I heard a soft voice next to me. I slowly looked up and could hardly believe my eyes. My mother had somehow walked up and was standing next to me. I jumped straight up, my two pets quickly forgotten, and threw my arms around her.

"Mommy!" I exclaimed laughingly, using my childhood name for her, "I'm so happy to see you again."

"My baby girl … it's my pleasure to see you again too," she answered, kissing my cheek and squeezing me in a hug.

Then just as quickly, I was struck with the thought that this was my mom – and the terrible memory of what had happed to both her and dad came rushing back.

"Oh mom … I've missed you so much," I whimpered,

"if only I had been with you and dad … maybe I could have done something to prevent …"

"No Katelyn, there was nothing you could have done," she whispered against my ear, "your dad and I were destined for that day … and it was not your destiny to be there. Destiny has brought you here today, but my precious little girl, Fate has much bigger plans for you yet to come."

"So then, does my being here now mean that I'm …" I slowly began asking.

"It means that you are transitioning my darling daughter … you are halfway between your mortal life and your immortal life. I wished to see you and talk to you before you became immortal," she answered with a smile, and pointing toward the house and the beach, she continued, "turn and look there."

I looked where she pointed and saw my dad, sitting in his favorite fishing chair, a newspaper in his lap and both of the cats, now resting, curled at his feet. He grinned at me and raising his hand, blew a kiss in my direction, just like he had done thousands of times before when I was a child.

"You are so important to me Katelyn," mom began, reaching and taking both my hands in hers, "your father and I gave you life … the first time … I carried you in my body for nine months and you became part and parcel of who I am. Now, you are about to receive life for the second time … a life that neither your dad nor I could have ever given you. You were and always will be my daughter and I love you as much now as ever. But you've made a choice – and a good one I might add – one that means I must surrender you and your fate to another."

"But mom … why … why can't we stay together," I asked pleadingly.

"Darling the world that your father and I now inhabit

is for those whose mortal lives have ended … this is where we live now … and forever. It's different to your world because your mortal life hasn't ended … it's merely changing into a different kind of life. You are becoming a new creature in that world … much as a caterpillar changes into a beautiful butterfly … and you will soon have the ability to live in two worlds – the mortal one, and the immortal one. And because you freely made the choice, I am happily able to freely let you go … to live, love and grow, in your new world."

"Does this mean I can come and see you and dad again," I questioned.

"Katelyn, you don't belong in this world … just as your father and I no longer belong in your world … you are only here for a short visit before becoming what you will be for eternity," she answered, "now that doesn't mean that your dad and I are no less real … we are always close, though you may not always feel our presence."

"Your father and I have discussed your decision regarding immortality, just as we did with any other major decisions you wanted to make when you were growing up, and we wish to honor your desire to join Mr. Dubois in immortality, and so we have given your decision our blessing. Just as we were responsible in the mortal world for raising you, teaching you, and seeing that you grew into maturity, so too is Mr. Dubois in the immortal world. I know that he loves you and will care for you – he will love you and see that you grow into maturity in your new life and new world – first as his equal, and just as importantly, as his mate. I love you my dear sweet Katelyn … for all time and eternity."

"I will love you and dad forever … I promise," I said.

"Now it's time for you to go," she smiled, "look

there."

I turned and saw James, smiling and standing close by us. He stepped over beside me and stood quietly, smiling at me. I looked back again at mom, and she once more kissed my cheek. He reached out his hand toward me, and my mom, still holding my hands, placed them in his hand. She took our joined hands and held them between hers.

"James, I'm placing the most precious thing I had in the natural world in your hands," she began in a low whisper, "now, as you take her into the preternatural world, I charge you to watch over, love, and care for her forever."

"I accept your charge Melissa," he answered with a smile, "and I promise that I will watch over and protect Katelyn for all of eternity. I take her as my mate and just as she was part and parcel of you in her mortal life, she will become part and parcel of me in her immortal life … from this day and forever."

"Katelyn, you don't yet fully understand the gift you are receiving," she spoke just as softly to me, "but you will before long … you will grow into it becoming strong and powerful in your new life, and so, for all eternity, I'm placing you in his care."

I looked into James' beautiful emerald eyes, and as a tear rolled slowly down my face at the realization of what had just taken place, my mom and everything around me began to fade back into the peaceful darkness … and I rested, comfortable and happy knowing that my parents had blessed my eternal decision.

Chapter Thirty

I had wanted from the day I met Katelyn to drink from her, but when I bit her and her blood exploded forcefully into my mouth, although it had been worth the wait, I was not fully prepared for the taste of it. The flavor of her blood was like none I had ever tasted, it was sweet and clean, filled with purity and innocence. It was so strongly succulent, so filled with her youth, her potency and most of all her love for me that I was very nearly overcome.

I wanted so desperately to take my time, to drink it in slowly, savoring and enjoying the pure goodness of it as if it were the very finest of wines. But, struggling against my very nature, I resisted that strong desire. I had to do this quickly, not just for her but for my sake also, I could not allow myself to become lost in the taking and thereby take the risk of also losing her. And so, resisting everything in my nature, I hurriedly drained her, almost completely, in just a matter of minutes, listening closely to her heart as it slowed to a near halt, leaving only just enough blood to keep it slowly beating at one to two beats per minute.

I heard her cry out to her heart in fear, coaxing it to work although there was very little blood left for it to pump. Her body relaxed becoming limp in my arms as the anguish of her plea tore through my soul. My dear Katelyn, though she didn't fully realize it at the moment, was now as close to death as she would ever be again.

I began loosening my hold on her, releasing her from the tight immortal embrace, and she silently cried out to me from the very depths of her being not to leave her. The absolute desperation and agony of her plea felt as if she had run a knife through my heart and twisted the blade. I understood how frightened she was in these first few minutes, not fully understanding all that was happening as the change began working in her. I too had experienced the very same fear that she was now feeling. But regardless of her fear, she knew, somewhere in the very depths of her soul, that I would not allow her to die, even so, her silent but emotional pleadings continued to tear through me breaking my heart in pieces.

I quickly opened the artery at the base of my throat and drawing her to it, began to replace her blood with mine. It poured into her mouth, filling it until it began to leak from the corners of her lips, then she reflexively swallowed, taking her first drink of immortality. Nature took over at that point and she drank deeply until she was filled. I waited nearly half an hour until my blood had absorbed itself from her stomach and began flowing through her before once again draining her. She again cried out silently, pleading with me for her life.

When I filled her a second time, our supernatural link fell into place and I sensed her as she began strolling, a bit hesitantly at first, through my mind and soul. I opened all my secrets and shared every memory and feeling of my life with her. In turn, I peered into her mind and saw her short but relatively happy life. The part that hurt me the worst though was witnessing her discovery of her murdered parents. I experienced along with her the terror and horror that filled her at the sight, followed by the pitiful sadness of her world unexpectedly crashing down around her and combined with the painful realization that she was now all alone … her against humanity.

I took her a third time, draining her to ensure that all of her human blood was purged from every fiber of her body and replaced with my vampiric blood. I was bringing her over in a thorough and precise manner, so when I filled her a third and final time, I both sensed and saw the change beginning to work in her as she pulled strongly at the open artery in my neck. It seemed that she was literally attempting to drain me as I had done her. When the change was complete in her, I wanted her to be strong and gifted, and so I had taken my time, nearly two hours from start to finish, while I drained and refilled her three times.

When I had finished filling her a third time, her body, still frail in its humanity, and unused to the powerful vampiric blood that now coursed strongly throughout her system, simply could not withstand the trauma of the change any longer. She heaved a final breath and sank quietly into a deep blackness as her body began to change, casting off its mortality and replacing it with immortality.

Then, having never witnessed this part of the change … only experiencing it from Katelyn's side … I continued watching, fascinated, as her body began to purge itself of anything it would no longer need … and I was very relieved that she had no knowledge of what was happening. My overpowering love for her flowed out and toward her as I continued watching the change carrying out its work, bringing about the marvel of second life in her. She appeared to be dead as she lay there, and had any mortal seen her, they would have declared her so. But my preternatural vision allowed me to see the first visages of immortal life beginning to show itself, and the things I saw transpiring were astonishing to me. I sensed the force of immortal life as it became a shield, surrounding and protecting her from any outside interference, including my own touch, while the vampiric blood continued to work the phenomenal singularity of immortality inside her.

Slowly the two small puncture wounds in her neck, now surrounded by a fierce black bruise where I had three times drained her life, began to grow smaller, finally closing, the bruise sinking into them as they did, leaving only smooth, unblemished skin behind. The light supernatural aura of life that only immortals have begun to show itself around her eyes, and then quickly spread covering her face and neck, finally enveloping her entire body. I smiled at the memory of our earlier conversation as I watched her little Tinkerbell tattoo that sat atop the ridge of her hipbone began to fade and finally disappear completely. I watched in amazement, absolutely astounded at what was taking place in her … the expectations I had held of what would happen as she changed were far exceeded as I witnessed her new preternatural beauty that was quickly developed and revealed to me.

Finally, I filled a pan with water and began bathing her, making ready for her to wake again to a new life. I lightly kissed her forehead, and began slowly and tenderly, carefully washing every inch of her body, making sure there were no traces of humanity left on her anywhere. Her face was soft and beautiful as I washed it clean, smiling at the memory of the passion we had just shared and the very special gift that she had bestowed upon me. I washed her arms, her hands and each of her fingers; kissing the palms of her hands and each finger individually. I could already feel the soft preternatural flesh forming, completely replacing her human flesh. I bathed her entire upper body, slowly and methodically, continuing on with her long elegant legs, and finishing my labor of love with her feet and toes. When I was satisfied that she was clean, I lovingly picked her up and carried her limp, nude body into another room just down the hall.

When I had placed her on the bed there, I silently went to the closet and took out the expensive black silk pajamas Charlotte Ann had purchased for her. She had chosen them along with the matching long black robe and slippers to be used just special for this occasion. Katelyn had already worn them several times, the first being the morning after the first night she had stayed with me, and again on every subsequent morning since. Her human scent combined with her expensive perfume, permeated them as I held them in my arms. I knew that her human scent, though soon to be so foreign to her, would linger as something familiar when she first awoke, giving her something from her old world to help her feel more at ease in her new world.

I affectionately dressed her in the pajamas and robe, then lying her back on the bed carefully straightened them out so she would be comfortable. I arranged her arms and hands, carefully crossing them on her stomach, tenderly rubbing each of her delicate, soft hands. I added the slippers to her feet and finally, gently lifting her head I silently brushed her long hair, splaying it out across her pillow and over her shoulders.

"Sleep now my eternal and beautiful young love, rest

easy while you complete your journey into a new world. I shall be waiting for you when you cross over into immortality and open your eyes again," I murmured as I gently kissed her soft lips. Then, listening to her heart, now beating strong and steadily at its new slower pace, I took a seat in a chair on the far wall and began to wait for her to wake.

Time began to pass … one hour … two … then three as I sat and watched every tiny change. Finally, a little after four hours, the room began to fill with the sweet fragrance of gardenias touched with a light scent of magnolias, I inhaled slowly and smiled happily at the new scent beginning to saturate the air. In no time at all it seemed, after hours of watching, the wonderfully tantalizing scent of mortal Katelyn was soon overpowered and overcame, until it was no longer detectable, by the scent of immortal Katelyn. I became aware of her beginning to rise up out of the darkness of immortal sleep. Finally, after nearly five hours of watching, I noted her eyelids begin ever so slightly to flutter. When she slowly reopened her beautiful blue eyes, this time on a new world and new existence, they were filled with the intensity of immortality, burning with the fiery glow of second life … my mortal Katelyn that I loved so much, was now my immortal Katelyn … new and changed … and together we would explore eternity.

Chapter Thirty~One

The deep death-like sleep that had been surrounding me began, little by little, to lift away. I could sense life gradually returning to me. The force of immortality moved easily through my body which now tingled all over from the new blood flowing in me. I felt uncommonly good, and extraordinarily strong, but still found myself unable to move. I continued to lie there quietly, not yet ready to open my eyes. All of my senses, now increased to a new height of awareness, were on full alert.

There was suddenly a new instinct in me that told me I had to be cautious and not move. I somehow knew that I was no longer in the room where I had watched as James took me and changed me. This was not the bed where he had drawn the life out of me and replaced it with a new life.

Even so, I knew exactly where I was. This was the bedroom just down the hall from where James and I had last acted out our passion for each other. I listened to my heart as it quietly thumped at its new steady pace. My chest rose and fell ever so slightly as I drew shallow breaths. I could feel all the differences in my body. I knew that I had changed now, but when, had it been last night or last week? I wasn't sure of the time frame.

The slightest touch of fear passed through me as I reached out with my mind to explore every part of this room. Was I alone … no … there was another presence here … one that was strong and imposing. Was I safe … I concentrated on it … yes … I didn't sense any threat. It was a presence I knew, with a peaceful comfort stemming from the center of it. Suddenly, as if a blurred picture had been drawn into sharply defined focus I knew it was James. I lay there in the darkness, my eyes still closed, and I realized that I had known him, rather than seeing or hearing him, by his scent.

Once I had firmly located him, the fear evaporated as quickly as it came. He represented safety. He was sitting comfortably in a chair across the room, his legs crossed, watching me. I'm not sure how I knew just where he was and what he was doing, but I did. I was acutely aware of every little detail around me. I could hear his slow, steady heartbeat now, and his easy breathing. He began to move … coming towards me, maybe? Yes, I was sure of it now. He was getting closer, I could feel him pressing in, but he still maintained his distance. I still did not move, unsure just exactly what was happening. I heard his soft voice in my head as he spoke, slowly, carefully, *"Katelyn … my love, you're awake now … open your eyes … look at me, darling."*

I suddenly sensed a hand moving towards me and everything in me screamed out – *'Danger!'* My thoughts came quickly as I assessed the situation, focusing on exactly where the hand was, and with reflexes faster than a striking cobra my arm shot out, catching it by the wrist as my eyes flew open and a quick hiss escaped my lips. As my new eyes quickly focused in the dimly lit room, I saw that it was James. I held his wrist in a crushing grip as I looked into his eyes.

He was unlike I had ever seen him; he was so amazingly beautiful now. He had a light aura surrounding him that I had never seen before, his eyes now glinted brightly … and his scent … his wonderful sweet manly scent filled the air of the room … I breathed it in trying to fully identify it … it seemed to be a mixture of sandalwood and sage … an ancient aroma that was both exotic and mysterious at the same time … and one that from now on I would know anywhere.

I began to slowly, carefully, relax my grip, and he smiled at me and said, "Well, your reflexes are certainly faster now and that's quite a grip you have."

"Sorry about that," I whispered, "I don't know why I did that."

"It's quiet alright … it was a protective move that's part of your new nature," he grinned.

I moved my arm back towards me, lifting it so I could see my hand as I flexed my fingers. And then the memory came flooding back to me … his strike … his grip as he held me … the sudden flash of fear … my blood flowing out … his flowing in … my eyes closing in that near death sleep. I could feel the change in me. I was a new creature … I was a vampire now, just like him. He stood stock still as I reached out, slowly and cautiously this time, to touch his face …

"Take your time my love," he whispered softly, "explore, touch, and learn, everything is new to you."

My fingertips lightly glided across his cheek. My touch was so sensitive now, I could feel everything. I moved my hand to my own face, again slowly letting my fingers explore every part of it. My skin felt like his, smooth and soft. He was still standing there watching me as I considered my new self, still not speaking, unsure if I could yet, or even what to say, if I did.

"I think I would like to get up, I want to stand," I thought to myself and suddenly found myself standing at the foot of the bed, my entire body tingling as energy roared through every part of me. I quickly looked around and then taking a glance at myself, saw that I was wearing my black silk pajamas, topped with the matching long black robe and slippers. I knew it was the same ones I had worn each and every morning after I had spent the nights here … I could smell the softly lingering scent of my perfume on them, only now it seemed overtly sweet … but overlaying that was something else … something strange, stronger and more potent … something that my new senses quickly identified as the scent of a human … then I realized it was my old human scent … a scent that was suddenly almost alien to me … different now … it represented what I used to be … not what I had become … still, in a way I didn't fully comprehend, I found it somehow strangely comforting to me.

"How did I do that," I asked surprised as I quickly turned towards James, who was still standing by the side of the bed, now with a big smile.

"You obviously decided you wanted to get up … and you did," he laughed, as he extended his hand toward me, "Welcome to my world … and your new life my beautiful love!"

I reached out and our fingers touched, interlacing into

each other's hand. I was amazed at how sensitive my touch was now … I could feel every part of his palm and his fingers. I looked up into his eyes and I saw his tremendous love for me flowing out. He took a step toward me, I met him and moved into his arms and we kissed, deeply and passionately. I felt the old tingle return as he easily held me. *"Mmmm …"* I thought, *"at least that didn't change."*

"This is so astounding, everything about me feels … different. I feel so … alive … I have so much energy!"

I held to him, and gently kissed him again. I moved my mouth lightly down his cheek and towards his neck. As I did I felt my fangs extend, tiny little points against my lower lip. I smiled at the feeling as I kissed his neck.

He pulled easily away from me with a short laugh, and said, "My, you do learn quickly little fledgling … but not yet, Katelyn … I understand the thirst and I will allow you to drink again very soon. But first let's walk out to the veranda. We have a lot to talk about and I have many things to teach you, and there's no time like the present, so let's begin."

I thought about the veranda and visualized the rear door. I suddenly found myself standing at the door, just as I had envisioned it, wondering again how I did that. James came up, it seemed, out of nowhere on my right side and joined me as I stood there.

"Before we step outside," he began slowly, "the light will seem a bit harsh to you until your new eyes fully develop and become accustomed to it. If it hurts too much, I'll bring you back inside until later."

I glanced cautiously through the glass panes of the big double doors and saw the veranda bathed in bright sunshine. Then I looked back at him and in a soft almost whisper said, "I think I can handle it … at least I want to try it."

"That's my girl," he chuckled, "fearless as always, never shying from the unknown."

Then reaching and taking my hand in his, he pushed the doors open and together we stepped outside into the bright afternoon sunlight. I abruptly cringed backward, and my knees buckled, barely able to keep myself from falling. The sudden pain that exploded throughout my body was completely unexpected. I felt as if someone had stuck a long sharp pin in my eyes. I screamed in agony, and jerking my hand away from his began grabbing at them. I quickly covered my face, hiding it with both hands as I struggled to stay upright.

"My eyes! They're on fire … I can't see … they feel like they're melting," I wailed, trying to press both hands into my tightly closed eyes as they burned with agony.

"It's alright Katelyn," James spoke softly, and I felt one of his strong arms wrap around my waist and the other under my knees, lifting me and taking me in his arms, "you are very sensitive right now to everything around you. The light won't hurt for long, but it will take a little getting used to it. Your body is still changing and it will take a couple of days for you to acclimate yourself to all the changes. Then you will be able to fully function again anywhere and anytime."

I rested my face against his shoulder as he held me in his arms, shielding my eyes against the brightness of the sun. He carried me to a chair, setting me down in its soft cushions with my back towards the sun. I slowly tried to open my eyes again and noted that there wasn't the blinding pain that facing the sun had been. Now it was more like just a grain of sand … that had been soaked in Tabasco … and wrapped in jalapeno pepper … and dropped in my eye … just a little discomforting.

In an attempt to take my mind off the pain in my eyes, I began to concentrate on how good the sun's warmth felt to me as its beams hit my shoulders and back through the vine wrapped trellises. The black silk of my pajamas and robe soaked up the warmth and quickly spread it throughout my body.

I continued to sit there, still as a statue, my new preternatural senses fully alert. I noted everything around me, and that I could distinguish every sound. I could hear the small birds in the trees, of course, but I could also hear small animals moving around on the ground. Suddenly I realized I could smell their blood too. I slightly raised my head, sniffing the air around me, trying to identify each individual scent.

James watched me in silence as I sat there, each moment reaching just a little further out from myself. I silently explored the rear of the house and the surrounding gardens, listening more than looking. I knew I was safe with James but there was something new inside me that made me want to confirm it for myself. After a few minutes of this exploration, I satisfied myself that I was safe. There was no danger around me, nothing but the sounds of nature. I began to relax and focused my full attention back on James again.

"You will note there are many things different now," he smiled lovingly at me, "and in the next few days and weeks, I will teach you everything. During the first couple of weeks, while the change continues, working and completing your transition, you will soon begin to feel more comfortable again."

"James," I started, slowly forming my words, thinking how to say this, "I don't understand how, but, I can *smell* you now! Your scent is softly sweet, but still masculine, like a mixture of sandalwood and sage, it was one of the first things I noticed even before I opened my eyes, how is that?"

He laughed happily at my question and smiled at me as he answered it, "Each of us has our own individual scent, I wish you could smell yours! Your human scent was wonderful to me, but now …"

"Yeah, well, if my human scent is that stench that's lingering around me," I interjected lightly fingering my pajamas and robe, "I'm afraid I don't find it to be as pleasing as you do."

"It'll go away soon and not bother you again," he grinned, "although I can say with authority that before long you will find the scent of humans to be, well, very attractive."

"If you say so …" I agreed.

"Katelyn, I sat up in that room and watched as you turned, as your mortal scent began to fade and your immortal scent developed and began to blossom out filling the room … it's like nothing I have ever smelled … your scent is a perfect combination of the sweet fragrance of gardenias and magnolias. I want to drink it all in and enjoy it."

A few days ago I would have blushed deeply at such a compliment.

"But remember," he added quickly, "that your newly discovered keen sense of smell is also how we track our prey."

I watched him as he sat back in his chair, relaxing and settling into the soft comfortable cushions.

"Katelyn," he continued, his love for me filling his eyes as he reached and gently took my hands in his, "my darling, you are now the youngest descendant of a very long line of preternatural beings. You have a great many strengths and no real weaknesses. You are my child now and I shall teach you of yourself. But more importantly Katelyn, you are my mate, my love for you is eternal, and from this day forward I will be your protector. I will provide for you and ensure that you have no lack. As long as either of us exists, whether we are together or separate, we will be connected, I will always be there for you. All you ever have to do is call out to me and I will come to you."

"My love for you is just as deep, James," I answered him looking into his eyes, "I pledged my mortal life and now my immortal life to you. I will always be here for you, my maker and mate, to protect you, to help you, to be with you, wherever eternity may take us. You know my parents would be proud of the choice I made."

"And they would be honored by you," he agreed.

We sat silently for a few moments, looking at each other, as the import of our shared vows sank in.

He broke the silence as he began, "You must learn now of yourself. You are completely and thoroughly an immortal being, but your body still has some changes to go through. You will soon need to rest as it finishes the process. I have made provisions for you a secluded resting place. A place where you will not be disturbed and you may come and go as you wish. Soon, like me, you will no longer need any rest or even to sleep. Then we shall hunt together and I will show you how to become successful and ensure your survival."

"Will I have to kill," I asked, still tingling all over, as the change continued its work in me.

"Yes, Katelyn, you will. It's in your nature, a part of you. You are a predator and you take life in order to live. When you kill, you will find that it is the most sensuous thing you will ever do. But, like any other part of your nature, you can learn to control the desire but only after you have hunted and killed the first time. I will teach you how to take only a little, but from many. But until our first hunt, I shall allow you to feed from me. That will sustain you and increase your strength. But nothing like what will happen when you take your first human blood."

"Before I go further, please allow me the liberty to tell you more about our kind, what I am and what you have become. There is no written history of our race, we just are. There is no real beginning and of course no end. Our kind has been here since the very beginning of time. We do not know who the first was and are not certain how they came to be. Some would say that we carry the Mark of Cain, but I'm afraid that neither science nor history allows that supposition."

"If you were to look carefully, there are references to our kind in the earliest written records of human history. There are depictions of us in the cave paintings throughout the world. There are clues of our existence throughout the ancient world – Egypt, the Persian Empire, and Greece. By the time the Romans had covered the known world, we were well known … and feared. We have lived in the shadows of day and the dark of night throughout history."

"There are some among us that are older than the centuries, even the millenniums. They have survived all that time and hold many secrets. They rarely make an appearance but if you should ever meet one of the old ones, it is an awe-inspiring event. The ultimate experience though is for one of the ancients to allow you to drink directly from them. That one experience will so completely alter your existence. You would become as they are, having more powers than you can imagine. You would become stronger than most of your kind, none of which would be able to withstand you."

"Have you ever seen or drank from one of them," I asked inquisitively.

"No, I've never drank directly from an Ancient," he continued explaining, "but I have drank from one who has and that one is much older than I am."

"There is an extraordinary life force that abides in each and every one of us. It fills us from the moment of our change, it sustains us, protects us, and we in turn pass it along to carefully chosen ones like yourself."

"There will be many things that you will face in your new life. We are not the only supernatural beings in this world, but we are the strongest and most powerful. Every other creature is subservient to us. Of all the beings you will encounter in this life, there is only one in the entire universe that is more powerful than our kind. He is The Ancient of Days, known to mortals as the Lord God, and is the only being that is all powerful. When He makes an appearance in this world, even the oldest and strongest of our kind bow to Him and acknowledge His Lordship."

"But, how do we know when that happens," I asked quickly.

"We will always know," he replied, "because 'The Watchers' will alert us to His imminent appearance."

"Who are these Watchers," I asked interestedly.

"The Watchers are a group of creatures, some say they are Angels, maybe fallen, maybe not, perhaps some of both who have been here since before the beginning of time. It is their duty to know what is going on in this world at all times, they watch and observe everything, everywhere."

"As you age, your strength and powers will naturally increase and you will gradually become attuned to all of the various life forces that are in this world. When you drink from one older than yourself, you share and then benefit from the strengths and powers of that one. Your strength is already exponential because of my blood inside you and as you continue to feed from me you will gain in strength. We will soon explore together and discover just exactly which powers you were born with. I suspect there are many because of your bloodline, but we have plenty of time for that. As you discover each talent, you will learn how to use and control it as you grow. You seem to have already discovered that you have incredible speed and have learned how to move from one place to another," he said with a smile.

"Yeah … 'bout that … will I move like that all the time now," I asked.

"No," he laughed, "you can if you wish, and it's certainly the easiest way to travel. As you have discovered, you merely visualize where you want to be, and you are there. It's something you'll learn to control and then walk and move slower, at a more normal pace."

"Now, the first and most important thing you must learn. The only thing that can harm you or any of our kind is fire or dismemberment. Your body will heal very quickly from anything else that may hurt you. But fire will destroy you and end your existence as will dismemberment. If your bodily parts are scattered … you cannot recover from that."

"I think it wise at this point to also warn you that should you cross paths with some human who fancies themselves to be a 'vampire hunter', or sometimes they refer to themselves as 'slayers', do not play with that individual. They carry all the usual toys – stakes, silver chains, holy water, etc. – none of which will hurt you but that doesn't stop them from trying to use them against you. Katelyn, they are zealots and dangerous, you must kill that person without mercy, because given the chance they will destroy you without mercy."

"If fire and dismemberment are the only things that will destroy me," I began slowly, trying to take in all he had just told me, "what about all the other things in the books and movies that are supposed to hurt me."

"They are all superstitions," he answered, "most of which were promulgated by our own kind to protect us. Humans often times destroy those things they don't fully understand. We have been called everything from the Undead, Lamia, Nephilim, blood-drinkers and even witches throughout history. The folklore allows us to prove that we are not what they think."

"Remember I told you I can see myself in a mirror. That's because I am solid and take up space, so there is something there to throw a reflection. Often times that alone will allay a suspicious human's curiosity."

"Some of the others that have been passed down include an aversion to crucifixes. They are merely a symbol of Christianity, having no power in and of itself. I can and have visited inside churches and chapels with no bitter side effects," he smiled, "in fact many of the older cathedrals and churches in Europe contain some of the most amazing and beautiful architecture you are ever likely to see."

"You can walk across running water," he smiled, "I'm not real sure where that one came from, but just the same if it proves to a human that you are like them, so much the better."

"But garlic … now that is another story entirely … garlic is very powerful, but another superstition that humans don't understand. You see it only tends to repel humans not vampires," he said laughing, "although it will assault your sense of smell if you get too close to someone who has eaten it."

A sudden peal of laughter rolled out of me as I pictured that in my mind. Then trying not to giggle too hard I asked, "Then what about wooden stakes and silver chains?"

"Stakes are only an inconvenience for you," he answered, "but they always end up badly for the poor fool who tries to employ one. Most of the time they end up sticking out of the chest of the attacker, which of course just adds to and strengthens the lore of it being a weapon to destroy us."

"Silver on the other hand, makes a very nice accessory, especially with dark clothing," he chuckled again, "silver is the color of the night, it's very feminine, and always associated with the moon. Our kind tends to gravitate towards it because it does symbolize the night where we spend so much of our time."

"Finally," he continued, "you don't need permission from someone to enter their home. You may do so anytime you wish, although if the person has manners they will invite you to come inside. There have been many times Katelyn that I have stood watch over you while you slept in your dorm room, protecting you from your nightmares," he smiled at me.

"So all those times I recall seeing your eyes, it wasn't a dream like I thought," I said, more statement than question.

"Katelyn, you have been under my protection since the very first time we spoke," he smiled.

I nodded and smiled, "Then I'm going to have to talk to you about that watching me in my bed thing … and not joining me … but thank you for taking away my horrible nightmares."

"You are very welcome," he chuckled softly, "and I

did enjoy the guard duty … you sleep so beautifully … but I'm afraid had I joined you, we would have greatly disturbed Lexi's rest … you do remember that she was in the bed next to yours!"

"Yeah, I suppose that would have indeed been a very rude awaking for her … even though she *did* get to watch you the first – and second – time that you took my pajama bottoms off," I chuckled.

"I seem to recall that she found it to be humorously entertaining, too," he added with a laugh.

"Meh, so she did … but I suppose it will give us happy memories to look back on and laugh about some day," I commented, "but James, all that aside, right now, I feel so very strange … inside and out … it's as if the whole world is spinning around in my head … I have so many questions I want to ask … and so much I want to say, but I'm not sure I know how … or what to ask and say."

"That's normal for now," he smiled at me, "remember that your body is still changing. You are transitioning from mortal to immortal, your mind is changing quickly and as such you may even seem a little confused at times. That will all go away while you rest. Katelyn, you are very much like a new born child right now. You are learning and getting used to being in a new environment."

"Come with me … I have another new experience waiting for you," he said, still with a smile, taking me by the hand, "besides, I think you have learned enough for today, it's time that you feed and rest. And, we are going to walk inside, slowly, this time."

Chapter Thirty~Two

I stood up easily from my chair, and immediately noticed that my movements seemed to be more graceful than before, almost fluid-like in motion. I stood for a moment, careful not to directly face the sun, and followed James into the house, my hand in his. I quickly became aware that in addition to my now flowing movements just how lightly I stepped, barely putting any pressure on my feet. I also took note that I made absolutely no noise as I moved. I continued holding his hand, staying close to him as we moved, feeling safety in his presence. We moved silently through the house and went into the huge library.

He went to one of the bookshelves near the fireplace and reached inside. I heard a faint 'click' and the entire section of shelves opened. They noiselessly moved backward and then slid behind the adjoining section of shelves. I watched, fascinated, as they moved and saw that they revealed a small room concealed behind them. He led me into the hidden room and there I saw … a coffin … resting on a low catafalque.

"Mmmkay … a coffin … yeah … guess I should have seen that one coming … but do I really *have* to get in that thing," I asked slowly looking at him.

"Don't let it frighten you, darling," he began with a smile, "you are only being affected by some residual human emotions. As you become less human and more vampire, they will fade away. Besides, it's only a temporary resting place while you finish the change. It's important that you have some seclusion at the beginning. Think of it as a type of womb if you will, one that I had custom made just for you, there's not another one like it in the world. It is constructed of African Blackwood, also known as Mozambique Ebony. It is the most expensive exotic wood in the world. All of the adornments are rendered in eighteen carat gold. The interior is lined with the finest handmade cashmere velvet from northern India. The embroidery all hand done with natural Tibetan silk."

"Yeah, that sounds nice and all … but me … in a coffin …" I murmured softly, silently contemplating it, "and I'm only twenty-one …" Then realizing I would be twenty-one forever and that I was thinking like a human – again – I quickly pushed those thoughts out of my head.

"Soon, probably no more than a couple of weeks, you won't have to use it any longer. But, it will always be here for you. There will be times, especially while you are young, that you will want to be apart for a short time, and when that happens it offers you total reclusiveness," he reassured me.

I stepped uneasily toward the coffin, reaching out to carefully touch it, letting my fingers move lightly across the top. I walked all the way around it, taking in every detail with my new preternatural eyes.

I had to admire its beauty, the wood was carefully polished to a deep black with a highly curved top. It glistened in the dim light of the little room. Every seam and joint was accented with decoratively carved molding. There were golden Seraphim bowed in prayer at each corner. Their feathery wings wrapped to the sides and stretched out along the bottom of the lid. It reminded me very much of a royal sarcophagus from the pyramids of ancient Egypt.

The handles, four to a side, were of black onyx, with gold embellishments, each attached to a rectangular golden plate. Each of the eight plates was finished in a different, high bas relief funerary scene with the words "Just Sleeping" engraved into the scroll work.

There was a solid gold plate accented with deeply engraved roses, set into the top and elegantly inscribed,

My Beloved Katelyn, Forever Young

I smiled at the plate, knowing that James had added that touch himself, and that special show of care made it personal, it made it mine. I knew he loved me deeply, and I also knew that now I was indeed forever young.

He opened the full lid for me and I saw that inside it was very feminine. It was lined throughout with the beautiful pink velvet he had described. The inside of the lid was heavily embroidered with a running vine of stunning red roses. A matching pink satin pillow, also embroidered with roses, lay at the head.

I carefully considered it, my emotions, mortal and immortal, clashing terribly with each other. I was really not sure just what to say … on the one hand, as an artist, I could appreciate its beauty … but on the other … well, nobody had ever given me a coffin before … then I smiled at him and said, "James, it's just … gorgeous … thank you so much!"

He looked at me and with a soft chuckle said, "I considered having cable and air installed but since it's only for a couple of weeks I assumed you could rough it."

"Oh! … No! … You did not just say that … you are so wrong," I laughed, feeling my sense of humor starting to reawaken, "No cable … why James, how will I ever survive without my favorite shows?"

He took me in his arms and whispered in my ear, "I think I can keep you distracted … allow me to illustrate …"

And he kissed me … deeply and passionately … producing strong tingles in all the right places.

"Yeah, that's distracting," I laughed when he finished.

"But now, before you rest, you must feed for the first time as an immortal," and with a swift movement he opened his neck with a fingernail.

When I saw the blood, I lunged at him, quickly forgetting about the kiss and the tingles, wrapping my arms around his shoulders and my legs around his waist. Locking him in my grip, I bowed my head to his neck and began drinking from him. The blood-lust rose up strong in me as his blood began filling my mouth. It tasted so sweet I never wanted to stop. I drank, pulling deeply as his life filled me, the strength and nourishment of it flowing throughout my body as it continued working the change in me.

While I drank, I began to relax, unwinding my legs from around his waist, standing on my own, but still holding him locked tightly in my arms. I felt so many emotions in me as I held him close drinking him in. His love for me was almost a physical entity as we stood there locked to each other. I literally felt his love as it flowed, along with his blood, into every part of my body. I could hear his heart beating at its slow and easy pace as I continued to drink my fill, hoping he could sense my never-ending love for him in return. There was no doubt in me that now, and forever, we would be a part of each other.

When I had finished feeding, I slowly brushed my tongue along his neck making sure to get every last drop. I watched in amazement as the open wound in his neck closed, completely disappearing. I stepped away from him, wholly sated, still licking my lips, wanting to savor every last touch of his taste.

"Now," he said with a gleaming smile, "it is time for you to rest," and he easily swept me up in his arms and gently laid me down in my new coffin. I cuddled into the soft luxurious velvet and folded my hands across my stomach, feeling perfectly at home.

He looked at me and said, "Don't be afraid when I close it, the lock is on the inside … right here … and only you can operate it; when you wake you can unlock it and open it back. I'll be waiting and listening for you, I will know when you wake, and return to get you then. Rest well and grow strong my love," he said with a smile and kissed my forehead as he lowered the lid.

The darkness was complete as I lay there. I heard the faint click of the bookshelves as they moved back into their position securing my resting place. I gently closed my eyes, unafraid now, as once again, the deep death-like sleep slowly covered me.

Chapter Thirty~Three

When I opened my eyes again, although the darkness was total, I realized there was no reason to be afraid. I was safely tucked away in the little hidden room behind the bookshelves in the library, lying comfortably in my new coffin – and I was a bit taken aback at just how comfortable it actually was. I smiled at the thought that now I had become a vampire – a truly life changing thing – and while there was no fear, there was however, a severe burning thirst, and I knew immediately I needed more blood; it was my strength, my life. I lay there considering the thirst, knowing I needed to get up, when I also remembered that I should explore my surroundings to ensure that no danger existed. I reached out with my mind to probe the small room, searching into every tiny recess of it, and just as I suspected, it was empty. James had promised me seclusion here.

When I was certain that the room was empty, I tentatively reached up and touched the top of my coffin. I heard a tiny 'whoosh' as the heavy lid, assisted by a small hydraulic support hidden at either end, effortlessly swung open. I sat up and with no difficulty stepped out onto the floor. The room was in total darkness but my preternatural eyes allowed me to see every detail of the little niche as I slowly looked around once again.

I reached out even further with my mind, exploring the library just on the other side. That's when I caught James' scent and at the same time felt his presence. I smiled knowing he was waiting on me. I decided to try my telepathy and see if it had survived the change in me also.

"James," I tried projecting my thoughts, *"can you hear me?"*

"Of course I can my love," his immediate, soothing response floated through my mind, *"I felt your mind sweep over me and knew that you were awake."*

"Uhh … a little help here," I continued, *"can you let me out, please?"*

"Why, do you really, really have to pee," he asked laughing.

"No!" I exclaimed and then stopping to think about what he had just said uncertainly asked, *"Am I supposed to …"*

"I hope not," he chuckled, *"but I thought I should ask since it was the first thing you said to Lexi the first time you woke up here."*

"James – of all the things for you to remember … You are so wrong for that," I exclaimed, trying to suppress a chuckle.

"Alright, I shall try to be serious again," he replied still softly chuckling, *"You try opening it first Katelyn, it's the same*

principle as moving from place to place. Think what you want to happen."

I considered his words for a moment, then directed my thoughts toward the back of the bookshelves, and whispered, "Open I want out."

Immediately I heard the faint little 'click' as they unlocked and began to move inward and to the side. That prompted a big smile as I stepped out into the library where James was waiting for me. Still excited about what he had just taught me, I turned and looked at the bookshelves and again whispered softly, "Close," and instantly they moved back into their place accompanied by the sound of the lock securing them shut.

"Now that's pretty cool," I exclaimed like a child that had just learned a new trick. Then I turned with a big smile looking at James for his approval.

"You did well," he said smiling back at me, "I knew you could do it!"

I crossed the room to him and gently wrapping my arms around him, kissed him lightly. He put his arms around me, and tenderly kissed me back.

"Ummm … there's that tingle again … he's going to have to do something about that … real soon," I thought.

"You must quit thinking about those tingles," he chuckled, "I promise, I'll take care of all of your tingles … in time!"

"James, stop reading my thoughts," I chided, "but, all tingles aside, my throat feels like it's on fire and I ache all over … I'm burning with thirst!"

"I understand young one, come and feed," he said lowering his collar and again opening his neck with a fingernail. I quickly put my mouth to his neck and began to drink, slowly wrapping my arms around him, holding him as I did.

His blood, the very life of him, tasted extremely gratifying as it filled my mouth, quenching my thirst. I swallowed the first time and the fire blazed up in me. I locked myself tighter to him, pulling as hard as I could; I wanted every drop of his sweet nectar. I drank until I was gorged, and sudden new life went roaring through my veins, filling every part of my body with new strength.

He gently removed me from his fountain and said, "That's enough for now, leave a little for me," he joked.

"Now," he continued, "let's explore some of your new found abilities and try some other things. You know how to move from place to place, but I'm sure there are other things – many that you haven't discovered yet – that you can do, too."

"Lead me on Lover, show me what I can do," I chuckled, as new energy, fueled by the fresh blood, zipped through me and like a dynamo inside me was producing endless stamina. I knew I could do anything James wanted me to right now. This new life was turning out to be better than I ever thought.

"Take a look at the door over there leading to the hall, now slowly open it so we can go through it."

I looked at the door and just like with the book shelves softly spoke, "Open, allow me through," and it swung open just as if there were a doorman standing there.

"Very good!" he said, "the same aspect holds true for anything you want to open or close. Now, an important point to remember is that if you close a door, or window, no human can open it again unless you allow it."

"The next thing we need to try is more than a gift; it is also a very dangerous weapon and can be used to protect yourself – fire. Let's see if you can do this. Take a look at the fireplace over there," he indicated with his hand, "think about being cold and you wish to be warm."

I looked where he was pointing and saw the fireplace stacked with several logs. I concentrated on the logs and whispered, "Light" … and the big chandelier hanging from the ceiling above us twinkled into life.

James was smiling at my confusion when it didn't work the way I expected, "Think about what you said and try another word. In every case, it's the words you use that are important, the words are the power behind your desire … your words will bring it to reality."

I carefully reconsidered the logs again, thought exactly what I wanted and then it came to me, "Burn!" I spoke out and the logs burst into a roaring fire.

"Again, very good," he smiled proudly, "If you should ever need to use fire as a weapon, defensive or offensive, you do the same thing. Simply concentrate on what, or who, you wish to burn. It's the only weapon you have to use against your own kind. But, it's also a weapon of last resort and should only be used when you have no other choice. But be very careful, it is a potent talent that can and will save your life if needed."

"Now," he continued, "let's go back to the veranda. This time we'll move the fast way and I'm going to increase the difficulty for you just a little. Take my hand … attempt to carry me with you."

I reached out, took his hand and thought about the veranda. I wanted to go there, and I wanted James to go with me … and we were suddenly there, standing beside each other just as I visualized. I also noted that the sky was quickly moving toward night and this time there was almost no pain in my eyes from the late evening sunlight.

"James, this is all so amazing … is there anything we

can't do," I asked.

"Very little," he replied, "although you are very young, you are extremely strong ... not only because of my blood, but also because of your bloodline, one that stretches back over six hundred years in length. Charlotte Ann was over a century old when she made me. In turn, her sire was over two centuries old, and I have waited over two hundred fifty years for you. Since each of us has made only one child, you have benefited greatly from the combined strength of three very old immortals."

"Most of the time, a young fledgling like yourself, cannot do some of the things you have already accomplished for many years. I knew that you would be a strong immortal and you have not disappointed me. I think you will soon discover that you have many other gifts and talents lying inside, waiting to be called upon. When you learn to call on them, it's then just a matter of learning to harness and control them."

"You also possess in you the ability to pass the gift along and make another immortal any time you wish. But, I would recommend that you consider well the individual you choose to turn. Do not do so without giving great consideration to the situation. Katelyn, you carry within you the gift of life, and it should be reserved solely for someone very close and very special to you. Just as I knew that you were special to me, you will know when to give this gift. It is the most precious thing you have, so never give the gift easily or lightly ... and when you do, only do so with the greatest love for the one receiving it."

"Now," he continued with a grin, "the night is early but I think it time that you begin discovering your new world, so let's take a short stroll together. We are going to walk around the grounds a bit and then venture toward the river for a closer look at it. I want you to begin to sense your surroundings, smell the air, the ground, and the different creatures that are all around us. Explore your new self and see just how sensitive you are to all the things around you. While we walk I want you to tell me what you see and feel."

Then he stood, and reaching for my hand, I followed him into the darkness. We reached the bottom of the steps and stood silently on the pathway. I looked around and noted that I could clearly see the flowers in the garden, the backdrop of trees at the edge of the property, and even hear the gentle movement of the individual leaves as the breeze softly tickled them. But the most astounding thing I noticed was that the darkness … wasn't that dark anymore. Instead it now looked to be made up of layers upon layers … hundreds of them … and each a different color. I looked into the night with the eyes of an artist, but saw the darkness with the eyes of a vampire … a new sight that now revealed every shade of blue that made up the strata. The layers of the night lying closest to the ground were the darkest shades of black … and as I followed the tiers with my eyes toward the crown of the sky, each level seemed to be only a shade lighter … a difference I instinctively knew that no human eye could distinguish. I looked into the night sky and saw literally millions upon millions of stars, unlike I had ever seen before, filling the clear panorama around me. The night had become a truly beautiful place … a place that now I felt more comfortable in than ever before.

I turned with an excited smile to look at James and when he met my gaze I noted that the pupils of his eyes were fully opened, only the tiniest circle of his green iris' were visible, allowing him to take in the smallest amount of light and see clearly in the darkness. I instinctively knew that right now my own blue eyes looked the same as his.

We walked along, hand in hand, in silence, as I continued taking in the sights and sounds around me. I could hear small animals in the area and although we were a distance from the river I noted that I could hear it plainly, even being able to discern which direction the water flowed as it moved toward the sea. I sensed a small disturbance in the air and looked up in time to watch as a huge owl swooped out of the tree line and into the tall grass, picking up its dinner. I watched, fixated on him as he climbed quickly back into the air with a large snake, twisting and turning in its own death throes, now gripped firmly in his talons. I continued to watch and realized that I was not hearing the big predator itself but the flow of air over its feathers as it returned, perching on the limb it had started from, and began devouring its catch.

"Do you see anything interesting," James asked with a smile as I turned to look at him.

"James, everything is so beautiful, I never knew the night held such secrets," I started, my smile growing, "There's so much to take in … everything has changed, it's all so new now … and I can see, hear, and strangely enough, I can feel everything around me. I actually think I felt the owl before I saw him!"

"You did," he replied smiling, "and as your senses and instincts develop you will be even more alert to what is around you. I saw the owl, sitting in the tree, onc predator watching another, from the time we left the veranda. He actually swept down and took his prey to prevent us from doing so."

"Yeah, well, I'd have let him have it … I've had my fill of snakes around here," I chuckled,

We continued our walk and I again felt like a child exploring its world for the first time, endlessly amazed at the sights and sounds of what was in it. We walked along the river hand in hand for a while longer, James allowing me to continue slowly exploring my new life and the world that went with it.

After about an hour he stopped and dropped my hand. Then turning toward me he said, "I want you to stand perfectly still … allow the darkness to concentrate around you … close your eyes and think about your surroundings … feel the earth under your feet, the sky above you, and the air that surrounds you, allow the elements to cover and hide you … now, breathe in the scents … slowly … think about all of it and tell me what you feel."

I did as he instructed, closing my eyes, fearless in the knowledge that he was right beside me. I stood as still as an oak, listening. I felt like my feet were becoming a part of the earth, like the rich ground underneath me was reaching out to me, claiming me as a part of itself. Then the darkness began to close in around me, not in a scary way but more like a cloak or covering. I could actually feel it covering and hiding me from the things I heard all around me. I felt myself disappearing into it, becoming a part of it, and I realized that nothing could see me unless I wanted it to.

"I feel … like I have become a part of the night," I began slowly, wonderingly, "I don't feel like I'm standing in the darkness anymore … instead, I've become a part of the darkness … acutely aware of everything that is happening around me."

"Exactly, my little love, and that is how you will hunt when the time comes," he spoke softly next to me, "now open your eyes and look around you again."

I did as he said and looked around me knowing that I wasn't just *in* the night but now I *was* the night. I looked at James with a smile at the change that was working in me. He smiled back at me and then unexpectedly he said, "Now Katelyn, follow me," and he disappeared!

I knew he wouldn't allow me to get hurt, and not wanting to look scared, I just stood still. I looked all around and when I didn't see him anywhere I closed my eyes and began to concentrate on him and search for his presence in the night. In a moment I felt him as if he were standing next to me. I opened my eyes again and began looking in the direction I had felt him. I quickly picked up his scent and followed it with my eyes to a tree several yards in front of me. I looked up and there he was sitting easily on a branch about thirty feet in the air.

"Well you found me quick enough," he chuckled low, "now come join me … jump … you can do it!"

I looked up and felt my body tense and like a coiled spring releasing, I jumped. Sailing effortlessly through the air, I landed on the branch right beside him, although probably not as gracefully as he had. He reached out his arms, putting his hands around my waist and steadying me as I looked all around. I was able to see for miles because of the flat terrain of the low country, noting the distant glow of Charleston's downtown and Port area lighting up the night sky. I suddenly felt the urge to laugh and giving it free reign I let the laughter boil up out of me. The waves of joy and happiness rolled through me as I sat there with his arms around me, beginning to fully realize my new world.

"Let's go now, Katelyn, we'll make our way back to the house," James spoke up after a couple of hours of sitting quietly together, observing the surroundings with me. I jumped with him to the ground, landing lightly on the balls of my feet and instantly stood upright. Together we began a slow walk hand in hand again, back to the veranda where we had started.

When we were seated safely back on the veranda James smiled at me and said, "Now, there is only one final thing we must discuss … and that is your financial security. You remember I told you that you would begin amassing wealth?"

"Yeah, you mentioned that," I said, "but how, and is it really that important now?"

"Not so much in our world, but it makes it easier to operate in the mortal world, and since you are my child, it is my responsibilities to insure that you have whatever you need to survive. I believe that you already have a bank account in Charleston," he asked knowingly.

"Yeah," I replied, "I have a little over five hundred thousand left from my parent's estate."

"That's a good beginning, but may I suggest that you take that, and entrust it to my agent in New York to begin investing and growing it?"

"I suppose so," I answered hesitantly, "but it's all I have James, will it be safe?"

"You have nothing to worry about, I trust her explicitly with all of my investments … I have been utilizing their services since 1753, just after my father's death. Let her oversee it and you can forget about it for the next hundred and fifty years."

"Oh," I looked shocked, "is she like us?"

"No," he said quickly smiling, "and she has no idea about us. She is just the current point of contact. But her investment firm has been around since before the founding in one form or another. If you will trust my agents Katelyn, let them become your agents, they will invest the money wisely and you will become very wealthy … they operate on the principle that if I, or in this case you, don't make money, neither do they."

"Now as to your current financial security, I have instructed my agent in London to establish a separate account for you in Bern, using some of my British funds. As such, you are now the proud new owner of a Swiss bank account with one hundred million dollars in it and there for your use at any time," he said with a demure little smile.

I was dumbfounded at what he had just said. I could not imagine that kind of money.

"Try to control your look of shock," he chuckled, "my agents also have offices in Paris, Berlin, Rome and, most recently, Moscow. So, should you ever be anywhere in the world and have need of cash, you only have to contact one of them and they will take care of anything for you."

"I … I just don't know what to say, James, I'm in shock!"

"Katelyn, I love you," he said, "and I will take care of you. Besides, that's only a small portion of what I have accumulated over the years and just enough to get you started."

"I love you too James, so very much," I said, feeling like I was about to cry, and suddenly found myself wondering if I even could, "but right now I feel suddenly overwhelmed. There seems to have been so much today … my new powers and how to use them … both as weapons and gifts … the gift of life … the secrets of the night … and now all that wealth … I feel like I just want to escape, can I go inside and rest now, please," I asked almost pleadingly.

"Of course you can, darling," he smiled at me, "you may rest anytime and for as long as you wish. Time no longer has any constraints upon you. But before you rest you should drink again. Your body is still going through some changes. Your new being is changing you, quickly using the blood you take to finish your transformation, and as such requires a greater amount of blood at the beginning. It's almost completely finished and you will be stronger when you wake. After today you should be able to tell a pronounced difference in yourself."

"Let's try a little experiment this time and find out just how much self-control you have. When you feed this time, try to take only a little amount, just a couple of swallows," he said smiling, "I want to begin teaching you how to control your blood-lust. I don't think it will be difficult, but let's see what happens."

I went to him and cuddled like a child in his lap as he again opened the artery in his neck for me. With one arm around his shoulder I bowed my head to his neck, gently placing my mouth over the wound he had opened. Pulling easily I took one large mouthful of his sweet, wonderful blood and swallowed quickly. I felt the energy begin to reinvigorate me almost instantly. Then I took another, smaller drink, quickly swallowed, and with great determination, I lifted my head up and looking in his eyes I smiled at him.

"Oh, wait," I quickly added and lowering my head back to his neck I very slowly and sensuously, with just the tip of my tongue, licked him along the still flowing wound, letting my tongue move playfully along the base of his neck and upward to his ear lobe and gently kissed it.

"How's that for self-control," I asked with a little laugh as I stepped away.

"You keep that up and you will make me lose mine," he said, shaking his head, "you amaze me, Katelyn, you were very strong and self-disciplined as a human but it usually doesn't carry over in the transformation, especially where feeding is concerned. But now, it is time for you to rest."

He walked with me to the library and I looked at the bookshelves, and quietly said, "Open," and they began their movement. I turned toward him with a very naughty smile, and playfully rubbing his chest said, "Why don't you go with me, we can find out what else carried over in my transformation!"

"Trust me darling, you are *not* ready for that yet, and besides your coffin isn't anywhere near large enough. But soon, when you are more completely changed and stronger," he smiled at me, "because you are going to need a great amount of strength and stamina for that occasion."

"Well then, here's a little reminder of what's waiting for you when you think I'm strong enough," I laughed and pulled him close kissing him very passionately.

"Against my better judgments you make me not want to wait," he smiled, as he continued to hold me in his arms, "but I know that you must rest, grow and gain your full immortal strength. Now before you go, I want you to know that we will have a guest when you wake up. Charlotte Ann will be arriving sometime today to join us for a while. There are some things that she, as a woman, can assist you with that I am unable to do as you complete the change. She has a very strong presence and I wanted you to know not to be afraid when you wake and sense an unknown being in the house."

I smiled, hugely excited at the thought of finally getting to meet her, but at the same time, I sensed a difference in my body and knew that I had to quickly get inside my secluded little hide away. My energy seemed to be draining fast, even after the quick drink I had just taken from James, and I needed to rest. I walked over to my coffin, actually happy to see it waiting for me. I opened the lid and happily lay down, stretching out comfortably and thinking how special I was to James for him to have gone to such great expense just for me. I snuggled comfortably into the soft velvet again, its fleecy warmth wrapping around me. I was warm, but comfortable as my silk pajamas settled lightly on my new skin. The last thing I heard, as I closed the lid and the welcoming darkness of sleep began to cover me, was the soft click of the bookshelves sliding back into place.

Chapter Thirty~Four

I am unsure how long I rested this time, not that it mattered anymore, because, at least for me, time had stopped; now and forever, it had indeed lost its importance to me. My sleep now is a very peaceful, very deep and dark, near death-like slumber that feels like a protective blanket surrounding me. When I begin to awaken, it gathers, as if it were folding itself from the four corners, and begins moving away from me.

When I opened my eyes I sensed a real substantial change just as James had said. It was not as tangible as the physical changes that had occurred when I first turned. Instead, I felt more powerful than I had before, as if there were a new dynamic strength inside me. I continued lying there in the darkness, adjusting to this newness that seemed to be almost slumbering as I did, lying in wait for me to call it forth.

I also noted that I was not as thirsty as I had been when I awakened last time. Although I knew I would have to feed soon, the intense burn at the back of my throat just was not there at this point. While I continued to enjoy the peaceful slumber I casually wondered what would happen if my resting place were ever disturbed, would I wake immediately, or would I just lie here defenseless. That would be something to ask James about.

So, with a stronger confidence than I had felt yet, I reached out with my mind to examine the room where my coffin lay hidden. When I found the room empty, as expected, I opened the lid back and stepped out into the darkness. I stood there basking in the thick shadows that now offered me so much protection instead of fear, feeling the latent power in me beginning to move as I did, giving me more vigor.

I recalled James had said we were to have a visitor, so I cautiously let my mind reach out beyond the bookshelves and tentatively probed the house, looking, feeling, waiting to see if I could detect a new presence yet.

I easily found her, and just as James had said, she was indeed a physically powerful presence. I quickly found her scent too, a sweet mixture of lavender and lilac. Like her presence, it was intense but softly feminine and nicely fragrant, definitely different from James'. I don't think I could have missed her even had I not been expecting her. She had such a force about her that I think I could have picked her out in a crowd of people. That thought made me stop for a moment and consider that perhaps that was how I could know another immortal anywhere.

I allowed my mind to linger around her rather than just passing over her. I suppose that in my newborn innocence I wanted to alert her to my presence. I waited to see if she sensed me, too, while still trying to conceal my exact location. There was a strong desire in me that wanted to let her know that I offered, and felt, no threat.

Unexpectedly, there came a strong response emanating out from the center of her toward me. It was a soothing comfort as she recognized my presence, and easily acknowledged no threat felt or offered in return. She moved over and around me, surrounding me like a soft hug from a friend. That was pleasing I thought, as her presence lingered, wrapping around me like a light blanket. I began to relax and then quickly let my mind move on searching for James. I found him very close to her, but her power and presence was so overwhelming that his presence was almost lost in it.

I was letting my mind hover around James when, out of the blue, the softest, sweetest voice I had ever heard spoke to my mind, *"Hello, Katelyn! I'm so glad you are awake now young one. I have looked forward to making your acquaintance for many months! Please come out and let me meet you."*

I suppose I was a little shocked at her boldness but suddenly learned that it wasn't just James and I that could communicate telepathically.

"James ..." I slowly asked, desiring his approval.

"It's alright, my love, please join us," he answered me.

I moved out of my little room, passing through the library, down the large hallway and into the main parlor of the house. Although she didn't speak to my mind again, I began to understand from her as I moved closer, that she knew exactly where my resting place was located and had chosen the parlor so as to be further away from it. She led me to know that she wanted to give me space and not cause me any undue fear when I woke. I suddenly realized the true sanctity of the resting place if one this old and powerful was not willing to risk disturbing it. I appreciated the courtesy and silently sent out a thank you to her for considering my feelings.

The two of them sat in the large parlor, smiling at me when I entered. She stood up and moved so elegantly that she seemed to glide across the room toward me saying, "Katelyn, I'm Charlotte Ann, and I'm so glad to finally meet you. James has told me so much about you."

Her voice was just as soft as it had been when she mentally spoke to me. She was very petite, as James had said, looking very much the same in stature as Lexi had been. But she was so absolutely, breathtakingly beautiful. The light preternatural aura that emanated from her added to her finely feminine features. She had a playfully mischievous smile that revealed perfectly straight, white teeth that invited me to come closer. Her brown hair hung to just past her shoulders and had a subtle hint of a curl to it. It framed her face, adding to her enticing beauty. She had soft brown eyes and baby-doll lashes. There was just the lightest splash of freckles across her nose and the tops of her cheeks. Her playful smile and youthful appearance all combined together to give her an incredibly voluptuous appeal … one that I instinctively knew she used successfully to draw her prey. There was no doubt that she was a mature woman, but she could easily have passed for an older teen or perhaps, as I had recently been, a college student.

She was dressed colorfully in a loose fitting sleeveless blouse that rested lightly on her shoulders. Her pencil skirt was short, coming to mid-thigh, and snug, but fitted her perfectly, accenting her small and shapely body. She was wearing a pair of stylish heels which added a couple of inches to her height. Her entire outfit highlighted the perfect marriage of her innocent, youthful looks and worldly seductiveness at the same time. Altogether it was a very dangerous combination and certainly lethal for her intended prey. I felt the kinship flowing from her when she hugged me, quickly making me feel comfortable with her closeness.

"I'm so happy to finally meet you too, Charlotte Ann," I replied shyly, "James has told me so much about you that I almost felt like I knew you before you arrived."

She took a step back and giving me an appraising head to foot look said, "Oh Katelyn, you are so much more beautiful than James described you … you have indeed made a stunningly gorgeous immortal … perfectly attractive and I can't wait for us to go shopping together, not to mention hunting! We should have no problem drawing our choice of fresh young men for dinner."

"But, I'm not so sure I'm ready to go back out in public just yet," I answered, a little hesitant.

"Oh, non-sense," she dismissed my objections with a quick wave of her small hand and a laugh, "you can't stay hidden away in this big old house forever. I think you are perfectly ready, you must let the world see what an absolutely beautiful immortal you have become … just probably not in those sexy pajamas … unless of course you happen to want an all you can eat buffet of hot blooded, horny young men lining up in front of you."

"Ummm … hot blooded … and an endless buffet, too … now there's a thought … and I do like the way you think," I said laughingly licking my lips as the thirst slowly rustled, rearing its head up in me.

"Don't forget horny … I did say horny …" she laughed, "But hot blooded horny young men aside, I promise to take just as good care of you as James would. I understand all about being new and the sometimes hardships it presents. Now, you do have something else to wear, don't you?"

"Yeah, I have some jeans and a few tee's put away upstairs," I said a little perplexed.

"I suppose we can make do with those until we go shopping," she said with a laugh, "but you'll quickly learn … and I'm sure James will agree with me … that I'm such a clothes whore, and I do style like nobody's business."

"I also have a couple of new, nicer outfits if I need them, but you gotta understand, clothes weren't exactly the main thing on my mind when this happened," I continued with a shy smile, sweeping a hand in front of my body to indicate my change.

"Yeah, I understand they weren't even on your body, let alone your mind, when that happened," she chuckled softly.

"James!" I exclaimed, looking over at him.

"Oh, sweetie, don't be embarrassed about it. I understand he's so terribly irresistible, and he's good too, isn't he … so very satisfying," she grinned, nodding her head in a knowing manner, and added a quick wink, "after all why and where do you think *he* was when I changed him?"

I giggled at her straight forwardness and had I been able to blush I would have been deep red just then. I found myself quickly warming up to her and beginning to like her more every minute as I grinned shyly back at her, nodding my head in agreement with a big smile. And then it hit me … what she had said about why and where she had changed him. Another huge grin spread across my face as I looked at her and said, "Wait a minute … you mean … you and him … before he was … did the deed … before you did that …"

"Of course we did, Katelyn … sweetie, it doesn't matter if it's the 1750's or the 2000's men and women are still men and women with the same desires and lusts they have always had. Regardless of the moralities of the time they will still do what they have done since the beginning of time. He just happened to do what men do so well that I felt I had to give him a little gift in exchange for all he had done for me … and of course so he could continue doing good things for me!"

I tried to stifle a laugh at her complete honesty as she added, "Did he happen to forget to mention that part of the story to you …"

"Yeahhh, 'bout that … I may have gotten the edited – heavily edited – version of that story," I laughed again.

"Well, it's safe to say," she winked at me, "that when I brought him over, he was in the exact same situation as you were when he brought you over."

I burst out laughing, "Nope, that's not exactly the version of the story I got."

"Well, he is a Southern aristocratic gentleman and doesn't readily discuss the details of his romantic liaisons," she added with a huge smile, "still, I couldn't very well let someone that good … that satisfying … just go away and become a forgotten memory under a tombstone somewhere."

"Well, I'm certainly glad you didn't," I said with a little smile playing around the corners of my mouth.

"My pleasure," she said as we giggled girlishly together, "I hope you get as much satisfaction from him as I did!"

"Yeah, so far so good," I grinned.

"Well, it only gets better … but that was over two hundred fifty years ago, and this is the here and now," she said bringing her story to a close, then lifting one eyebrow and looking at me with a mischievous twinkle in her eyes continued, "but since James is my child, and you are his child, that logically makes you my granddaughter, which is good … it means I get to spoil you … just don't you dare call me 'granny'!"

"Well you certainly don't look the grandmotherly type at all … so shall I just call you 'nana' instead," I said with a laugh.

"Ah, no … you shall not," she answered, struggling to hold back a laugh, "but I do admire your keen sense of humor!"

Then she turned back to James, who might have been looking just a tad bit uncomfortable at our recent exchange, and laughing said, "James, I'm taking my granddaughter shopping."

"Charlotte Ann …" he started cautiously, "please … you know I could never say 'no' to anything you wanted, but please don't range too far afield. Remember she hasn't hunted yet and we don't want to cause any problems."

"That's alright, I know of a wonderful little boutique downtown that should work just fine for us," and turning to me with a wink continued, "you and I will plan an extended shopping trip soon. When you have hunted for the first time, then we shall have our time together. We'll take a month or so and take in Chicago, San Fran, and Los Angeles. Have you ever shopped down Rodeo Drive … oh, we can be so extravagant … maybe even grabbing a couple of those haughty salespeople to eat while we're there."

"Yeah … well … that sounds like fun and I would love to go shopping with you … but all this talk of hunting and feeding has made me a little thirsty … James," I said turning toward him, "I haven't fed since … was it yesterday?"

"Katelyn, please allow me the honor," she interjected, her voice now very serious, "You are as much my blood as James', please come and feed from me young one. I will gladly open my heart and my mind, withholding nothing from you. Allow me to share my strength and my gifts with you, child. There is so much more I can show you and tell you as you feed than is possible with mere words."

I looked quickly at James and he nodded with a smile saying, "It will be an enjoyable experience for you."

Charlotte Ann moved closer to me and with a swift movement opened the artery at the base of her neck. I bent a little and putting my lips to her small neck started to pull. She wrapped her arms gently around me holding me close. The instincts in me swiftly took over and I locked my arms around her holding her tightly, pulling her closer to me. Her heart pumped her blood at the steady immortal pulse, quickly filling my mouth. I began to swallow over and over as it rushed into me, filling every part of me. It tasted very sweet, like James', only it was different … more like the taste of very old wine, aged to perfection. I drank like one dying of thirst, pulling strongly at her neck; I wanted to take all of it. It tasted so good I didn't think I could make myself stop at just a couple of mouthfuls.

She opened her mind to me and said, *"Drink, my child, long and deep, take all that you want, fill yourself with my life. Let it infuse every part of you. Let the strength of my oldness take away the weakness of your youth. Be strong and let nothing harm you."*

I looked deeper into her mind and she carried me back over nearly four centuries of time, sharing so much with me. The things she had seen and done were absolutely amazing. Such an experience, words alone cannot begin to describe it.

When I had filled myself, I raised my head from her neck and she smiled at me and said, "You have just received the blood and strength of at least three very old immortals from me. Allow the powers and wisdom that are contained in it to flow through you, making you to be as if you were a very old immortal yourself. Your strength is many times multiplied over that of any fledgling you may happen across. Let wisdom guide you, child, use your powers and strength wisely and nothing will ever harm you."

"Now, if you would like to sit here with me on the couch, I will share with you the beginning of my story …"

Chapter Thirty~Five

I was born in London in the year 1606, a full year before England began settling Virginia."

"Well, that certainly puts your life in a new perspective," I whispered, remembering my high school history class.

"My family was a prominent shipping family at the time. I was born the youngest of six children – with three brothers and two sisters. My father owned twelve large cargo ships and still went to sea as the Captain of the largest of them. My mother, as was normal in those times stayed at home, oversaw the house, the servants, and raised the children."

"I was always a little different than the rest of my brothers and sisters. I was always looking for excitement, the most headstrong, the most adventurous, and in my opinion, the prettiest. Although I was a girl, I enjoyed being with my father on his ship and walking the surrounding docks holding his hand. I delighted in the sounds and the smells of the waterfront."

"And by the way," she added looking at me, "I still enjoy a good hunt along the docks. The only thing that's changed in four hundred years is the size of the ships. We'll have to make it a point to hunt the waterfront together. I think that you would enjoy it there, and I'm sure the two of us would make a very successful team."

"That sounds like it might be fun … especially with you," I laughed, "I can't wait!"

"I promise, it'll be an enjoyable hunt," she smiled as she continued her story, "I learned a great deal about life growing up around my father and his ships. While I was a child, the crew of my father's ship, many of which had no families themselves, adopted me as a kind of ship's mascot and acted like I was their own child. Many of them brought me all kinds of little trinkets from their vast travels to the many ports of call around the world. I sat for hours when they were in port listening to the yarns they spun of faraway places."

"My imagination ran wild as I tried to picture the people and places they talked about. They told me of people with red, yellow and black skins. They talked about places that had fruits and other things to eat like we had never seen in England. They even told me about a tree, found in the islands of the West Indies, called the Tree of Death, one that would kill a man in a matter of hours from just a touch. As I grew and matured, entertained by their tales, I wanted more than ever to be like my father and be a ship's Captain."

"I think that my father finally realized as I continued to grow and age that I had no interest in being married and having children, still he held out hope that one day my mind would change and I would give him a grandchild. He desperately wanted me to be like my sisters, to marry and have children. But he knew that the time for that was growing shorter. He also knew that I was past the prime child bearing age – that most girls, like my sisters, were married and having children by the age of twelve or thirteen. It was a rare occasion indeed that a girl reached my ripe old age of fifteen without having a husband and several children."

"Twelve or thirteen," I asked looking at her in disbelief, "that's so young to be married, not to mention having kids!"

"Times and customs were very different then than they are today Katelyn," she smiled at me, "you must consider that the average lifespan in the early 1600's was only some thirty-five to forty years for a man. Most women only lived into their late twenties, many not even making it that far because they died giving birth."

"So, hoping to change my mind before it was too late," she continued with her story, "and knowing that I sought adventure and wanted to expand my world, father approached me with the best birthday present I have ever had. His newest ship, a fast galleon named the *Charlotte Ann*, was nearing completion and he was planning a short trip for her maiden voyage. So with my sixteenth birthday approaching, he offered me the opportunity to go to sea with him for that expedition … to say that made me the happiest girl in England would have been a huge understatement."

"Likewise, saying it made my mother happy was an even larger understatement. She was anything but enthused with the idea of me leaving, especially on a ship – that was full of men. What she didn't take into consideration though was that since those men all felt like they had had a hand in raising me, I was probably the safest woman on the planet. My father further calmed her concerns by assuring her that it was only a short trip and perhaps after I had had my adventure I would finally want to settle down, be more like my sisters, marry and give them grandchildren. Together they hoped that when it was over, it would cure me of my desire to be a seafarer."

"Since most of the crew had watched me grow up, they were enthusiastic about having me finally make a trip with them. They actually thought of me as their 'Good Luck Talisman' because the ship had been named after me. They rationalized that with the namesake actually onboard it would be an easy voyage and no harm would befall them."

"I was so excited I couldn't wait for our sailing day to arrive. The plan was that we would sail down the Thames and cross the Channel to France. There we would call on the port of Calais, then down the Normandy coast to Le Havre. Once we had taken on a full cargo we were bound for Athens, Greece. When we arrived in Athens we would unload our cargo, take on another cargo and return straightway to London."

"So, in the early summer of 1622, with the hope of fair winds and following seas we departed for 'parts unknown' as I happily referred to our destination. Those four months were the most enjoyable time of my human life and when we returned, I was anything but cured of my desire to travel the world."

"Sadly, fate soon dealt me a terribly tragic blow. My Father's ship left on a voyage in 1624 bound for China and the Spice Islands of the far-east and never came back. The only thing I would ever know for certain was that my father was never coming back to me. I grieved continuously, the days soon became months and then turned into years."

"My mother had to sell the shipping company by my twenty-first birthday in order to survive. She kept the huge manor house in the country outside London and split the remainder of the proceeds with us children. I decided to take my portion, packed a trunk and left on a tour of England, hoping to find a renewed happiness. Little did I know what an adventure I was setting out upon."

"In the spring of 1628 I departed on my tour of the country. I began with a trip south to Portsmouth, hoping that at that great seaport I might discover news of my father's ship. Sadly, there was no record of his ship being seen or heard from since leaving four years earlier. I finally accepted there was no hope left and departed for the northern part of the country. I spent the summer and fall in Cambridge, living in a boarding house. That was where I met Ferdinand, the most intriguing man I had ever met, and my life changed … literally forever."

"He treated me like a young lady, showing me special favors and before I realized it I had fallen madly in love with him. I enjoyed the special treatment Ferdinand lavished on me and grew to appreciate his romantic behavior."

"Then one day in early September, he asked me to accompany him for a ride in his carriage. I was flattered and gladly accepted his offer. We drove out into the countryside and stopped for a snack of bread, cheese and some wine under the shade of a giant old tree.

After a glass of wine he asked my permission to kiss me … I quickly and happily agreed … blushingly allowing him the privilege. He took me in his arms and ever so lightly kissed my lips. I closed my eyes and became lost in the wonderful reality of kissing him."

"Suddenly my eyes popped open at a sharp pain in

the side of my neck. I struggled to get away and see what had happened but he pulled me tighter against him, holding me there. I was filled with fear and thrashed frightfully trying to fight him off but he only pulled me closer and held me tightly to him. I didn't understand what or why this was happening to me."

"Abruptly I realized that Ferdinand had cut my throat and I had never even seen the knife … and what was worse, he was drinking my blood. This man that I loved with all my heart … one that I couldn't believe had come into my life at my age … was killing me and there was nothing I could do about it."

"Then he did the unexpected, lowering his collar and opening a gash at the base of his own throat. I saw his blood begin pouring from his throat as he pulled me toward the river of red. I was inexplicitly drawn toward the glimmering flow but at the same time horribly disgusted by it. Still, I was so weak at this point, that no matter how repulsive I thought it was, I didn't have any choice as he guided my mouth to his throat."

"When he had pulled me to him, he said, 'Drink now my little wounded one, and you shall live and never die'. I felt his blood begin pouring into my mouth and down my throat. I tasted the coppery earthy taste of it as it filled my mouth and I swallowed to keep from choking on it. I felt suddenly tired and my eyes grew heavy, I closed them and drifted off. When next I opened my eyes it was as the immortal you see me as today, almost four hundred years later."

"I didn't return to London again until 1750, over one hundred and twenty years later, making sure that by then all my family and friends were long dead. I left London again in the spring of 1753, and started back north to Cambridge, to the place of my second birth. Then early one afternoon while taking a walk in the afternoon sun, I stepped into the path of the most handsome young man I had ever seen. His lips looked to be so very soft and kissable … and his eyes … oh his eyes were the most intense emerald green you could ever look into …"

Chapter Thirty~Six

A couple of weeks had passed since I had turned and began not just a new life, but an entirely new existence. There was so much to know and learn about who and what I had become that I became a student all over again. I learned so many things from James and Charlotte Ann about my new life.

They were both extremely patient with me and I grew more comfortable day by day. During the first two or three weeks of my new life I fed only from them, one or the other would go hunting and when they returned, much like a baby bird in the nest feeds from its parents, they would feed me. They both insisted that until I was ready to hunt on my own, feeding only from them would strengthen me and help in my maturing process. My strength did grow very quickly from their constant care. I began to spend less and less time in my coffin, as I discovered that I no longer had the need or desire to sleep. Charlotte Ann even mentioned to me that it had been fifty-eight years since she had so much as taken a nap.

I ventured out into the city with Charlotte Ann a few times as she helped me transition back into the mortal world. Our trips usually started in the early evening, a couple of hours before sunset, because my new eyes were still adapting to the sun. We would walk together through the streets and crowds of downtown Charleston, often times arm in arm like the friends we were quickly becoming.

We shopped in all the little specialty shops and boutiques in the historic district, buying clothes and shoes. Thanks to her I soon had a completely new, and expensive, wardrobe to choose from for any occasion. We spent time casually chatting with people in the stores about the weather and upcoming events in the area, generally appearing to be nothing more than a couple of the local college girls.

Charlotte Ann used these times for instruction in my new life. She taught me how to scent blood when I hunted … the difference between male and female, young and old. She also taught me the scent of sickness and disease. I soon learned the unique smell of menstrual blood, and the reason for its distinctive smell, was that it was no longer living human blood, but dead blood that contained no life.

Many times when we were in the shops, we would brush up against someone, or lightly touch their arm or hand during our casual conversations. They never suspected that they had just come in contact with two potentially very dangerous immortals. When I was feeling especially comfortable in our outings, we would drop into one of the restaurants to have a drink together as I continued learning to become at home again in the human world. I soon came to realize, and to appreciate, just what a rare and wonderful gift I had been given.

I sat at the dressing table in my room quietly looking at the reflection of myself in the mirror, contemplating all the changes that had taken place in me when I turned. My preternatural vision was able to pick up every detail of my new self. When I was mortal, I had known that I was a beautiful young girl and had been told as much all of my life. Although, at the same time, I had also been taught that it was socially inappropriate to boast of it. So, I had never thought much of it or flaunted it in front of others; it was just there and not that important a detail to me.

Now, I considered the reflection in the mirror of what I had become. The physical changes were all minuscule but when added together, they created an indescribable beauty that I had never seen before. My physical beauty had been so enhanced as to be nearly breathtaking. It was the kind of beauty that in a human girl would have frightened many men away from approaching while at the same time causing other men to do anything to possess her. But this preternatural beauty, admittedly frightening in its perfection, was now a part of my draw. It was the instrument I would use to beckon to my prey. It contained an attraction that would make my prey want to come closer, to try to possess me if possible.

When I was mortal my eyes had been a stunningly deep electric blue. They had remained that same blue in the change but now they held a penetrating gaze with an intense shimmer as they reflected the light. I looked closer at them in the mirror, thinking they appeared enticing, tempting the beholder to come closer. They had the same intensity that I had first noticed in James' eyes.

My fangs were tiny, since they only had to penetrate a victim's skin deep enough to puncture one of the two main arteries in the neck. They were extremely sharp though, like the two precision surgical instruments they were. They extended and were only visible when I wanted them to be seen. I had not yet had the opportunity to use them since I was still feeding only from James and Charlotte Ann. James had refused to allow me to try them out, saying that he was fully capable of opening his own veins for me. He insisted with a smile that the first time I actually used them would rank among the topmost memorable events of my life and should be saved for my first hunt which he had promised he was working out the details of it and that it would be coming soon, too.

My hair was still the same dark brunette I had been born with, but now it had become fuller and thicker. It looked impeccable, just as it had that last day of my human life when Ashleigh had trimmed it and set it in place. It framed my face and shoulders and extended half way down my back in picture-perfect waves. It was soft and silky as I ran my fingers through it noting that it had taken on the look of a lion's mane. It was lighter now and moved easily, actually billowing softly in the breeze like the hood of a cobra, as I walked. When I brushed it, it developed a shimmering shine, again part of the draw for my prey.

My skin was cool and soft to the touch, satiny smooth and completely flawless. I no longer had the deep tan that I had worked on for so long. But, neither did I look chalky and pale like the classical movie vampire. Instead it had lightened to a natural medium tan resulting from the Cherokee blood of my maternal grandmother. When I did go into the sun, its warmth felt good and comforted me, flowing into every part of my body. When I fed, my skin developed a healthy glow giving me more of the deep tan I had when I was mortal. Feeding also produced an enjoyable warmth that lasted for many hours afterward and seemed natural to the casual touch.

I smiled silently as I continued studying my reflection in the mirror, awed at how everything about me combined together to make me the perfect bait for the hunt. My thoughts were interrupted as I sensed James moving up the stairs and toward my room. I turned on my little dressing bench towards the door to greet him.

"Good morning," he said as he came into my room, "I see that you are up already."

"Oh yeah," I answered as I stood, still in my pajamas and stretched, arching my back, "Actually I haven't slept in the last couple of days, instead only lain on the bed and rested. You know James, I really like my coffin, it seems to feel more natural to me now than in the beginning, but it's so good to be back in a real bed again."

"And," I added with a coaxingly seductive smile, "unlike my coffin, the bed is plenty big enough for more than one … and has lots of room to move around in …"

"We shall certainly have to explore that possibility very soon," he smiled back, "but in the meantime, I'm here to give you something better than sex," he said with a smile.

"I wouldn't know," I said, flashing a devious smile, "I haven't had any in nearly three weeks and if I have to wait much longer I'm likely to forget what it is!"

"It's like riding a bicycle dear, you never forget how it's done," he smiled back at me, "but I promise, before long you will have your first chance at preternatural sex, and it *will* be worth the wait!"

"I hope you're right," I said and glancing at his neck asked with a smile, "Is breakfast ready?"

"Not today, Katelyn, like you said, it's been a couple of weeks since you turned and you have gotten very strong during that time, adapting well to your new life. I could not be more pleased with your progress. Now, however, I think it's time for my little 'Virgin Vampire' to lose her vampire virginity. So, I'm taking you hunting this afternoon … and I have a very special surprise in store for you," he said with a devious grin.

"Oh James, that's wonderful news! I can't wait, my first hunt, this is what I have been looking forward to … I'm so excited, please tell me all about it," I begged, momentarily forgetting about the promise of sex, as I jumped up like a child at Christmas, leaping across the room toward him.

"Watch it," he smiled, reflexively catching me in mid-air, both his hands circling my waist, he gently set my feet back on the floor, "you should be more careful jumping like that. You still don't realize the full range of your own strength yet!"

"If you keep touching me like that I'll show you how strong I can be," I purred as I cuddled against him, quickly kissing his lips, "now quickly, please tell me all about the hunt, I need to get my mind on something else!"

"If I told you what it was it wouldn't be a surprise now would it! But, I promise you shall enjoy this hunt, it will be one that you will remember forever and not just because it's your first time."

"Hummm … well, maybe I can make myself wait then," I said trying to act sad and stuck my bottom lip out in a little pout. But then brightened up just as quickly and asked with a laugh, "Please, do tell, what should the stylish and well-dressed vampire wear to go hunting in?"

"Well," he answered thoughtfully, "I've arranged for them to be waiting for you, so you won't have to attract and lure them to you. Perhaps you should present yourself as a wealthy young college student from a large city, so something classy but just a touch provocative. Suppose you wear a silk top with a short skirt to showcase those long beautiful legs? I think your intended prey will more than appreciate that look."

"Hummm … let's see now … wealthy – check … young – check … college student – check … yeah, I think I can pull that off without too much work," I chuckled, "now, you get out of here while I get dressed."

"Why should I leave, you're about to take your clothes off, or are you suddenly a prude," he asked getting playful again, "besides, there's no part of that tremendously beautiful body that I haven't seen, touched, kissed or petted," he grinned, as he slowly took me in his arms, giving me a light kiss, his hands sliding easily down my back to gently rest on my behind.

"Yeah, well, that was before, when I was mortal," I grinned back at him, enjoying the closeness and the feel of his arms around me, "now I'm a predator …" I tried to give my best growl, only to break up laughing as I cuddled closer to him, "and unless you're planning on finishing what you're starting you'll have to leave. Because if *you* stay much longer," I smiled threateningly, "and *I* get undressed, *we* may not go hunting … at least not outside of this bedroom! Now, stop distracting me," I laughed playfully, swatting at him, "I have to get dressed."

"Alright, alright, I'm leaving," he laughed and disappeared almost faster than my new eyes could follow him, leaving me standing there, suddenly so stinking horny I didn't think I could stand it. I had seriously enjoyed sex as a mortal, but now, one of the aspects of this new life, besides the untold powers and accented physical abilities and attractions, the immortal had also awakened in me a serious sexuality that I didn't know I possessed before. And like it or not, although I suspected he would like it, James was going to have to take care of that nearly constant tingle he produced in me – and soon!

Thankfully, I had a good assortment of clothes to choose from so I chose a sleeveless, low cut, pink satin blouse that fit just so and paired it with a short, tight, black pencil skirt that came to just above mid-thigh. It showed off my long legs to an advantage. I finished the outfit with a pair of open toed short heels, which made me just a shade over six feet tall.

I shook out my hair, until it perfectly framed my face and shoulders, resting easily down my back. I stood in front of the long dressing mirror, turning completely around and thought to myself, *"If I do say so myself, girl, you are awesome … classical, sexy, and showing just enough to create interest … and if I can't draw somebody's attention with this … they're already dead …"*

I turned and glided easily down the stairs to the front parlor where James was waiting for me. I smiled, half curtseyed, twirled around once and asked, "So, how does your little 'Virgin Vampire' look now, am I dressed properly for the hunt," I asked with a big smile.

"That look makes me want to eat you myself," he winked at me.

"You hold that thought until later," I giggled and winked back, "I'll be your dessert after the meal!"

"I suppose we should probably get started while I still can," he laughed, "Come over here and put your arms around me, it's a bit of a trip, so I will carry you this time."

"Where are we going," I asked.

"Some place special, a couple of hours away," he answered with a smile, "your first meal as an immortal should not only be memorable, but exclusive."

I felt us as we seemingly lifted away from the floor, not really flying, but not solidly anchored to the earth either. It felt as if we were moving through space but not time. This was a new sensation for me and I sort of liked it, so I cuddled closer to James and enjoyed the trip.

Chapter Thirty~Seven

fter what seemed like only a few minutes I felt us anchor back to the earth. I untangled myself from James, smoothed out my skirt, and looked around to see if I knew where we were. We stood on a pockmarked street in an old, broken down neighborhood that as far as I could tell could have been just about anywhere.

"Okay, I can see the memorable part … kinda be difficult to forget this place … but I could have sworn you said exclusive too," I chuckled looking around at our new surroundings.

"Be patient my love," he grinned, "you'll soon understand both the memorable and the exclusive."

The late afternoon sun was starting to sink lower in the sky and a few people were beginning to move around. I turned and looked questioningly once again at James.

"Don't worry, I have us shielded, none of them can see us," he said, "Come, we're going to that little tan house down on the right close to the end. I've already done a little 'pre-hunt' and set it up for you. When we go inside I'll be introducing you as 'The Girl' they asked for to entertain them tonight."

"James! Ewww … yuck …" I whined, "you didn't tell me you wanted me to act like a prostitute," I said with a hurtful look.

"You know I wouldn't do anything to humiliate you, Katelyn," he replied, "and how you wish to perform is totally up to you. Those two are yours … and they are already dead, they just don't know it yet … so however you wish to make that happen is completely up to you. If you wish, you may go in, rip out their throats and drain them dry. But, I don't think you would want to kill them too quickly, you wouldn't derive nearly as much pleasure in it if you did, especially when you hear the back-story that comes with them. It's your first kill and I want you to take great pleasure and thoroughly enjoy yourself. I assure you that you will appreciate it in the long run. Now, take a look in the window and I'll tell you a little more about your intended prey."

I looked through the window and saw two, large, well-built young men, both shirtless, one lying on a couch and the other stretched out in a worn out old chair. But the stink that wafted from the house thoroughly assaulted my new sense of smell.

"Whew!" I whispered, "What is that stench?"

"Oh, just some recreational drugs that they've been experimenting with. Don't worry, it won't hurt you, your system will filter it right out of their blood."

"The one on the couch is named Terrance and the other one is Anthony. They were both just recently released from jail and they are planning on having a very special celebration tonight. It seems they benefited from a loophole in the legal system. They were both indicted for a robbery and double murder they committed a year ago last April in a small grocery store over in Marietta, and for some reason the charges were dropped."

My blood ran cold and I felt an intense anger rising inside me as I realized just which robbery and double murder James was referring to. I sensed the blood lust begin to move through me and almost overtake me. My fangs came down and touched my lower lip at the thought of who these two really were and what they had done.

"Now that you know that, do you think you can better entertain these two 'gentlemen'," he added with a knowing smile.

"Oh, I think I know exactly what to do …" I snarled and turned to look at him about to continue when he stopped me.

"This time, Katelyn, I'm delivering your dream, one that you have waited for very patiently. Darling, I promised you their deeds would not go unpunished. You will always remember your first kill and I wanted it to be especially extraordinary for you. Now, don't allow the anger to overtake you or you won't get nearly the pleasure this promises. I've said that revenge is a dish best served cold … the dish is cold now … so go and serve your revenge my love. Enjoy … no … I want you to savor this kill."

I forced myself to calm down, my anger cooling somewhat. The blood lust settled in me and my fangs slowly retracted … for the time being.

"The one on the couch, Terrance, was the leader; the

other one, Anthony, was the shooter. You may take them however you wish, and remember, as you drain them, you will be able to open your mind to them, if you want, revealing who you are, what you know about them, and why they must die. Now, my little 'Virgin Vampire', bon appétit … happy first … and second … kill. I told you it would be memorable and exclusive."

A short snarling growl rolled through me as we started into the house, and this time I didn't laugh.

"Gentlemen, greetings," James announced as we stepped through the door of the trashy little hovel.

"Game face, Katelyn," he whispered to me, so low neither of them could have possibly heard him.

"I believe you gentlemen are planning a special celebration tonight and asked to have a lady to share the evening with you? I promised you a memorable evening with a lady the likes of which you have never experienced. Does this young lady suit your fancy," he asked looking toward me.

Suddenly, both of them were up and on their feet in a flash, each with his own huge smile covering his face. The two 'gentlemen' looked at me from head to toe like a couple of hungry tigers. They never realized that the real tiger was looking back at them with a sheepishly shy smile, and sparkling, deep blue eyes.

"Oh, man …" Anthony almost moaned, shuddering all over with happy anticipation, "I'm gonna enjoy me some of dis high class hoe! Baby, me and you, we gonna do us some real cel-e-brating tonight!"

"Awww … not so fast now, sweetie," I said playfully, the blood lust beginning to tingle through me again. I decided to get fully into the act … after all mom and dad had paid for the acting classes so no need to let them go to waste. Turning to Terrance and putting my finger on his bare chest, I began running it down toward the top of his jeans and said, "You look like a natural born leader to me, I think I want you first baby boy … can you lead the way tonight?"

"Yeah," he laughed big, "I'll lead you … right to that bedroom … I can't hardly wait to get inside you!"

I looked at him with a big smile and slowly, seductively, licked my lips. Then with a twinkle in my eye and a soft, sultry voice, I wrinkled my nose at him and replied, "Oh, you got that one backward, baby boy, I'm the one that can't wait to get you inside me!"

Then turning back to Anthony with a wink and smiling really big I said, "Oh, don't look so sad, darling, I like to finish with a good strong shooter … and that looks like you! I just want to save the best for last!"

I casually reached and scooped another beer out of the cooler on the floor, handed it to Terrance, then grabbed him by his hand and started toward the little bedroom door giggling as I said, "I've got a big surprise waiting for you just behind that door!"

He turned and laughed at Anthony, tossing over his shoulder, "Sloppy seconds for you tonight, bro!"

I laughed with him and turning back to Anthony with a meaningful wink, and laughing my way through the bedroom door said, "Don't you worry, sugar, good things come to those who wait … I'll just be getting good and warmed up for you … I promise, I'm saving the best for last!"

I thought James was about to choke trying not to laugh at my performance.

Before I could close the door good to the bedroom Terrance starting stripping out of his jeans, saying "Com-on, baby, get those clothes off. I didn't pay good money to see you dressed!"

"Whatever you wish," I smiled in answer and taking off my top, wiggled my skirt down and stepped out of it, then folded them and laid them on the end of the bed.

"Girl, you are even hotter without your clothes … I am really going to enjoy this," he lustily eyed my nearly naked body.

"Not nearly as much as I am," I whispered, "but slow it down, just a little bit, let's you and me savor our time together … you don't want to get all over excited and have it end too quickly do you? Besides, didn't my friend James tell you this was my first time out … that I'm a 'virgin' at this?"

"Oh, I loves me some virgin tail," he leered nastily.

"Then let's make this special for both of us, stretch it out, and make it last a little bit. I want to make sure you get everything you deserve so you'll remember me for the rest of your life," I said with a sexy, lusty voice. "Now, come on over here Terrance, let me wrap my arms around you and introduce you to my special kind of loving."

"Yeah well, by the time I'm finished with *my* special kind of loving, you'll be begging me to stop," he grinned.

"We'll see who's begging … but first," I smiled, stepping into his arms, and whispering against his ear "I have a special question … what does sixty-eight mean to you?"

"I don't know … I'll play … is it your 'safe word' … or better yet it means you're gonna do me and I'm gonna owe you one," he laughed.

"Oh, I'm definitely gonna do you … just not the way you expect," I continued my soft whisper, "you see Terrance, sixty-eight was the amount of dollars in the cash drawer at my parents store when you robbed and murdered them last year!"

Before he could react, I tightened my arms around him and bit swiftly into his neck, just under the ear, and caught the carotid artery severing it. I held my fangs in him for an extra moment allowing him to feel the strong sting and the shock of my bite as it spread throughout his body. I retracted my fangs and his blood gushed into my mouth … and it was the best thing I had ever tasted.

I was overtaken with pure pleasure as waves of sensualness rolled through my body at the taste and feel of human blood, hot and coppery, filling my mouth over and over as I drank deeply, swallowing again and again. I opened my mind to him and showed him my parents, covered in their own blood, lying dead on the floor of their store, and revealed to him that I was their daughter … and his executioner.

A short growl escaped me as I continued pulling on his neck, forcing his heart to give up every drop of his foul life to me. I heard and felt his heartbeat getting weaker. I smelled the fear that suddenly filled him causing his heart to try to pump the blood even faster and then it quickly began to slow again. A final short whimper of despair escaped his lips just before he died. My body shuddered in near orgasmic pleasure as I took the last couple of pulls from his neck, ending his life.

I released him, not losing a single drop of his blood, letting him drop quietly to the floor. I quickly moved his body over into the corner, and sat him in a slumped position with his head lying down on his chest, looking for all the world like he was passed out. I set the beer bottle up in his hand for extra effect.

It was all over in what felt like mere seconds but it had actually taken about six or seven minutes to drain him completely. But the new strength I felt rushing through my veins was amazing. The fresh blood I had just drank so thirstily nearly brought my body temperature almost normal. I could feel my heart beating at its new and unrushed pace, my body absorbing the nourishment I had just taken. I licked my lips and turned, smiling, as I started back toward the door.

I opened the door slightly, smiling at Anthony. I brushed my upper lip with just the tip of my tongue and with a coy smile said, "I'm all warmed up now and ready for the main course! I really need a strong shooter, how about it big man, you ready to come in here and get what I've got waiting for you?"

"Damn, that was fast, Terrance! I thought you was a better man than that, bro!" He laughed rushing into the room, almost dancing with excitement, to his own doom.

"Awww Anthony … Terrance just wasn't up for the long haul, and sadly he didn't last nearly as long as I wanted him to … he was, umm … 'finished' before he could satisfy me, and then he just passed clean out over there in the corner. And he only filled up me less than half way, too. But, I just know you'll be so much better … I bet that you can fill me all the way up, sugar, that's why I saved you for last. Do you think you can last longer than he did and fill me up?"

Moving quickly, he was out of his clothes and glancing over his shoulder said, "Hey, bro, you just sit right there and watch how a real man does it and makes this woman glad to be here." Then turning back toward me with a little twinkle in his eyes and smiling a devilish grin said, "Baby, I can last as long as you want me to," then reaching down to rub himself smiled, "jus' you looky here at dis big ole Nawth Jawgee black snake … bet a pretty little white city girl like you ain't never had no experience with something like this!"

"Oh, I've had some experience with large snakes," I laughed, "and that snake don't look like it's too dangerous to me!"

"Yeah, well why don't you just get down on your knees and start sucking on it … see if it don't turn into one of them 'spitting cobras'," he leered at me.

"Oh trust … I definitely plan on doing some sucking … and believe me, this pretty little white city girl can do things to you that you never imagined possible."

He eagerly put his arms around my waist, my trap closing swiftly behind him. I smiled and stepped closer, putting my arms around his shoulders, cuddled closer to him and listened to his heart beating quickly in his chest. I smelled his blood rushing through his arteries. I bowed my head to his neck and whispered softly in his ear, "Ummm … I gotta say, you smell so good … better even than Terrance!"

"Yeah and I like that perfume you got on, too, baby … now let's get to part about getting you on your knees!"

"My perfume is called 'Katelyn's Revenge' … and I wore it tonight, just special for you … but I'm afraid I won't be getting on my knees … not for you … murderer!"

Then faster than he knew what was happening, I buried my fangs deep into his neck. He tried to struggle, to get loose from my embrace and get away. My regular strength would have been more than he could have ever withstood, but after the fresh blood I had just taken my strength was easily too much for him. I held him tightly to me as I drank, pulling hard on his stinking heart for every drop of his defiled blood I could get, and this time I drank slowly, taking my time, and luxuriating in the taste.

I opened my mind and replayed the entire scene for him from my parents' store letting him know who I was. I looked into his mind and saw the pleasure he had gotten as he ruthlessly killed my helpless parents. His happy memories caused painful reminiscences of that terrible day to tear through me. I forced myself to drink even slower, making it last, torturing him now, as I slowly escorted him to death's door.

Before he could die, I drew back from him, letting him see my face, full in the blood lust, my fangs extended, and my eyes shot through with red. "I finally got you, you bastard! Blood for blood," I snarled at him and sinking my teeth again went for the final kill, happily knowing that as he died, the terror in him had been so much greater than either of my parents had experienced.

Then just as I was about to release him and let him fall to the floor, he produced an explosive sound of flatulence and emptied his bowels in a pile on the floor beneath him.

James chose that moment to open the door, and scowling as he looked around said, "Oh Katelyn … in the name of all that's holy, what did you do?"

"Nun-uhhh … that's all on him – literally," I chuckled, "I guess he just got really scared and couldn't help himself … but, they don't all do that … do they?"

"Sometimes you'll get one that is so scared their bladder will let go," he grinned and added, "but I suppose that you just have to be different and do things on a grand scale, don't you?"

"Yup, that's me – go big or go home … and oh yeah, memorable!" I laughed.

James laughed out loud at me, "Definitely memorable, but I have to ask have you been watching dirty movies? Where did you get all that from?"

"I'm not real sure ... and no, I haven't been watching dirty movies, thank you very much! They have … uh, had … so I just pulled it right out of their minds. I didn't even have to think about what I was going to say, it just started coming out when I got close to them."

"Humm … really," James asked, "that's very interesting. There's only one other immortal I know of that has that kind of talent. I think maybe Charlotte Ann gave you more than you realize."

I reached and took my clothes off the bed, quickly putting my top on, and sliding my skirt up over my legs, tucked it in, and straightening it all out commented to James, "You do know that when I get back I'm going to have burn these clothes right?"

"Then perhaps this shall help replace them," he answered with a smile, and reaching, taking my hand, he placed a stack of folded bills in it. I counted it and found five one hundred dollar bills, six fifty dollar bills and ten twenties.

"What's this for," I asked confused.

"These two paid five hundred dollars each to have an experience like they had never had … with a girl like they had never had … and received a promise of double their money back if they weren't pleased. And since I don't hear either one of them complaining … am I to assume that you delivered on the promise?"

I laughed out loud as I held the money and looked down at the two bodies of my parents' murders and said, "No, I don't hear either one asking for their money back either!"

"In my day it was customary," James began to explain to me, "for a condemned man to pay the executioner to ensure the job was done correctly … I think you earned it, so enjoy it."

"I will … I think Charlotte Ann and I will go shopping when we get back," I laughed.

"As you wish, but before we leave, we must clean up your meal and dispose of them," he said pointing at my victims, "I suggest we just burn the house down, maybe the landlord will be happy to get rid of them. Any ideas," he asked.

I thought about it for a minute, smiled and said, "Since they lived together and died together, perhaps it's only fair they go into eternity together … let's leave a little parting gift, I'll take one, you take the other."

I reached and grabbed one of the bodies by the arm and tossed it across the room to land on the small bed.

"It's a good bet the fire won't totally destroy the bodies, so let's leave them in bed together, wrapped lovingly in each other's arms for eternity," I said as I began to pose the first body. After we positioned their bodies together, arms and legs wrapped lovingly around each other, I stepped back and admired our handiwork.

"That's perfect," I laughed harshly, "I'm going to leave their families a little something they'll never forget about them just the way those two left my parents for me to never forget."

"Katelyn, you are indeed the devious one," James laughed at me, "I think I've created a real monster!"

"Revenge can be such a motivator," I laughed wickedly.

I watched in fascination as several times James began to call fire, gathering it in the palm of his hand, forming it into a ball and tossing it about the tiny house. The flames began to spread quickly throughout consuming any trace of our having been there. When the flames had taken secure hold of the house, I wrapped my arms strongly around him, and closed my eyes, remembering his warning about fire. When I reopened them again in a few minutes we were back in the main parlor at Whitehall where we had started from just a short time ago.

Chapter Thirty~Eight

James and I stood there together in the main parlor for a moment as I reoriented myself after the long trip. I had never made such a trip since my turning but it was just the same as moving from the bedroom to the veranda, only a few extra minutes.

I was gorged with the fresh blood of the two murderers running through me and my skin was glowing all over with a healthy shine. The energy was still ripping through me, my strength seemed unending. The feeling of my first kill was exhilarating, my first taste of human blood incredibly delightful. It had produced in me a feeling that was so sensual, so intense, it was very near to orgasmic. I examined myself as I stood there and thought, *"I really am a vampire … I have hunted … I have killed … and most importantly I have avenged my parents!"* That thought sent an absolute rush throughout my entire being, knowing that now, my parents could finally rest in peace.

Just then Charlotte Ann walked into the parlor and with a knowing smile looked at me and said, "Well, Katelyn, I see that you've hunted and fed … I'm so happy for you … and from the glow of your skin you must have taken blood that was full of guilt and wickedness … so what did you think … how was your first time?"

"Oh, Charlotte Ann, it's absolutely incredible … almost indescribable … well except for the part where the victim lost control of his bowels just before he died."

"Yeah, I hate it when they do that … it just ruins the ambiance of your meal," she chuckled.

"I know, right … but, other than that, the thrill of the kill is the most sensuous thing I have ever felt," I continued, "not to mention as it turned out, they paid handsomely for my company … which means that I've got a thousand bucks for me and you to go shopping with!"

"I think we can do that," she laughed, "the 'executioner's coin' is always an enjoyment in the market!"

"But Charlotte Ann, human blood is so different from what I have gotten from you and James. I had no idea how wonderfully satisfying it could be. I really truly feel like I am changed and different now. This first kill will always be very special to me too, it had a unique revenge aspect to it that made it all the better. My victims really had it coming …"

Then beginning with the tragedy of my parents, I told her the entire story of how those two had played into my life. She listened attentively to me as I recounted in minute detail the entire scene in that little house tonight, reliving again how their deplorable lives had ended.

"I'm so happy you had a good first kill, one that shall be a memory you carry with you forever … and it sounds like you have a bit of the actress in you, too … that will serve you well in your hunting activities in the future," she smiled.

"Well, I did take a couple of Theater classes in college," I chuckled, "I figured there was no need to let them go to waste."

"You're a girl after my own heart," she continued, "now, if you don't mind some advice, you know that you don't always have to kill after the first time, but when you do, always go for the blood of the guilty … those who have done the most wrongs … the ones that are a plague on society. You must attempt to not take the life of an innocent … and never under any circumstances take the blood of a child. Although both are much sweeter, and very addictive, the young and the innocent are undeserving of the fate we are able to give them."

I let that lesson begin to sink in, considering what she had said when James looked over to her and asked softly, "Did you find him last evening, was he in the usual place?"

"Yes," she said nodding, "I didn't get very close, but I don't think he is quite the problem we thought at first."

"So then he's just a vagabond, as I thought?"

"Well, to an extent, yes, but I'm beginning to think he is just lost."

"Ummm … excuse me, who are you two talking about," I asked.

"There exists the possibility of a small problem Katelyn and I suppose it best that we include you in this," she began, "James … would you?"

"Katelyn, there appears to be a renegade vampire, probably just a nomad, stalking the area," he said simply.

I looked at him shocked, wondering how such a thing could be since I had no real concept of anything other than my very small new world. I had just never considered the possibility of other immortals being around.

"You see," he continued, "besides assisting with you, he is another of the reasons I asked Charlotte Ann to come here. I became aware of his presence just before you were turned. I thought perhaps that he was only a wanderer passing through. But he has remained, so I knew he would have to be approached and, shall we say, encouraged to leave. I knew that might prove a little difficult for me because I would be preoccupied for some time helping you through the change. Since Charleston is not only my hunting grounds but also my home he is therefore my problem. I asked for her help to locate and monitor his movements before any other problems could arise. She's been following and closing in on him since she arrived while we decide how best to approach him."

Then turning back to Charlotte Ann he asked, "So then, what are your thoughts about him and how to handle him?"

"He seems to me to exhibit the traits of one who was changed by accident and left with no teacher. He spends most of his time in that small club downtown, just sitting and watching. I think he sleeps during the day since I have never sensed him except at night. If he is a traditionalist, then the best time to approach him will be early evening, just after he has risen, when he will be at his weakest, and before he can feed. He is young, probably changed in the last thirty to fifty years, and either does not have much power or doesn't know how to use what he has. I suggest we go this evening and do whatever we have to do to settle the matter."

"Very well, then," he nodded in answer, "we shall be there when he arrives this evening. We have the advantage of both numbers and strength, and there's only one of him … odds that would make any immortal, especially a weak one, consider well his actions."

"James, is he dangerous, will you be safe, and what about me, where will I be and will I have a role to play in this?"

"Of course I'll be safe, and you will be right with us and protected as well. Besides, what else would I do with you ..." and chuckling softly added, "lock you in your coffin and say 'naughty vampire, you can't go!'"

"That's not very likely to happen," I snickered, and quickly kissed him, "and now that I've had my first kill, when we get back I'm going to show you exactly what being a 'naughty vampire' is all about."

"Now children ..." Charlotte Ann laughed softly, then with a wink looked at me and added, "and if you happen to need any tips and pointers, I've got three hundred seventy five years of 'naughty knowledge' so ..."

"Oh I can't wait to have that conversation," I grinned at her nodding happily.

The three of us arrived at the little club about an hour before dusk and settled into a table along one side, between the front entrance and the back wall. There were already some early customers at the bar and scattered around the various tables. The large central dance-floor was mostly empty, although I suspected it would fill up after the guests had some drinks in them.

I decided why not try a little drink with a human ... one where I *had* to stop ... just to see if I could ... so I began to casually look around, gauging the patrons, deciding if there was the possibility of another drink for myself. I had certainly attracted more than the passing notice of several of the young men and even caught the interest of a couple of the girls. I chuckled softly to myself as I remembered Charlotte Ann's reference to them as a buffet line.

I picked out one of the single guys, glanced at James and quietly asked, "Can I go take just a little drink, please?"

"Give it a try," he answered, "just don't go too far, we have other, more important, business to attend to here."

I reached out to the one I had chosen making solid eye contact and he blushed. He wasn't overly handsome, but certainly desirable enough. *"Ask me to dance when the next song begins playing,"* I spoke softly to his mind. I was going to repay him with a little celebrity in exchange for what he was about to give me. With what I had in mind, his friends that were with him were about to become very jealous. The next song was perfect for a slow dance and he walked nervously towards me and looking cautiously at James, asked if I would dance with him.

"I would love to," I answered smiling, and easily moved into his arms as he gently began swaying me around the floor. He was a pretty good dancer too and I cuddled closer to him letting him feel every part of my body against him. As his friends watched, my arms circled his back and I drew him closer to me. I lightly kissed his cheek and then bent close to his ear as if to whisper a secret. He stiffened just the tiniest bit as I easily slid my fangs into his neck. His blood was hot and thick as it gushed into my mouth quickly filling it.

"Ummm … I made a good choice," I thought to myself as I took two good mouthfuls and stopped. It wasn't much, but enough to warm me and increase the still lingering healthy glow of my skin I had from earlier in the day. Then I lightly brushed my tongue over the tiny wound on his neck to close it.

As the song ended I whispered into his ear, "You will

only remember the pretty girl and the dance, nothing more. I think you are tired suddenly and should probably sit down."

He returned to his seat with a smile, suddenly a man among men, and was quickly surrounded by his friends. I returned to my friends, too, smiling hugely at what I considered my monumental success. James and Charlotte Ann both smiled with me at the secret.

She spoke softly to me as I again took my seat, "You certainly are good to be so young! That talent will work well for you in the future."

We didn't have to wait much longer, and I actually felt his presence just before he entered the front door. It wasn't nearly as strong as with James or certainly not Charlotte Ann, but somehow I knew inside that another immortal was close.

He entered and went to a table near the back to sit. I knew that Charlotte Ann was masking our presence so he would have no idea we were there. I casually sat back, not the least bit frightened, and watched him to see what I could make of him.

He looked all alone and sad as he sat there looking around, obviously searching for a victim. Although he appeared to be brooding, I smiled as I suddenly realized that he was pretty. It was obvious that he had been very young, probably no more than a teen when he was turned. His features were those of a young boy but still retained a slightly girlish look to them. Then I suddenly remembered that he was a predator like myself, very dangerous, and that could very well be his draw.

He looked to be only a few inches over five feet. His clothes, though clean had a dirty, worn look to them. His blondish, brown hair was cut in an older, shaggy, style but looked good just the same. His eyes were soft brown, and dull, lacking any light or intensity. His lips looked soft but without the hint of a smile. I realized that although he appeared innocent, he could no doubt be a very dangerous killer.

Then with no warning I heard Charlotte Ann speak to him with her mind, *"Hello, young one … you look as if you have lost all hope,"* she simply said, *"why are you so downcast and sad."*

He looked up startled, unsure of or unbelieving what he had just heard. The slightest shadow of fear crossed his features as he continued looking quickly around him trying to locate the source of this unexpected intrusion.

"There's no need to look for me, you aren't allowed to see me until I want you to," she continued, *"but be assured that I mean you no harm and pose no threat to you as long as you do what I say. Please remain calm and just listen."*

He was evidently very frightened now, but did as she said. He looked down at the table top, an air of defeat covering him, and simply nodded his head in understanding. That's odd I thought, he can apparently hear Charlotte Ann, but either can't or doesn't know how to answer her.

"Now young one, kindly stand up and slowly walk outside, I will meet you there, I only wish to talk with you, and again I mean you no harm," she finished.

He got up very slowly and began moving dejectedly toward the door. I picked up a fragment of his thoughts when he walked past us, *"destroy me … be free … gladly … finally …"* He had the voice of a child, and as he passed our table, never seeing us, I physically felt his fear.

I looked at James and Charlotte Ann and asked, "Did either of you pick up his thoughts just now, he thinks we are going to destroy him."

"While that may be an option, it will be the last one," she said and got up to follow him out the door. James and I waited another moment or two and then went together following Charlotte Ann. I was actually excited to see what would happen next. This was beginning to feel almost like a hunt and I sensed the blood lust stirring in my chest.

When we got out to the street, I saw that he had turned into a small alley and was slumping against the side of the building with Charlotte Ann was standing on the sidewalk in front of him. His fear was so strong now I could smell it radiating out from him.

James, moving with preternatural speed crossed behind her and came up on her far side. I followed, moving just as quickly, and closed in on her near side. It looked like the both of us had suddenly just appeared out of nowhere, covering her sides. The new one suddenly realized that he had not one, but three supernatural beings standing in front of him.

"Please," he begged pleadingly, "if you are going to destroy me, do it quickly. I've endured all the pain I can stand."

When he spoke, I could hear the desperation in his voice and that I had been correct in my assumption that he had not been much more than a child when he was changed.

Charlotte Ann spoke quietly, "Be calm, young one, I told you we mean you no harm," she slowly reached out her hand and gently laid it on his shoulder, calming him, "What is your name, fledgling, and how did you come to be here?"

He looked at her, still frightened, and said, "Dale, my name is … used to be … Dale … Dale Krause. I'm here because I'm alone now; I have been wandering from place to place because I don't know what else to do."

Then I saw tears of blood spill over his eyes and run down his face as he begin to cry frightfully like the little child he appeared to be. I suddenly learned that immortals do cry, and I was seeing genuine tears of despair from this one.

Charlotte Ann said to him, "Come with us Dale, we must return inside and there we shall continue our talk."

He hesitantly moved away from the wall and walked slowly with the three of us around him. We went back into the little club where the noise level was beginning to climb high enough that we could talk and ensure not being overheard. We chose his table and the four of us sat down, the humans all around us little realizing that a literal court was taking place in front of them.

"Dale," Charlotte Ann started, "I want you to tell us your story, and remember, the details are important to me – and ultimately to you – so please don't leave any out, regardless of how unimportant they may seem to you."

"There's not a lot to tell," he started to say, "I'm not even sure how I got this way, it just happened one night."

"How long ago," she asked soothingly.

He looked away for a moment, recalling and gathering his thoughts, and began, "1978 … a Friday night … I remember that," he looked up smiling, "because I had been at the pizza parlor, celebrating my sixteenth birthday with my girlfriend and some of our friends. It was late when we came out, and split up to go back to our homes. I was alone, walking toward my house when this man came up to me and asked for directions. I was telling him what he wanted to know and he suddenly jumped on me and quickly pushed me to the ground. I suppose I was knocked unconscious, I don't remember, but when I woke up I was like this," he finished with an almost plaintive cry, extending his hands outward.

"Did this man stay with you," James asked, speaking up for the first time.

"Yes, sir," Dale answered politely, nodding his head, "he told me that he was a vampire and that he had made me one, too. I thought I was having a nightmare, I just didn't know I wouldn't wake up from it. He said that he was tired of existing and hunting alone. He wanted a companion and had chosen me because he thought I was pretty."

"Where did this happen," James quietly continued.

"I lived in Renton Junction, a small mining town in western Pennsylvania, with my family. He carried me far away and told me that my life had ended and my family would never find me. I didn't know what to do, I felt so completely lost. He taught me that we were now creatures of the night, that we lived only at night, and died again when the sun rose. I learned that I had to dig a new grave each morning before sunrise, cover myself, and sleep all day until dusk. He told me that I had to stay with him, and kill if I was to survive. I felt like a prisoner."

"What is his name," Charlotte Ann quietly interjected.

"Was … it was Charles," he answered her, "he kept me with him until the beginning of last year. Then one night in Boston, after we had hunted and fed, we saw a burning building as we walked along the waterfront. We stopped to watch it as the firefighters tried to put it out. He suddenly turned to me and said, 'You must take care of yourself now kid,' and he ran into the fire. I listened to his screams, and watched him dancing in the flames as he burned. I was too afraid to follow him and do the same thing so I just stood there, all alone, lost, not knowing where to go or what to do. I had been completely dependent on Charles and now there was suddenly no one to guide me."

"I was lonely and started wandering around in the night, always finding an old cemetery somewhere before dawn to sleep. I looked for, and found, fresh graves when I needed new clothes. When I rose each night, I moved further along, searching the darkness, even calling out to see if there were more like me, but only emptiness and silence met me. I knew what Hell must be like."

"When I arrived here, I was tired of traveling so I decided to stay. I would either discover someone like me or find a way to destroy myself. I don't know how to do what was done to me, and wouldn't even if I knew how, but I was determined not to continue alone in this terrible existence any longer. Now, suddenly, three of you show up all at once. I'm not sure whether to be relieved or scared. And that's pretty much my story," he finished, "now, please, I beg you again, if you are going to destroy me, do it quickly, please set me free of this curse."

"How could a maker so callously lie to a fledgling, you poor thing, you shall not die at our hands, innocent one," she spoke her verdict softly to him.

"My name is Charlotte Ann," she continued, "this is James and his mate Katelyn," revealing our names to him for the first time, and extending her hand to him she said, "come young one and travel with me now, it's time for you to discover at last what a wonderful gift you have been given."

Then turning to James, she said, "I think perhaps we should return home now, with your permission, of course."

James simply nodded to her.

She reached her hand toward Dale, he slowly, frightfully, put his hand in hers and the four of us departed for Whitehall.

Chapter Thirty~Nine

When we returned to the main parlor at Whitehall, Dale simply stood and stared, awestruck at the majesty and splendor of the room surrounding him. He was literally speechless at the sight. Finally he spoke, his sweet little voice ranging half way between the child and young man that he must have had when he was changed, "You … you actually live here," he asked disbelievingly.

"Well, not technically … I in fact live in New York City," Charlotte Ann chuckled, "This is actually James' and Katelyn's home … but I tend to come and go as I please. While we are here, they have welcomed us in as their visitors."

That was the first time I had heard Whitehall called my home and my name used in equality with James. It quickly brought a smile to my face and created a very good feeling in me. James and I continued to watch and listen as Charlotte Ann began telling Dale the things that he would need to learn about the life he had lived over the last thirty plus years.

"Dale," she began with a soothing voice, "you must first understand that what happened to you that night was not your fault and it goes without saying that it obviously was not your choice, either. I deeply regret that you lost your human life before you had an opportunity to live it. But our world does have a small share of rogues that do not adhere to authority or traditions. I understand that your first thirty years or so have been difficult, so let's make the rest of eternity more pleasurable for you."

"Eternity …" Dale asked confused, "but that's … forever. Charles said that we usually only lived less than a century, then we would began to crumble and die. How can that be?"

"Young one," Charlotte Ann continued smiling, "there is so much you must learn. This life that you have been born into is eternal. You will live forever … a youth in appearance to be sure … but certainly for much more than a century."

"Look around you and consider the three of us … I am close to entering my fourth century … James is nearing three hundred years in this life … and Katelyn's bloodline is over six hundred years in length."

I quickly noted that she mentioned the length of my bloodline, not actually revealing my age to him and found that to be interesting.

"While we are certainly not the oldest of our kind," she smiled at him, "we are certainly more than a century … and there are others among us who consider us to be fledglings," she laughed easily.

She extended her hand toward him and he easily set his hand in hers. She looked at him and continued, "Although I did not sire you Dale, from this night forward, if you will allow me, I shall take you as my responsibility and guide you as if you were my sired son. I will arm you with knowledge and help you develop the wisdom you will need to survive in our world. I will make you my companion and protect you. So come now, let's set out on a new path together, one of learning, growing and maturing."

"May I please ask a question," he interjected, still looking around, "where will I go to ground at in the morning. The time is getting close and I must begin to prepare."

"As I have said, there is much that you must learn, young one," Charlotte Ann smiled patiently at him, "your first lesson is that you do not require sleep any longer. Sadly, that is a lesson you should have been taught long ago. You no longer have to dig a hole in the earth to repose. If you do desire to rest you may do so in a real bed in one of the upstairs bedrooms."

"But … the daylight … it will burn me … it's so awful … please don't let me die that way," he asked pleadingly.

"You may find the sunlight to be a little uncomfortable at first, but it will not harm you my little one, on that you have my word. But, before we introduce you back to the daylight and the mortal world there is one small detail we must attend to, and that before you rest or do anything else. Please, little one, don't be offended by this, but you stink," she said softly, "we must get you upstairs, into a hot bath and wash the smell of the grave off of you …"

I stifled a little giggle, hoping he didn't hear it.

"Then in the morning we shall take you shopping for

some new clothes to wear. You no longer have to rob the dead for clothing. We shall properly outfit you as a modern teenager should look for your return to the daylight."

"James," she continued, "do you or Katelyn have something that will make do until we can finish shopping?"

We both nodded to her, trying to be as nice as possible to our new guest.

"Very well," she said, "come along with me now, Dale. Let's begin again your transformation. You must feed and then we can begin to take care of some things that should have been done when you were born to this life." She took him by the hand and led him away, up the stairs.

When they had disappeared up the stairs and I heard the 'click' of the door to one of the bedrooms close, I turned to James, and with a lustful smile said, "Now *you* come with me, we must also go upstairs and take care of something that should have already been done, too." I reached, took his hand in mine and leading him toward the stairs added with a playful laugh, "I believe I said something to the effect of showing you what a 'naughty vampire' I could be when we returned home!"

We spent the rest of the night together in my bed, having the most tremendous time of my new life! I had waited, maybe not patiently, but waited, for this first new experience. I remembered all too well the intensity of my last night as a mortal with James and wondered if it really could get any better. It could … and did … dramatically! My first time after becoming an immortal actually was more memorable than my first time as a human … of course that's not saying a whole lot either. Everything about me had changed when I turned and it didn't take long to discover that, along with my increased libido, my sense of pleasure had also been greatly heightened.

I had thought that sex with James was great when I was a human, and I suppose that for a human it probably was. But, as an immortal, words could not describe the new feelings that he brought out in me. My body ached deeply for him; I wanted him more than ever. I was completely lost, disconnected from myself as he made love to me. The two of us were wrapped passionately around each other, the world that surrounded us was completely forgotten in our love for the other. I had never delighted in him so much and for so long. The enjoyment he was providing for me at the moment was happily returned as I learned the true meaning of immortal pleasure. I also discovered a little nugget he'd neglected to share with me before I turned … male vampires didn't really need a recovery time either. I felt that my change, my turning, was completed now, as together we consummated my new life.

James slowly demonstrated to me all the delights of immortal mating. The familiar tingle that he had so easily caused in me when I was a human now turned to a full-fledged roar. My sense of feeling had so increased that when his fingers slid across my skin it felt like they were dragging electricity along with them. That electricity translated into pure pleasure throughout every part of me as his soft fingers explored every inch of my new, and very sensitive, preternatural skin.

As he gently took me in his arms, I opened myself to him and he easily slid into me, filling me … the pleasure he was giving me was absolutely wonderful! I could not believe the sensuality of immortal lovemaking. We moved deeper into the throes of pleasure and I realized that it was me that had changed and not him. We quickly became one with each other and the sensation of being filled like never before was indescribable.

He pulled me tighter against himself, kissing me passionately, filling me, making me complete. I suddenly wanted more and more of him; I arched my back upward against him trying to get him deeper inside and squeezed my muscles tighter around him.

He began to pick up his pace, moaning in his own pleasure, as he pushed harder and deeper into me, nearing his own release point. I quickly tipped over the edge into one of the most colossal orgasms I had ever had. The waves of pleasure went ripping through me with unbelievable speed gripping me in their hold. I had never felt so much pleasure at one time. I clawed at his back and screamed out his name!

Then, just as we both reached the top of the mountain together, the absolute height of enjoyment and pleasure, the most incredible and unexpected thing happened. The blood lust suddenly rose up, tearing through me just as strong and powerful as the physical lust. I had to have blood … I had to feed … it would complete our act of love!

I wrapped my arms tighter around him, drawing him closer to me, my fangs came down, and I bit into his neck! His blood gushed into me, hot and wonderfully sweet. It filled my mouth, over and over, as I swallowed again and again, drinking deeply. The taste and feel of his blood as it flowed down my throat and into me only intensified the feeling of the quaking temblors already moving through my body. I tried desperately to pull every bit of his essence into me.

When I bit him and his blood began to flow into me he forcefully thrust as deeply into me as he could, groaning with pleasure. He stiffened in my grip, not making the smallest movement, as I pulled hard at his throat. When I had drank my fill, he groaned and I felt him empty himself inside me, strong and powerfully. He throbbed in me, trying to push deeper, groaning loudly, as he pumped again and again deep inside me. When he had finished he went limp in my arms, pulling out of me and rolling away with another pleasure filled groan. I rolled with him, staying as close as I possibly could, still licking slowly at his neck, still tasting his blood. I just could not believe all the sensations pouring through me at that moment.

The fulfillment of physical lust and the satisfaction of the blood-lust all at the same time combined to make a unique and unforgettable experience. The massive orgasm I experienced did extraordinary things in my body and was even greater than what I had become accustomed to in the past. Couple that with his blood ripping through every part of me at the same time … I just did not want it to ever stop! I actually found myself breathing hard, gasping for useless air.

I could feel the happy twinkle in my eyes as I looked at him and smiled as he playfully asked, "Well … was that worth the wait?"

"Wow! I had no idea it could be that good! The taste of your blood was so pure, so much more powerful than ever before! I had feelings and sensations in every part of me that I have never had before. It intensified my pleasure like I've never felt, it did things in me I had no idea it could do," I said, my breathing returning to its almost normal nothing.

He grinned slowly and his eyes lit up, and said, "That's just the beginning … wait until the next time … I'll take your blood just as you reach the precipice … then it will be your turn to experience a most special immortal pleasure. You have no idea how wonderful that sensation is just at that moment, just as you release your passion … to have someone taking your blood, your literal life, out of you as your body writhes in excitement. It is very probably the most intense act of immortal passion possible … and by the way … thank you so much for the experience!"

"If it gets any better than what I just had I don't know if I can stand it …" then with a sudden naughty smile I glanced sideways at him and added, "and since I know now that *you* don't have to recover … what if *I* don't want to wait?"

"If I may quote Charlotte Ann, 'You have so much to learn, young one'," he laughed back, "and good things do come to those who wait!"

I lay there wrapped in his arms … my love … his love … our love … for each other a more tangible thing than ever before. I felt more like him, more a part of him than ever before. The night slowly passed us by, and all I wanted as I cuddled against him, enjoying his closeness, was to be even closer to him.

The quietness closed in around us until somewhere, in another part of the house I heard Dale's small childish voice as he breathed out a soft, satisfied and pleasurable laugh.

I glanced over at James with a smug smile, and asked, "Do you think she …"

"Plucked his cherry …" he smiled knowingly, "yes, she most certainly did."

"Hummm … I'm gonna say she not only plucked it … she crushed it beyond all recognition … but do you think he even knew he could …"

"He had no idea …" he answered with a chuckle.

"Bet that was an experience he wasn't expecting," I giggled softly at the thought of that scenario and cuddled closer to James whispering softly, "and you got to admit, *that* certainly gives a whole new definition to the term 'Virgin Vampire', doesn't it?"

Chapter Forty

Later the next morning, I walked into the main parlor where the three of them had already gathered. Charlotte Ann looked at me with a big smile as I came in and said, "You and those silk pajamas! Do you plan on staying in them forever?"

"No longer than I have to … isn't that right lover boy," I answered smiling and looking playfully at James, "while they do make me feel especially sexy when I wear them, after last night, I'm quickly learning to enjoy *not* wearing them!"

"They do make you look especially sexy," James added with a salacious grin, "and make an immortals fangs extend!"

I recalled what he had said last night about biting me.

Now I had to contend with a very pleasant tingle in all the right places and a conversation at the same time … a conversation that I needed to quickly turn the direction of until later.

"Good Morning, Dale," I said turning to him with a huge smile, "you certainly look different this morning."

"Good Morning, Katelyn," he replied timidly, looking at me with a bashful smile. I noticed immediately that his soft brown eyes had life to them this morning. They now held the intense sparkle that should have been there all along. I knew that, among other things, he had fed from Charlotte Ann during the night. His immortal aura was brighter and his skin still had a slight glow remaining to it.

He was wearing some clothes that James and I had found for him. A pair of gray sweat pants and one of my college tees, they were both old and didn't fit him very well but they were at least clean … and he smelled much better, too. I noted now that he smelled of cinnamon and cloves as I silently registered his individual scent for future reference. He still looked a little uncomfortable. He kept eyeing the windows and the sun beaming in through them. He was trying to stay in the shadows and as far away from the direct sun as possible.

"Don't worry, Dale," I began, and attempting to ease his fear, stepped over into one of the bright sunbeams streaming in through the windows, and standing comfortably, grinned at him, "see, told you it won't hurt you, just maybe sting your eyes a little until you get used to it again."

His looks were very deceiving. Although he looked every bit the young teenager, I remembered that he had been an immortal for more than a decade when I was born … and between his mortal and immortal lives, he had nearly fifty years of life … more than twice my own … just no experiences to go with it. But I was determined to make him my friend.

"Did you have a good night," I asked with a knowing smile, "did Charlotte Ann introduce you to some of the finer points of this life?"

Dale looked down at the floor and had he been able to blush I'm sure he would have been beet red. He was probably still in shock from all his new experiences.

"I … I didn't know I could do … *that*," he whispered softly, "Charles always said that we were dead."

"Well aren't you glad he lied," I continued with a chuckle, "there is a first time for everything … and you got the first time of both worlds at the same time! Sex is pretty fun isn't it?"

"Yeah, it was certainly an experience … lots of fun," he half smiled, still looking bashfully at the floor.

"Now, Katelyn," Charlotte Ann laughed softly, "Dale has a lot of new things to learn … and he seems to learn quickly … of course having a pretty good teacher also helps!"

"Yeah I'm pretty sure that anybody, spending an entire night alone in a bed with you, would have a truly life altering experience," I chuckled.

"You can be assured of that," she laughed and turning to James continued, "James I want to thank you and Katelyn so much for your kindness to us and allowing us to stay with you. However, I think that Dale and I will be leaving today. We are going to move back into my apartment in New York. We have so much learning to do to get him where he needs to be. It's probably better if we have our own home for a while."

"One of the first lessons we are going to have to work

on is learning how to take only a little when he feeds and not kill. I need to take him hunting where there are an abundance of humans, just in case there's a little mishap. Besides, drinking and not killing makes having a social life so much easier."

"Charlotte Ann, you know that you are welcome in our home anytime," James said with a knowing nod to her, "and that goes for you as well, Dale."

"Thank you, sir, for having me in your home, I've enjoyed it," he spoke just above a whisper.

"Bet you did," I chuckled giving him a hug and lightly kissing him on the cheek, "Dale, I hope the next time you are here that you'll feel more comfortable and at home. Maybe by that time, you will be adjusted to the daylight and able to take me for a walk in the sunshine."

Dale smiled his cutest teenage smile, "Katelyn, I'll try my best to be able to take you for a walk the next time I'm here."

"I'm so sorry that we didn't get to spend a few days together shopping like we talked about Katelyn," Charlotte Ann spoke up, "but I promise we'll plan on it again, soon. Since you like pajamas so good, the next time you are in the city, we'll make it a point to visit Vickie's Boutique. I'm sure we can find you something there that James will think makes you absolutely mouthwatering!"

"That sounds like something to look forward to," I smiled back at her.

"Mouthwatering indeed," James interjected with a smile, "when would you like us to visit?"

"Anytime you wish," she smiled, then turning back to me continued, "and by the way, little granddaughter, check your account in Bern when you get the chance. I spoke with my agent in Paris this morning and had him transfer matching funds to it for you."

I suppose I had a very human reaction, my jaw dropped at what she said, and I started to say something but she stopped me short.

"Oh … Katelyn … don't … we'll just call it a little memento of your first hunt," she smiled, "it isn't much, but you do have to have something to start with in order to build on it. And in the meantime, until you build it up some, I promise that neither James nor I will laugh at you for being poor!"

Thankfully James broke in here to lighten the moment asking her, "So I suppose we'll see each other at the Ball next month?"

"By all means, I wouldn't miss it," she laughed, "and will you be in drag again this year?"

"Probably … that's the one time of year I almost have to do that," he started and that's where I broke in.

"Whoa … stop right there … what are the two of you talking about this time …" and looking at him I asked pointedly, "and what does she mean about you being in drag?"

"Oh, I'm sorry Katelyn, she's referring to the annual 'All Hallows Eve Ball' at The Palace. They bill it as a Halloween party. It's a formal event and one of the biggest social occurrences of the year in our world. There's usually several hundred immortals from around the world in attendance.

"Drag …" I asked with interest, raising my eyebrows.

"It's not exactly the kind of drag you are thinking about," he smiled, his eyes sparkling, "I call it 'Vampire Drag', but it's really just formal wear. It's the only time of year that I go all out with the traditional black tux, opera cape, top hat and cane," he explained with a smile.

"Alrighty then," I laughed, suddenly relieved, "I can deal with vampire drag!"

"I'm planning on having something special there for you to commemorate the event too," he promised with a smile.

Charlotte Ann and Dale quickly took their leave at this point and left James and me standing there alone, together. I moved into his arms and kissed him.

"James, I love you so much, but right now, it's really been a full two days," I said still holding him and recalling everything that had happened, "I feel like I need to go rest."

"That's to be expected love," he replied, gently stroking my back, "you are still growing and you've used a lot of energy so I'm sure you probably do need a rest time to recover your strength. Will you be upstairs?"

"No," I said thoughtfully, "I believe I'm going to go behind the bookshelves. I think a little alone time to consider everything that's happened, as well as some rest, is needed."

"Very well, but come and feed before you go," he smiled, "drink long and deep, darling, you need it to replenish your energy ... you seem to have really exerted yourself last night."

His blood began to flow into me and I could feel it moving quickly into every part of my body, tingling to the tips of my fingers. I knew that he would hunt and feed while I slept so I took more than usual as I felt his wonderful strength begin to renew and rebuild my own vigor.

When I had finished feeding from him, I went into the library, opened the hidden room, and went inside to my coffin. I don't think it had ever looked as inviting as it did now. It was my own private world, the one place I could be completely secluded to rest and think without the slightest worry of being disturbed. I opened it and quietly lay down, snuggling into the soft, comfortable velvet.

I had so much to think about as I closed the lid and set the latch. The Change was complete in me … I was fully an immortal now … my human life was a thing of the past. My gifts, abilities and even physical strengths were continuing to become more familiar to me every day. I was well on the way to becoming as strong as James and Charlotte Ann. Although I still needed a little rest, from now on it was just a matter of fine tuning and learning the use of all my new found talents. I closed my eyes on those thoughts and felt the deep, peaceful stillness of immortal sleep begin to cover me.

Chapter Forty~One

Five weeks passed since Charlotte Ann and Dale had returned to her New York home. James and I had the entire time with each other and we spent it mostly at home and around the estate. James made good use of our time together by continuing to teach me things about my new life. I sharpened and honed the skills and powers I had been born with, learning to use and control them to my benefit and becoming stronger day by day.

The days were spent learning and the nights were spent hunting with James. We hunted together almost every night. I began to get better and more proficient at the skills I had been taught. I killed frequently during those first few weeks after the change, regularly gorging myself with blood. With each subsequent kill I became stronger, more powerful, and my kills became cleaner and neater. I'm not a 'ripper' like some immortals are; instead I only make two small punctures using my fangs and always close them up afterward. When I killed it was always in the outlying areas of the city, usually around the docks and the port, both areas where a body wouldn't raise too much interest.

I also learned that since Charleston is a huge tourist town I could always go into the historic district downtown for a 'grab-n-go' snack. There's a steady supply of fresh, new and usually delicious guys to choose from in the local bistros and specialty shops. I just had to be very careful not to kill in those areas. After all, I wouldn't want to mess up the tourist trade … they're good for more than just the money they bring to the area.

Additionally there are several college campuses in the area around Charleston and, as James had taught me, they did indeed prove to be good hunting grounds, especially when all I wanted was a quick drink. I was able to effortlessly blend in having recently been a student myself. I felt comfortable there and actually was able to easily carry on conversations with others who thought me a student like themselves. I became the perfect predator.

It was in and around the downtown area and the several colleges that I refined my ability to take a little drink and move on. I fed well in both vicinities, although I never have and never will kill, unless I absolutely have to, in either of the two locales. James was still astonished that I had so quickly mastered the ability to take only a small amount of blood but from several different victims in a night.

I became incredibly adept at silently prowling the rooftops and back allies of the city carefully choosing my meals. I will admit that the small sip here and there can be fulfilling and even satisfy the hunger, but the kill … and it will be difficult to understand this unless one is an immortal … the kill is something that is extremely exhilarating. The taste of blood that is filled with guilt is different and so much more satisfying than that of a common tourist or student. As I have said I tried not to kill too close to the center of the city or the schools because that would certainly have drawn undue attention. But there was one night in particular in which I had a hunt and kill that, as it turned out, was very nearly as gratifying as my first two kills. I not only took a life that night, I saved one as well …

I had been hunting alone all evening, James and I had gone in separate directions, and I had already fed extremely well, several times in fact. It was a couple of hours after midnight and I was casually roaming the rooftops and back areas of the dorms at one of the local colleges looking for another small drink before returning home for the evening when I heard what sounded like a little girl's voice some distance away. I stopped to listen and noted that she was crying fearfully, so I moved closer to the sound, carefully listening, to find out what was causing her distress.

I silently took up a spot on the roof above an alleyway where the dorm dumpsters were located and looked down on a scene that made me smile. I inhaled the scent of two types of blood wafting upwards on the air drafts, one completely innocent, the other brimming with guilt. The innocent blood, though mingled heavily with the smell of fear, was so enticing, so fresh and sweet, so tempting. The smell of the other, the guilty blood, made my mouth water and I felt my fangs come down. I breathed it in knowing that I was soon to feed again, but better yet, I was going to kill when I did.

I quickly delved into the thoughts of the man … they were very vivid and so overwhelmingly filthy as he thought about how much fun he was going to have with this obviously new little girl he had found. As it turned out, this hadn't been the first time he had done this sort of thing either. The memories of what he had done to his several other victims, and what he planned to do to this one who was so much more young, tender and fresh, than the others, flooded his mind, and he became aroused far beyond his expectations.

He was much bigger than the girl was, and had her cornered next to the dumpster, away from the streetlight and standing in front of her, blocking her escape. I wondered that she could actually be a college student; she looked incredibly young, resembling a mere child, so tiny and fragile standing against the dumpster. I quickly picked her name, Jessica, from her thoughts and that she was extremely terrified and felt powerless "*… it's my first time away from home … why did I have to take the trash out this late, I knew better … nobody knows I'm out here and it's so dark … I've never even done what he wants to do … and he's not going to let me go either … I'm so scared … so alone out here … I wish I had never come here … I wish I was back home, safe with my mom and dad …*"

She was crying harder now, like the frightened child she appeared to be, the tears streaming down her face, "Please don't do this to me mister … please … just go away and leave me alone … I don't know who you are … I won't tell anyone, I promise," she begged softly through her tears.

"I just love this," he growled, "all you pretty little young things running around here looking so good, shaking those tight little tails and acting like you're so much better than everyone else … but *I* know the *truth* … you're just waiting on a real man to come along and do you! Why, you're so sweet and fresh, you just look good enough to eat," he laughed at his own joke and took another step toward her.

"Ummm … and so do you," I spoke softly and quietly as I landed silently behind him from the roof, "What … you want to eat a pretty young girl … try me … I like it that way … but I must warn you … I bite back! Come on big boy, leave the child alone, have some fun with a real woman," I said with an enticing smile, "because I certainly plan to have some fun with you."

"Wha … who … where did you come from," he demanded spinning around, suddenly confused and feeling not so in charge now. The little girl looked around him at me and her eyes grew even bigger with fright.

"Oh it doesn't matter where I came from," I laughed, "although it would appear that you're not the only predator hunting on campus tonight are you?"

He started to step away, making a futile attempt at a run, but I reached out and grabbed him, wrapping my hand around his throat and squeezing. I easily lifted him so that the toes of his shoes barely touched the pavement.

"Don't be in such a hurry to leave," I smiled at him, squeezing just a little tighter, "this party is just getting started … and it would be so rude of you to leave before introductions are made. You wanted to know who or what I am … well, I'm certainly not going to tell you who I am, not that it would matter anyway. But now what I am, I'll answer that one for you!"

Just then the girl saw an opportunity to escape and she started to move. I spoke quickly and sharply to her, raising a finger on my free hand in her direction, "Jessica, please … stay right where you are and don't make any sudden moves … you smell so very delectable … and that puts you in great danger until I finish what I am about to do … so please for your own safety do as I say … just stay right where you are, remain perfectly motionless and you will be safe … from both of us." She froze in place trying to squeeze herself tighter into the corner formed by the dumpster and the brick wall.

I was still holding the man up with my other hand wrapped securely around his throat and looking into his eyes. "Oh be still," I said sharply, tightening my grip on him as he continued desperately trying to get away, "and take it like the 'real man' you said you were!"

"Now then … where were we … oh yes, we were talking about what I am," I said thoughtfully, pulling him closer to me so that we were eye to eye, "I'm your worst nightmare, the thing that leaps out of the darkness when you least expect … I live in the shadows, watching and hunting the darkness for vermin like you … I'm the one who rides the pale horse, you know me as Death, and I promise you, hell follows close behind me."

Then making sure my back was turned to Jessica I smiled, flashing my fangs at him and said, "See those … no living human has ever seen them … so what do you think that means for you?"

"Please," he started begging me, struggling to choke out the words around my grip, "just let me go, I promise I'll never do anything like this again, I'll leave and never come near this place again."

"Yeah 'bout that, you're pretty much right, and you'll never come near this place again either," I mused quietly, "but tell me why should I let you go, we're both hunters, you and I, and you obviously understand the hunt. You found your prey … and I found mine. You have no choice about releasing your prey because a bigger predator came along and forced you to do it. Unfortunately for you, there is no bigger predator to come along and force me to release my catch. Besides, it's not like you were about to let her go willingly because she asked – or should I say begged – in fact, if you had left her alive, you would have left her dead inside … you were about to destroy her future and you weren't going to show her any mercy … now convince me why should I show you any?"

I let him see the blood lust begin to rise in me as my eyes changed from blue to dark red. The front of his pants suddenly showed a widening dark spot as the fear completely overtook him and his bladder let go.

"Oh Jesus," he started whimpering, "Jesus … Jesus … this can't be real … *you* can't be real …"

"I assure you, I'm very real and it's a little late now for prayer," I laughed at him, "after all, you're already dead … and there's nothing you can do about it."

I matched my viciousness to his as I pulled him to me. Ripping aside his collar, I wrapped my arms around him and sank my fangs deep into his neck. He tried to scream as his blood exploded into my mouth, hot and strong, deliciously guilty. I bit him several times in an effort to cause him as much pain as I possibly could. I swallowed again and again, drinking deeply from the severed artery in his neck. I felt the sensuality of the kill building and finally breaking as the waves of pleasure washed over me. I held him tightly as I drained every drop of his blood, again not losing a single trickle. When I had taken the last of his guilt ridden blood I began ripping and tearing at his throat nearly decapitating him before dropping his body at the side of the dumpster.

Once I had started this predator down the on-ramp to hell's highway, I turned my full attention toward the frightened girl. The fear that was still running rampant in her caused the scent of her blood to be even stronger, rising up from her like steam off of a hot pool. Even gorged as I was, her blood still smelled deliciously wonderful, so innocent, so tempting; the scent of a mere child. I breathed it in like the sweet bouquet that it was … and then with every bit of willpower in me, forced the blood lust away.

"Oh my God," she whispered softly to herself, her eyes growing wide in pure terror, "a vampire … they do exist … a real, live, honest to God vampire is standing right in front of me … and this one isn't sparkling … she's not even smiling …"

I took a couple of slow steps toward her and crouched down in front of her, resting one knee on the ground. She was still very scared, and couldn't believe what she had just witnessed. Continuing to hold her spellbound, I reached out and gently laid my hand on the side of her face and smiled. I looked into her pretty grey eyes and saw the fear reflected in them, her heart was thundering loudly in her small chest, and her breathing was in short ragged gasps of terror. She opened her mouth to scream and before she could I released a wave of comforting safety over her and watched as she became calm. Suddenly all she saw was another student just like herself, with sparkling blue eyes, smiling and kneeling easily in front of her.

I opened my arms and taking her in a hug, drew her close to me. I gently nuzzled into her hair as I held her in my arms, again breathing in the tempting scent of the youth and innocence of a child. I staunchly refused the natural urge to allow my fangs to descend and instead began whispering into her ear, "Jessica, I am indeed a vampire, just like you've said, but I'm also a young girl just like you, so you don't have to fear me. What you just witnessed was me preventing you being horribly raped and possibly murdered. I killed the man that frightened you … you are safe now … he will never threaten you again."

I felt her tiny body, still trembling with untold fear, melt against me in total surrender, as she began to cry uncontrollably on my shoulder. I drew her closer and began rubbing her back, trying to reassure her. She begin snubbing as she tried to stop crying, and her shaking begin to slow to almost nothing as I continued whispering calmly to her, "Jessica, in just a few minutes I'm going to wipe away your memory of him, me, and this portion of the night. When I do, you must return to your room, go to your bed, and sleep. Do you understand me?"

She nodded on my shoulder so I took her and held her at arms-length and looked deep into her mind, receiving quite a shock at what I found there. She was indeed very young, barely fourteen and a science and math prodigy. She had only just arrived on campus the week before to attend special summer classes for the extraordinarily gifted and talented.

I kept her locked in my thrall, our eyes fastened to each other, and she never moved as I gently began wiping her memory of the night, replacing it with something better.

"Jessica, you never left your room all night … you were never at the dumpsters … you will not remember seeing or experiencing any of this, not even in a faint dream. When you wake in the morning, you will remember having a series of wonderfully sweet dreams … a very restful night dreaming of home and those you love and miss … something that you look forward to returning to again soon."

When I had completed changing her memory of the night, she relaxed in my grip. I hugged her once more … breathing in deeply and forever committing to memory the scent of the pure innocence of a child … then gently kissed her on the forehead and spoke softly, "Dear sweet little Jessica, may you have many, many years before you stand and look death in the face again … now go quickly, may you be successful in all you do, be at peace little one, and stay safe."

I leaped silently back to the rooftop and out of her sight, watching her as she dreamily made her way back into the dorms.

Chapter Forty~Two

When the body of my last particular victim was found, he was identified by police as a known child sexual predator that was wanted in three States in connection with several rapes of young girls. The authorities attributed his death to some kind of an animal attack due to the manner in which I so viciously killed him for attacking an innocent little girl. Still, after that night, it became evident that James and I should conduct our hunting far away from Charleston. We decided that for the next several weeks, it would be to our advantage were we to restrict our hunting activities southward to Beaufort and the Hilton Head area and northward to Myrtle Beach and beyond, leaving everything in between unscathed with the exception of the quick drink.

Only once during that time did I come close to

actually killing again. We had gone down to South Beach, to SET, the most exclusive dance club in Miami to feed and dance the night away and while it wasn't completely intentional it also wasn't completely accidental either.

I love to dance, and have been a dancer since I was a small child, continuing my lessons throughout high school, and I still enjoy showing off my moves. Probably because due to my tall, slender build, I was never endowed with a very large chest, so my legs and butt are two of my best endowments. I don't mind showcasing my legs either … and thanks to so many years of dance classes and cheer, I not only have a rock solid core, but also a tight, firm butt and well-toned legs that allow me to rock a pair of low-rise skinny jeans like it's nobody's business.

I've found that nightclubs are an ideal location to show off my assets while I hunt, their dance-floors often being very crowded, which makes them a perfect setting to take prey without drawing undue attention. When I find and take my prey, we simply look like any other couple making out while we dance.

When James and I weren't feeding we sat together at a table and acted like the lovers we are. He likes for me to show off and look very sexy when we go out, and of course with the added allure of the immortal, I am more than a little appealing to both men and women. It's that draw that attracts the attention of my potential prey and makes feeding a much easier task.

James, on the other hand, is so very handsome and his immortal attraction so strong, that he almost immediately draws the attention of just about every woman in the place. It seems that anytime a man, especially one as good-looking as he is, shows up with an attractive woman, all the other women want to know what it is about him. So I suppose in a manner of speaking, I work in partnership with his immortal draw to make feeding a little easier for him, too.

We had both dressed to appear like we were out on a date. I was wearing a short, shiny satin half-sleeve blouse that I had tied open in front. It fully revealed my flat smooth tummy and lean sides. I had paired it with a very short, snug, designer skirt that rode just on my hips, and a pair of strappy sandals. I had certainly put myself on display and after several hours my skin had developed a nice warm glow in return for my efforts.

On this particular night I had danced several times with a wide variety of men. All of whom had treated me like a lady, since this was the best club in town. I in turn, had treated each of them to a very close and personal dance, being careful to take only a small drink from each, and quickly closing the wounds left by my fangs. James and I had pretty much taken our fill and were preparing to leave for the night. So my near accident can be explained by the actions of the victim himself.

I usually pick my victims, mentally suggesting to them that they ask me to dance. This specific man however, decided he wanted to dance with me. He had been in the club most of the night, usually drinking alone, and so had become quiet inebriated. I had seen him watching me and couldn't help but notice how he had undressed me with his eyes every time he looked at me. I had homed in on his thoughts, which were dirty, extremely crude, and directed right toward me. Of course, it wasn't physically possible for him to have successfully accomplished what he was imagining … honestly, I'm not sure any mortal man could, but just the same I had passed him over several times in making my choices.

Between his imagination and the alcohol he finally

got up enough nerve and approached me, completely ignoring James sitting there beside me, and was very insistent about wanting to dance with me. I looked at James with a little twinkle in my eyes and silently said, *"Why not, I suppose I could call him dessert."*

"Humph, going sugar-free tonight," he silently laughed.

We moved out to the dance-floor together and he quickly took me in his arms drawing me close against him. As we danced, his hands began roaming over my back and sides, finally coming to rest lightly on my butt. I gently moved his hands away saying, "Look, all I want is to have a quick enjoyable dance and go back to my boyfriend."

"Forget about him," he slurred as he laid a hand back on my butt and squeezed, "you can go home with me and have a much better time."

"Oh, I don't think either one of us would really enjoy that," I quipped.

"Oh, think about it," he persisted, "I'll make sure you enjoy it!"

"You really don't want to do this," I warned him again.

"Baby, you are such a fine woman, the most beautiful in the club. Now come on, give me just a little kiss. Once you kiss me you'll forget all about him," he kept on.

I spoke a silent warning to James with a little laugh saying, *"Gonna need some help here in a minute, I may need some assistance restraining myself!"*

"I'm watching, and listening, do what you have to do," he flashed right back.

"If you absolutely insist on kissing me," I told him, "we're going to do it my way and I like to start with a little neck nibbling."

"Now that's better," he slurred again.

I had allowed myself to get angry at this buffoon, so I struck hard. I wrapped my arms around him, pulling him close, and holding him tight, I sank my teeth deep into his carotid. I knew I should have stopped after two mouthfuls but I didn't. I just kept drinking, pulling his blood into me. When I heard his heart begin to slow I knew I had better quit or he would have a really bad ending to his night.

I quickly licked his wounds to close them and whispered in his ear saying, "You are very lucky I don't just kill you, remember that the next time you have those kinds of dirty thoughts about some girl. When you wake up again, you'll only remember that you suddenly felt weak and couldn't stand up anymore. You'll tell your friends that you drank too much and are probably lucky to be alive."

I dropped him to the floor and let out a tiny squeal that I needed help, he had passed out. Several of his friends came running to him and I disappeared into the crowd. James and I quickly took our leave and began our trip back to Whitehall.

Later that night, after we had gotten back to Charleston, I apologized to James for almost going too far.

"Don't let it bother you, he was just an obnoxious drunk human" he said, "I would have killed him for you if you had asked. We could have shared our first meal together in Miami instead of New York!"

"Humph, you might have liked that, but I would rather we share something a bit more pleasant-tasting! I really don't mind having a little bourbon in my blood … I just don't care for blood in my bourbon!" We both shared a laugh at my little joke.

"Speaking of New York, I've been thinking, how

would you like to go up to the City? It's only a week until the big ball and I believe I did promise you a trip to the theater and perhaps we can find something more delectable there. I need to pick up something I ordered from a friend and besides, it'll give you the opportunity to get together with Charlotte Ann and go shopping," he smiled, closing the deal.

"You had me at shopping with Charlotte Ann," I laughed, kissing him passionately, "I'm ready to go any time you are."

After we arrived and settled into James' huge suite at the Waldorf, I immediately called Charlotte Ann. We left for our postponed shopping trip right away, laughing like two school girls. She took me straight to the original Vickie's Boutique, on 5th Avenue. We went in and she introduced me to Vickie herself.

"Oh, hello Charlotte Ann, it's so good to see you again! I had no idea you were back in town," Vickie said smiling.

"It's good to see you again, too, Vickie," she began with a smile.

"And who is your beautiful friend that you have brought along?"

"This is Katelyn and she's up from Charleston for a visit."

Then turning to me, extending her hand, said, "It's so nice to meet you Katelyn!"

"Hi Vickie," I smiled at her, "it's really my pleasure to meet you! I've been a fan of your work for a long time."

"Katelyn is my friend James' new companion. You do remember James don't you," Charlotte Ann asked with a smile.

"Oh, I surely do, and what a handsome gentleman he is," she smiled, "and Katelyn you certainly are the lucky one!"

"Katelyn is a pajama girl Vickie," Charlotte Ann began with a smile and a quick wink, "and she absolutely loves wearing them when she's lounging at home. Do you think you could find her a nice outfit and maybe even a special little naughty something for entertaining James!"

Vickie took a step back, looked me over carefully, taking in every detail as only a master seamstress can, and smiled.

"Katelyn," she said, "you are perfect, so tall and slender! I have the most impeccable pair of pajamas just for you. They are imported English satin with silk trim, done in a medium blue that will absolutely agree with your beautiful eyes. They have a corresponding, open sheer robe that's just a shade lighter, and the cutest little matching slippers. Allow me to get those for you and then we'll talk about the naughty-wear!"

I modeled the pajamas when she brought them out. They had an ideal fit and the soft satin felt so good against my skin. The top had a wide half-sleeve, and was loose enough to be comfortable and just short enough to show an occasional flash of my tummy when I moved. The bottom was fitted and sat just below my waistline, hanging comfortably on my hips. It flared out to a nice flowing leg that accented my small waist and height. The little sheer robe was just that – sheer. It was like adding a see through veil and bestowed a touch of mystery to the entire outfit.

I looked at Charlotte Ann with a giggle and asked, "Do I have to take these off?"

"I'm sure James could very easily persuade you," she commented dryly with a smile.

"Now, the lingerie is a completely different story," Vickie said with a smile, "follow me I have a private fitting room for my special customers."

"I'm right behind you," I laughed, "I can't wait to see what you have!"

"I've just recently received a bolt of the finest Chantilly Lace, handmade in Belgium, from the best natural Chinese silk," she said looking over her shoulder as we walked, "this particular pattern is very retro, dating back almost three hundred years. I personally made this outfit myself for just a special someone like you. You're about the size of one of my models so this should be absolutely perfect on you."

She handed me one of the cutest, smallest negligee's I had ever seen. I decided to buy it as soon as I saw it but I tried it on anyway. I looked at the mirrored walls of the fitting room and was more than pleased! It was black, of course, and consisted of a soft, corset style bra with a layered tier that came to just above my waist. The panties were cut in a French bikini style and sat low on my hips, just barely hinting at the hidden treasures that lay beneath. Both pieces had a red silk thread working its way throughout and were accented with the Chantilly lace. The separate silk sheer, again accented with the red thread working, was made completely of the Chantilly lace that Vickie was so excited about. I loved it and couldn't wait for James to see me.

"Thank goodness for that Brazilian," I thought as I stepped out of the dressing room to model it for the two of them.

Vickie was all smiles, looking somewhat like a proud parent, as she took in her handiwork.

"Katelyn, you look undeniably stunning," she laughed, "and I'm sure that James will agree with me on that. But, there's just one little thing that will make that outfit perfect for you … you may tell James I added it just special for him … I'll be right back!"

When she returned she was carrying a set of big fluffy, feathery angel's wings, "Here you are," she said, "add these to the outfit for that finishing touch … enjoy them … they're on me!"

I couldn't help but laugh at the seeming irony of the wings. Charlotte Ann, with a twinkle in her eyes, and laughing quickly added, "Bet you won't ask 'Do I have to take these off'?"

"I don't think I'll have to worry about that," I giggled, "I suspect that James will take them off for me."

We all three laughed heartily at my comment. Then Vickie wrapped each of my new things in her specialty boxes and Charlotte Ann and I headed off back to the Waldorf.

Chapter Forty~Three

Later that night, I lay cuddled in James' arms, my new angel wings and little lace creation thrown haphazardly in a heap beside the bed. I'm pretty sure he liked the new outfit as much or more than I did. In fact, the little nightie had really brought out the playfulness in him. It was like discovering the joys of each other's body for the first time. We had both outdone ourselves trying to see who could give the other more pleasure. James of course won out in that contest. After all, he did have nearly three centuries of experience over me. Besides, when he wins, I win … because he would never leave me unsatisfied or wanting more.

He had been right about that one moment of overwhelming immortal passion, too. I was caught up in our playing, concentrating on making him happy, when it happened. I had taken the topmost position this time and I soon felt myself begin to move toward my release point. I began to focus on what was happening in my body as the extreme pleasure continued to increase. Rocking in unison together, I leaned into him, letting my hair fall like a curtain around our heads, shielding us from seeing anything but the other's face.

He sensed the beginning throes of my orgasm and pulled me tightly against himself. Kissing me passionately he began thrusting upwards into me, deeper and stronger as we continued to move together in perfect rhythm. His lips barely touched my chin, the tip of my nose, and my eyelids. He began lightly tracing the tip of his tongue along my jaw line, nibbling at my ears. He kissed my neck and shoulders, his soft fingers tracing along the tops of my shoulders and upper back as he held me, driving me closer to the edge with his tender loving. He picked up his pace, moving closer to his own release point as I continued moving faster and faster toward my climax. I moaned softly in happiness as the first of the fireworks of orgasm slowly begin to trace into the sky.

Just at the point I completely let myself go and tipped over the edge into another in a long line of 'The World's Greatest Orgasms', he wrapped his arms around me and pulling me down on top of him, bit my neck and began pulling mouthful after mouthful of my blood into himself. I literally exploded with pleasure as he stayed at my neck continuing to slowly drink from me.

The pleasure of his bite was so concentrated inside me that I was literally unable to move as wave after glorious wave of powerful orgasm rolled through me over and over again. The terror that had been in me the first time he bit me was nowhere to be found. This time it was replaced by the most rapturous joy I had ever felt as my life was literally being sucked out of me. The orgasmic fireworks, complete with rockets and bursting star shells, climbing into the sky above me, were a thousand times better than the biggest New Year's Eve display ever. When it began to recede away I became totally limp in his arms and couldn't move for several minutes, not that I wanted to anyway. As I lay there on top of him, the pleasure slowly ebbing away, he began lightly rubbing my back and shoulders and I casually thought to myself, *"It's a good thing I don't have to breathe; I don't think I could if I had to!"*

Finally, when I could move again, I cuddled in close to his side as he wrapped his arms around me once again. He continued gently rubbing my back and shoulders with his soft fingers, letting them run easily through my hair. I was wiped out, but absolutely glowing from our lovemaking.

I looked at him in awe as we lay there together, his beautiful green eyes sparkling in the near darkness of the room. I kissed him, barely touching his lips, and whispered to him, "I love you more than life itself James DuBois, thank you for loving me enough to share this wonderful gift with me."

Then I slowly reached out and tenderly traced his jawline with my fingertip. I quietly chuckled laying there against him as I thought about us and what a couple we were.

"What are you thinking about," he asked casually.

"Oh, just you … me … us," I answered, still snickering, "I never thought I would fall in love with an older man … and you've certainly given a whole new meaning to loving an older man!"

"But I'm only twenty-eight," he chuckled, pulling me against him and kissing me again, "just seven years older than you."

After several minutes of total silence and continued tender petting, he turned toward me and softly spoke, "Katelyn, tomorrow morning we have to make a visit down to the diamond district. I want to buy you something …"

"James, you really don't …" I started to say.

He stopped me, gently laying a finger on my lips, "You don't understand … I fell in love with you the very first time I saw you in the bookstore. I knew then that you were my life, the eternal mate I had waited so long for. Now, you are eternally a part of me, forever, and I want to give you something to show my love for you. I want everyone who sees you to know how lucky I was to find you and to see the visible symbol of my love for you … please?"

"James, if I didn't love you so much … yes … I suppose so …" I whispered, smiling back at him and wondering what kind of pretty little diamond ring he had picked out for me.

We spent the remainder of the night lying together, with some light conversation, interspersed with several more rounds of intense lovemaking, then followed by the enjoyment of our closeness and the coolness of our bodies against each other.

The next day we made our way down to a little shop in the diamond district and walked in.

"Mr. Dubois, good day to you, sir!"

"And to you, also, sir," James answered with a smile, "Mr. Weissmann, this is my Katelyn I've told you about."

Mr. Weissmann turned to me and extending a hand said, "Ah, Miss Katelyn, it is indeed my pleasure to finally meet you in person. Mr. James has told me so much about you, but he was still unable to fully describe your beauty to me!"

"Thank you, sir," I said, taking his hand and slightly bowing my head since I was unable to blush at such a compliment.

Weissmann was an older man; he looked to be in his sixties or seventies. His hair was snow white and he wore thick glasses low on his nose. He spoke with a soft European, probably German or Russian, accent. He possessed the air of a kindly old grandfather that just made you want to hug him.

"Mr. James," he said, turning back to him, "I have the pieces you asked me to make for you. Please excuse me while I bring them from the back."

He returned in a few minutes carrying a large rectangular, black velvet jewelry case and set it down on his counter. Then turning to me he continued, "Miss Katelyn, you shall indeed stand out when you premier these at the ball."

He opened the case toward me and I was taken aback at what I saw inside. There on the velvet bed was the largest collection of beautiful gems I had ever seen, in either of my lives. The necklace itself was large and would easily cover my throat and upper chest. It was a waterfall necklace made up of four leaf clovers, crusted in diamonds with a large blue sapphire in the center of each cloverleaf. There were three stones, one large emerald and two smaller rubies, hanging beneath each of the five largest cloverleaves. Stretched out at the bottom of the case, was a matching bracelet of clover leaves, again a large sapphire in the center of each and surrounded by crusted diamonds.

A pair of earrings completed the set. They were made up of one large diamond with an emerald and two rubies hanging beneath to match the necklace.

"They … they're very beautiful … no, that doesn't even begin to describe them …" I said stunned.

"I'm delighted you approve of them … a world of meaning lies in this box, Miss Katelyn. It is a collection made up of four of the most precious gemstones known to mankind, the very bones of Mother Earth," he began explaining as he pointed out each stone, "the blue sapphires are said to be the connection to the spiritual world, often called the stone of prosperity, it helps you achieve your aspirations. The diamonds that surround it are the symbol of innocence and changelessness; the emeralds, one of the rarest of all gemstones stands for hope, persevering love and eternal life; finally the rubies, more prized above all the other stones, symbolize love, bringing contentment and peace to its wearer."

Weissmann smiled again and looking at James said, "Just as you asked, each clover leaf is made up of a ten carat sapphire and is surrounded with five carats of smaller diamonds; the emeralds are all three carats each and the complimenting rubies are two carats each. The bracelet is exactly half the weight of the necklace. The earrings are one carat diamonds with three-quarter carat emeralds and half carat rubies. The entire ensemble being set in eighteen carat white gold to give it added strength."

"The price … as we agreed," James asked.

"Of course, sir," Weissmann quickly said.

"Very well, I shall have payment transferred to your account."

Weissmann gently closed the case, handed it to me and said, "Miss Katelyn, I hope they serve you for many years and may each of the stones bring its true meaning into your life. May the love they absorb from you be passed down with them to your daughters and granddaughters."

"Thank you, so much," I said, still unsure of what to say.

Then as we started out of the door, Weissmann called to me, "Miss Katelyn, should you ever find yourself in the city and have need of jewelry for an event, please feel free to come to me. I shall see that you have whatever I have for however long you may need it."

Chapter Forty~Four

When we got back to our suite it was time to get ready for the Halloween Ball. Charlotte Ann had helped me in the search for a proper evening dress for the occasion. It was a full length, black silk affair handmade in Paris and tailored by one of her friends to fit me. It was really gorgeous, a low-cut, sleeveless, backless formal dress. It was form fitting to my body, drawing in tightly at the center to accent my waistline. There was a full length split on the left side from my upper thigh to make walking a little more comfortable.

When I had put it on, I added the jewelry James had just given me, the necklace fit perfectly from mid-throat and across my upper chest, the earrings hung lightly from my ears and the bracelet rode comfortably on my right wrist.

The outfit was completed with a ladies half cape of black velvet with a cranberry satin lining that, supposedly, was to keep my arms warm in the night air.

James was resplendent in his best 'Vampire Drag' as he called it, which was really just formal evening wear. His tux was black with a gray vest, the half coat being cut tightly at the waist and with long tails. His shirt was white with a lace ruffle at the throat and cuffs. He wore a beautiful, flowing, full length two tiered opera cape that was made of fine wool that matched mine in color, over his tux. He finished his ensemble with a top hat, white gloves, and a silver-topped walking stick.

"Have you ever wondered what goes on under the vampire's cape," he asked with a devilish grin, opening it and spreading it wide.

I stood looking at him and thinking how absolutely hot he looked in – and out – of his clothes, before I answered him with a seductive smile, "Do you really want to go out tonight, because if I take the time to find out what happens under that cape, we probably won't be going anywhere anytime soon!"

"Yes, we must go," he smiled back, "it makes coming home that much more appealing. Besides, you know, I am introducing you tonight as my new mate. That will give us ample excuse to make an early but tasteful exit."

When we arrived at the ball a doorman deftly held the limo door for me and James as we carefully exited. He glided into The Palace with me on his arm. I looked around and was shocked at the number of immortals I saw intermingling in the grand lobby. Everyone was dressed in the finest evening wear but I quickly noticed that James seemed to be the only one in full 'vampire drag' complete with cape, top hat and cane. It swirled gracefully around him as we walked, everyone carefully moving aside as we made our way toward the Grand Ballroom.

"Look around you," James spoke softly to me, "this is the only time you are likely to see this many immortals gathered together in one place."

"And no one suspects that we are different from anybody else," I asked shockingly.

"Of course not," he smiled at me, "it's Halloween in the mortal world, everybody is supposed to look pale and fangy!"

I chuckled and tried not to snort at his comment.

We were met and greeted by Charlotte Ann and Dale, both dressed in the same formal evening wear as most of the others. I was pleasantly surprised at how good Dale looked.

"You do know that you had better stay close to him," I whispered to Charlotte Ann, "he cleans up really well and looks just absolutely yummy ... if he were a mortal, I'd certainly be tempted to take a drink."

"Now Katelyn, you know I've warned you about innocent young mortals," she answered with a little laugh, "but although he does look like a yummy young mortal, he isn't, and yes, I do have a very special 'After the Ball' event planned for him later!"

"I'd be willing to bet that it's very similar to the same event I have planned for James, too!"

We shared a girlie laugh together as we entered the Ballroom and the doorkeeper bowed to James and Charlotte Ann saying, "Your table is prepared, please come this way."

The four of us followed him to a table at the very front. It was set for only four. I had noticed that most of the tables seated eight and some, towards the rear, even ten.

There was a big brass band set up on the stage, a dance floor had been left open in the center of the room and a huge crystal chandelier hanging above, glittered with reflected light. The band was playing an assortment of classical swing, jazz and slow dance music. I was taken aback at the decor. But my surprise was about to be jolted again as the lights came down and the Master of Ceremonies stepped to the center of the stage.

"Ladies and Gentlemen," he began, "welcome to the annual 'All Hallows Eve Ball'. Before we begin it is with great pleasure that once again I introduce to you the Lord and Patron of our yearly event. Please make welcome James Thomas Dubois … The Master of Whitehall Manor."

I must have looked shocked at this and then a small spotlight centered on our table as James stood to a soft applause. He looked around him, smiling as his fangs flashed brilliantly in the dim light.

"And in addition this evening, we are to congratulate him on what is a very special occasion in our world, one that many have waited decades, and a couple of us a century or longer, to witness … he is accompanied tonight by his new mate," the MC continued, and turning toward me, extended his hand, "originally from Marietta Georgia, please make welcome the newest member of our world, Miss Katelyn Melissa Corbin, the Mistress of Whitehall Manor!"

I sat there shocked as James reached his hand toward me to stand beside him. I smiled as I stood not knowing what else to do. As the audience softly applauded, I shyly moved closer to him and he gently wrapped his arm around me and whispered, "Show your fangs darling, it's alright and expected here."

I began to feel a little more comfortable, secure with his arm around me, as I stood there next to him looking around. Following his example I extended my fangs and smiled brightly at the crowd. Their applause erupted loudly for me.

I sat back down as quickly as I could and looked at Charlotte Ann. She flashed her perfect smile at me and said, "I assume James forgot to mention that you are a part of our version of the 'Royal Family', such as it is. Not to worry," she continued with a smile and a soft laugh, "soon you and I shall sit down and I will outline the hierarchy of our world to you."

The first dance was reserved for me and James. We moved onto the dance-floor as the band struck up a happy tune. He held me close as we slow danced around the floor, passing by all of the tables that lined the edges. I put my arms around him, trying to get closer as we whirled and turned around the room. He was still wearing his cape and I felt it as it flared out and encircled both of us, protecting me as if it were a shield.

He looked down at me and softly said, "Katelyn, darling, you are the most beautiful woman in the world … the center of my universe … and I am so happy to call you my mate!"

Then he kissed me on the lips as we continued our dance. Everybody and everything in the room disappeared as his kiss became more passionate. I felt it to the center of my being and began to get weak as he held me there, wishing we were somewhere else. I felt the familiar tingle rise up in me and move throughout my body. I looked up at him with a cunning smile and said, "So, is *this* what happens under the vampire's cape?"

"Not even close," he replied with a smile, "but if you liked that just wait until we are alone."

"I can't wait," I smiled happily back at him lightly

kissing his lips. We began another circle around the dance floor, slowing as the music slowed, our dance coming to an end. He kissed me again and when he did I returned his kiss, hot and passionately, not caring who watched. The audience burst out with wild applause as we finished our dance and returned to our table.

We stayed for only a couple of more hours, dancing with each other several times. Charlotte Ann introduced me to more than a few of her friends from Europe, whom she said would be nice to know in the future. Just after midnight we made our exit, returning quickly to our suite. I had really enjoyed myself but was happy to get back and more than ready to change out of the evening dress and into my new pajamas.

When we got back to the suite and after we had settled a little, I slipped ahead of James into our room to start changing when I noticed his beautiful black cape draped across one of the several wing back reading chairs scattered around the bedroom. A smile slowly crossed my face as I stood there, forming an idea. I finished undressing and quickly slid into a pair of tiny, black, lacy panties I had bought while I was at Vickie's. Then I put the cape on over my shoulders, carefully fastening the clasp to hold it in place. The soft, cool satin felt good against my bare skin as I walked toward the bedroom door.

"I have alerted the pilot that we will be returning to Charleston in the morning, Katelyn," James said from the other room, his back turned toward me, as I stepped out of our bedroom.

"That's sounds good, I'm ready to get back home," I replied with a sultry voice as I stepped back into the main room, "but we still have tonight."

James glanced up and actually looked a little

surprised when he saw me. I was standing across the room from him, wrapped in his cape and wearing my best impish grin. It was almost too long for me, the end of it just touching the floor. I smiled naughtily at him and said, "You said something about showing me what goes on under this cape when you're wearing it … come with me and allow me show you what goes on under it when *I'm* wearing it."

"Somehow I believe that your version is going to be much more interesting than mine," he answered with a huge grin.

I moved closer to him and opened the cape wide revealing nothing but me and my sexy little panties underneath. I heard him growl low as he slipped his arm around my back between me and the soft satin pulling me close to him. My entire body shuddered with happy anticipation as he kissed me passionately and I returned the same kiss to him adding my own low growl to it.

"You do know that I'll never look at that cape quite the same way again," he chuckled softly as he kissed me a second time.

I quickly turned him loose and clutching each side of the cape in my hands flared it out and put my arms back around him, covering both of us in its lavish folds, and drawing him closer to me, I lightly kissed his lips again and whispered naughtily, "If you'll follow me into the 'Little Vamp's' bedroom, I'll show you what magic lies under this cape!"

"I shall follow you any place you wish to go," he laughed.

I pulled him quickly into our bedroom and closed the door behind us. After several hours of slow, fun playfulness combined with a considerable amount of steamy, passionate love … that was all very satisfying I might add … I gently kissed his lips and with a coy little smile softly asked, "What did you think of my version of what goes on under the vampire's cape?"

He answered my question with a happy groan and another deeply passionate kiss.

Chapter Forty~Five

When we returned to Whitehall, we spent the next six and a half weeks solely with each other. Our relationship, although strong from the very beginning, needed that time for just us. We grew even closer and bonded tighter than ever before. We spent a great amount of that time together exploring the four hundred seventy-eight acres of the Whitehall estate. James pointed out to me all the little secrets the property held, including a couple of hidden lairs in case we ever had to use them.

One afternoon as we stood together on the veranda looking out across the property I turned to James and with a playful smile, almost laughing said, "James … let's go running … we'll play 'catch me if you can'," and laughing like a little girl, I leaped off the steps with him right on my heels.

For the next two hours we ran and jumped, dodging in and out among the trees and fields. We played 'tag' and 'catch' with each other and whenever he would catch me, something I allowed him to do often, I would drop and roll around the grass, taking him down with me. Then after a few minutes of some very intensely passionate petting we would start our game all over again. I had never laughed as much and had so much fun in so short a time. When we stopped for a minute to look at each other and smile, James unexpectedly upped the ante on me.

"You want to try the swamp," he laughed, "we can jump through the trees and around the creeks and streams!"

"What are you waiting for," I laughed as I bounded off toward a huge old pine tree and launched myself toward the top of it. I surprised myself at how agile I had become as I landed gracefully among its topmost branches. We were soon playing another game of 'tag' as we bounced and leaped together from tree to tree, enjoying ourselves to no end, moving deeper and deeper into the swamp.

Suddenly, just below me, I caught a flash of brown out of the corner of my eye, and knew it was a deer. I felt my fangs extend as I leaped in its direction, a soft growl escaping my lips as I easily landed on top of it, straddling it as I brought it down. It kicked frantically as I held it and began tearing into its throat. I quickly found its jugular and tore into it, holding the madly kicking deer as I began to drink. Its frightened heart pumped its lifeblood quickly into my mouth. I drank and drank, enjoying the feel of the fresh hot blood, which, unlike human blood, was filled with the taste of the wild and untamed. It poured down my throat, and I didn't lose a single drop, finally stopping only when the deer's heart stopped pumping.

I stood to my feet as the fresh blood coursed through me, leaving me feeling refreshed and ready to run again. I turned around to find James and found myself looking right into his eyes. They flashed and twinkled in the light as he looked at me and laughed, shaking his head, "Katelyn, you never cease to amaze me. You have taken so naturally to your new life … I sometimes find it difficult to believe how easily you have acclimated yourself … it's almost as if you were born to it the first time … I'm so proud of you!"

"Do you think maybe it was because I had a good maker and teacher," I laughed as I cuddled close to him and kissed him, the blood from the deer still fresh on my lips. I reached for his hand and led him to a nearby water oak and we sat down at the base of it amid the large roots. I settled between his legs, propping my arms on his upraised knees, and leaned back against his chest. He wrapped his arms around me and for the next couple of hours we sat and talked quietly with each other. Finally a peaceful stillness fell around us while I enjoyed his closeness.

"James," I said softly after a long silence, "I want to go hunting again."

"Very well," he answered me as we stood up, "would you like me to join you or do you wish to go by yourself?"

"I think I'm going alone, I have something special in mind that I'm looking for. I have a taste for something I've never had," I whispered, as I stepped into his arms, and looked into his eyes, "something I have to be very careful with … I'm going down to the college, I think I'll find what I'm craving for there."

"I know what you are going for, and you are likely to find it there. But, you must be very careful, it is as addictive to us as heroin is to humans, don't allow it to draw you in too deeply," he replied, kissing my forehead, "I hope that what you find will be as satisfying as you hope it to be … enjoy yourself and good hunting!"

Later that afternoon I arrived on the campus of one of the larger close by colleges to begin my hunt. I quickly found the student longue area and settled into a comfortable chair. I was watching and waiting for something special, something different to come walking into the commons.

While I sat there patiently waiting I thought back about the alluring scent of the innocent blood of Jessica, the little girl I had recently rescued. I had fought so desperately against my nature not to take her that night, but since then I had been distracted by the memory of her blood and the pull it had since exerted on me to taste virtuous blood … to see what was so appealing about the innocence of it. It was that untouched purity or something very similar to it that I was hunting and it didn't take long to find someone that interested me.

I smiled to myself as I watched a young boy walk into the lounge and start toward the snack bar. He was just what I was hoping to find. He was close to my height with a nice medium build, appearing healthy and strong from work. His hair was the lightest corn silk blond, so fine it moved with every step he took. His eyes were the prettiest baby blue and his cheeks were still ruddy with his youth. I felt a thrilling excitement begin in the center of my body as I thought about the freshness that was lighting his features. He absolutely radiated an innocence that I hadn't seen in some time.

The blood thirst began to stir in me and I felt the tingle as I struggled not to allow my fangs to extend. When he walked past me I looked up at him, making solid eye contact and smiled shyly. He blushed deep red and I caught the scent of his blood. This boy was so fresh, so entirely innocent, and the thirst roared up in me, the blood lust ripping through every fiber of my being. I wanted him and I wanted him now.

"Well, hello there pretty boy," I thought to myself with a smile, *"I think I just found exactly what I have been looking for!"*

When he returned with his soda I smiled at him again and knowing he was bashful spoke up, "Hi there would you like to sit here with me for a few minutes?"

He blushed again and flashed a shy smile, showing pretty white teeth, "Who, me," he asked uncertainly looking around before answering, "Well, sure, I suppose so."

I quickly picked up his thoughts, he couldn't believe that such a beautiful girl had not only noticed him but was talking to him. I smiled at his thoughts, knowing this was going to be a very enjoyable afternoon … for both of us.

I continued smiling and playing along, "My name is Katie," I introduced myself, using the shorter, junior high school version of my name, as I offered my hand to him, "I'm new here and don't really know anyone."

"My name is Ryan," he began, blushing bright red again, as he lightly took my hand.

The scent of his blood was driving the blood lust to a near frenzy in me. It was the same intoxicating and inviting scent that had risen like steam from little Jessica and I couldn't wait to get a taste of him. I knew I would have to be so very careful when I finally did. He was so innocent he was almost childlike, and it would be a real test of my ability to take just a small drink and stop. The blood lust was tearing through me and I again had to fight the urge to not allow my fangs to extend. It was a struggle not to wrap him in my arms and take him right here. I was fighting nature and I knew that if I wasn't careful nature would soon win.

"I just moved here from Georgia," I offered, trying to start the conversation and get closer, "are you from Charleston, Ryan?" I savored his name as it rolled off my tongue, again breathing in his soft scent.

"Oh no, I'm from up in Virginia, my folks have a dairy farm there," he continued as he began to feel a little more comfortable, "I'm a freshman this year, what about you?"

"Oh you certainly are fresh," I thought to myself, and with a smile I continued, "No, I'm a senior this year, but like I said, I'm new here. Would you like to show me around if you have time?"

I had to get him out of here and someplace where I could feed ... and soon. I certainly didn't want to kill this beautiful, innocent little boy, but I definitely planned to enjoy more than just my usual little sip of that precious, sweet blood. Although he wouldn't remember my little sip later, I decided to give him a memory that would boost his own self confidence in return for the pleasure of the drink he was about give me.

We walked outside and I reached and took his hand in mine. I looked into his eyes and released a wave of pure relaxation toward him. I started searching his mind for any place where we could be alone, then I hit on it ... his room. His roommate was a senior and had moved out into town so Ryan had it all to himself. He would never have spoken his thoughts out loud, but he was thinking to himself how much he would like to have me alone in his room, although he didn't have any idea of what to do with me if he did.

"I think we can arrange that," I thought to myself, *"and I know exactly what to do."*

"Ryan, do you think maybe we can go up to your room for a little while," I asked as I continued looking into his eyes, holding him captive to my wishes. He was locked in my thrall and completely under my power now and only too willing to do what I asked.

We went directly to his room and once inside I moved closer to him. I took him in my arms and gently kissed him on the lips and he melted against me. I smiled as I began to easily rub his back. His heart sped up with my game and the scent of his blood exploded in my nostrils once again.

Then taking the game a little further I began planting some very erotic thoughts in his mind and quietly said to him, "Please Ryan, take your shirt and jeans off, let's lay down for a few minutes, I'm going to do something to you that will make both of us feel very good."

As if locked in a dream he began to undress and moving across the room, lay down on his little dorm bed. In his mind's eye he saw me completely undressed and exploring his body. I watched with fascination, smiling, as the bulge in his boxers began to grow to a full erection. I slowly stretched out next to him, allowing my fingers to wander leisurely over his smooth chest and stomach. I lightly kissed his lips and quickly moved downward to his throat and his neck. His pulse rate increased, raising his temperature and continuing to fill my nostrils with the sweet fragrance of his blood. I could feel the sudden warmth of his body even through my clothes and I pressed closer to him. He was indeed hot blooded and I savored the thought of how he would soon share that warmth with me. I kissed him again gently on the lips and whispered, "Ryan, sweet, innocent Ryan, you smell so wonderful, I can't wait much longer for this."

He tried to talk but was so wrapped up in my control that he found it difficult to pull an intelligible thought together, "I … I'm not too sure … I've never … I don't know much about this …" he finally stammered.

"That's alright Ryan," I whispered, my tongue tracing the outer curve of his ear, "I'm in complete control of everything and I promise you'll never experience anything as intense or satisfying as this again."

He put his arms around me as I continued to feed the pictures into his mind. I breathed on his neck and he groaned in pleasure. Then as I slowly ran my tongue over his neck just below his ear, I eased my hand down across his stomach and began to lightly stroke his inner thigh. I wanted him to enjoy this as much as I was. His own mind began to take over and he added to the pictures I was ingraining there. He shuddered with pleasure as his mind allowed him to enter me and plunge into my body. He became lost in his feelings tightening his arms around me.

I was unable to restrain myself any longer and I sank my fangs into his neck, quickly retracting them as his blood shot strongly out of the tiny wounds, filling my mouth. It was unbelievably sweet, so fresh and full of pure, untouched virtue. The taste was incredible, like nothing I had ever tasted, sending shivers of near orgasmic pleasure throughout my body. I drank slowly and deliberately, nuzzling at his soft neck, taking my time, licking at the now slowly flowing blood and savoring every sweet drop of it.

I continued planting very passionate pictures in him, as I held him there enjoying the deliciousness of his delightfully virtuous blood. I continued drinking from him, swallowing over and over, knowing I had to make myself stop before I went too far. Taking one final pull from his open artery I carefully licked his neck to close the small holes where my fangs had penetrated.

Finally, reaching deep into his mind and searching out his darkest hidden fantasy, I softly whispered into his ear, "Ryan, you are the most astonishing lover … so pleasing … you are so delightful and have satisfied me in so many ways!"

I breathed on his neck again as I slowly licked it one more time, getting one last tiny taste of his sweet, untainted blood. I reached down and touched the inside of his bare thighs with my fingertips as I continued pouring the erotic pictures into his mind. I trailed my fingers slowly up his leg toward his smooth stomach, stopping only for a moment to massage the straining bulge in his underwear. I continued playfully rubbing him and he began to moan with pleasure.

He suddenly stiffened and groaned, "Oh my God … Katie … this is so much better than I ever imagined it could be!" And arching his body strongly upward, he jerked again and again, releasing his pent up desire and filling his underwear. I smiled as I slowly began circling my fingertips around his stomach and across his chest.

"Ryan, you won't remember what I have just done," I spoke softly to him, looking deep into his eyes, "or ever know how much you have pleased me, but you will remember the incredibly pretty young girl that came to your dorm room, made love to you, and left you asleep in your bed. When I leave you, you will sleep deeply, resting peacefully and when you wake up you will have a new, stronger confidence in yourself. You will easily find a wonderful new girlfriend, she will be the perfect girl for you, and you will be a good lover to her. Now sleep my sweet, innocent little boy and regain your strength."

I slowly stood up next to his bed, running my fingers through his soft hair brushing it away from his eyes. "Thank you Ryan, so very much," I whispered, again lightly kissing him on the forehead, and gently closing his eyes with my hand.

Then I silently disappeared out of his room and quickly made my way back across campus still savoring my first taste of innocence as his delightful blood continued rushing through me, warming me and giving my skin a nice soft glow.

James was waiting for me when I returned to Whitehall, "How did your hunt go," he asked with a smile.

"It was wonderful … and the easiest hunt I've ever had," I replied as I melted into his arms, "I found exactly what I went after, too. My victim was completely innocent and his blood was sweet, pure, and virtuous."

"Ummm … you've been playing the role of a succubus," he said still smiling, his eyes twinkling, "I can still taste the innocence on your lips and the glow absolutely gives you away … but were you able to constrain yourself … did you leave him alive?"

"Of course I did," I laughed kissing him again, "I mean I took more than just a small sip, probably three of his eight pints, and I had to force myself to stop at that. He'll be weak for a few days but should recover very nicely."

"Do you understand now what Charlotte Ann says about the appeal of innocent blood?"

"Yes, I do, but that innocence only satisfied one desire and the purity of it created another, much stronger, desire in me," I smiled at him as I cuddled closer and softly kissed him, "I don't know if it's the innocence and purity of the blood … but right now I am so incredibly turned on. Take me to bed – have sex with me – don't be slow and gentle … take me fast and hard … I want you … I need you … do something for me that an innocent little boy could never do!"

I laughed like a school girl as James picked me up, tossed me over his shoulder like I was a sack of potatoes, and carried me to our bedroom. He made love to me hard and fast, he took me again and again … and to greater heights than I think he had ever taken me. I returned his loving with a wild abandon. When we had finished, I refused to turn him loose, holding him close against me, enjoying the physical closeness of his body. The remainder of the day was spent in each other's arms as again and again we made love throughout the rest of the afternoon and late into the night.

Early the next morning, with a devilish smile, and looking into my eyes he whispered, "Darling, you absolutely must go hunting again … and often!

"Ummm … you liked that did you," I breathed softly.

James continued over the next few days to teach me more of the things I needed to know to survive in my new life, fine tuning many of my new found skills. Together we ran, lightning fast, brushing the edges of the river, the swamplands and into the trees. I easily followed him as we leaped across gullies, creeks and small streams. We jumped up into the trees, grabbing and climbing the trunks, then leaping from tree to tree. I learned how to move across great distances without ever touching the ground. When we got thirsty, we fed on the wildlife … the deer, the fox, the rabbit … whatever happened to be close to us. None of it was as good or fulfilling as human blood, but it did suffice until we went on a proper hunt.

This was one of the best times that I had had with James. I learned, grew stronger, and discovered new gifts and skills. I felt myself becoming more and more like him every day. I was happy, just being with him. We laughed and played together like two children. I had never known a love as strong as what we had between us.

One afternoon as we roamed the grounds near the rear of the estate I came upon an old cemetery. It was surrounded by an ornamental iron fence with a gate in the center of one side. It appeared to be clean and well kept. There were huge old trees growing all around it and giving it shade.

"James," I quickly called out, "come over here, look what I found. It's an old cemetery of some kind. It looks so well cared for, let's go in and look around!"

"The grounds men care for it at my instruction, keeping it trimmed and free of intruding overgrowth," he commented as he joined me.

I started to open the gate and turned to look at him as he stood beside me. I saw the shadow of an old pain flit across his face. I realized instantly where we were and I felt like an intruder.

"Oh James, I'm so sorry," I said taking his hand, "I didn't know what this place was, I shouldn't be here. Come, we'll go somewhere else."

"No," he said slowly, "we should go in. I haven't visited her since the fall of 1752. I need to pay respects to the love of my human life. Come, I will show you where she and my daughter rest."

He opened the gate and entered walking slowly, his head bowed. I followed behind at a reverent distance. We crossed the paths that led throughout between many of the old headstones. Then, toward the back of the enclosure we came upon an elaborately carved headstone. It was much bigger than any of the others that surrounded it.

James stepped up to it, looking at it while I maintained my respectful distance. This was his moment and I did not want to intrude any further into it. After a few minutes of silence, he turned slightly toward me and extended his hand for me to join him. I put my hand in his and silently stepped up beside him. The stone was engraved simply with their names:

Mary Elisabeth Johnson Dubois
1729 – 1748
Newborn Daughter, Mary
1748

I looked at him and saw tears of blood forming in his eyes and beginning to spill over onto his cheeks as his love of over two hundred fifty years reached out of him and across time to her.

"Katelyn," he spoke softly, putting his arm around my waist and drawing me close to himself, "this is Mary Beth, she was once the center of my human life and I loved her more than life itself." Then turning back towards the stone he continued, "Mary Beth, this is Katelyn, she is the center of my preternatural life and I shall love and care for her, as I did you, for eternity. We shall go now, and not further disturb your rest. May you rest in continued peace my first love."

We turned to go, I put my arm around his waist, and out of nowhere, felt a gentle breeze envelope and swirl around us as we walked away. I sensed that somehow, across time, she had given her approval and acceptance of me.

Later I led him to our bedroom and said, "James, I have come to you so many times when I was sad and hurting and you were always there for me. Now allow me to comfort you while you are sad and hurting."

I took him in my arms and not willing to interrupt his most private thoughts, silently held him the rest of the day and all night. I never once broke the silence, allowing him to roam freely through his memories, hoping my touch would help bring healing and close the old scars that had been inadvertently opened that afternoon.

The next day James seemed like his old self again, almost as if nothing had happened.

"Katelyn," he said as we walked through the manicured gardens at the rear of the house, "Thank you so much for yesterday. You have no idea what it meant to me and how you have helped me."

"But, I opened so many old wounds," I started to say.

"You didn't do it on purpose," he said, "and it was best that it happened. I have had a huge hole in my soul for over two hundred sixty years. I thought that by never going near that place again it would go away, but it didn't. Then, yesterday, I was forced to come face to face with it."

"I feel like I can now move on with my life, it's as if I finally accepted her blessing to do so. She is no longer a part of my life so I can now close that chapter and look to the future. You are now the true center of my life Katelyn, and together we have a grand future in front of us. I shall be making some changes in the next few weeks that will reflect the new center of my universe."

He smiled at me and I felt his love fold around me like a blanket.

"Now," he said with a huge smile, "let's go hunting, I need to feed. There's a big festival and street dance downtown and we can pass right through the center of it, feeding until we are glutted. What do you say?"

"I'm thirsty," I laughed, "what are we waiting on?"

"Katelyn," James called out to me one day soon after, "come quickly, I have something to show you!"

I went to the main parlor and when I walked in I gasped as if I had breath. There, over the huge mantle where the portrait of he and Mary Beth had hung was a new painting. It was a life size, oil on canvas, of me and James, mounted in an elaborate gilded frame. We were dressed in our formal wear from the ball at The Palace.

"Oh, James …" I started to say, "it's so beautiful … but the other painting … what …

"It has been moved to another place of honor, so that the new center of my universe will meet any visitors. Come closer," he said, "see the plate ..."

I walked over to the new painting and, tracing the engraving with my fingertips, read the golden plate attached to the frame:

James Thomas Dubois and Katelyn Melissa Corbin
The Master and Mistress of Whitehall Manor

I stood there, shocked, unsure of what to say, and finally just said nothing. I slid my arm around his waist and pulled closer to him as we stood there looking at the portrait, knowing I would never have to share him again.

Later that day my phone rang and I saw Lexi's picture on the screen. I was happy to hear from her but wondered at the unexpected call.

"Hello there, Lexi!" I said cheerfully as I answered the phone, "it's so good to hear from you, how are you?" I hoped that she wouldn't notice any change in my voice, not that it was a big one to begin with.

"Katelyn, it's so good to hear your voice again," she started, "how have you been, is everything good on your side of the pond?"

"It's wonderful," I started, "since you left I have moved in at Whitehall and James and I are traveling and just having the time of our lives! How about you, what's going on in Berlin, do you still like it there?"

"Oh Katelyn, it's so wonderful here," she gushed, "it's everything I ever hoped it would be, but I miss you so much!"

"I miss you too, Lexi," I laughed, "all the fun we used to have together, going out and being together, just the two of us, it was so great!"

"Well, since you miss me so much, I have some good news for you," she giggled, "I'm coming home for a couple of weeks and I want us to get together for some of that time. I don't know what we'll do or where we'll go, but I want us to spend some quality girl time together!"

"Lexi, that sounds absolutely wonderful, but I thought you would be gone for the next two years, how are you going to get away," I asked happily but thinking to myself that this was going to present a big, unexpected problem for me.

"We have a two week break between classes here, so I thought I'd use it to come home and visit everybody. Besides I have been feeling a little down and the university doctor thinks it's just a bad case of homesickness," she giggled happily, "anyway, I'll be home next Wednesday. Can you and I plan on getting together for a four day weekend?"

"Sure thing," I said trying to keep an upbeat sound to my voice.

"Great, then I'll see you next week, tell James I said hello, love ya, Katelyn," she said and was gone.

I stood there looking at the picture of her on my phone smiling back at me and wondering what to do now … was I ready to see Lexi, or, more accurately, was Lexi ready to see me?

"Uhh, James," I called out, "I have a little problem here!"

"What is it," he asked joining me.

I related the phone call to him from Lexi and her wanting us to spend the weekend together.

"What do I do," I pleaded, "I probably shouldn't see her yet, all the changes in me will still be obvious, it's only been a few months, how will I explain them to her?"

"Just tell her its healthy eating," he chuckled.

"James! I can't do that she'll want to know what I'm eating!" I laughed.

"So tell her," he grinned.

"No! I can't do that either! I can just hear that conversation," I chuckled.

"'So Katelyn, what are you eating that makes you look so healthy?'" I said, perfectly mimicking Lexi's tiny musical voice.

"'Oh, you know, a couple pints of blood a day,'" I continued, "'I usually end up with either an O or A positive, usually from some smoking hot guy … although I will take a girl if she happens to have AB negative!'"

"'That is so cool,'" I continued switching back to Lexi's voice again, "'I would never have thought blood would make you look so vibrant! Are you ready to let's go dancing now?'"

I sat back and looked at James with a huge smirking smile on my face.

"I was just kidding!" he chuckled at my theatrics.

"I know, and so was I," I chuckled.

"But seriously, Katelyn, why do you concern yourself with a problem that may not even exist? Why don't you and Lexi go up to the city? I'll have our suite at the Waldorf cleared for the weekend, you can call Charlotte Ann for back-up, and the three of you can go shopping, catch a performance at the Metropolitan and just have an enjoyable weekend. Besides," he added with a salacious grin, "maybe Vickie will have some new creations for you!"

"You're awful," I said with a laugh, "but maybe you're right, and since I'll be there anyway, I'll certainly stop by her shop and see what she has … who knows, maybe this time I'll come home with horns instead of wings!"

"Humm … a horny vampire … one can only hope," he replied with a little laugh.

"James, you are such a man … besides I don't need Vickie to make me a horny vampire, you do that quite well on your own," I winked, cutting my eyes playfully at him, "now go away, I have to call Charlotte Ann and get her ready for this," I added a smile as I scrolled up her number.

When she answered I quickly explained the situation to her and asked for her help with the problem. "Dale and I will be thrilled to watch over the two of you, and I'll be more than happy to spend time shopping with you," she replied, "there won't be any problems, I promise. If Lexi has any questions I'll help you explain anything she wants to know about."

"Charlotte Ann, you are the best, thank you so much," I laughed relieved, "I can't wait to see you next week, bye now!"

I felt so relieved after talking to Charlotte Ann, knowing that she would be there to help me in case of any awkward moments. I felt a lot better now about me and Lexi getting together too, and I really looked forward to having a good time with her. I waited until the next morning and called Lexi back to tell her what I had thought about for our weekend.

"Good Morning, Lexi!" I gushed happily as she answered her phone, "I'm so excited about you coming home next week, I just had to call back and tell you what I came up with for us."

"Ummm …. Katelyn, it's four in the afternoon here … I'm still in Berlin remember," she laughed happily, "but good morning to you just the same!"

"Oh, sorry," I said, "I wasn't thinking about the time difference, anyway, how about we get together next weekend like you said, we can take Thursday through Sunday and go up to New York. You can drive up to Whitehall and we'll leave from here."

"Alright," she laughed, "That sounds good to me, I can't wait to see you again Katelyn!"

"I'm really looking forward to seeing you again, too," I smiled, "I'll have some entertainment lined up for us by the time you get here … love you, Lexi, see you soon!" I said ending the call.

Chapter Forty~Six

The following Thursday just could not arrive fast enough for me, and I became more excited as the time grew closer. James decided that we needed to have my skin tone looking perfect when Lexi arrived. We could get by with some subtle changes but not something as drastic as the tan she was used to seeing me sport. I just could not be the least bit pale so I needed to feed, and feed good, in order to get, and maintain, a healthy glow.

My dad had been a proud, former combat Marine, and had always taught me that whenever you have a problem that needs fixing quickly you call on the Marines … so that's just what James and I did … we called on the Marines. We went up to Camp Lejeune, North Carolina on Wednesday before Lexi's arrival the next morning. During the course of the night I drank deeply from several young, battle-hardened Marines. When we returned to Whitehall I was literally glowing all over. My skin had the most beautiful and healthy radiance to it and I was now ready for the trip with Lexi.

When dawn arrived, so did a very happy and excited Lexi. "I'm sorry to have arrived so early," she apologized grinning, "but I guess I'm still on Berlin time!"

"That's alright," I laughed hugging her, "it's wonderful to see you again and be back together! Just think of how much more time we'll have together! Let's get started, James has already alerted the pilot and has him ready and waiting for us. All we have to do is get there, unpack in the room, and then we have the next four days to pack in all the fun we want!"

We drove out to the local airport where the smaller Gulfstream was ready to go. Lexi and I talked, laughed, chattered and giggled the entire flight. She told me all about Berlin and how she had traveled to several different countries when she had time away from her teaching duties. In turn, I delighted her with the stories of mine and James' weekend excursions to Miami and New York, omitting certain small details of course, and in no time at all it seemed, we arrived in New York.

"James has called ahead and had our suite readied for us for the weekend, we'll be staying at the Waldorf …" I started just as the pilot called back that we were beginning our final approach to New York.

"Whoa, you mean THE Waldorf," she asked, looking at me, "as in the Waldorf-Astoria?"

"Yeah, James owns one of the upper floor suites, so when we get ready to use it, he just calls up to be sure it's empty when we arrive. It's really awesome," I continued, "we stayed there for the big Halloween bash over at The Palace last October."

"Wow," she said, "I've never even been in a place like the Waldorf, it sounds like we are in for a big time this weekend!"

"Lexi, we can go anywhere or do anything we want to, although I did make a few plans, I hope you don't mind. Oh, and the best news of all, there's a family friend, Charlotte Ann, that lives in the city and she'll be spending some shopping time with us. She knows all the great places to shop!" I saw a little hint of sadness cross her face at that and quickly added, "Oh, don't worry, you and I will have most of the time to ourselves!"

"Now that sounds like what I wanted," she smiled big at me, "I don't care what we do as long as we do it together!"

We arrived and settled into our suite. Lexi was thrilled when I gave her the huge master en-suite. Soon after, I called Charlotte Ann and she agreed to meet us for a quick shopping trip.

When we met at one of her dressmakers, she silently asked me, *"How are things going, any problems yet?"*

"None, so far," I answered back.

"Lexi," I said, "this is Charlotte Ann, she's a very special friend of ours and knows the city better than GPS. So if we have any questions about where to go or what to do, she's our answer!"

"Hello Lexi, it is so good to meet you," Charlotte Ann said, taking her hand, "Katelyn has told me so much about you, it seems almost as if the two of you are sisters. I hope that you have a weekend that you'll remember for the rest of your life," and turning to me asked, "What are the two of you planning to do all weekend?"

"I thought we would go dancing tonight, maybe get

in a little drinking," I winked subtly at her, "the only other firm plan is to attend the Met Saturday night, everything else is up in the air."

"But first, we have to find a dress for Lexi for the Metropolitan performance. I'd like to find something similar to mine," I said smiling as another idea began forming in my head.

After a couple of hours we left the shop with Lexi's new dress. It was done in beautiful black crushed velvet with black silk trim and cut to perfectly fit her small body. It wasn't too low cut in front, but was backless and with heels made her seem taller than she was. She looked like a beauty queen in it, and she smiled to match. I couldn't wait to finish it out.

"Lexi," I said as we walked down the street together, "We have to stop in at Vickie's sometime this weekend and see her. I know she'll have something special hidden away."

Then I turned and looked at her with a salacious smile, "Do you maybe need something a little bit naughty for a special boy back in Berlin?"

"There's no one at the present time but I suppose it might not hurt to find and have a little 'just in case' tucked away for the future," she giggled, "but right now I want one of those New York hot dogs that guy is selling! They are supposed to be the best in the world … c'mon, let's treat ourselves!"

"Oh, you go right ahead," I said, laughing, "I'm not sure I could handle one of those this time of day! But when you finish eating, let's go drop our things at the hotel. I have someplace I want to take you."

The hotel driver met us when we came back down,

and we settled into the comfortable seat for the ride as he asked, "Miss Corbin, where would you like to go?"

"Will you please take us down to the district, to Weissmann's on 47th street," I instructed.

It took us about forty-five minutes to get there through the traffic but when we walked in Mr. Weissmann met us with a big smile and a greeting, "Miss Katelyn," he exclaimed, "it's so wonderful to see you again, and you've brought a friend!"

"Good afternoon, Mr. Weissmann," I smiled happily, "it's good to see you also, I hope you are well?"

"Oh, in perfect health," he replied, "and I hope you are still enjoying your gift?"

"Oh, yes sir, they are beautiful, and truthfully, that's why I'm here today," then turning to Lexi, I said, "this is my friend Lexi Gordon. She's visiting for the weekend from Berlin."

"Ach, Guten Tag Fräulein Lexi, müssen Sie Deutsch sprechen," Weissmann said with a huge smile, extending his hand to her.

"Ja, das tue ich, aber leider nicht so gut wie Sie," she answered him with her own smile.

"Ah, sehr gut, und wie geht es Ihnen heute," he beamed.

"Ich bin heute sehr gut, danke der Nachfrage," she smiled back at him.

"It's always such a pleasure to meet someone that speaks my native language, Miss Lexi," he continued, switching back to English, "welcome to my humble shop!"

Then turning back to me he said, "How can I help you ladies today?"

"Mr. Weissmann, we are attending a performance at the Met Saturday evening, and I was wondering if perhaps you might have something that Lexi could wear for the night?"

"Of course I do," he said, and turning to her asked, "Miss Lexi, what will you be wearing?"

He listened intently as she described her dress, smiled broadly and said, "I have just the thing for you," then turning back to me, "it will perfectly complement your ensemble! Please excuse me while I step in the back to get it."

When he returned he was carrying another of his black velvet jewelry boxes which he placed easily on the counter, "I have just this morning finished these and they could not have a better young lady to premier them," he said smiling at Lexi. He turned the box toward her and opened it. There inside, was another beautiful collection of diamonds and emeralds. Lexi stood there, speechless, her eyes growing huge, much as I had done when James had given me my jewels.

"The choker," he began, "is two inches wide, made of twenty-two carat white gold and crusted with forty-five carats of diamonds, the two bands of emeralds at the top and bottom consists of fifteen carats each. Both of the bracelets are one inch wide, half the weight of, and exactly match the necklace. The earring strands are each made up of three diamonds and two emeralds, each a one carat solitaire," he smiled as he slid them toward Lexi, "They look as if they were made just for you and will compliment your beauty wonderfully! I can't thank you enough for showcasing them for me."

"Oh, Mr. Weissmann," I said happily, "I knew I could count on you, thank you so much!"

"I hope that you ladies have a wonderful time at the Met, it's a great time of year," he said smiling, as we left to return to the hotel.

Later that evening, after dressing up for a night on the town, we went out dancing. Lexi and I had decided to make tonight our 'Girls Night Out' part of the weekend so we had spotted and chosen this particular club earlier in the day and waited until later in the evening to make our appearance. It was a great place, a retro 80's style disco in the center of Mid-Town and it was packed. The music was especially good tonight and I moved through the dance-floor, dancing with several different partners. I had danced for several hours and fed until my skin was absolutely glowing again.

Afterward, I sat comfortably, relaxed in one of the padded leather cocktail chairs at our table. I easily swiveled the chair just the tiniest bit from side to side as I slowly sipped on my girlie drink with the umbrella and enjoyed the music. I casually wondered what James was doing this weekend without me and realized how much I missed him. I'm sure he was off on a hunting expedition of his own somewhere.

Lexi and I were dressed to kill, pardon the pun, and we were certainly drawing more than our share of attention tonight. We had outdone even my usual attire for clubbing.

I was wearing a pair of designer low-riders that sat extra low on my hips and were just tight enough to still move easily in. I had added a thin black leather belt, suggestively left unbuckled and dangling in the front. I paired them with a sleeveless, dark burgundy satin top that was tied open in the front. Between the two I was showing a lot of skin tonight. I had brushed my hair until it shined, bouncing as I walked. My eyes and my smile were brighter than ever, reflecting the dimmed lights of the club.

Lexi was a bit more conservative but still very fashionable. She was sporting a silver satin spaghetti strap top that was cut low in front with a half back. It was a little short and revealed just enough of her mid-riff to spark the imagination. It sat on top of a pair of snug fitting, custom low cut black jeans. She had highlighted her outfit with a pair of mid-thigh black boots with the tops rolled down to the knee, and a thigh length red sash, the combination making her look a bit like a buccaneer of old. The entire outfit of course had been custom tailored to fit her small body and she looked like she had just stepped off the runway.

I watched as she danced, smiling at her various moves. I knew that she was a very good dancer but I was a little surprised at what I saw; she must have been practicing while she was in Berlin. She seemed to enjoy showing off her moves on the dance floor. I smiled, watching her as she cuddled closer to her current partner as the music slowed. He reluctantly released her and she headed back to our table for her drink.

"Katelyn," she began as she dropped tiredly into her chair, "I'm having so much fun tonight! I haven't danced this much in a long time," she laughed as she took a long pull on her drink. Then she laughed excitedly, and grabbing my hand said, "C'mon, dance with me, let's you and I hit the dance floor and show them how it's done!"

Together the two of us totally redefined the term 'Dirty Dancing' and we sure drew a lot of interest. Finally after about three songs each of us was picked off by a couple of hot guys for the next set. I used the opportunity to feed again and after about an hour on the floor made my way back to our table. I sat there again casually watching, smiling at Lexi, as she continued dancing with several more young men, knowing she was thoroughly enjoying every minute of the evening.

Suddenly I sat bolt upright as I noticed the man she was currently dancing with … he was an immortal … one of my kind … and was obviously on the prowl for a victim. It was obvious from his actions that a small drink was not what he had in mind … he was looking for a kill … not that it would have mattered in any case because he had Lexi.

Then for the first time ever I looked at Lexi through the eyes of a vampire, and I saw that she would make the perfect victim too … she was young, pretty, dressed nicely, and had just the right amount of innocence with a touch of naivety blended in that would make her blood deliciously gratifying … and as the blood lust began to tingle through me, I knew I had to force myself to stop thinking about my best friend in those terms … and I had to do it now before it could develop any further.

I continued to watch as he held Lexi close while they danced. I noted his movements as he began to move toward a darker corner of the dance floor. I saw her eyes glaze over as he drew her into his thrall. Then he refocused on her neck, getting closer to her, lightly kissing her cheek. I knew I had to intervene and do it quickly … because *his* next kiss would be *her* last kiss.

I concentrated my thoughts and spoke silently and calmly to him, *"Excuse me, but the human girl that you are dancing with is with me … and I would appreciate it if you would please return her to me now."*

He suddenly looked up, away from Lexi, surprised to hear one of his own. He quickly located me, and appraising me, spoke back, *"Ah, but she's with me now … and it is the way of the world, the stronger takes from the weaker … now run along young one, there are plenty more like her … you can find another one."*

For a split second all I could think about was Lexi's safety and how close she stood to disaster. So I replied back to him, *"If you even think about taking just the smallest drink from her, I will destroy you before you can take the first sip!"*

He looked up at me again, this time with a look of annoyance and smiled as he replied, *"You can't possibly hurt me young one, I'm a great deal older than you are, so please, I'm trying to be nice to you here, you don't even want to think about it. Now like I said, be a good little girl and run along now."*

And his calling me a little girl just pissed me off! I stood up and looking in his direction felt the fire begin stirring inside me. I raised my hand in his direction to burn him where he was standing. But before I could say or do anything more I heard another voice, calm and soft, speak up, *"Oh foolish one, you really should pay closer attention to who and what is around you. Katelyn is indeed young, but she's not a little girl, and much stronger than you think ... my blood flows in her ... believe me when I say she can easily destroy you ... and if she doesn't, I certainly can and will ... it is very unwise of you to underestimate her power ... now, as she said, the girl is with us and under our protection ... may I suggest that you take your hands off of her and move on ... because I won't think twice about incinerating you where you stand, fledgling!"*

I knew Charlotte Ann's voice immediately without looking. I had no idea she was anywhere close by, but I was certainly glad to hear her. Although I had never heard her speak with the authority she was using now, there was no doubt she meant every word.

This new one looked quickly around, trying to locate her, recognizing the sound of her dominance, but I knew she was hiding herself from him.

"Do you insist upon a demonstration, or do you wish to

leave peacefully and hunt elsewhere," she asked again, *"final warning young one!"*

As if he suddenly realized who he was talking to, he bowed his head and said, *"Charlotte Ann, m'lady, I'm so very sorry, I didn't realize ..."*

"Go!" she cut him off sharply. Suddenly understanding the danger he was in, with preternatural speed he left Lexi standing alone on the dance-floor looking around for her partner, oblivious to the danger she had been in just seconds before.

"Thank you, Charlotte Ann," I spoke silently out to her.

"It was nothing," she chuckled softly, *"I just really didn't want to see you turn him into a torch in front of Lexi, it might have scared her. Now that all is well again, I think that Dale and I shall return to our own dancing, just call if you need me, otherwise, enjoy the rest of your evening!"*

I went and brought Lexi back to the table, telling her we had to leave immediately and made an excuse of hearing about a fight in the club. We went straight back to the hotel, and were both soon in our pajamas. It seemed just like old times as we sat and talked and laughed again, completely safe now.

"Katelyn," Lexi started with a smile, "I'm so happy for you. I just knew that everything would work out for you and James. You seem so much happier than I have ever seen you."

"Lexi, he's such a wonderful man," I smiled back at her, "he's so good to me and loves me more than I have ever been loved in my life. He has even helped me heal from the wounds left by my parents' deaths in a very unique manner. That man has literally turned my life into something different. I can certainly see myself staying with him forever!"

After a couple more hours of girlie talk, we sat silently for a while, enjoying our closeness again. After a while Lexi turned back to me, and looking closely, tilted her head just a little and said, "You know, there is something that is different about you Katelyn … and I've been trying to figure it out since I arrived, but I just can't quite put my finger on it."

I was suddenly alert to her choice of words as I thought, *"hum … out of the mouths of babes … you don't know just how right you are."*

"You've changed somehow. I don't know what you've done," she smiled, "but you look more beautiful than I have ever seen you. Your tan is not quite as dark as it was the last time I saw you but your skin has the prettiest glow to it now. You have to tell me what you do to make it shine like that!"

"I didn't realize," I said, trying to play it off, "I'm trying to take better care of myself now that I'm with James … so it could just be healthy eating … you know, none of those street vendor hotdogs!"

"Maybe before I go back to Berlin you'll share some of your healthy eating secrets with me," she smiled questioningly, "because whatever it is you're doing, you really look better than I've ever seen you … and Katelyn I didn't think you could ever look any better."

"Well right now, I'm too tired to look like anything, let's call it a night and go to bed before the magic wears off and I turn into a pumpkin," I laughingly stretched big and feigned a yawn, determined to end this conversation as quickly as possible before it could develop any further.

We both went to our separate bedrooms and before long Lexi went fast asleep. I moved quickly and quietly toward where she lay, and stood in the shadows of her room, listening as she slept. Her breathing soon settled into a low, steady rhythm. I smiled as I listened to the sound of her heart beating in slow even beats and I knew that she was sleeping soundly. I took another step and stood beside her. I smiled to myself, as I replayed the fond memories of our friendship over and over in my mind. I wondered at how someone could remain so innocent and carefree. Her sweet face was completely relaxed as she continued to drift deeper into sleep. I very carefully brushed the hair away from her face with my fingertips as I watched her. Then I silently leaned over her and ever so lightly touched my lips to her forehead, and spoke to her mind, *"Sleep peacefully and take your rest my innocent little mortal friend."*

I straightened up and stepped away from her bed, back into the darkest corner of the room. I stood there, still and silent as death itself as the night passed, quickly moving toward the new dawn. I continued my protective watch over my dearest friend, the one I considered my sister, while she peacefully slept the night away.

Our weekend ended all too soon and we began preparing to leave for Charleston. Lexi came into my room as I packed carrying the black velvet case from Weissmann's.

"You had better take these," she began, laying the box on the foot of the bed, "I can't imagine what they're worth but I suspect Mr. Weissmann would like to get them back pretty quickly … but I really did enjoy wearing them," she added with a little girl giggle, "I felt so 'uptown' all dressed up for the Met."

"Lexi," I began, giving her a close hug, "I want you to know that you are my best friend in the whole world. I don't know what I would have done had you not been there to help me through the most difficult time of my life."

"Oh, Katelyn," she said as she hugged me back, "you've been so good to me, too! I'm so fortunate to have such a special friend as you. I've had such a wonderful weekend. Thank you for all you've shown me. It's been so much fun just being with you again. I can't wait until we can do it again!"

"Now that's something we will plan on for sure," I laughed, "the next time you get a week away from school we'll spend it in Miami!"

Then I turned and picked up the jewelry box and handed it back to her, "I want you to take these Lexi … they're yours … my gift to you for all you've been to me. Every time you wear them I want you to think of our special friendship."

"But Katelyn …" she began.

"Don't 'But Katelyn' me Lexi," I laughed, "you know I'll win … and besides I've already spoken to Weissmann and arranged payment."

"Thank you … so much," she said, hugging the case to her chest, the tears beginning to brim in her eyes.

"I love you Lexi," I said, "you're very special to me."

She hugged me again and a tear began to roll down her face.

"Oh, Lexi, don't do that, I can't cry, it will ruin my make-up," I laughed, knowing what else it would ruin if she were to see my red tears.

Chapter Forty~Seven

It had been three weeks since I had returned from my weekend trip with Lexi to New York. I had spent the day in Charleston, and had just returned from an especially successful hunt in the lower historic district. I was in the library, allowing the fresh blood to work its way through my body, when my phone rang. I was a little confused when I saw Lexi's picture on the screen so I picked it up and answered with a cheery, "Hello Lexi, are you still in the States? I thought you would be back in Berlin by now."

"I … I won't be going back, Katelyn," she said haltingly, and I heard the sound of hopelessness in her voice, "you remember I told you that I had been feeling kind of sickly, so I went to see my doctor and had my yearly physical a little early before I went back … the tests came back today … Katelyn," she slowly said, dropping her voice to a whisper, "I'm dying …"

There was a complete silence for what seemed like an eternity before I was able to say anything, and finally, disbelievingly, I choked out, "That can't be Lexi … surely there's been some kind of a mistake … you got the wrong test results."

"No Katelyn … there's no mistake," she continued, "my doctor here in Savannah, has diagnosed me with a quickly replicating blood and bone cancer. It was the reason I've been feeling weak and sickly. He said that if they had caught it two months ago there might have been some hope."

I felt my soul begin to tear apart as my heart broke silently in two. I continued listening to her as she spoke, now crying softly, through her tears. I wanted so desperately to try to comfort her, but I didn't quite know what to say. After all, what are you supposed to say when your best friend has just told you they're dying?

"But, Lexi … there has to be something they can do, are you sure," was all I could think to say.

"The doctor said that I'm terminal, and at this point, there's just no help possible. He said that I have at best, some six to eight weeks left. They offered me treatment, but said it would only make me sicker, so I turned it down. I have decided that other than medications to help fight any pain I'm going to refuse further treatment. Katelyn, there's just no need to make this thing any worse than it already is … besides, I don't want to be buried with a wig … although if I did, I could finally have hair that's as long and pretty as yours," she laughed nervously and then fell into silence.

I sat there, an immortal suddenly being flooded with mortal emotions. I held the phone silently for a few seconds, unable to talk, not knowing what to possibly say now. Lexi was more than my best friend … she was like a sister to me.

"Oh, Lexi …" I started crying, unable to hold my own tears back any longer, "I just can't believe what you're telling me. When we were together in New York, there was just no signs then of the sickness. How did it happen so quickly? I'll talk to James, surely he knows a doctor or someone that can help you."

"Katelyn," she said as her voice caught in her throat, "when Dr. Richardson told me the test results this morning I literally felt my life, and all the plans I've made for it, suddenly implode on me. You are the first one, after my parents, that I've called to break the news."

Her news had upset me severely and not just because we were such close friends. My parents had died only a little over a year ago and now it seemed that death was to come calling close to me once again. I was well acquainted with death by now, so often being the harbinger myself. I simply was not accustomed to it coming so close to me personally. I could hardly believe that Lexi was sick enough to be dying.

"What did your parents say about it," I asked.

"My parents naturally are devastated at the news," she continued, "I'm their baby, and now I'm dying … quickly … I won't even be here to celebrate my dad's birthday this year."

I heard her start to cry again as she tried to continue, "They immediately said that they would sell everything and pay for any treatment to save my life … that it's just not natural for a parent to have to bury their child; it should always be the other way around. I told them I appreciated that they loved me that much. But Katelyn, they have struggled financially and gave up so much just trying to pay for me to go to college. I know they will never have enough money to pay for that kind of treatment."

I listened, now crying uncontrollably, as her news sank deeper into me.

"Katelyn, you and I have to have some time together … and soon … before this thing progresses any further … I want us to be able to say 'good-bye' to each other in person …" she said now weeping unrestrainedly, "I haven't figured out how to say that just yet though … Katelyn, you're my sister and my best friend … how do I say good-bye … to you … and everyone else … please tell me how to do that …"

There was another moment of quietness on the phone. I was speechless, I had no idea what to say as I sank deeper into despair with her.

"I want to see you again, Katelyn … quickly … to spend time with you just like we always have … I want us to laugh and giggle together again … I want to feel like everything is going to be alright …"

"I promise you an entire day together," I said, "we'll go anywhere and do anything you want to do Lexi."

"That sounds like fun," she said slowly, "I have to go now, Katelyn, I'll call you back later … I promise … but right now all I want to do is cry … and I feel like that's all I can do … I don't know what else to do … I feel completely lost and helpless … I have to take time and just cry … for myself … and for my family and friends … I love you so much, Katelyn."

Then she was gone, the phone in my hand went dead, as my best friend went to be alone and mourn her brief life.

Chapter Forty~Eight

My face and throat were streaked with little red trails where the bloody tears had rolled across my cheeks and down my neck. I was torn to the very depths of my soul at the news Lexi had given me. I felt like I wanted to wail out in torment. Anything to try to make the excruciating pain in the center of my chest go away.

The hurt in me was so intense it brought back vivid, unwanted memories of my human life. There had only been one other time when I had felt that same kind of hurt. Now, as then, I realized there was nothing I could do but endure it. I silently wondered if the hurt would heal quicker in this life than it had in my other life. So I just sat there in silence, holding my phone and looking at Lexi's smiling picture on the screen, as the tears continued to flow down my face.

I looked up at James when he came into the library and crossed over to where I was sitting. When he looked at me, he paused and I saw a fleeting shadow of concern cross his face. He quickly recovered and asked, "Katelyn, what's wrong darling … what's happened to upset you … why are you crying?"

"James," I whispered through the tears, "it's so terrible … I just received a call from Lexi … and she told me that she's dying. Her doctors said that she has a blood and bone cancer that is incurable at this stage. She said that it's so far advanced she only has about two months left. She's been my best friend and I feel so helpless … just like with my parents, there's nothing I can do to help!"

I moved into his arms and pulled him closer to me. The anguish rippled through my body and the tears began all over again, unable even to speak, all I could do was cry into his shoulder at the thought of losing my closest friend forever. He held me close, and gently petted me. I felt safe there, wrapped in his arms, but like a small child, so pitifully vulnerable.

"James, please, can we help …" I asked, recovering my voice, "she's like my sister and I don't want to see her die … is there anything we can do … do you know of any doctors that we can send her to that can save her life … I'll give everything I have … I'll empty my bank accounts to pay for it for her."

"Katelyn, sweetheart, stop crying now," he whispered to me as he easily stroked my back, "it will be alright. But darling, at this point, even the doctors I know can't help her."

And the tears started fresh again, my sobs wracking through me as my last hope evaporated.

"But Katelyn, there is something *you* can do to help

her, *you* have the ability save her life."

"What can I possibly do, I don't know where to suggest she go, or what doctor to see, I don't even know what to say to her to comfort her," I said as the tears started all over again, "she asked me to tell her how to say good-bye … and I've got no idea what to say to her."

"Katelyn," he spoke lovingly but with a touch of sternness in his voice, "please stop crying and look at me."

I stepped back from him, forcing the tears to stop, and looked up into his deep green eyes. They were so peaceful and calming to me, just like they had always been.

"Katelyn, you are no longer a human so please stop thinking like one … remember what you are … you are an immortal … one that carries the Fountain of Youth, the very Gift of Life, inside you … why don't you offer that gift to Lexi?"

"The Fountain of Youth … the Gift of Life …" I asked sounding dumbfounded, looking questioningly at him, still too shocked to realize just what he was saying. He continued looking into my eyes, silently comforting me in his arms, smiling and waiting.

Then as understanding slowly crept back into my mind, my thinking and emotions began to clear immediately as they changed from that of a weak, hurting mortal to that of an immortal again. I knew exactly what 'The Gift of Life' and the 'Fountain of Youth' meant. I began to consider it and all that it meant … that Lexi could become an immortal like us. There was indeed something I could do to help her. My heart leapt with joy in me as the idea came to full realization.

"Can I really do that," I asked hesitantly, "I mean … I know you said I could make another … but I'm still so young, it's not been quite a year since I turned, would it work?"

"Katelyn, you have had the ability to reproduce since the very first day that you awoke," he started, "and your bloodline is solid and strong. Additionally, you have mine and Charlotte Ann's blood still fresh in you … that alone should give Lexi a huge advantage and an absolutely smooth transition … that is if she opts to accept your offer. But in the end, whichever she may choose, life or death, it has to be her choice … if she chooses life, you may give her life … but if she chooses death then you must abide by her decision and allow her to die."

"Assuming that she will accept the gift, will you help me to change her," I asked, as a small glimmer of hope began to rise up within me.

"I will be here, but you won't need my help. Just as hunting and feeding came naturally to you, this will also. You have it inside you, you know how it's done, it's a part of what you are," he reassured me.

"Then I have to call her right now, and ask her to come up immediately, she has to know there's an option, that there is hope!" I threw my arms around him, hugging him close and loving him that much more.

When Lexi answered her phone, I tried not to sound too excited or bubbly, "Lexi … I need to see you … now … we need to talk," I slowly said, "I have some wonderful news … can you please come up to Whitehall as soon as possible?"

"I suppose I could come up there tomorrow morning, but do you think I can maybe stay a day or two, if I need to, so I can regain some strength," she asked.

"Lexi, Whitehall is as much your home as it is mine. You can stay here as long as you want, anytime you want. But first we have to talk about your life … and how to save it … this is more important than you can possibly imagine …

I'll see you in the morning … I love you Lexi … don't ever forget that," I said as I finished the call.

Chapter Forty~Nine

The next morning Lexi arrived early and I ran down the front steps and met her at the fountain before she could get to the porch. So much had changed in the three weeks since I had last seen her. Outwardly, she looked good, the picture of health, just like always. No human would ever have thought she was so near death. But with my preternatural senses, I smelled the scent of death on and around her and I saw the shadow of it on her face as it worked its insidious way into her. I knew that unchanged, the end for her wouldn't be far away. Strengthening my efforts not to cry, I wrapped my arms around her. I would not allow her to see my bloody tears, she wouldn't understand them yet.

I held her in my embrace, her small body trembling

throughout against me as I tried to comfort her. Then she broke my heart all over again and nearly brought the tears I was trying so desperately to hold back when she whispered to me, "Please don't cry right now, Katelyn … I've already cried enough for both of us … let's just be happy for a little while … just like we were last month in the city."

"I'll try my best, Lexi, I really don't want you to see me cry," I replied and with another quick hug, continued, "let's go sit on the rear veranda, the morning sun is there and it's going to be a beautiful day. Do you want anything … something to drink or a snack," I asked as we settled down to visit.

"No thanks," she answered, "I just want to sit here with my sister and talk … I want every minute I can get with you. You and James have been so good to me Katelyn. You've been the sister that I never had and he gave me my life's dream … maybe later, if he's here, I can spend some time with James and talk to him, too. Y'all are both so much a part of my life … so special to me … and I have so much I want to say to you … to both of you … but it seems I have so little time to say it."

"Lexi, I was so hurt when you called me yesterday … I just could not believe that you were suddenly that sick … I mean we had so much fun together just three weeks ago!"

"Well, now I'm enjoying day by day, and Katelyn, right now I want to enjoy today with you," she smiled happily. We sat there in the sun together, moving as it moved, and talked and laughed just like the first time we went to the beach together; just like the sisters we had become. Pretty soon we were lost in our stories and jokes with each other as we remembered all the things we had done together. Before we knew it, a couple of hours had passed swiftly away.

While we continued sitting there together, Lexi reached into the bag she was carrying and took out her velvet jewelry case, laying it carefully on the table in front of her, with a sad smile, she gently patted it and then slid it toward me.

"These are the diamonds that you gave me … I love them and think they are so beautiful and there's nothing in the world that would ever get these from me, but it seems that I won't be needing them much longer …" she swallowed a tear as she continued, "so I want to give them back to you now. All I ask in return is whenever you wear these in the future, please take a minute to think about and remember me … how much I loved you … and that I will always be your sister and we will be friends forever!"

She struggled to hold back the tears as she reached for a Kleenex out of her bag. A single tear escaped her eye and gently rolled down her cheek and unable to hold them back any longer she began to cry softly before continuing.

"While I'm on a serious note," she almost whispered, "I want to ask a huge favor of you."

"Lexi, you know I'll do anything you ask," I answered with a smile.

"What I'm going to ask may be difficult for you Katelyn … you've been more than my friend, you've been my sister … so when the time comes … I want you to say a eulogy at my funeral service … please Katelyn, do that one last thing for me."

She sat looking at me, trying, unsuccessfully, to snub back her grief and blink away the tears filling her eyes.

"Lexi, if and when the time comes, I'll do as you've asked me to … but in the meantime, why don't you hold on to these …" I gently pushed the box back to her, "you can give them to me later, before you leave if you'd like … but that's little details … we can take care of them later."

We sat in silence for a few moments, each with our own thoughts. Then feigning a deep breath, I began to slowly offer her an alternative to death.

"Lexi, I want to ask you something. I know you said this thing is terminal, but do you really want it to be the end, do you want to die, or given the chance would you rather live … and I mean really live … a long, long life?"

She looked thoughtfully at me, then shifted her gaze outward across the gardens, and exhaling slowly, spoke softly, "No, Katelyn … I really don't want to die … but I guess I really don't have any choice in the matter either … so I've accepted this thing and while I'm not totally at peace with it … it is what it is … I'm dying … but, yes, of course I would love to live and have a long life, and if I were given the opportunity at a complete cure, and never have to worry about it again, I would do, say, or offer anything, just to be able to live."

"When Paul, that's Doctor Richardson, told me the diagnosis yesterday morning," she continued, "I think I literally felt all of my hopes and dreams crash down around me. I've suddenly realized just how young I really am … I just turned twenty-two last month … I've thought about all the things I haven't done and just how much life I'm supposed to have in front of me … and it's just not right Katelyn … I shouldn't be getting ready to die … I should be getting ready to live and enjoy my life … it's just not fair … so, no, I don't want to die!"

Snubbing back tears, she took in a long, deep breath and continued, "I've always lived a sheltered and protected life," she said glancing back at me before returning her gaze to the fish pool, "my parents considered me a gift and have always tried to keep me safe from life … but death is the one thing they couldn't protect me from."

"But, you know, I was thinking … and you do a lot of that when you are facing death … one of the things I've never had … and really missed out on … was a real, true, loving relationship with someone. I wish that I could have found a good solid relationship like you found with James."

"It's not like I haven't had a couple of boyfriends," she continued quickly, "I had one most of the way through high school … or maybe he was just a friend … anyway … and then I dated this guy for just a short time in college … but all he wanted was something physical. He didn't want to wait on me to be ready, so that didn't last very long at all."

Then wiping away the tears that rolled down her face again, she looked at me, blushed and slowly dropped her eyes as she continued, "I never knew that talking about end of life and all the things I haven't done would be so hurtful … but I want to tell you something … and don't you dare laugh at me Katelyn Corbin … but I've never even had sex. I mean, I wanted to, but I wanted it to be something special … something extraordinary when I did … so I kept saying that I'd wait to find the perfect boy … then at the perfect time and the perfect place we would do it … and it would be perfect and memorable … now, it's too late to think about checking that little item off my bucket list."

"Lexi, it's a lot of fun … the sex, that is … I promise you it is, especially with the right man, one that you really care about," I smiled at her, trying to lighten the mood.

"Yeah," she smiled big at me, "I remember you telling me about the first time you and James did it!"

The two of us broke up laughing.

"Yeah, I still haven't forgotten that," I chuckled softly, "but Lexi, maybe you haven't missed out on it yet … in a new life, one where you're not sick anymore," I continued softly with a smile, "maybe you'll be able to find that special one … you know … the one that makes you get all wet and sends tingles throughout your body … and then you can have that lasting relationship … along with having and enjoying the best sex ever and all you want, any time you want it."

The two of us laughed like a couple of pubescent school girls at my comment. Her tears this time were tears of happiness as she laughed with me over my joke. She refocused her gaze fully on me, and for just a moment her musical little voice returned as she smiled and said, "You know, Katelyn, you make it all sound so good … a new life that is … something to really look forward to …" and then jokingly added, "You don't by chance happen to have a miracle to offer me so that I can enjoy that new life … do you?"

Our eyes met over the table and I felt like I was looking into her soul when I answered her, "As a matter of fact, Lexi … yeah, I do have a miracle for you … but only if you want it … I can offer you an entirely new life … but you have to ask for it."

"Katelyn," she said slowly, looking intently at me, "I know you love me, and that you would do anything I asked you, but what can you possibly do? Unless you or James happens to know a really good doctor … you can't even offer me an extension on this life, let alone a completely new one. There is no cure for what I have and I've accepted the fact that I'm dying … and that's that."

"Lexi, what I'm about to tell you is going to sound unbelievable and will shock you at first, but before you react, please think about what I'm telling you. The only reason I am about to share this with you is because you are dying, and we both know it."

"Sometimes, the things you see, the people you know, aren't always what they seem on the surface. They may indeed be the same people you know, but just under the surface they are someone totally different. Do you remember when we were in the city and you said to me that I was different … that I had changed? There was more truth in that statement than you could possibly have realized at the time."

"Lexi, I have a huge secret that I've been withholding from you, something I am never supposed to reveal to a human, but I'm not worried that you would betray my confidence by telling anyone else. Besides, if you did, no one would believe you anyway. I have indeed changed, just as you noted … I may look like Katelyn, talk like Katelyn, and even act like Katelyn … but Lexi, I'm no longer the same Katelyn you knew when we roomed together and when you left for Berlin."

"Katelyn …" she started slowly, "I really don't understand what you're talking about, but you're starting to scare me, please don't do that."

I reached across the table and gently laid my hand on her forearm and released a wave of relaxation towards her and she immediately became calm, "There's nothing to be frightened of my dear friend, so please don't be afraid of me Lexi … but the change that you noticed in me is what happened when I became a vampire …" I paused for just a moment looking steadily into her eyes, to allow that to sink in before continuing.

She looked at me with a steady gaze, and slowly a little grin grew across her face, "Whew … so you're just a vampire … I can live with vampire … it could have been worse … I mean you could have tried to tell me you had become a werewolf," she laughed happily.

I heard James chuckle lightly in the distance, I knew he had been listening in on this conversation, awaiting Lexi's decision, and I remembered our conversation when he was revealing his nature to me.

"What is it about werewolves," I asked no one in particular … and quickly recomposing myself, looked at her, and allowed my eyes to begin sparkling just the tiniest bit.

"It's true, Lexi," I continued calmly, "I've been changed for several months, it happened just after you left for Germany. And that's why I wanted so desperately to talk to you today … to tell you that you don't have to die … I don't want to see you die … you're more than just my best friend, you're my sister, too … and I want to offer you a gift, one that can only be offered to a very special person … Lexi, I want to offer you the gift of life so that you can live and not die …"

Lexi looked at me disbelievingly, and lightly shaking her head said with a soft laugh, "Katelyn, you had me going there for just a minute … and that's good … you've made me laugh and that's made me feel a little bit better … I just wish it were true … I would so love to believe you … and be able to live."

I crossed my arms and smiled at her, I could feel the immortal stirring and beginning to rise up in me. I allowed the aura to shine through me, changing my outward appearance. I felt my eyes change to the deeper blue that drew in my prey. When they changed and began to reflect the light, I knew they were sparkling brightly in the afternoon sun … and cutting her off mid-sentence … I smiled at her, letting her see my fangs extended … something I had never allowed a living human to see before.

Then I quickly retracted them, dimmed the aura and willed my eyes to return to normal so as not to unduly frighten her, replacing it all with my perfect human smile that she knew so well. For just a moment of time the shadow of unbelief, quickly followed by fear, replaced the shadow of death on her face, another tear rolled silently down her cheek again as the reality of what I had just shown and shared with her sank in.

She stared at me, her mouth hanging open for just a minute then slowly said, "Oh … my … God … Katelyn … you really are a vampire … but … but how …"

Then an even deeper truth hit home and she looked at me questioningly, "James …"

I slowly nodded my head and quietly said, "He's my maker … and now my eternal mate."

"Katelyn, please tell me what all this means," she sniffled through her tears as another flash of fear passed through her.

"Lexi … what it means is that you are a very special person … it means that James and I love you so much that neither of us want to see you die … it means that I'm offering you the Gift of Life, call it the Fountain of Youth if you will because it's a real life that never ends. It's an offer that is only given to those you deeply love and it is never made lightly … but ultimately Lexi … the choice has to be yours … I can't choose for you … you have to ask for The Gift.

But if you do, I will change you myself to be like me. I will make you an immortal, a vampire if you prefer, so that you don't have to suffer this terrible thing that has come upon you. If you choose not to accept it, well, then you know what awaits you … so I'm literally giving you the choice of your own life or your own death."

She dropped her eyes, looking at the floor, thinking, taking in all I had just said. It grew suddenly quiet and she looked away from me, to the yard, the trees, back down at the porch and then, barely above a whisper, she began speaking, as if thinking out loud about what I had just said … I listened patiently as she analyzed her circumstances, getting her thoughts in order, "I'm going to die, that's a given … and probably soon … but if I allow you do what you say you can do … I will at least be alive … I don't understand just exactly how … and I don't know anything else about it … but I trust you to tell me everything I need to know about what's going to happen to me."

Then she slowly looked up, directly into my eyes, and with a weak smile and tear filled eyes, but strength in her voice asked, "Katelyn … I don't want to die, so will you please give me this gift so that I can live … tell me what I have to do … and how do we make this happen?"

"It's probably best that we don't go into all of the details right now, but you just said that you trusted me," I said letting her know that I had heard her soft musings, "Basically, I will take away the dead, disease ridden mortal life that has infected your body, a life that is about to end, and replace it with a living, powerful, immortal life that will go on and on forever. I promise, there will be time, afterward, when time no longer matters, to explain the details and answer all of your questions."

She closed her eyes for a moment and slowly nodded her head in acceptance.

"Then come with me, the three of us need to talk," I stood, offered her my hand, and mustering every ounce of trust she had in her, she placed her little hand gently in mine. I led her through the big rear door, down the grand hallway and into the main parlor where James was waiting for us.

Chapter Fifty

After I had finished my revelation of a new and supernatural world to Lexi and she had made her decision to allow me to change her in order to save her life, the two of us stood and went inside. We walked together down the hall and toward the parlor, and I lightly squeezed her hand that I was still holding for reassurance. James had been waiting there, listening to our conversation on the veranda, and anticipating her decision. He greeted Lexi with a hug, then the three of us took a seat and for the next several hours we talked. During that time we continued to prepare her for what she had chosen to do … to become … while we continued to reveal more about the supernatural world to her.

Since she knew less than nothing about the

supernatural world to begin with, I knew from my own experience that many of the things we shared with her were just too much for her human mind to comprehend just yet. In order to make things easier for her we only touched on the highlights of what was about to happen. I continued gently holding her hand while she sat there silently listening, intent on trying to remain calm. When she assured us that she understood what we were saying and what she would go though we began to delve a little deeper into the things of the preternatural world.

"Lexi," I began, "you are about to go through a lot of changes as you turn from a human being to an immortal being. I want you to know everything that will happen, just like I did when I turned, so that you can know what to expect and how to deal with it. Although you will look, walk and talk just like the Lexi you are now, you will be different … a completely new person … and anyone who knows you well will immediately notice the difference … just like you noticed the differences in me while we were in New York. So I suppose that brings us to the first issue we must deal with … your parents."

She looked questioningly at me, then James and slowly asked, "My parents … what do they have to do with this?"

"They really have nothing, and yet they have everything, to do with it Lexi," James spoke softly to her, "your new life is indeed a new beginning and you must necessarily break all ties to your mortal life. You have made the decision to become an immortal, now you must make the decision to see it through. You may alter your decision at any time until the change begins, and if you choose to do so, I will ensure that you only have memories of a fun filled day with Katelyn, sharing your lives and memories together. You can then return home and share the last few weeks of your life with your parents."

"However, should you decide to see it through, to become an immortal and share the lives that Katelyn and I have, you must necessarily break off any contact with them … I realize that will probably be the second most difficult decision you will have made today … but in return, you will have an eternity to live, you'll be forever young and forever pretty …" he smiled softly at her and she blushed brightly at his words as he continued, "so think about the decision you have made, then if you still wish to take this path, Katelyn and I have some ideas about how to make it a little less difficult for you."

I could see the shock on her face as she sat and listened to what he had just told her … she couldn't ever see or talk to her parents again … I knew she was struggling with the idea of understanding going through life without seeing them again.

"I … I can't ever see my parents again," she asked hesitantly.

"Probably not face to face and be able to talk to them," he said slowly.

"But, they're my parents, and I love them and …" she started to say, the tears welling again in her eyes as she suddenly realized the devastating impact that her sickness was having on her life.

"I understand that, Lexi," James said, "but how would you explain your sudden recovery … you are about to become incredibly healthy and vibrant looking. Then, twenty or thirty years from now you will have to explain why you still look like you're twenty-two."

"So, I'll really look like this forever," she asked.

"I'm twenty eight years old, Lexi, and I look now just

like I did when I was changed and entered immortality in the spring of 1753," James smiled at her. "But as long as your parents are alive, you will be in a position to provide for them and see that they lack nothing in their lives … only you must do it anonymously and from a distance … and life being what it is, in about fifty years or so the issue will take care of itself."

"So then, it's all true … all the legends and what they say about vampires …" she stopped mid-sentence and looking at both of us asked, "is that what we call ourselves?"

I quickly noted that for the first time she had included herself in that question, I suppose it indicated a subconscious acknowledgment that she was now, or at least soon would be, one of us.

"Oh no, it's not all true … you can eat garlic and look at yourself in the mirror," I chuckled.

"Just don't get too close to the mirror after eating the garlic," James quickly added with a laugh, "and after the first couple of weeks you don't ever have to sleep anymore, either."

"And since you don't have to sleep you can use all that extra time having the best sex you ever dreamed of …" I added looking at James, my eyes sparkling and smiling happily.

"Katelyn!" she exclaimed … and blushed deep red again.

"Well … you can," I said still grinning happily, "and you may call yourself whatever you want to … vampire … immortal … or just plain Lexi."

"And as long as we are talking about it, you don't have to worry about the wooden stakes, silver chains, running water or not getting invited into someone's house, either."

Then she looked up at James and with a chuckle and a huge grin asked, "No sparkling …"

"Definitely no sparkling," we both laughed in answer.

"But what you are going to be is pretty much the most superior supernatural being in this world," I continued with a happy smile, "well except for God that is … nothing is greater than Him."

"Okayyy … as long as there's no sparkling I guess … but what about my parents," she became serious again, "what will I tell them, how will I explain not coming back home to them?"

"Lexi, your parents are expecting you to die … and so you shall … at least to them. And here's how …" James quietly began explaining.

I saw the hurt and felt the emptiness filling her as she listened intently to the plan James and I had made. But, like a drowning man, whose desire to live is stronger than the specter of death, she reached out, grasping at any straw available … picked up her phone and made a terribly difficult call to her parents. She told her mom that James knew a doctor in Europe and that she was going to a hospice in Austria. She said that she would have to fly out that afternoon in order to begin the medication and treatments that went with it. She tried to sound upbeat and happy with the news but struggled to hold back tears throughout the call. Finally, telling her mom good-bye and that she would call if she was able, she ended the call.

Six weeks later, Lexi's parents received notification of her death in Austria. The telegram informed them that she had died quietly and painlessly in her sleep. They would receive her ashes, personal effects, and a final letter she had written to them the following week.

James and I, with a little help from Lexi, sent her parents a huge living arrangement of purple Orchids and Morning Glories, her favorite flowers, for her funeral. Afterward they could be planted in her small backyard garden and continue to live and grow in honor of Lexi's memory.

And thus ended Lexi's mortal life.

Chapter Fifty~One

fter the phone call to her mom and more crying while I held her wrapped in my arms, Lexi began to settle down and seriously consider the new life she was about to embark upon. Then for the next few hours the three of us sat together as first James and then I began to explain, in depth, all that was about to happen. She said that she understood about the change and what would happen to her as she became an immortal.

We all knew there was much more that she would have to learn after the change. Whereas I had had several weeks to learn about it and talk to James about what would happen in my case, Lexi just didn't have that much time to learn about it. But she trusted both of us, and we again promised to teach her all that she would need to live and survive as an immortal. Together James and I would help her grow into her new self. We continued to sit together, letting the finality of her decision and the entire situation sink in to her.

Finally, after a while, with my arm still around her, I rubbed her shoulder and said, "Let's you and I go up to my room. You'll want to change clothes and get into something a little more comfortable. Besides, you'll want your jeans and shirt when you wake up again," I smiled at her, "I have a robe you can wear for the next few hours."

I reached and took Lexi's hand in mine again as we started upstairs to my room. When we got there I stood by casually chatting with her while she undressed. I knew it didn't make her uncomfortable because when we had been roommates we had both seen each other numerous times with and without our clothes on. She changed out of her clothes, folded and laid them on my dresser. I had picked out one of my nicer embroidered silk robes, a deep burgundy one that would have been a 'shorty' robe had I been wearing it, but on her it came just to her knees. I held it open for her while she slid her arms into the sleeves and then watched as she tied it loosely around her waist. I smiled as she wiggled around in it allowing the folds of the soft silk to slide along the skin of her shoulders, back and thighs.

"It's so soft and comfortable Katelyn," she commented lovingly caressing the sleeves and front, "probably the most expensive robe I have ever worn … do you think maybe I can keep it … for afterwards?"

"Normally I would say yes," I answered, "but I don't think you'll want it afterwards. It will of course be covered with your human scent … which would normally be a good thing … something from your old world to be a comfort for you as you enter your new world. But due to the leukemia,

I'm afraid it will be also have the stench of death all over it."

I watched her face fall in disappointment as she looked down at it and I quickly continued, "But I promise, I'll have something much better and more to your liking when you wake up … besides I have plenty of robes that you can choose from later."

"I suppose, if you say so," she answered dejectedly, "but it sure is nice."

"Just wait … you'll see … I promise," and chuckling added playfully, "you ain't seen nothing yet!"

We took a seat on the side of my bed and got comfortable where I once again explained in detail what I would do to make the change take place in her. She was about to cease being a human and become an immortal … a vampire … and I knew what a staggering thought that was. Then with her hand in mine, she smiled at me and we started down the hall. I knew that she trusted me completely as I began leading her toward a new life. She padded along silently on bare feet, the highly polished oak floors muffling our steps as we walked together.

I led her to one of the huge bedrooms on the upper level of Whitehall. The room I had chosen was dimly lit. The huge plantation style blinds on the windows were closed and only a small amount of sunlight was allowed to filter into the shadows of the room.

I sensed a shiver pass through her and felt her fear trying to overcome her when I gently closed the door behind us. There was a distinct 'click' as the lock snapped in place and she looked at me with eyes full of dread. I watched as tears began to roll down her cheeks and felt her sense of helplessness as we stood in the quiet, still darkness of the huge room.

"Lexi, please don't be afraid of me," I softly

whispered as I turned back to her and again took her hand in mine.

"Katelyn, I'm not afraid of you …" she whispered back, through her tears, "I would never be afraid of you, but in just a few minutes I'm going to die … and that's a difficult thought to deal with because I don't know what to expect … please tell me again what it's like …"

"No, Lexi, you're not going to die …" I spoke softly and caringly as she looked up into my eyes, "you're going to live … really live … and experience life like never before."

I reached and tenderly wiped the tears off her face with my fingertips as I continued speaking in soft, comforting, tones, "It's almost like taking a nap … you'll just drift off to sleep. I promise I will stay right here with you the entire time. You'll be able to feel my presence and know that I'm close to you. Then when you wake up I'll be right here waiting on you, I promise."

I looked into her soft brown eyes, our gaze steady and began drawing her into me. I opened my arms toward her and she relaxed as I took her in my arms, wrapping them gently around her. I held her in a loving embrace, petting her, calming her shaking body, as we stood there.

I kissed her cheek and nuzzled into her hair. Then I softly ran my tongue along the side of her neck to deaden any pain caused when my fangs penetrated her skin. I gently and carefully sank my fangs into her neck, skillfully breaking through the skin and into the carotid artery, holding them there for a few seconds before retracting them. I felt her arms tighten around me, holding me tighter as she realized what was happening. Bitter tears filled my eyes when I heard her heart beat increase, driven by fear, as I took the first mouthful of my best friend's blood. Although I knew this had to be done, it broke my heart to have the taste of her blood filling my mouth.

Then as I held her tightly in my arms continuing to drink, draining the life out of her, I felt my own acrid tears, tinged with blood, began to roll down my face. And for however short a time, I no longer felt like the predator I had become … instead I felt like an angel of mercy … giving a life, instead of taking a life. This was something I had never experienced and I suddenly realized just how special this moment was … literally for both of us … I was giving birth, and she was being born. Right at that moment of realization, I had never loved anyone as dearly as I did Lexi. When I felt her knees buckle and her body sag, I easily lifted her, like my child that she was becoming, taking her gently in my arms and holding her close to my heart while I continued what I had begun.

I slowly and methodically took her through the three stages that would complete her transition. The first time, her blood tasted rank and fetid from the sickness that worked in her body. I quickly replaced her dead disease ridden blood with my own living blood and as it worked its way through her the first time, I could feel the thing that now lived inside her. It was the one responsible for making this moment happen … its invasion of her body had led us to this point … and I hated it, and what it had caused, more than anything I had ever hated. I could feel it as it began writhing in agony … I knew when it began to die, unable to withstand the onslaught of the powerful vampiric blood that now flooded it.

The second time her blood was sweeter, cleaner, as I took it back out of her. Our minds melted together and we became one, knowing each other like never before. I saw the happy memories of her short life … her parents … her home … and her dream of school. These were quickly followed by the unbelief, and the fear that permeated her when she heard the news of her impending death.

The second time I gave her my blood I could feel the immortal strength beginning to grow in her. I knew what she was feeling as the third time I pulled my blood out of her. This time it was pure and cleansed and there was no remaining trace of the disease that had tried so desperately to take her life.

The third time I gave her my blood, I felt the strong pull on my heart from her as she took from me. I knew that she was trying to fill herself and drain me dry. I had taken death from her and now, this time, she was taking life from me. Soon her mortal body would be unable to handle all the supernatural changes that were happening inside it. While the change continued its work in her she would sink into the deep immortal sleep. Then when she woke again, she would be a changed being. She would still be the same Lexi I had known and loved, only with a new and better life, one that would never end, and she would be like me, a preternatural being … immortal … a vampire.

When she was fully enveloped in the deep sleep and the change began working in her, I carried her tiny body and easily laid her on the bed. I took the robe she had been wearing off of her and discarded it. Then I began to wash and bathe her to ensure that no blood remained anywhere on her body.

When I had completed bathing her, and some other small details that had to be done before she awoke, I carefully redressed her in a pair of pale yellow silk pajamas with lemon yellow satin trim and matching slippers. They were her favorite color, and I had hurriedly purchased them before her arrival earlier this morning. I brushed her hair away from her face and then listened to her heart as it began to beat again. It slowly gained in rhythm to its new thirty-five beats a minute, and then her breathing began to slow until it came to a near stop.

I felt James' presence surround me and as it covered me in his love, I turned and saw him standing, watching me. I moved into his arms, cuddling against him as another bloody tear moved quickly down my face, "How long will it be?"

"Not long," he said consolingly, and then smiled at me, "her heart is beating powerfully. It sounds as if she is going to be strong and gifted … just like her mother."

I stood there with James holding me and waited as Lexi continued her transformation. She lay there calmly and peacefully while I watched the change take place in her. I was intrigued as she turned, carefully noting each of the physical alterations, one by one, as they took place in her body.

In a few hours, I felt her began to wake, her mind rising up from the deep, dark sleep, then slowly sweeping over me as she silently explored the edges of her new world just as I had done when I first woke.

In a short time, when she felt comfortable, her eyelids fluttered, and she slowly opened her soft doe brown eyes. They now glistened gently with the new intensity of immortal life as they reflected the subdued light of the room. She looked around her for the first time taking in all the details of the room with her new preternatural vision, then settled her eyes on me, and smiled.

I reached out taking her small hand in mine, and with a loving smile welcomed her to eternity, "*Now* we shall be friends forever …"

The Beginning
of
The End

Thus Ends

Katelyn's Chronicles

Book One

of

The Grand Narrative

Known as

The Epic Saga

of

The Master of Whitehall

Don't Miss Book Two of

The Epic Saga of

The Master of Whitehall

Lexi's Legacy: The Epic Saga Continues

'Lexi's Legacy' is the exciting sequel to 'Katelyn's Chronicles'. After being diagnosed with terminal cancer, Lexi discovers an unexpected cure from an unlikely source and two best friends become eternal friends. Lexi tells her tale of life and love, lost and found. She relates her experiences as she leaves behind her human life and begins her journey into a new immortal life. No longer the shy, sheltered young girl from book one, Lexi radiates strength and power in her new life as she grows into her own woman.

The Epic Saga of

The Master of Whitehall

Continues with Book Three

Dale's Descent: A Journey into Darkness

'Dale's Descent' continues The Epic Saga of The Master of Whitehall with Dale's tragic and heartbreaking story of a young teenager, born and raised in the mining region of western Pennsylvania. He was illegally attacked, turned and kidnapped by a rouge vampire on his sixteenth birthday. He relates his story in a soulful manner, full of hurt and disappointment as he watches all of his dreams and aspirations fade away. It is a story of redemption that begins with lost love, an unfulfilled life, and an evil influence.

Discover how it all began

The Epic Saga of

The Master of Whitehall

Charlotte Ann's Coven: The Beginning

In the long awaited prequel to The Epic Saga of The Master of Whitehall, Charlotte Ann Erickson has decided that at long last she must tell her story; one that is shrouded in the fog of myths and imaginations. It spans four centuries, and has been a closely guarded secret in the past. She reached this decision primarily because she feels it is long overdue for humans to hear some hard truths about the immortal world. When her story is told, watch, as once again, she quietly fades away, back into the mists of folklore and fantasy.

Don't miss the intriguing conclusion

The Epic Saga of

The Master of Whitehall

James' Journey: The Interlude

In this highly anticipated final installment, James Thomas Dubois, The Master of Whitehall himself, narrates his tale and brings the classic love story of the epic saga full circle. Travel with him across the centuries as his transformation from human to vampire; untrained fledgling to powerful immortal unfolds. The story of James' life, both mortal and immortal, illustrates the role Fate plays as it guides him toward that one special day in the twenty-first century that will forever change his life, and finally fulfill his destiny.

Meet a brand new member of the family in

Hannah's Heartache

A Master of Whitehall Novelette

Hannah Richards has her life all planned out, she was born and raised in tiny little Waycross, Georgia, and she wants nothing more than to spread her wings and fly away. She wants to experience life and find out what the world outside of Waycross holds in store for her. All her plans are about to come together … until she goes to the State wide cheerleading finals in Savannah. After arriving in Savannah, she wakes to find herself thrust headlong into a new world … and it's anything but the world she expected …

Jennifer's Ghost

A Tale of Ghostly Love

Set on the South Carolina Coast

Meet Jennifer, an almost thirty single girl who suddenly finds herself summoned to an attorney's office in Beaufort, South Carolina. Once there she discovers that she is the sole heir to her Aunt's estate, a beautiful nineteenth century cottage that sits atop a bluff overlooking the beach on a small coastal island. She is thrilled at her inheritance but soon dismayed when she finds that the cottage comes complete with its original owner … who died in 1864. Find out what happens when the two of them come face to face …

~ About the Author ~

The author was born in the upstate of South Carolina and has spent the majority of his life there. He joined the Navy immediately out of high school. During a six year span he had the pleasure of visiting many different countries. After returning home he attended The University of South Carolina graduating with a double Associates Degree with Honors. He completed his education at Presbyterian College in Clinton, South Carolina where he earned a Bachelor's Degree in History. He has since worked in the education field as a teacher and in various management positions in industry. He is now retired and currently lives alone.

His current works include the award winning epic saga of *The Master of Whitehall,* a sweeping six volume narrative set in historic Charleston and the surrounding Low Country of South Carolina.

His short stories include *Jennifer's Ghost,* set in beautiful Beaufort, South Carolina, *Hannah's Heartache,* a Master of Whitehall novelette, set in Savannah, Georgia, and Taylor's Tale, set in Charleston, South Carolina.

All of the books, *Katelyn's Chronicles, Lexi's Legacy, Dale's Descent, Charlotte Ann's Coven, James' Journey, Jennifer's Ghost* and *Hannah's Heartache* are all available in both print and e-book formats.

Should you wish to receive a personally inscribed and signed copy of any of the books please contact the author directly via e-mail at author@prtcnet.com, or Rick H. Veal on Facebook.

www.ingramcontent.com/pod-product-compliance
Lightning Source LLC
Chambersburg PA
CBHW030842030726
47495CB00005B/1334